Daughter of Magic

C. Dale Brittain

DAUGHTER OF MAGIC

A Baen Books Original

Baen Publishing Enterprises
P.O. Box 1403
Riverdale, NY 10471

ISBN: 0-671-87720-8

Cover art by Darrell K. Sweet

First printing, May 1996

Distributed by Simon & Schuster
1230 Avenue of the Americas
New York, NY 10020

Printed in the United States of America

CONTENTS

PROLOGUE

She was slimy, streaked with blood, squalling, and so small I could hold her in my cupped hands. She was the most beautiful girl I had ever seen.

The midwife whipped her away from me, washed and dried her tenderly, then laid her, wrapped in a blanket, on Theodora's breast.

"Thank you," said Theodora weakly. Her face was pale with exhaustion, but she looked, if possible, even happier than I felt. "You can take a rest now."

The midwife looked at me distrustingly, as she had for the last two hours, but closed the door behind her as she left. I sat down beside Theodora, brushed the sweaty hair away from her forehead, and kissed it gently. Our baby found the nipple, stopped crying, and began to drink.

"We'll call her Theodora," I said, touching the baby's impossibly small fingers with one of my own.

Theodora smiled but shook her head. "We'll do no such thing."

"But I thought that was your mother's and grandmother's name before you."

"And further back than that. But if our daughter and I both have the same name, either you'll call her Theo or some such foolish nickname, or else you'll start calling me Mother. That's what happened to my parents."

I laughed. "I'm unlikely to start thinking of you as my mother. But we'll name her whatever you like." I handed Theodora a cup of water, and she drank deeply. "I thought childbirth was supposed to be easy for witches."

She looked at me in amusement over the rim of the cup. "I'm never going to persuade you I'm not a witch, am I. But I gather you have never seen any other woman give birth?"

"Of course not. And the midwife almost didn't let me be here."

"Fathers aren't usually welcome. But this was an easy birth in comparison to most. Even with the best magic, neither birth nor death will ever be painless."

I nodded. "Death I know about."

"And now you know about birth." Our baby was drinking more slowly now, and her eyes were half closed. Theodora stroked her tiny tuft of hair as if in wonderment. "Her hair's going to be lighter than mine, almost chestnut colored."

The same color, I thought, that mine would be if it hadn't turned white when I was twenty-nine.

"I hope her eyes stay blue," added Theodora.

I had a vague sense that babies' eyes, like kittens', changed color in a few weeks, but I didn't say anything.

"We'll name her Antonia," said Theodora.

"An excellent name," I agreed. I would indeed have agreed happily to anything. Such an obviously perfect child would have given beauty even to an ugly name. I imagined for a moment all the wonderful things that Antonia would do while growing up. "We'll have the bishop baptize her."

Theodora too had almost started to doze, but at this she opened her eyes and frowned. "I don't think the bishop will want to baptize an illegitimate child himself."

"The bishop and I have been friends for twenty years, and he likes you. He'll be happy to."

"And aren't you worried about what the wizards' school will say if one of their graduates publicly acknowledges his liaison with a witch?"

Since I had no intention of worrying about what the school did or did not think appropriate, I stayed with the topic of the bishop. "It's certainly not Antonia's fault that her parents were heedless. And—" I hesitated, not wanting to put pressure on Theodora while she was weak. But I had to say it. "We can still be married."

I needn't have worried about putting pressure on her. She just smiled and leaned back against the pillows, closing her eyes. "We've already been through all this, Daimbert. I can't let you destroy your career as a wizard by marrying me."

I should have known she would say that. I kissed her on the cheek. "Just remember I love you," I whispered, but both mother and baby were already asleep. Carefully I adjusted the blanket around them. I had no way of anticipating that five years later I would decide I had to kill a rival for Theodora's affections.

PART ONE

Miracle-Worker

I

The clash of swords shattered the night stillness. For a second I tried to incorporate the sound into my dream, but then I sat up abruptly to hear the clang of steel on steel with waking ears. My casement windows opened onto the castle courtyard, and the sound came from the direction of the gate.

In a second I was out of bed, my heart pounding wildly, fumbling with numb fingers at the door latch. We *never* had armed violence here in the kingdom of Yurt. The night watchman had for years been only a formality, but this sounded like real fighting.

But by the time I was out in the courtyard, the cobblestones cold and hard underfoot, the clashing had stopped. The night and silence were ominous.

I flew through the courtyard toward the gate, shaping a paralysis spell for whomever I would find. A lantern burned where the night watchman should be standing, and by it was a large indistinct lump. A cloaked and hooded man bent over it, apparently tying it up with a cord.

"Who are you?" gasped the indistinct lump in the night watchman's voice.

Two more seconds and my spell would be ready. But the hooded man spoke first, as though in mild surprise, and at his voice the watchman gave an amazed laugh. "I am Paul, your king. I thought I was well known to you."

I dropped to the ground, abandoning my spell, caught between anger and relief. The watchman seemed to feel the same way. "But, sire! Why didn't you tell me who you were rather than attacking? I might have killed you!"

"Yes indeed," said King Paul cheerfully, pushing back his hood. "The king of Yurt came very near to being killed by his own watchman! And very pleased with you I am, too. But you probably don't want to lie there bound all night."

He saw me then. "Good evening, Wizard," he said, looking up from undoing the knots he had just finished tying. "I decided not to spend another night at that old ruined castle I've been exploring but to come on home."

I took and let out a deep breath. "I hope you realize, sire," I contented myself with saying, "that you came very close to being trapped at best by a paralysis spell—or even transmogrified into a frog." The problem with being Royal Wizard was that I was supposed to have mature wisdom to offer my king but was not in a position to spank him as though he had been twenty years younger.

"Then I have both a competent wizard and a competent night watchman," Paul said cheerfully. "Have you ever been to the ruined castle, Wizard? It's over in the next kingdom, but I think you'd find it very interesting. I'll just take care of my horse; I left him outside the moat. Good-night." And he disappeared back out the gate.

I helped the watchman up. He rubbed his wrists where

they had been chafed by the cord and retrieved his sword. "And I helped train him myself," he said with pleased pride.

This was not my own reaction. Paul had been king only a few years, and if he thought testing his castle's defenses by putting his own life in danger was nothing more than a joke, then he needed to find more to do to keep himself occupied. Either that, the thought struck me with depressing force, or else the castle's main source of mature wisdom was going to have to teach him some.

But my first thoughts the next morning were not for Paul. "My, uh, my *niece* would like to visit me here at the castle, my lady," I told the queen mother. "That is, if it's all right with you."

She looked at me, puzzled, her head cocked to one side. "I don't think I knew you had a niece, Wizard." I willed her to understand though not daring to say more. The queen knew about Antonia—or should. "How old is the girl?" she asked.

"She's five."

The queen blinked, long lashes over emerald eyes. The matronly mother of the king, she was still the most beautiful woman I had ever met, much more lovely than Theodora although with none of her intelligence and wit.

"Oh," said the queen in sudden comprehension. "Of course, Wizard. We would be delighted to have your, uh, your *niece* visit the castle. The duchess's daughters will also be visiting this week, although I myself will be away. Does the girl have a nurse of her own or should I ask the constable to engage one for her stay?"

"Oh, she won't need a nurse," I said. And I hurried up to the pigeon loft to send Theodora a message that I would be coming in two days to see her and pick up our daughter.

Theodora lived, as she had since I first met her, in the cathedral city of Caelrhon, in the next kingdom over from Yurt. She had Antonia all dressed in a new blue dress when I set the air cart down in the narrow street outside her house two mornings later. The air cart was the skin of a long-dead purple flying beast, which would still fly if given magical commands. I tethered it to a ring by the door and ducked inside.

"I'm all ready," said Antonia gravely. "I packed my bag all by myself."

I hugged her and kissed Theodora, who sat at her sewing. She gave me a one-armed embrace but did not get up. Her curly nut-brown hair was even more tousled than usual. "We don't have to leave right away," I said.

Theodora used her teeth to rip out some basting thread. "I'm supposed to have these dresses ready by tomorrow," she said distractedly. "I'm glad you're taking Antonia now."

"But I could help you pin seams," said the girl. "I'm very good at pinning seams," she explained to me as though it were a great secret.

Theodora smiled. "I know you are. But go with the wizard. They'll all think you're beautiful in your blue dress when you reach Yurt. Aren't you looking forward to living in a castle for a week?"

It was the castle that decided it for Antonia. She had never been to Yurt. She marched out toward the air cart, then darted back in to grab her bag and, somewhat belatedly, kiss her mother good-bye.

Theodora kissed me too. "I'll see you both next week. She really is a good girl, Daimbert," she added, "but make sure she gets enough sleep. She'll keep herself awake for hours if you let her."

And so, rather abruptly, rather than having a pleasant day with the woman I loved, I found myself leaving for home with the daughter with whom I had never before spent more than brief periods alone. A moderately skilled wizard, with access through the Hidden Language to the same forces that had shaped the earth, I felt at a loss before this serious-eyed young girl. I wanted this to be a wonderful week, an opportunity to gain the affection and confidence of someone who might not even be certain I was her father.

Boys I thought I knew about, from memories of my own childhood and from watching Paul grow up, but girls, I thought with something approaching panic, must be different. It was all very well for Theodora to say that she needed to get to bed on time, but what was involved in getting a girl to bed? Nightgowns and toothbrushes, I was sure, played a role in this, but how about her hair? Did I brush it? Was I supposed to rebraid it at night or in the morning? And did I even have the slightest idea how to braid hair?

I lifted Antonia into the air cart, climbed in myself, and gave the command to lift off. Her self-possession cracked for a moment as the cart rotated and rose above the twisting streets of Caelrhon. She clutched my leg and looked up at me—was it *supposed* to sway like this? When I smiled and the air cart's flight leveled out, she smiled back, reassured.

She stood on tiptoe to look over the edge as we soared above the construction for the new cathedral and across the green hills toward Yurt. Our shadow darted up and down the slopes below us.

"When I grow up and become a wizard I'm going to be able to fly like this myself," she said confidently. This had been something else I had been hoping to discuss with Theodora today—the question of when and how the daughter of a wizard and a witch should start learning magic. "Why do you think Mother always makes me wear blue?" she added.

"Because it looks so good with your eyes," I suggested.

Antonia's eyes had in fact never changed color, remaining a brilliant sapphire blue.

"I don't think so," she said, thinking it over. "I think it's only because Mother's own favorite color is blue. *My* favorite color is yellow. What's yours?"

"Blue," I said, thinking I would have to buy Antonia something yellow to wear.

I had expected that she would sleep on the couch in the outer room of my chambers, but Gwennie would not hear of it. "A little girl alone with a wizard?" she said. "You'd probably have a nightmare and turn her into a frog by mistake. Of course, you'd be very sorry in the morning, but think how *she'd* feel!"

Antonia, holding my hand, looked up at me and laughed, but with the slightest questioning look, as though wondering if Gwennie was right and she might unexpectedly find herself an amphibian.

I had the vague feeling that Royal Wizards in other kingdoms were treated with more awe and respect than to be accused by the castle staff of doing transformations by accident. "I wouldn't do anything to harm her, Gwennie," I tried to argue. This would have been easier if I had dared tell anyone Antonia was my daughter, but the queen was the only person in the castle who knew. "And you can't very well put a little girl like this in a room by herself."

"I sleep in a room by myself at home," Antonia piped up.

Gwennie, daughter of the cook and the castle constable, had been destined for the kitchens by her mother, but herself had always intended to replace her father. Indeed, since her father had been so sick the past winter, she had taken over more and more of his duties, supervising the other servants, arranging accommodations for visitors to the castle, and keeping the accounts and the ledgers. Senior members of the staff had smiled indulgently, assuming it was only a temporary situation. Knowing Gwennie and her determination, I knew better.

"I'll put her in the suite with the duchess's daughters," she announced, forestalling further argument—besides, the duchess's daughters probably knew all about hair brushing. "They've just arrived, and they were very interested to learn you had a niece. And I've already told you, Wizard," she finished loftily, "that in carrying out my duties I prefer the name of Gwendolyn."

The duchess's twin daughters, three years younger than King Paul, were delighted when I brought Antonia's little bag to their suite—a doll's smiling face poked out of the top of the bag. "We already said we could take care of the girl," the twins told me. "So you don't need to worry about your niece at all, Wizard. Oh, Gwennie, before you go, we're going to need more towels."

"Of course, my ladies," she said with a respect she never showed *me*.

"We know an old man, set in his ways, doesn't want youthful female companionship!" they added, going into giggles that I found highly inappropriate.

Antonia held on to my hand, looking up at them gravely. They had grown into handsome women in the last few years. Both the twins had inherited their father's height, being very tall, but physically the resemblance between them stopped there. Hildegarde was blond like her father, whose principality she would someday inherit, and Celia was slim and dark-haired like her mother, after whom she would one day be duchess of Yurt. They had always shared a unanimity against outsiders, which when they were little had even taken the form of a secret language, but I had the feeling that as they grew up their personalities had begun to diverge.

"What an adorable little girl," said Hildegarde. "It's hard to believe she's related to you, Wizard."

"Where did you get those big blue eyes, sweetheart?" asked Celia.

"I was born with them," said Antonia very seriously, which made both the twins start laughing again.

"I'd better warn you, Wizard," said Hildegarde with a grin for her sister, "that if you leave the girl with us too long Celia may make her into a nun, of *much* too pure a mind to want to associate with some magic-worker."

"And who was it," Celia shot back with an answering grin, "who was saying just today how much fun it would be to teach a little girl to use a sword?"

Antonia looked up at me again. "I haven't seen any swords yet," she said in anticipation. "Will I see a dragon too?"

"I'll keep the girl with me though dinner," I said and escaped.

As we walked back across the courtyard, Antonia asked thoughtfully, "Do you love other ladies besides my mother?"

"Of course not!" I replied, shocked.

"Those ladies are very pretty," she said in explanation.

I had tried to tidy my chambers for her arrival, but she immediately clambered onto my desk and started leafing through papers, telling me she was looking for good magic spells. When I lifted her down and threw the papers into a drawer she crossed straight to my bookshelves and started to climb, working the toes of her small shoes in between the volumes.

"Here, I want to show you something interesting," I said quickly, taking hold of her again and planting her in a chair. "And, Antonia, I don't want you on my shelves."

"But Mother likes to climb," she objected.

"Not on shelves. It's very dangerous. She'll be angry at me if you hurt yourself."

"What are you going to show me?"

"A unicorn," I said, throwing the spell together as quickly as I could.

II

And so I spent much of the afternoon working a series of magical illusions that I hoped would amuse a girl. She watched very seriously without commenting at all, but she did snuggle up next to me while I told her a few stories from my experiences in the fabled East and in the borderlands of the wild northern land of magic. However, she kept being disappointed at the absence of dragons in my stories.

"We've only ever once had a dragon here in Yurt," I said, "years and years ago, before the king was even born. It almost killed me." For a number of reasons, I did not think the details appropriate for her.

But instead of asking me more, she jumped up, listening with an eager expression. "I hear a swordfight!"

My heart gave an abrupt thump, but the faint sound of swords during the day, carried into the castle from outside, was perfectly normal. "Someone's practicing," I said. "Do you want to go see?"

Antonia ran ahead, chestnut-colored braids bouncing against the back of her blue dress. On the grass outside we found King Paul and Hildegarde, fencing with swords and light shields.

In a leather tunic and men's leggings, her long blond hair tied back and eyes flashing, Hildegarde had a magnificent figure. She was as tall as the king, well muscled but not the least bit unfeminine. I would have found the sight of her before me highly distracting, but Paul apparently did not. He concentrated on his fighting, moving lightly, landing all his blows on her shield while deftly parrying the strokes she rained less discriminately on him. For ten minutes they circled each other, fighting while more and more of the staff came out of the castle to watch.

"*Very* good," the king said as Hildegarde got an unexpected advantage for a moment and forced him to retreat a few steps. "But don't drop your defense," he continued, his sword moving constantly as he spoke. "Because if you do—" and with a sudden twist he jerked the blade from her hand.

Antonia was watching openmouthed. I doubted a seamstress's house in town offered anything like this much excitement. Hildegarde dipped her head and lowered her shield. "That stung," she said, flexing the fingers of her sword hand. "I think you got in a lucky blow."

"In part, of course, I did," said Paul, pushing back sweaty hair and ignoring his audience. "I've had a lot more experience. But in part I'm just stronger than you are. Your footwork is fine, your stamina is fine, and your reach is longer than a lot of men, but you just don't have the upper-body strength you'd need."

"Father keeps telling me the same thing," she said glumly, retrieving her sword.

Paul smiled and put an arm casually across her shoulders, as though she had been a youth in knighthood training rather than a stunningly well constructed young woman. "I think it's time we got cleaned up for dinner. I'll try to think of some exercises for you to build your muscles."

At dinner my daughter demonstrated excellent manners, sitting beside me with a copy of *Thaumaturgy A to Z* bringing her up to table level. Afterwards I took her to the twins' suite—Hildegarde had been transformed back into a modestly attired aristocratic lady for dinner—

and told them to make sure Antonia got to bed soon.

King Paul was waiting at the door of my chambers when I returned. "I'd like to talk to you, Wizard," he said, frowning.

Good. This was my opportunity to impart some wisdom—if I could only think how to tell my liege lord diplomatically that he had been behaving like a fool. Acting in front of the staff as if he did not notice that Hildegarde was not a boy was perhaps insufficient cause for comment by itself, but I hadn't forgotten him allowing the watchman to attack him in good earnest. I pressed my palm against the magic door lock and let him in, leaving the door open since it was such a pleasant June evening.

Paul flopped down on my couch and stretched long legs out before him. "You know, Wizard," he said, "sometimes it seems that you're almost the only person in the castle not trying to get me married."

"Married?" This was certainly a different topic.

"My Aunt Maria and half the ladies in court seem to bring the topic up every day. Mother's the worst, of course." Even his frown could not obscure the fact that Paul was extremely handsome, golden-haired, superbly muscled, with his mother's emerald eyes and ready smile and his own grace and confidence in everything he did. "For the longest time she was trying to marry me to the daughter of King Lucas of Caelrhon. Not that Mother—unlike Aunt Maria!—ever said anything explicitly. But have you noticed how many times in the last year the little princess has been invited to the castle? And there were always hints, suggestions that now that I was king it was time to start giving some thought to the heir who would one day be king after me."

"And you don't like the princess?" I asked.

"There's nothing to like! I'm sure she'll be fine when she grows up, but it's quite a stretch calling her a woman rather than a child. How could I possibly be interested in someone like that?"

"It would certainly make sense to your mother," I suggested, "forging anew a dynastic tie between the twin kingdoms of Yurt and Caelrhon. After all, her own husband is the younger brother of King Lucas."

Paul pulled a jeweled-handled knife from his belt and flipped it into the air, caught it, flipped it up and caught it again. I had never been quite sure how much he approved of his mother's second marriage, but that was not what was bothering him now. "I thought a king was supposed to be able to do whatever he wanted," he said gloomily. But then he abruptly smiled for the first time since entering my chambers. "But I *can* keep on with my horses. I've got a dozen foals sired by Bonfire now, and I'm going to backbreed some of the fillies to him. The stables of Yurt will one day be famous."

"And you've been able to do a lot for educating the children of Yurt." I knew that Paul had, from his own resources, laid out a great deal in addition to the amount the royal treasury had always expended on books and teachers' salaries in the schools scattered across the kingdom.

He waved this away as barely worth mentioning. "I guess I just don't want to feel that everyone considers me a stallion myself, interesting only if I'm fathering the heir to the throne."

The topic of fatherhood always made me feel as though my ears were burning. Traditionally wizards neither marry nor have children, being considered wedded to institutionalized magic. Although I had managed to carry on as Royal Wizard of Yurt in the five years since Antonia was born without either Paul or the wizards' school learning she was my daughter, this was a charade I could not continue indefinitely. Part of my decision to bring Antonia to Yurt was a vague feeling that once she was here I might find a way to resolve the issue.

The king did not seem to notice my confusion. "I think I finally made Mother understand that I'm not about to marry a thirteen-year-old girl, but rather than giving me a little peace she invited the duchess's daughters to come visit! I'm sure she thought she was very subtle, being away with her husband at the royal court of Caelrhon while the twins were here, so as not to appear to be putting any pressure on me, but it's still obvious why she invited them. I thought the three of us, the twins and I, had made it clear years ago that none of us wanted to marry each other, but apparently we're going to have to do it all over again."

"Are you quite so sure they wouldn't want to marry you?" I asked.

Paul crossed his booted legs and smiled. "Of course not. We've known each other all our lives. Neither one of them wants to marry anyone. Celia just wants to study her Bible, and Hildegarde intends to become a knight."

This was news to me, though maybe it shouldn't have been. "But women can't be knights!" Or, for that matter, wizards, I added to myself. But Antonia had said she was going to be a wizard.

Paul laughed. "Try telling that to Hildegarde. *I've* never had any luck changing her mind."

So far I hadn't been able to work in any discussion of the fact that a king without an heir should not imperil himself for a joke. But fathers, I told myself, had to act responsibly even if no one else did. "Aren't there *any* adult princesses who would consider marrying you, even if the twins won't?" I asked. "After all—"

He didn't give me a chance to finish. "Of course there are, Wizard," he said, looking at me levelly. "Last winter, when I spent several months in the great City by the sea with those relatives of Mother's, there were ladies enough who would have been more than willing to marry me or, for that matter, do anything else I wanted." He shook his head in disapproval—or a good imitation. "Incomprehensible, of course," which I thought showed a remarkable lack of insight. "Not a few of them even had royal blood! I expect wizards don't get proposals like that, so you won't know how startling it can be."

I prudently kept silent.

"So of course there are women of appropriate rank who will have me—the problem is that I wouldn't be willing to marry any of *them*. If I ever do decide to get married, it's going to be to someone who excites me to the very core of my being, someone who feels as though she and I were two halves of the same whole, waiting from before our births to be reunited: *not* just someone who would be politically appropriate. So what do you think, Wizard?"

His green eyes sought mine. I wondered briefly if he might be someone who would never find women romantically attractive, which would of course make the succession much more problematic. Without any good answer, I looked out toward the twilight courtyard and stammered, "Well, a king of course, that is— I mean, minds have been known to change—"

But whatever Paul was hoping I would say, it was not what he had been hearing from the queen and the Lady Maria. "I really don't know what you should do, sire," I said, meeting his look. "You certainly shouldn't force yourself to marry someone you find less appealing than your horses. And you can't look at every woman you meet with both of you wondering if *this* is the one. Perhaps after a period of time—"

Paul rose before I had to carry this inadequate advice any further. "Well, at least I know I have one more ally in the castle," he said, settling his belt. "Maybe I'll go see Gwennie." He ducked his head to go out through my door.

"Gwennie?" I said, startled. "But she—"

"She should be done with her evening chores by now. She's always been a good person to talk to—almost as good as you, Wizard," he added generously. "She was the one who helped me decide how to break it to Mother the other year that I wasn't going to marry either of the twins."

And he was gone, leaving me looking thoughtfully after him. That Gwennie was the daughter of the cook and the castle constable was only one of the reasons why I did not think her the best person with whom the king might discuss the question of whom he should marry.

When I went to find Antonia in the morning, she was wearing a yellow scarf belonging to one of the twins and finishing a big bowl of porridge with gusto. "Guess what, Wizard!" she said with an excited smile. "Hildegarde and Celia are going to teach me to ride a horse!"

"It's very good of you, my ladies," I began, "to help take care of my, uh, niece, but you really—"

"We *want* to do it, Wizard," said Hildegarde.

"They were going to teach me to read," said Antonia, "but I told them I already knew how."

"Then later today," said Hildegarde cheerfully, "we'll teach her how to deal cards off the bottom of the pack."

"What?!" I glared at the twins while Antonia grinned in anticipation.

"It can be a very useful skill for a lady," said Celia, affecting a serious tone, "learning how to spot cheating so she will not be tricked herself. So we'll see you this afternoon, after our ride. Now, if you'll excuse us, we need to put on our riding habits."

"Make sure the door is tight," I heard Hildegarde say as it swung shut in my face. "He's an old man. The shock of seeing us dressing *couldn't* be good for him." And all three of them—including, I was mortified to hear, my daughter—began to giggle.

Since it looked like I wasn't going to spend the morning trying to make Antonia feel as comfortable with me as she apparently already did with the twins, I instead went to look for Gwennie.

I found her in the kitchen, slicing mushrooms for lunch. We grew mushrooms in the castle cellars, and the cook made excellent soup with them. If Paul had not yet persuaded his mother that he was unready to marry anyone, Gwennie had yet to persuade her own mother that she would never be a cook.

I worked the pump for her. "Antonia seems happy that you put her in the suite with the twins, Gwennie— uh, Gwendolyn," I said.

But her frown had nothing to do with Antonia or with whatever I chose to call her. She shook the water from a handful of mushrooms and moved her knife so fast I could scarcely follow. "Paul told me he'd talked to you yesterday," she said after a quick glance around showed her mother and the kitchen maids all at the far side of the room. That she called him simply by his name, without his title, and didn't even seem to notice that she had, told me how distressed she had been by their conversation.

"I can't see him marrying a child princess any more than he can," I said encouragingly.

"But she might be the best person for him," Gwennie said, pushing away a strand of hair from her face with a damp wrist. The knife flashed again. "If he told the queen he'd marry her when she was five years older, then he wouldn't be bothered in the meantime by a parade of other candidates. And in five years, anything—" She stopped herself. "The girl would have to be better than the duchess's daughters." She allowed herself a smile. "I'm sorry, Wizard. I shouldn't be talking to you like this."

"Better me than anyone else," I said, working the pump again. Wizards in royal castles have always been in somewhat of an ambivalent position, with a power beyond that of kings if they cared to use it, yet on the paid staff like any servant. Most wizards manage to cultivate airs of authority and mystery that make everyone, from kings to stable boys, treat them with deference. In spite of twenty-five years of intermittent trying, I had never gotten anyone at Yurt to treat me with deference and had decided it was not worth the effort.

"I didn't tell Paul any of this, of course," Gwennie said, scooping mushrooms from the board into a bowl.

"How about telling him not to challenge an armed man for fun?" I said, but she wasn't listening.

"If I started telling him the same things everyone else is saying," she said, "he'd stop coming to talk to me." Although Gwennie and Paul were almost exactly the same age and had played together as children, I had imagined they had grown apart in the last fifteen years. Perhaps I was mistaken.

"So don't you agree, Wizard," she said, looking at me with serious eyes that should have been bright and laughing, "that the best thing for him to do would be to marry the little princess? She's certainly of a suitable station for him"—with only the slightest catch in her breath—"and I'm sure will be well trained to become a gracious queen of Yurt and mother of Paul's children."

She turned away abruptly at that, making the gesture into rinsing off her knife with more than necessary energy.

The thought flashed through my mind that if Paul was going to wait until someone grew up, then even

Antonia might someday be old enough for him. But the illegitimate daughter of a witch and a wizard would never be of suitable station for a king—even less than the daughter of a cook and castle constable.

III

The twins and Antonia came back from their riding lesson in the early afternoon. When they left they had been on two rangy geldings and a shaggy little pony, but they returned with Antonia sitting in front of Hildegarde, half asleep, and the pony led behind. A wilted chain of daisies was around the girl's neck.

"I want to tell Mother I can ride now," she roused herself to tell me. "Can we go see her?"

"Not right now, but you can tell me," I suggested, carrying her into the castle.

"I can make the pony stop and go forward and even gallop," she murmured into my neck. "Hildegarde didn't want me to gallop but I did anyway. I only fell off once."

"She falls very well for a child," said Celia, which I did not find nearly as reassuring as it was doubtless meant to be. I held Antonia close and stroked her fine hair.

Having left her asleep with the duchess's daughters I returned to my chambers, feeling on edge and unable to concentrate on the spells I was trying to perfect for entertainment over dessert tonight. Instead I wrote Theodora a brief message to be sent on the carrier pigeons, telling her that Antonia's first day in Yurt had gone well, leaving out all mention of cheating at cards or falls from ponies, and saying I sent love from both of us.

As I came down from the pigeon loft in the tower, Gwennie met me. "You have a telephone call, Wizard."

For a second I imagined it was Theodora. But she

had never wanted me to install a magical telephone in her house, saying she would have no use for it—and since it would have been hard to conceal my relationship with her if I was always talking to her on the phone, I had to agree she had a point.

The call was instead from my old friend the bishop of Caelrhon. "Joachim!" I said with pleasure. It had been ages since we'd talked. Even when I visited Theodora in the cathedral city he was usually too busy with his duties for me to want to bother him. "How good to hear from you!"

His face was a tiny image in the base of the glass telephone: black hair streaked with gray at the temples, enormous and compelling dark eyes, and an expression of great seriousness—except sometimes when he was talking to me. I had long ago decided that I should count it a personal virtue rather than a failing that the bishop of the twin kingdoms of Yurt and Caelrhon seemed to find me more amusing than he did anyone else.

"I would like your advice, Daimbert," he said, not smiling now. "There is something, well, strange going on here."

"How strange?"

He hesitated. "It's hard to say. A miracle-worker has come to town."

This didn't sound like the sort of thing to concern a wizard. "But that's good, isn't it? Why do you need *my* advice?"

The bishop hesitated again, just long enough for me to start to wonder if it might be serious after all. Joachim didn't frighten easily. "I'm not sure he is really working miracles," he said at last. "He might be working magic. But he has started to acquire a following. I need to know if he is a fraud or has truly been touched by God."

Wizards could easily tell the supernatural from the

natural forces of magic, I thought somewhat smugly, even if priests could not. The situation did not sound nearly as worrisome to me as it apparently did to the bishop, but it was always good to have an excuse to see him. And using my magic to help him would be much better than sitting around Yurt wondering who was going to marry whom. "Of course, Joachim. I can come right away."

Even as I spoke it occurred to me that if I had just brought Antonia to Yurt in order to get to know her better, I could not very well abandon her for quick trips to Caelrhon, even if she did seem to be spending more time with the twins than with me. But perhaps now might not be a bad time after all. She was napping anyway, so if I went at once I would miss dinner with her but should be able to solve the cathedral's problems for them, see Theodora this evening, and still be back first thing in the morning.

There had been a time, I thought as I went to look for the twins to tell them I was leaving Antonia with them, when I could not, as wizard of Yurt, have had anything to do with magical occurrences in the kingdom of Caelrhon. But for the last few years the Royal Wizard of Caelrhon had been a good friend. He lived in the royal castle, not in the cathedral city itself, and he had told me with exasperated firmness that if the cathedral was overrun with nixies he would just as soon have me deal with it myself. I was probably one of the few wizards in the western kingdoms to get along well with a bishop.

I met Hildegarde in the middle of the courtyard, just coming back from the weapons shop where she told me she had left off a mail shirt for repairs. "Of course, Wizard," she said casually. "Antonia will have so much fun with us she won't even realize her uncle is gone."

I peeked in a minute at my daughter: sleeping deeply, her cheeks flushed and her doll's perky face next to hers. Celia sat reading her Bible nearby. A sweet scene, I thought, heading out of the castle for the flight to Caelrhon.

But Celia caught up with me. "You're going to see the bishop?" she asked, low and intense. I was startled to see the change in her from the carefree young woman of just a short time earlier. Perhaps there were sides of her that did not come out when Hildegarde was there. "Take me with you, Wizard."

It would mean going in the air cart rather than flying myself, which would have been faster, but I couldn't very well refuse. Hildegarde could certainly watch over my daughter by herself—though I wondered if she might indeed have made her into a warrior by the time I came back. In ten minutes Celia and I were rising above the towers of the royal castle, and the air cart began the steady flapping of wings that would take us to Caelrhon.

I studied her as we flew. She sat in the skin of a purple flying beast, whipping along a quarter mile above the ground, the wind tugging her midnight hair free of its pins, with no more apparent wonder at the experience than if she had been taking a horse to the cathedral city. She wore a simple dark dress that accented her slimness and her ivory skin, and I thought that it didn't seem right that someone so young and pretty should be so glum. Her eyes were focused inward, as though concentrating on something she needed to do or say.

When she spoke it was clear that whatever speech she was preparing was not intended for me. Instead she said, "I gather you and the bishop have always been friends, Wizard?"

"Most of the time for twenty-five years," I agreed. "Institutionalized magic and institutionalized religion normally have no use for each other, but Joachim and

I have managed to be friends in spite of each thinking that the other one is seriously misguided on certain important points."

But Celia was not interested in the millennia-old tensions between wizardry and the church. "All I really need is an introduction," she said, "a chance, maybe only for a quarter hour, to talk to him directly. I've tried reaching him before but have always been put off by one priest or another, who just tell me I'm being silly and shouldn't bother His Holiness."

"And *are* you being silly?" I asked lightly, trying to take some of the sharp intensity from her face.

She did not smile. "It's not silly to know what you want—what you were meant to do. The only trouble is with others who think they can plan your life better than you can for yourself."

I nodded, not sure what I was agreeing to but thinking of Paul.

Celia and I were shown into the bishop's study after only a short wait. A shaft of late afternoon sunlight lay across the floor. Joachim stepped out of the shadows to meet us, tall and sober in his formal scarlet vestments. He lifted an eyebrow, mildly surprised to see a young woman with me.

I introduced her. "Forgive me, Celia, for not recognizing you at once," said the bishop politely. "I am always happy to see any of my spiritual sons and daughters, but I fear I have not spoken with you properly since you were quite a bit younger."

She knelt, overcome, to kiss his episcopal ring, something I myself had always been able to justify not doing. "Please, Holy Father," she said in a low voice, "don't send me away before hearing me. Don't leave, Wizard!" as I stepped toward the door, as though frightened of being left alone with the bishop. "I know you have business of your own here, and this—this should only take a minute."

Joachim blessed her, his hand resting lightly on her hair. "Rise, my daughter. Sit beside me and tell me what troubles your soul."

Celia gave me a quick glance as though for moral support, looked next at the crucifix on the wall as though hoping it would provide the support I clearly would not, gulped twice, and began. "Holy Father, I want to be a priest."

This was the same surprise to Joachim it was to me. Fortunately Celia kept her eyes on her folded hands. "When did you make this decision, my daughter?" the bishop asked kindly.

"I've always known it," she murmured bitterly, as though already hearing rejection in what sounded to me only like friendly interest. "Or, at least I've known it for several years. I was meant to serve God. I want to devote my life to bringing the absolute light of good and love to those around me. My parents expect me to get married and become a duchess, but I cannot."

"It would be hard for you to be a priest," said Joachim thoughtfully. "Since the time of Moses and Aaron, the priesthood has been entirely male. There has certainly always been a place in the Church for pious widows and virgins, though they can usually best serve God as cloistered nuns."

Celia was no widow, but she was most likely a virgin—though that was not really for me to know.

"There is," the bishop continued, "as I am sure you know, a nunnery in the kingdom of Yurt well known for its rigor and purity."

"I am *not* going to be a nun," said Celia, quietly and distinctly. "I intend to bring God's message to laymen and women, *especially* women. They'll listen to me when they would never listen to some male priest."

Joachim looked toward me, eyebrows raised, over her lowered head. I shrugged my shoulders with no idea what to say to her—especially since I thought she had a point.

"You're the bishop," Celia went on when he did not answer at once, determined to get in everything she had come to say. "You're the supreme religious leader in the area. You can accept whomever you want into the seminary without having to answer to anyone."

"It is true that I have no direct superior," said Joachim, "but that does not mean that I answer to no one. Above all, of course, I answer to God and to the church structure He has ordained, then to my own conscience, and then to all the other bishops in this region of the western kingdoms."

"And in none of this—"

"In none of this," said the bishop, "do I see women priests."

He spoke quietly, gently, but with a firmness that would have kept even me from disagreeing. Celia blinked hard, but no tear escaped her eye. She was, after all, the duchess's daughter.

"Then I guess I'll go see if I can hire a horse to return to Yurt," she said expressionlessly. "Thanks for the ride, Wizard."

But Joachim put a hand on her arm as she started to rise. "Do not leave spiritually dissatisfied. I need to speak now with the wizard, but you and I can talk more later. You were planning on staying in Caelrhon this evening anyway, weren't you, Daimbert?" He knew all about me and Theodora, the only person besides the queen of Yurt who did. "If you would like to stay tonight in the cathedral guest house, I am sure it can be arranged," he added to Celia. "A way should certainly be found for someone who feels herself called by God."

She nodded without looking up and let herself be led away by an acolyte.

"A true daughter of the duchess," I commented when the door closed. Duchess Diana of Yurt had always done exactly what she liked and had never been comfortable herself with the life of the noble lady. She seemed to have passed on several key personality traits to her daughters.

IV

"Now, Joachim," I said, "tell me about this problem you're having. Somebody is working miracles, you say?"

He turned quickly from frowning at the door where Celia had just gone. "Yes," he said, shifting his attention to me. "And if they are truly miraculous, the man may be a saint. But somehow, something about him does not seem true."

I sat down opposite him. "How long has he been here?"

"Only about two weeks," said the bishop as though in careful consideration. "Some say he arrived with the Romneys, though no one has seen him with them." The Romneys wandered from place to place throughout the western kingdoms; I had noticed their caravans and horses outside the city walls as we flew in. "But already he—"

"Give me an example," I prompted when he paused.

"What they are already calling his first miracle," said the bishop, drawing back so that his eyes were shadowed, "was saving the life of a little dog."

"A *dog*?"

"It belonged to a boy who lives down in the artisans' quarter, near the river—that is where this man seems to make his headquarters."

That was where Theodora and Antonia lived. Faint

unease prickled the hairs on the back of my neck.

"It had slipped its leash and run right under the wheel of a cart. The carter was very sorry, of course, but there was nothing he could have done. The boy picked up the dog's body—some say its ribs were crushed, some that it was already dead. But as the boy, sobbing, was carrying his dog home, this man stopped him, very kindly. He took the dog from him, cradled it in his own arms a minute—scores of people claim to have been eyewitnesses—and returned it to the boy alive, unharmed and barking."

I shook my head hard. "That's not magic. Magic's never had any control over the earth's natural cycle of life and death. We can prolong life but not restore it when it's gone."

"Yes," said the bishop quietly. "For that you need the supernatural, the power of the saints—or of a demon."

I took a breath and released it slowly. This had suddenly become much more serious. I had imagined someone who had picked up a few scraps of the Hidden Language somewhere, trying to make a living by producing rather pathetic illusions and passing them off on the credulous as miracles. But this person had *better* be working real miracles. The other possibility was black magic, which meant he had sold his soul to the devil.

"Listen, Joachim," I said. "There are a couple of very good demonology experts at the wizards' school. I'll telephone them—one will certainly want to come if this man is working with a demon. And that way—"

"No," said the bishop, low and firm. "I told you, this man may be a saint. I don't want him accused of black magic if he is, certainly not by one of the masters of your school, someone with no respect either for religion or the Church. That is why I sent for *you*." I had never had a whole lot of respect for the Church either, but I declined to mention this now. "I must find out where he draws his power, but I would not want him falsely accused—even martyred. The truly holy man," and he paused for a second, looking past me out the window, "must always seem profoundly strange to those caught up in the petty affairs of the world."

I considered for a moment, tapping my fingers on the bishop's desk and making myself stop when I realized what I was doing. I had the spells, of course, to detect the supernatural, but those spells would not by themselves indicate if a supernatural power was demonic or divine. "You must have made inquiries," I said. "What else have you found out?"

"I did more than make inquiries. I went down to the artisans' quarter to see him."

"And did you meet him? How old a man is he?"

"It was hard to tell his age," said the bishop, his dark eyes distant. "He was tall and gaunt, with a face that looked as though he did not know how to smile."

I didn't like this at all. I had once met a demon taking human form, and this is just what he had looked like.

"That is," the bishop continued, "until he *did* smile and his whole face was transformed by joy and beauty."

Not a demon, then, I said as persuasively as I could to the cold sensation at the pit of my stomach. A demon would not smile joyously at meeting a bishop. That is, unless the bishop himself was sunk in sin—a possibility I thought I could safely disregard.

"I spoke with him for close to an hour," Joachim went on. "He has something of an accent; at first I thought he might be a Romney but he's not. He told me he was highly honored that I had come in person to see him, denied any particular merit of his own, and tried to dismiss the whole story of the little dog by saying that he expected the saints had heard the boy's prayers."

This sounded like what a genuine saint would do. I tried to be reassured.

"So I was reassured," said Joachim. "He wouldn't tell me his name, saying it was of no importance, and I did not press him. Instead we spoke of the love of God for all His sons and daughters, even fallen and sunken in sin as we are. He seemed to have thought very little before about religious precepts, considering he told me he had been brought up as a Christian, but he told me he would start attending services at the artisans' church. In the days since I have heard he has become something of a favorite of the children of the quarter."

Including Antonia? I wondered in panic. "But something else happened or you wouldn't have telephoned me."

The bishop nodded and his enormous eyes found mine. "The children started bringing him, so the story goes, their broken toys, and he fixed them by passing his hand over them. One girl's doll had fallen in the fire, and he restored the charred remains to new, and better than new."

Could this possibly have been Antonia and *her* doll?

"This was not, of course, in the same category as restoring life, even the life of a dog. So I next began to wonder if perhaps he had told me truly, that the dog's recovery was due to the boy's prayers and not to this man's own merits. He could be working magical illusions out of good if mistaken intentions, I thought, restoring the appearance alone of wholeness, knowing the children would be too confused or frightened to accuse him of fraud when their toys became broken again in their hands as the illusion faded. I even thought it might be some kind of magic different from your school magic— the Romneys' spells, perhaps, or even witchcraft."

"The Romneys don't know any magic," I objected. "And witchcraft— Have you been talking to Theodora?"

I must have sounded irritated, because the bishop gave a small smile. "I speak with her often, of course—she is, after all, one of the best seamstresses working for the cathedral—but I would not say anything to her about magic that would sound accusatory without speaking to you first."

"So that's why you called me? To ask me about witchcraft?"

"No. I called you, Daimbert, to keep me from possibly making a very serious mistake."

Dustmotes danced in the horizontal light from the window. The sounds of the city were very far away as I waited for him to continue.

"Priests—and bishops—deal with good and evil every day," he said after a long pause. "But rarely do we see absolute good or absolute evil. Instead we see gradations of gray, virtuous paths followed only because they are not very demanding at the moment, sins fallen into because of laziness or a desire for some temporary advantage rather than because of a soul turned to darkness. Young Celia imagines herself a priest moving in a halo of white light. In fact, priests move daily through petty and rather sordid sins: lust, selfishness, lies half-believed by the person who tells them, much of it caused by greed and boredom among the wealthy and by ignorance and misery among the poor. It has come to this, Daimbert," leaning toward me, "that when I find myself meeting a man who is either very holy or else working with a demon, who represents true good or real evil rather than a gray somewhere between, I no longer trust myself to tell the difference. That is why I called you—you are one of the very few whose judgment I trust."

So far I had a king and a bishop trusting my judgment—now all I needed was to do so myself.

"I had almost persuaded myself," Joachim went on,

"that we were just very blessed in having a holy man here in Caelrhon, when the incident with the frog occurred."

It had been over twenty-five years since that transformations practical exam. Most of the time now I was able to discuss frogs without any self-consciousness. But the bishop's use of the term "incident with the frog" brought back all the embarrassment of that long-ago disaster. Even after all this time, I had never worked myself up to telling him about it.

"It may not be true," he continued. "There seem to have been only a few witnesses, and the stories that filtered up to the cathedral do not agree on all points. But in essence— A boy brought a frog, a live frog, to the miracle-worker and asked if he could kill it and then bring it back to life. And the man did so."

Faint in the distance I could hear the cathedral organ playing, bass notes vibrating on the lower edge of audibility. "That," I said slowly, "does not sound like a holy man to me."

"Or to me," said the bishop.

V

And that was why, when I would rather have been visiting Theodora, I was trying to find a miracle-worker. Sunlight still lingered in the long June evening as I walked down by the river. Theodora's house was only a few blocks away, but I did not want to worry her before I knew if there was something to be worried about.

The dockworkers had gone home, but children playing along the river's edge were happy to talk to me. "I haven't seen the Dog-Man today," one boy told me, "but I saw him yesterday. He's my friend. Are you his friend?"

"I've never met him," I said vaguely.

"But everybody knows the Dog-Man!" the boy protested.

Other children also happily talked to me because, I suspected, that way they could plausibly ignore the faint but clear calls of mothers wanting them to come home to bed. They said the man could sometimes be found in a little shack on the docks. But no one seemed to have seen him recently, and the shack—which didn't even have four walls, much less an intact roof—was empty of all except a faint but definite trace of *both* magic and the supernatural.

I shook my shoulders hard to try to dispel a feeling of unease. Magic and the supernatural were very rarely found together. Attempts to locate magically whoever lived in the shack told me there was no other wizard in the city—or, if there was, he was shielding his mind by very powerful spells. Scared off by my arrival now? I wondered. Or perhaps by my brief appearance in the city the day before? There was so much in the stories Joachim had told me that seemed contradictory that I felt I had to meet him before I could draw any conclusions.

And suppose the bishop was right, and the magic he was working was not the result of an abortive training at the school but rather of something closer to Theodora's witchcraft? But in that case, was the supernatural influence from the forces of good—or a demon?

I wouldn't know unless I found this man. When half an hour's walking and further probing failed to produce him, I decided to check with the Romneys. This magic-worker without a home or a name must have some place to spend the night, and the Romneys had always been generous toward others living on the fringes of society.

Their vividly painted caravans were drawn into a circle, in the center of which were horses, goats, and several mothers nursing their babies. It was growing dark at last, and their campfires flared bright. Most of the children, laughing with a flash of white teeth in dark faces, were playing an elaborate game that seemed to involve a great deal of running, screaming, and ducking in and out between the caravans. One woman shouted at them futilely in the Romney language.

I spun an illusory golden cord around the waist of a boy as he raced by. When he did not slow down the cord became a snake, ruby-eyed, winding its way up his arm and vibrating its tongue at him. He stopped at once, staring amazed and putting his other hand right through it as he tried to seize it. "Very good, Wizard!" he called then, spotting me.

The children now ran to circle around me. I spoke quickly before the adults could tell them to give me no information. "I'm looking for someone they call Dog-Man in the city," I said as casually as I could. "He's another magic worker, they say, and I wonder if he's here in your encampment. I'd like to meet him."

"I heard about Dog-Man," said one girl. "Someone said he smashed a pot and put it back together again."

This certainly didn't sound like any magic they had taught *us* in school. "But where is he now?" The Romney woman was bearing down rapidly on us.

The children looked at each other, shrugged, and laughed. "We don't know! We haven't seen him. Have you seen him?"

They scattered then, laughing and squealing. The woman, scowling under her red scarf, looked after them and then at me as though wondering whether to strike me with a Romney curse or offer to tell my fortune.

"I'm looking for someone," I said ingratiatingly, "called Dog-Man. He's just been here a couple of weeks but is already gaining a reputation as a miracle-worker." When she continued to frown, I added, "I'm a friend of Theodora's."

Theodora the Romneys all knew. The woman's expression suddenly cleared. She smiled broadly, flashing gold teeth below a lip that sprouted a long bristle. "You're her wizard friend!" But she shook her head. "I have never seen the Dog-Man myself. He has not visited our camp."

I spun her an illusion of her own, a bracelet of scarlet blossoms, thanked her, and headed back through the darkening air toward the lights of the city. First I would go by the episcopal palace and leave a note for the bishop, telling him of my lack of success in finding the man but suggesting hopefully that he might have left Caelrhon as inexplicably as he had arrived. Then I would go talk to Theodora. I had wanted to keep her out of this, but she might be the only person who could help me find someone who very clearly did not want to be found.

Simultaneously I knocked at Theodora's door and called to her directly, mind to mind, so she would know who was outside her house at this hour of the evening. "It's me."

She swung the door open hard, her amethyst eyes round. "Antonia's fine," I said rapidly, realizing too late how startling it must be to have someone at her door from whom she had just gotten a pigeon-message saying he was forty miles away. "Everyone's fine. Antonia is safely in Yurt with the duchess's twins. But the bishop needed to talk to me, and I couldn't miss the opportunity to see you." I took her face between my hands and kissed her. "Did you get those dresses done on time?"

She smiled then and pulled me inside. "It's wonderful to see you, Daimbert. I'm sorry that I was too busy to talk yesterday. Yes, I got the dresses done on time." I had told her more than once that I had plenty of money from what they paid me in Yurt and that she needn't sew for a living, but she had always insisted that she wanted to support herself.

Theodora cleared a space on the couch, wadding cloth

scraps and loose threads into a bag, piling pattern pieces on the table, giving me quick, happy glances as she worked. I knew enough to stay out of the way. She lit the magic lamp that she *had* agreed to accept from me and smiled again as the room was flooded with warm light—showing more cloth scraps scattered across the floor and under the table. Also under the table was a worn toy dragon. "It's a good thing," Theodora commented, "that wizards aren't any tidier than seamstresses, or you'd *never* want to visit me. So how is Antonia liking Yurt—and the duchess's daughters?"

We settled ourselves comfortably, my arm around Theodora and her head on my shoulder. She had always alternated between being affectionate and good-humored as she was now, and being—well, not lacking in affection, but somehow distant, as though wanting to keep some aspects of her life independent from me. I told her how Gwennie had insisted that it would be improper for Antonia to stay in my chambers, and how the twins seemed to enjoy her.

"She seems happier with them than with me," I finished, finding it coming out more plaintively than I intended.

"She loves you, Daimbert," Theodora said in reassurance. "She's just more used to women. That's why I'm so glad you're having a chance to be together."

If we ever did. I realized Antonia, happy to sit on my lap but not laughing at my most amusing illusions, had the same inner private reserve as her mother.

"And what did the bishop need?" Theodora continued. She kissed the corner of my cheek. "This is probably not what a wizard likes to hear, but one of the best side-benefits of knowing you has been the opportunity to become, at least a little bit, friends with a bishop."

She laughed as she spoke, but there was an emotional note to her voice when she mentioned Joachim that sounded as though she rated him more highly than any wizard. But I dismissed this thought. I was just being irritable because I was worried about the purported miracle-worker.

"There's someone working magic—or something— here in Caelrhon," I said abruptly. "The children call him the Dog-Man. Do you know him?"

Theodora turned in the circle of my arm to look at me. It was full dark outside now, and the lamp made wavering points of light in her eyes. "It's not any magic I know," she said quietly.

I pulled her closer. "Then you've met him? Is he really working miracles? Or—" and found I couldn't say it.

She shook her head, her hair moving against my beard. "I don't know what he's doing. I've not met him in person, only sensed his mind. There's something about him that is, well—not right. I can't say that he's evil, but there is nothing about him like the force of good that flows from the bishop."

Joachim again. I kept silent.

"A lot of the children in the neighborhood have made something of a pet of him. I've gotten to know the children well through Antonia, and they talk to me about him. He's been living in a little shack on the docks, made from scrap lumber, and the children bring him food from home. I told Antonia I didn't want her down there. I don't think she's disobeyed me yet. . . . That was part of the reason I wanted her in Yurt now. But I couldn't tell you that yesterday, with her standing right there."

This sounded to me too like an excellent reason to have Antonia in Yurt. The castle had had a giant pentagram put around it by my predecessor as Royal Wizard. Unless someone had moved the stones over the years, no demon would want to enter the castle because he would be unable to leave again. "I tried without success to find the man. No one has seen him since yesterday."

Theodora went still a moment, slipping her mind away into her own magic. "I don't find him either," she said then. "Maybe he's gone."

That was fine with me. Maybe he'd left Caelrhon for a kingdom where the Royal Wizard would spot him before the local bishop did, where no one would be too squeamish to call for a demonology expert. "Then I don't have to worry about him anymore," I said, finding Theodora's lips. "Say! You know you're always worried that Antonia will wake up—"

She laughed, pushing me away with hands on my chest. "I'll kiss you as much as you like, as loudly as you like—but wouldn't that be disgusting, to make big smacking kisses just because no one is here to overhear them?—but that's it. Remember our agreement."

I leaned back, exasperated. "I don't remember making an agreement that would last this long."

"Yes, you do," she said teasingly, though I was not about to be teased back into good humor over this. "I know the bishop explained it to you. We have sinned, been penitent, and been forgiven, but that means we must be even more careful. We are not married, and we cannot act as though we were."

"So we made one mistake," I said in irritation, "one big mistake six years ago, and now it's going to ruin the rest of our lives?"

"We have Antonia," she said mildly. "I would not call her the ruin of our lives. She is rather a reason for us to be supremely grateful."

"And do whatever the bishop tells us," I grumbled. Maybe I should have been angry with Joachim, but this all seemed like Theodora's fault. "Since when does a witch pay so much attention to a Church that considers all magic dangerous—*especially* women's magic?"

"Since when does a wizard come racing to town the instant a bishop telephones him?" she shot back.

But then she looked at me, gave a smile that brought out the dimple in her cheek, and took me by the ears and kissed me on the eyelids. "Don't be angry, Daimbert. I get so little chance to see you. I want to talk to you about what's happening in Yurt. Let me make us some tea."

She was right, I thought, watching her light the fire for the water and forcing myself to stop frowning. I didn't want to waste this time with her by arguing. The easiest answer, of course, would have been to get married, but I no longer dared ask her. She had always refused, always would refuse, saying it would be the ruin of my wizardry career. But sometimes, like now, I wondered if that was the real reason. As fond as she was of me, I apparently did not "excite her to the very core of her being," or whatever it was King Paul was waiting for: she herself did not want to marry me.

"Are you sure there isn't somebody else?" I asked, trying to make it sound like a joke and not succeeding.

"Of course not," she said briskly, getting out cups. "I promised you years ago that you would be the only one."

When people got married, I thought gloomily, they promised to forsake all others and cleave only to each other. Theodora seemed happy with the first half of that promise but not the second. I was a wizard, with powers supposedly so great that the only reason I served a king rather than being a ruler of men myself was the service tradition of institutionalized magic. Yet here I was stymied by a witch and a five-year-old girl.

PART TWO

Lady Justinia

I

"A flying creature is coming," Antonia told me calmly. She had tugged open the door of my chambers, looking in from the sunlit courtyard to where I was finishing a late breakfast back home in Yurt. "Do you think it's a dragon?"

I was past her and out into the courtyard in a second. Something small and dark, flying much too fast to be a cloud, approached from the south. I snatched her up as I tried to put a far-seeing spell together. "I always wanted to see a real dragon," she said.

But it was not a dragon. It was a flying carpet.

Dark red with tasseled corners, it flew purposefully toward the castle, hesitated and rotated a moment overhead, then plunged down to land in the middle of the courtyard. On it, feet shackled together, stood a young elephant. As I watched in amazement it raised its trunk and trumpeted, the sound echoing from the cobblestones.

But the elephant was not all the carpet carried. A person was also seated on it, surrounded by boxes and parcels that tumbled off as the carpet came to a stop.

"In the name of all-merciful God," came a high woman's voice, "is this at last the kingdom of Yurt, or have I passed quite beyond the fringes of the civilized world?"

I stepped forward cautiously. I had only ever seen elephants once before, years ago on our quest to the East. The woman rose with a swirl of black hair that reached to her waist. "This is indeed the kingdom of Yurt," I said, keeping an eye on the animal.

Antonia, who had been staring in as much astonishment as I, elbowed me as though to remind me of better manners. "Welcome to Yurt!" she called out. In a confidential undertone she added, "That's an elephant, Wizard. Mother showed me a picture of one in a book. They aren't dangerous unless they step on you."

The woman smiled then, her curved lips crimson, black almond-shaped eyes taking in both me and the girl. Her eyelids were painted an iridescent blue and her red silk blouse was nearly transparent. I found myself tugging at my jacket and standing straighter. "I am Daimbert, the Royal Wizard."

"At last," she said, stepping from the carpet. "Thou art exactly the one I sought. By my faith, it seems an age since my feet have touched the earth. My elephant requires hay and water. And aid my servant in bringing the baggage to my chambers."

Antonia saw the servant first. I had taken him for one more parcel until he unfolded himself to stand up and— My daughter gasped in my ear. He was not a parcel but not a man either. This lady's servant was a shiny metallic automaton.

He started gathering up packages, one in each of his six arms, and waited, staring silently out of flat silvery eyes toward me for directions. The elephant wrinkled the leathery skin all along its back and looked around the courtyard. "I'm sorry, my lady," I managed to say. "I don't know who you are."

"Justinia, granddaughter of the governor of Xantium,"
she said as though surprised that anyone should not
know. She reached with a jangle of bracelets into a
leather bag. "But here. This message is for thee."

The parchment was written all over in indecipherable
characters. But I had seen something like this before.
A few quick words in the Hidden Language, and the
letters scurried across the page, changing their shapes
and forming themselves into legible words.

It was from Kaz-alrhun, the greatest mage in the
eastern city of Xantium. I had known him years ago;
when our party from Yurt had been in the East he had
saved all our lives. It seemed that he was now asking
for the return of that favor.

"May God's grace be on you, Daimbert," the message
ran. "This letter will introduce to you the Lady Justinia
of Xantium. She is the governor's granddaughter and
my own distant niece. Certain political events in Xantium
have put her in line for assassination, so it seemed safest
to remove her far from the city. I learn that the king of
Yurt I knew is dead, but I am certain the court of Yurt
will welcome her for old friendship's sake. Justinia is
not a princess, as the governors rule only in the name
of an Empire gone fifteen centuries, but she should
be treated like a princess."

I looked up from the parchment. Justinia was gazing
around her. "This castle is most fair!" she exclaimed.
"It is like unto a child's toy!"

The arrival of a flying carpet in the courtyard, laden
with an elephant, an eastern governor's granddaughter,
an automaton, and all their luggage, had naturally
attracted attention. The chaplain, short and fussy,
scurried up beside me. "Do you think she can possibly
be a Christian, looking like that?" he asked in a loud
whisper, both shocked and intrigued.

Justinia overheard him. "Of a certainty I am a

Christian," she said haughtily. "*All* of Xantium's governors have always followed the true faith."

King Paul and Hildegarde came in across the drawbridge, practice swords in their hands. Paul stopped dead as Justinia turned with a swirl of her skirt. I wasn't sure he even noticed the elephant. "Welcome, Lady," he stammered as she favored him with a devastating smile. "I am the king of Yurt."

His sword dangled unheeded and his mouth came partly open as she gave a deep, graceful curtsey, her head lowered but her eyes giving him a look of assessment. "I am honored to meet thee, most high king," she said then, one eyebrow cocked and an amused twitch to her lips. "I was told the king of Yurt was a boy. Verily my uncle the mage has inadequate information." I decided I didn't have to worry after all that Paul might not find women romantically attractive.

"I desire to learn all the quaint customs of the West," Justinia continued. "Now here is another wonder!" looking Hildegarde up and down. "Is the royal guard made up quite entire of such women? Are they perhaps bred for this purpose? This one is of a certainty a fine specimen! Or is she perhaps thy concubine?"

"No, she's my cousin," said Paul with an embarrassed laugh, not looking at Hildegarde. She hooked her thumbs into her belt and frowned, as if not entirely sure what about the Lady Justinia she found insulting.

Gwennie came hurrying up at this point, before Justinia could ask us further about our western customs. "This lady is a very important visitor to Yurt from the East," I said hurriedly. "Her great-uncle once did all of us a great service. Could you find her some appropriate accommodations?"

"The stables should suffice for my elephant," said Justinia. "He is still quite young."

"Welcome to Yurt!" said Gwennie, as polite as

Antonia in spite of her surprise. She gave the king a quick glance and looked away again. "What a lovely dress, my lady! And what a, well, unusual way to arrive! Come right this way; the best guest chambers are in the south tower."

The automaton stepped off the carpet with a jangling of joints to follow them. Gwennie gave a sharp gesture behind her back and several servants sprang forward, somewhat belatedly, to pick up the rest of the baggage. Paul remained stock-still until Hildegarde took him rather firmly by the elbow.

I looked thoughtfully after the Lady Justinia and Gwennie. As I recalled, in the East slaves were common, and even trusted servants might throw themselves on their faces to kiss the ground at a master's foot. But the lady did not seem to mind the relative informality of Yurt's staff.

The automaton returned in a moment to unshackle the elephant. Highly dubious stable boys led it away, leaving the dark red carpet by itself in the courtyard. The elephant stopped at the watering trough, drank deeply, then shot a trunkful of water across its back and all over the stable boys.

"Maybe I can see a dragon some other time," said Antonia, to reassure me in case I thought her disappointed. "But I've never seen an elephant before. Or a flying carpet either."

"I rode on one once," I said, "all the way, hundreds and thousands of miles, from the East back to Yurt." Antonia looked at me with new respect.

Five minutes later, while I was examining the carpet and wondering if I might be able to keep it long enough to learn how the underlying spells worked that made it fly, Gwennie came racing back from the south tower. Paul and Hildegarde had gone outside again, although the king had appeared distracted enough that I thought the duchess's daughter might have a chance to defeat him today.

"Do you know what she said?" Gwennie demanded. Her eyes were wide and voice high. "She said she thought it very 'quaint' that Yurt has a woman as vizier! And then she asked if I would 'bid the slaves' to come draw her bath!"

"And what did you tell her?"

"I don't think we have slaves," provided Antonia.

Gwennie smiled for a second and ruffled the girl's hair. "We don't. That's what I told her. I did tell her I could assign her a lady's maid for her stay. She started to pull herself up, as though about to tell me I was a worthless vizier who should throw herself into the moat at once, but then she relaxed and said she was sure she could cope with some 'inconveniences' while fleeing for her life, especially since she also had her servant. Have you ever *seen* anything like that creature, Wizard?"

"The mage Kaz-alrhun makes automatons; I assume it's one of his."

Gwennie shook her head. "If *I* was fleeing for my life I wouldn't be worried about a slave shortage! I'd better send her a maid before this fine lady has to resort to something as degrading as pumping the hot water herself. Now, let's see, which of the girls would be both skilled and obsequious, and unlikely to be spooked by that thing. . . ."

The maids Gwennie referred to as "girls" were all older than she was. I smiled to myself as she turned on her heel, her mind apparently made up.

But she stopped for a second. "I'll tell you one thing, Wizard," she said in a low, intense voice. "That lady would make a *terrible* queen of Yurt."

"How about a ride?" suggested Antonia, tugging at the tassels on the carpet. "I wasn't scared in your air cart," she added when I did not answer at once.

"All right," I said, giving her a conspiratorial grin. "It's not our flying carpet, but the Lady Justinia won't be needing it for a while. And I think I still remember the magical commands to direct one of these things. . . ."

I seated myself, Antonia in my lap, and gave the command to lift off. The carpet shot upward, far faster than the air cart, and headed rapidly south. The girl's braids blew back into my face. "All right there?" I asked cheerfully, holding her closer.

"This is exciting, Wizard!" she shouted over the wind's roar. Birds dodged out of our way. "Can we take Mother for a ride too?"

"We'd better not—it's too far to get to Caelrhon and be back before anyone misses the carpet." And besides, I was supposed to be spending time alone with Antonia this week. Was it my fault that I too would rather have been with Theodora?

"And I'm looking for something," I added. I slowed the carpet's flight with a few words in the Hidden Language, and we hovered while I put together a far-seeing spell to examine all the distant clouds in the sky before us.

If Justinia was the object of an assassination plot, I wanted to make sure she had not been followed to Yurt. Since Kaz-alrhun had entrusted her safety to me, I had to make sure she wasn't killed in our best guest-room. The mage, I thought, had probably done his best to get her off unnoticed, and he might not have told even the governor himself where he was sending her, but I didn't like to take chances.

"Nothing there," I said to Antonia after a minute. "Just clouds."

"No dragons?" she said, making it into a joke.

"No. Dragons would probably come from the north anyway. Let's get back to the castle."

As we shot back home a chilling thought struck me.

Suppose the arrival of the miracle-worker in Caelrhon—and his abrupt disappearance yesterday—were somehow related to the Lady Justinia's arrival in Yurt?

But I could not think of a plausible connection. He had already been in Caelrhon when Justinia left Xantium, and I could not imagine that anyone in the East would have learned where she was going and gotten an assassin here so far ahead of her arrival. And the lady herself was unlikely to have spent the last few weeks in hiding, disguised as someone who healed broken dolls and dead dogs.

II

"I hope you realize," said Zahlfast testily, "that I can't send a demonology expert from the faculty racing off to Yurt unless you've actually got a demon! We have classes here to teach."

When Antonia had been whisked away by the twins to take a nap after lunch, I had gone to telephone the wizards' school. So far I wasn't having any luck getting help there. Zahlfast, second in command at the school, had long ago become my friend in spite of my disastrous transformations practical in his course. But the faintest suggestion that I was being drawn into the affairs of the Church had always riled him.

"Of course," I said quickly. "I'm not asking for anyone to come here now. But since this magic-worker appeared suddenly and inexplicably in Caelrhon and then disappeared again just as inexplicably, I wanted to warn you in case he suddenly shows up again, working his miracles or whatever they are—with or without a demon—in some other part of the western kingdoms."

"Well, certainly no other wizard has said anything to us about a—what did you call him? A Cat-Man? And do you know what we would do," Zahlfast continued, an edge to his voice, "if there *was* a strange magic-worker in your region, one there in fact as well as in rumor? We'd ask a nearby wizard to look into it, someone experienced: one, say, who'd had his degree twenty-five years or so. . . ."

"Oh, I'm investigating all right," I said lamely, though there wasn't a lot I could do unless the Dog-Man came back. When Zahlfast rang off I stared gloomily at the stone wall before me, short of good ideas.

Part of my problem was that I felt too close to this situation. The irrational feeling kept nagging me that the Dog-Man had disappeared from Caelrhon in order to bring evil to Yurt. Zahlfast thought I was overreacting, and maybe I was, but I could not take any situation lightly when it could affect my daughter. Although wizards were usually in fierce competition with each other, in this case I would have been willing to admit to deficiencies in my own magic to get the help of another skilled wizard.

I thought briefly of Elerius, generally considered the best student the school had ever produced. He had learned or guessed quite a bit about Theodora and me, and he might even feel he owed me a favor since I had never told anyone several secrets I had learned or guessed about *him*. But on the other hand I had never quite trusted him, and when we last met our relationship could hardly have been called cordial.

This was *my* problem. Zahlfast didn't want other wizards investigating purported miracles in Joachim's cathedral city any more than the bishop did. As long as the man didn't return—and as long as nothing touched Antonia—I could act as though I was on top of the situation.

In the meantime I intended to learn more about the plots against the Lady Justinia and how the decision had been made to send her to Yurt. After all, the mage had sent her specifically to *me*.

Out in the courtyard I was startled to see a small blue-clad figure, carrying a doll, walking purposefully toward my chambers. I ran out to meet her.

"There you are, Wizard," Antonia said, looking up at me with pleased sapphire eyes. "I was just looking for you."

I had to smile back, although all the dangers a child could get into wandering around a castle by herself flashed through my mind. "I thought you were with Hildegarde and Celia." Theodora, I thought, must have to be constantly alert to what our daughter was doing; maybe having her away in Yurt was a welcome respite.

"I like them," said Antonia as I hoisted her onto my shoulder. "But they wanted me to take a nap, and I didn't want to. I came here to see *you*, Wizard, not some ladies." So she had been regretting not spending more time with me while I was regretting the same thing! "Celia is sad," she added as I walked toward the south tower. "She wants to be a priest and the bishop won't let her."

And Hildegarde wanted to be a knight and Gwennie the queen of Yurt, and it didn't look as though any of them stood a chance. "What do you want to be, Antonia?"

"A wizard. I already told you that. Do you think," she added thoughtfully, "that it would help if I talked to the bishop about Celia? He's my friend."

I gave her a bounce, tickled to hear such adult concern in a child's high voice. "He's my friend too, but I don't think it will help for *anyone* to talk to him." A cold thought struck me. "You aren't by any chance also friends with—with someone they call Dog-Man?"

"No," she said regretfully. "Mother said I couldn't play with him anymore. But my friend Jen got her doll burned all up," she added with enthusiasm, "and he fixed it. That's what I'll do when I'm a wizard: fix toys for people."

This was certainly a novel motivation for becoming a wizard. But I did not respond because we were now at the Lady Justinia's door. Gwennie had put her in the finest rooms the castle had to offer guests, the suite where the king of Caelrhon stayed when he visited.

Her automaton answered the door, stared at me with its flat metallic eyes for a moment, then motioned us inside. Antonia, staring, squeezed me around the neck until it was hard to breathe.

Justinia rose from the couch and came to meet me. I managed to loosen Antonia's arms from around my neck and gave a reasonable approximation of the formal half-bow. "I trust you are finding everything satisfactory, my lady?" I said. From what Gwennie had said, she had better be. "Now that I hope you've had a chance to settle in, I'd like to learn more of why you had to leave Xantium."

She waved me to a chair and reseated herself but did not seem immediately interested in talking about her affairs. Antonia perched on my knee. "That cold meat at luncheon, O Wizard," Justinia asked, "prepared in a most bland style: was it perhaps beef?"

"Of course it was," Antonia provided, with an air of showing off her own superior knowledge.

Justinia smiled. "Know then, my child, I have had but brief acquaintance with beef. It is eaten rarely in Xantium."

Antonia thought this over. "How about chicken? How about bread? How about onions?"

But I interrupted before they could go into culinary comparisons of east and west. "Since the mage entrusted you to me, my lady, I hope you will allow me to ask what foes forced you to leave home, and what likelihood there is that they will follow you here."

Justinia gave a flick of her graceful wrist, jangling

her bracelets as though to dismiss such dangers as unimportant. "It is the old controversy between my grandfather and the Thieves' Guild, of course," she said in a bored voice. "It was destiny's decree that the controversy arise again. All believed it settled a great many years ago, when I was but very small, back when—" and for a moment her voice became faint "—back when they assassinated my parents."

"What's assassinated?" Antonia asked, but I shushed her.

"My grandfather the governor declared that the thieves were becoming far too frequent on the streets of Xantium, even in the harbor which was forbidden them, and that he would shut down the Thieves' Market if they could not conform to their earlier agreement. The Guild replied that they could not be responsible for the doings of non-Guild members, and that the governor's taxes on their Market had risen most exceedingly. Tensions were such that— Well, my grandfather did not desire the lives of any of his family again used as negotiating tokens."

"I understand, my lady," I said gravely, glad Yurt had never had anything like this deadly political maneuvering. But then the wizards of the western kingdoms would never allow it to come to this. "But why did you come *here*?"

She had been playing with her rings while she talked, but now she turned to look at me over a half-bare shoulder with her dark almond-shaped eyes. "It is very far from Xantium. Or if I may speak boldly, from anywhere else."

This was reasonably accurate; Yurt, one of the smallest of the western kingdoms, would not normally be a place of which anyone in the East had heard. But our quest fifteen years ago had alerted a number of powerful people, not just the mage Kaz-alrhun, to the existence of Yurt. I hoped that none of them would be people in contact with the Thieves' Guild.

"Wait a minute," I said. "I thought the mage operated out of the Thieves' Market himself. Why should your grandfather trust him?" I had no intention of being manipulated into being part of a devious double-edged plot against a lovely young woman.

"When one's life is in most dire danger," she said in a tone that sounded not young but very old and weary, "one trusts no one." She nodded toward the automaton. "That is why I brought him with me."

And the mage had doubtless made the automaton as well. I had been able to work with him in the East because our purposes coincided, and we had eaten his salt—I wondered how long the beneficial effects of *that* were supposed to last.

As I left the Lady Justinia's chambers one of the castle servants met me. "You have a telephone call, sir," he said, looking anxious. "I think—I think it's from the bishop."

"Tell him I'll be right there!" I darted across the courtyard, delighting Antonia, who was riding on my shoulder again, and opened the door to my chambers. "Stay here," I told her. "I'll be back soon. Don't leave for any reason."

"All right, Wizard," she said agreeably. "Or should I call you Daimbert, the way Mother does? Would you like that better?"

I closed the door without answering and hurried to the telephone. Whatever the bishop had to tell me, I did not think Antonia should hear it. But I immediately began to imagine the harm she could do to herself in my rooms, starting with pulling down a bookshelf on top of herself.

The bishop was actually smiling. "I must apologize,

Daimbert, for bothering you yesterday. The man has returned, and I believe all my questions have been answered."

"Well, that's wonderful," I said in amazement. "But— What happened?"

"He came up to me in the cathedral after the noon service," said Joachim. "As you can imagine, I was quite surprised." So was I, but I almost dared be encouraged. A demon would not, I thought, enter a consecrated cathedral to talk to a bishop. "He told me he wants to be a priest."

"A *priest*?" First Celia and now the Dog-Man. I tried unsuccessfully to tell from the tiny image of Joachim's face if he actually believed this or was only trying to persuade himself of it.

"He told me he has powers in himself he does not fully understand, but he feels God has called him and he wants to be trained to use those powers to help others."

I myself didn't believe a word of it. If what I had sensed down by the docks was accurate, this man had the highly unusual combination of magical abilities and contact with the supernatural. A holy man who could heal a wounded dog, maybe. A magic-worker who had the power to fix broken toys, just possibly. But this man had, if the stories were right, begun to kill just to restore life, and he did not dare talk to a wizard.

At least Antonia was safely in Yurt. "That's good to hear, Joachim," I said, because I didn't know what else to say without more information. "Let me know how it all works out." As I returned to my chambers I thought that this man, whoever he was, seemed to have found the one certain way to defuse the bishop's suspicions.

His questions might all be answered, but mine were just beginning. I found Antonia sitting in my best chair, legs straight out in front of her, poring over a book as though actually reading it. I smiled and reached for my copy of the *Diplomatica Diabolica*.

Leafing through it was not encouraging. I sneezed from dust; it had been a long time since I had had this volume off the shelf. It confirmed what I already knew, that a demon in human form would not be able to wander, unsummoned, into a cathedral. But a person who had sold his soul to the devil, who was using the black arts for supernatural effects, would still be able to do all the ordinary things, like enter churches, that the rest of us did, those of us who might well be damned but didn't know it yet.

The book, being written by and for wizards, did not directly address the question the bishop might have asked, whether someone who had sold his soul could still save it by becoming a priest. But it was not encouraging. The book didn't offer any way out at all for such a person—short perhaps (and only perhaps) of skilled negotiations by a demonology expert.

I reshelved the volume slowly, wondering if a demon would have too much sense of self-preservation to let the person who had summoned it spend time in close association with the saints who always clustered around churches. Saints, I told myself hopefully, should be perfectly capable of returning a demon to hell all by themselves, no matter what the book said.

"What's this word, Wizard?" asked Antonia.

I realized with a start that she was not just pretending to read but was actually reading *Elements of Transmogrification*. "It's the Hidden Language," I said, scooping the book from her lap and returning it to the shelf. "Your mother and I will teach it to you when you're older."

She jumped down from the chair, indignant. "I was *reading* that! Give it back!"

"No, no. I'm sorry, Antonia, but it's really not suitable for you."

Tears started from her sapphire eyes, and she stamped a foot hard on my flagstone floor. "It's not *fair*! You can't just take my book away! Where's my mother? I want my mother!"

I picked her up, trying to soothe her, but she wiggled free and began to cry in good earnest. "I was *reading*!"

"You're just cranky because you didn't have your nap," I said encouragingly, feeling panic set in. "Maybe if you have your nap—"

"*I am not cranky!*" she shouted, tears pouring down her cheeks.

I gave up trying to calm a distraught little girl and lifted her from the floor with magic, startling her so much she stopped crying for a moment, and flew across the courtyard with her to the twins' suite.

III

They were both there, Hildegarde wearing her leather tunic and sword belt but sitting disconsolately in the window seat, and Celia reading her Bible with an aggrieved angle to her chin as though finding things in it different from what the bishop had told her.

"You haven't seen Paul, have you?" Hildegarde asked me, but not as though she really cared. "The king really liked Justinia's dress," she added over her shoulder to her sister. "Maybe you should get one like it, Celia, if Father ever takes us to Xantium as he keeps saying he will," but even this teasing sounded halfhearted. "Here," to Antonia. "Stop crying and I'll let you hold my knife."

I was horror-struck, but Antonia gulped back her sobs and reached for the knife. Hildegarde closed the girl's small fingers around the handle. "Hold it very carefully," she said, "so nobody gets hurt."

"The wizard wouldn't let me read my book," said Antonia, looking at me from under lowered eyebrows and holding the knife in a way I would have called threatening.

I stood back a safe distance. "I think the king went riding after lunch," I said to Hildegarde. Paul tended to react to anything which he had to think over by taking his stallion out for a miles-long run. Even if he didn't end up exploring some ruined castle or scenic waterfall, he might be gone for hours, occasionally even days. No one, not even the queen mother, had ever been able to persuade him that a king should have an escort when galloping around the countryside. Besides, no other horse in the kingdom could keep up with Bonfire.

"Earlier he'd said he was going to show me some exercises. But I guess," Hildegarde added with a deep sigh, "that he was just humoring me. He doesn't think I can be a knight any more than anybody else does."

Either that, I thought but did not say, or Lady Justinia's arrival had distracted him so much he had forgotten everything else.

"I *was* going to be a wizard," said Antonia with a dark look for me, "but now I think I'll be a knight too."

"Knights need their naps," said Hildegarde, unfolding herself from the window seat. "Don't I remember tucking you in over an hour ago, you little scamp? And then," with a laugh, "I looked up and saw you out in the courtyard with the wizard!"

"What's a scamp?" asked Antonia.

"Scamps are mischievous people who have a mind of their own," said Hildegarde. "I used to be a scamp myself." I was surprised she put it in the past tense.

Antonia allowed herself to be taken off to bed in a much better mood than I could have anticipated a few minutes ago. Hildegarde casually slid the knife from the girl's hand back into her own belt.

"Celia," I said when the others had left the room, "I need you to do something for me."

"Of course, Wizard. Do you need to leave the girl with us again while you go somewhere?"

"No," I said slowly, "but I would like *you* to go somewhere for me. Down in Caelrhon there's a man—someone whose name I don't know but who has been nicknamed the Dog-Man—who wants to be a priest too. I wish you would talk to him."

Celia put her Bible down very slowly. "Is this a joke, Wizard?" she asked as though not quite sure whether to be irritated. "I remember the tricks you used to play to amuse Hildegarde and me when we were little. Because if you think you can make me forget—"

"No, no," I said before she could make this any messier than it already was. "I'm absolutely serious." Some of the tricks I had played on the twins had been pretty good, I recalled; I should try them on Antonia if she was still speaking to me. There was the one where I pretended to snip off a girl's nose with my fingertips, then presented a plausible illusory nose for her inspection, or the one where I tossed a butter knife in the air, went to catch it, gave a bloodcurdling yell and presented my arm with the hand "cut off," that is made magically invisible. . . .

But I shouldn't be distracted. "This man, Celia, has apparently persuaded the bishop that he has been touched by God, but I'm suspicious of him. He's hiding from me—which is part of the reason I'm suspicious. So I need someone who has a pure religious vocation, but someone who doesn't automatically agree with the bishop on everything, to find out more about him."

"More about him?" said Celia, sounding bewildered.

"Find out why he's suddenly appeared in Caelrhon, how he's doing what look like miracles—but maybe aren't—learn how deep are his religious convictions: all the things the bishop is unwilling to ask him."

She gave me a level stare. "You're asking me to do something behind His Holiness's back?"

"Well, yes, I guess so. But I can see," I added hastily, "that it was probably wrong to ask you, that—"

"I'll do it, Wizard."

"You will?" I said, startled.

"Women often understand people, *both* men and women, better than men do," she said firmly. "This way I may be able to help the Church if your suspicions are accurate." She suddenly grinned. "And if I can show the bishop my powers of spiritual discernment, he may realize he's made a *big* mistake. Now, tell me more about this man."

An hour later Celia rode away from the castle toward Caelrhon, telling me she hoped to be back in a few days and would send me a pigeon-message in the meantime if she discovered anything interesting. Hildegarde decided at the last moment to go with her, announcing that no future duchess should ride across two kingdoms without an armed warrior to accompany her and protect her. The twins had ridden up from the ducal castle unescorted, and Celia had dismissed my suggestion that a few of the castle's knights ought to go with her to Caelrhon, and without Paul there to back me up there was no way I could change her mind.

As I watched the twins' horses disappearing, I hoped that the bishop would not be too insulted at my sending a woman to prove him wrong.

Antonia, still partly asleep, came out with me to see them off, trailing her doll behind her. "Before I took my nap, Wizard," she said, "you picked me up without touching me and lifted me high in the air. Is that magic? Can you do it again? And you have to teach me how to do it to Dolly."

With the duchess's daughters gone, Antonia ended up on my couch that night in spite of Gwennie's concerns. I was sound asleep when the clang of sword on sword resounded in the courtyard.

Not Paul again! I thought, swinging my feet reluctantly out of bed. But it could not be the king returning to the castle late because he had been here for dinner, too absorbed in the Lady Justinia even to notice that the twins were not there until someone else asked about them.

There came now a hoarse shout and the high winding of a horn—the watchman's alarm signal, which I had never actually heard used before. The horn's note blew a second time, then abruptly was cut off. This wasn't just someone playing a joke on the night watchman. He was in serious trouble.

"Stay here!" I cried to Antonia, who was sitting up, wide-eyed and clutching her doll. I slapped a magic lock on the door as I swung it shut behind me.

Justinia's elephant trumpeted in the stables, and shouts and clangs came from elsewhere in the castle—I was not the only one to hear the watchman's horn. But I was the first to the gate.

And saw row after row of warriors marching in across the drawbridge: shadowy, armored shapes, naked swords in their hands, and eyes that I could have sworn glowed in the darkness.

This couldn't be real. It *had* to be a nightmare. But waking or dreaming I had to do the same thing: defend the castle of Yurt.

I shouted spells in the heavy syllables of the Hidden Language, and the first warriors stopped as though they had run into a wall—which indeed they had. But their feet kept on moving as though trying to push themselves through. Their eyes still glowed and their swords were ready if my spells weakened for even an instant.

Someone ran into the little room by the gate where the bridge mechanism was worked and cranked the wheel to raise the drawbridge. Beyond its end, I could see in the dim light more warriors advancing. The ones on the bridge slid off into the moat as it rose, but the ones behind them kept right on marching, straight into the water as though not even noticing the bridge's absence.

The portcullis slammed down as I started looping binding spells around the warriors trapped between the gate and my magical barrier. One by one they stopped moving as my spells caught and held.

I paused to catch my breath. Magic is hard physical as well as mental work. It had been very close, I thought, but I had gotten out into the courtyard with my spells in time.

There was a shout from the wall. "They're coming up!"

Swords and glowing eyes loomed against the starlit sky. Knights with lances swarmed to the battlements to thrust back into the moat men—or monsters—that seemed to have no individuality, no awareness of their surroundings, only a need to keep on coming.

They appeared to have marched underwater across the floor of the moat and be coming straight up the wall by finding fingerholds among the stones. The knights' lamps made crazy patterns of light and shadow among the castle's defenders and whatever was clambering up toward them.

I would have to wait to catch my breath. The thought flitted through my mind that Hildegarde would be very sorry to have missed all this.

"By the saints!" someone shouted. "It's as though they're directed by the devil himself!"

King Paul was in the middle of it all. I threw spell after spell onto the advancing warriors, raw terror lurking just beyond my shoulder. "Shall we make a sortie, Wizard?" the king asked me quietly.

"Magic's stopping them," I gasped. "Don't try fighting them with steel—they look like they'd keep on fighting even with their heads cut off. Where's the watchman?"

"That dark shape on the ground just inside the gate," said Paul. "He's not moving."

I paused for a second to wipe my forehead and cautiously lowered the magical barrier I had thrown up around the first warriors through the gate. They were now all secured by binding spells. Several people rushed to examine the watchman.

"He's dead!" said a knight in amazement. I was not amazed. If the watchman had not blown his horn with his final breath, if I had been only a few seconds slower getting to the gate, there would have been a whole lot more people dead by now. Yurt had always been a very peaceful kingdom. It looked like it wasn't anymore.

IV

It took me half an hour to get all the warriors, both inside and outside the walls, immobilized with magic. We lowered the drawbridge again, and knights carried the ones who had made it into the courtyard back outside. They used grappling hooks to retrieve the rest from the moat; being underwater had not taken the light from the creatures' eyes. The swans from the moat had all retreated to dry land, hissing and flapping their wings menacingly if anyone came near.

Though the knights tried to pry the swords from the warriors' grips, they held on far too tightly, even encased in my binding spells. I didn't count, but there must have been at least a hundred of them. Whatever they were, I thought, studying them by lamplight with fists on my hips, they weren't human. Human in shape, holding swords in human hands, they had no minds inside their heads or souls behind their eyes. The sweat on me was cold now that I had finished my spells, but it was more than that that made me shiver.

"Demons incarnate!" gasped the chaplain, clutching his crucifix. He took a quick look and then retreated. The whole castle was roused and milling around the courtyard—everyone, that is, except the Lady Justinia, whom no one had seen.

"Not demons," I said slowly. Several lay on the ground by my feet, no longer struggling against my spells but watching me with glowing eyes. "Demons would not have been stopped by my spells. But they're not alive either. They look like they're made from hair and bone."

"Can magic do that?" asked the chaplain, hovering a short distance behind me as though not wanting to approach but not wanting to appear to retreat any further either. "Can it make life?"

"Not life. But there are spells in the old magic of earth and stone that can give the semblance of life. They don't teach those spells at the wizards' school, but back in the old days of apprenticeships wizards used to learn them, and I think they still use them over in the Eastern Kingdoms, beyond the mountains."

"How would you make such creatures?" asked the chaplain, coming one step closer and sounding interested in spite of himself.

"The traditional way," I said, then paused for a second to renew a binding spell that seemed tattered, "was to use dragons' teeth."

There was a long silence. "*You* didn't make them, did you?" asked the chaplain as though trying to make a joke. When I turned to glare at him, in no mood for a joke, he added hastily, "Well, I trust you did not, my son, but in that case who did?"

"I have absolutely no idea." It must be linked with the Lady Justinia's arrival, I thought, but I was not about to say so until I had better evidence—no use having everyone in the castle treating with suspicion someone whom the mage had entrusted to me.

Then I remembered who else had been entrusted to me. Antonia! Where was she in all this? Yelling at one of the knights to call me the second any of these unliving warriors showed signs of breaking out of my spells, I raced back into the castle and to my chambers.

She had lit the magic lamp and was sitting in my best chair with a blanket wrapped around her. "What happened?" she asked, round-eyed. "And why," with a wrinkling of her chin as though trying to keep back tears of terror, "did you leave me all alone?"

I snatched her up and held her close. "I'm so sorry, Antonia," I murmured, stroking her hair. She was shaking and clung to me—no cool self-possession now. "But right here was the safest place for you. Some warriors tried to invade the castle, and I had to stop them."

Slowly she stopped shaking as I held her. "I could have helped you," she said then, pushing herself back to look me in the face. "I can do all sorts of spells. While I was waiting for you I turned Dolly into a frog."

A quick glance at her doll showed it unchanged: a rag doll, embroidered with a smiling face I found almost aggressively adorable, wearing a silk dress doubtless made from the scraps of something Theodora had sewn for a fine lady of Caelrhon. "Soon you'll be a witch like your mother," I said encouragingly.

For some reason I didn't like the way that sounded, but we were interrupted by a shout from the courtyard. "Wizard!"

I bounced Antonia back into bed. "Go to sleep," I said, trying not to sound too rough. "I may be busy the rest of the night." And I darted out across the drawbridge to find one of the armored warriors pushing itself to a sitting position and raising its sword.

A few quick words of the Hidden Language restored

the binding spell, but I thought, looking at the twitching collection of creatures before me, that there was a limit to how long I could keep them imprisoned. I had worked my spells fast, using shortcuts wherever I could, and the spells that made unliving hair and bones—and maybe dragons' teeth—into manlike shapes were a lot stronger than mine. It would only be a matter of time until they all broke free again unless I found a way to dismantle them.

And I couldn't do that and keep my binding spells going at the same time. I needed help.

"Do we have enough chains to chain them up?" I asked King Paul. Brute force might supplement magic in the short term. He took some of the knights to look while I hurried up and down the rows between the creatures, renewing spells and blinking in the lamplight as exhaustion pricked the backs of my eyes. But I could not let up my concentration for even a second. Warriors with swords in their unliving hands could have slashed me in two before I even realized my spells were weakening.

The king managed to persuade everyone but the knights to go back inside once they realized the immediate excitement was over. The chaplain, showing a calm authority I had not expected in him, took away the body of the watchman for last rites. By the time we had the warriors all chained together—and twice a knight of Yurt just missed being badly wounded while he tried to fasten links around a creature that had almost managed to wiggle free of my binding spell—dawn had streaked the eastern sky pink. Not too early, I thought, to make a phone call.

There was only one person worth calling. I gave the glass telephone the magical coordinates of Elerius's castle.

It took several minutes before the wizards' school's

best graduate appeared in the phone's glass base. While I waited for him I tried to think how to frame my request for help so it wouldn't sound as desperate as I felt. Elerius, though school-trained, had years ago also learned enough of the old magic from a renegade magician who had been hiding out high in the eastern mountains that he himself could give dead bones the semblance of life. I probably could have too, given enough time, but Elerius's skills were so unusual that he had even been invited to give a series of lectures on the topic at the school.

He came to the phone at last and looked at me quizzically, his eyebrows making triangular peaks over tawny hazel eyes. His look always made me feel disconcerted but his tone was friendly. "What is it, Daimbert? It *is* good to hear from you after, what has it been, several years at least, but I assume you must have a serious problem to call me at such a time!"

"Well," I said with assumed joviality, "sorry to awaken you at this hour and all, but we do have a little problem—" I gave it up; after all, I *was* desperate. "Please, Elerius," I said, not caring how pathetically I begged. "You've got to come to Yurt. We've been invaded by scores of warriors who move without life. I've got them in binding spells for the moment, but I can't dismantle them by myself. Please!"

He did not hesitate. "Of course," he said soberly, with an expression that was probably supposed to convey reassurance. It was going to take more than an expression to reassure me. "I shall leave within minutes and be there in two hours—maybe less."

"Wizard!" I heard a shout from outside. I slammed down the receiver and darted back out, nerving myself to face the entire horde come back to life and motion.

But none of the creatures were moving. Instead, as the dawn light touched them . . .

At first I did not dare believe it, but it was real. For a few seconds the sunlight showed them clearly, human in no more than shape, faces unfeatured except for their eyes, and then they began to disintegrate. As though melting in the sun, their hands shriveled away from their hilts, their eyes lost their glow and fell back into their sockets, and their struggles against my spells ceased abruptly. Their armor and swords rusted away as I watched until they were no more than fragments, like something dug up from an ancient burial mound. Their limbs collapsed, with a rattle of chain, into piles of scrap.

I closed and opened my eyes, saying a prayer of thanks to whatever saint might listen to wizards. Where a few minutes ago the grass had been spread with warriors who had very nearly killed us all in our sleep, it was now scattered with acrid heaps of bone and hair.

The knights of Yurt sent up a triumphant whoop. King and knights were haggard with exhaustion, and I was trembling all over, hardly able to stand in the weakness of relief. I still wore what had once been my best yellow pajamas, now ripped and filthy rags. High up in the courtyard wall I could see a light burning in the window of the chapel where they had laid out the body of the watchman. "That," I said to myself, "was too easy."

Elerius had already left for Yurt by the time I telephoned his castle again. Well, maybe he could help me determine where these warriors had come from, I thought, putting one set of bones aside for later magical analysis. The knights threw the rest onto a bonfire they built in front of the castle. The smoke rolled into the dawn sky, dense and black.

I went back across the bridge and into the castle. The people King Paul had sent to bed a few hours earlier had all reappeared, complaining about the horrible stench of the smoke. They should be glad, I thought, they had nothing worse to complain about, and decided to talk to the Lady Justinia before Elerius arrived.

No time yet for exhaustion. First I stopped by my chambers to wash, change clothes, and check on Antonia. She was sound asleep, lying on her back with her mouth slightly open and her doll held tight to her chest. I touched her cheek lightly with a finger on my way back out the door. *This* was the reason I would have died quite cheerfully if my death had kept the warriors out of the castle.

Justinia's shiny automaton stood guard before her chambers, a sword at the end of each of its six arms. It stared at me from flat eyes, expressionless but implacable. I was not going to get by unless she wanted me to.

I called, "You can open the door, my lady! The warriors are gone!" There was a long pause, during which I tried magically probing the spells that gave the automaton the semblance of life. It whirled its swords menacingly but did not move away from the door. As I expected, the spells were intensely strange and intensely complicated; it would have taken me weeks to duplicate them, even with a passive automaton before me. At least it did not dissolve in the sun's rays. But then I would not have expected anything made by Kaz-alrhun to have that kind of flaw.

The door swung open at last, and dark eyes glinted at me. I must have looked unthreatening, for Justinia said a quick word to her "servant" and motioned me inside.

Her chambers had been transformed since the day before. She must be planning to stay a while, I thought, for she had unpacked, spreading the flagstone floor with mats and pillows and hanging the walls with silk curtains. The flying carpet lay placidly in front of the hearth. Oil lamps burned in the room's corners.

Justinia pushed the door quickly shut behind me. "Was it as I feared?" she asked, not succeeding at all this morning in sounding nonchalant about mortal danger. "Have my grandfather's enemies found me already?"

"I'm afraid so." I told her about the undead warriors out of nightmare, shaped to advance and to kill but without enough knowledge or will to stop at the edge of a moat or to try to run from a wizard's binding spells.

But partway through the telling, I noticed she began to look first surprised, then disturbed. "But this cannot be!" she broke in. "There is no one in Xantium who would make such soldiers! These magical arts are forbidden!"

I was sure there was a distinction to be drawn somewhere between making warriors of hair and bone and making metallic automatons, but I did not want to get into arcane comparative legal systems. "Are you saying, my lady," I said in astonishment, "that these warriors, such as have never been seen in Yurt before, invaded the castle as soon as you arrived but have nothing to do with you?"

"Most certainly," she said, tossing her head imperiously. "Perhaps my uncle the mage chose poorly when he sent me to such a perilous kingdom."

Either she was lying to me, I thought, about the likelihood that her enemies had sent them, perhaps because she was so terrified that she did not dare admit the true extent of the danger even to herself, or else she, with her own unaided magic, had caused this attack.

But there was nothing of magic about her, other than the automaton and its spells, and it seemed unusually counterproductive for someone to use mindless warriors to attack a castle where one was staying oneself.

"I shall try to see that you are not bothered further

by such disturbances during your visit, my lady," I said stiffly and rose to go. The automaton watched me all the way out.

The courtyard was packed. I turned, highly surprised, to see expressions of delight on every side. Smiling at me were all the knights and ladies, the castle staff led by Gwennie and her mother, and Antonia, still in her nightgown and trailing her doll.

"Here he is!" cried King Paul. "The hero of Yurt!"

A shout rose from everyone there. But I saw now the forced edge to the smiles, the grim realization behind whatever triumph this was supposed to be, that the watchman's death was the first time since long before anyone could remember that someone in the royal castle had been violently killed.

Paul, still streaked with black from the bonfire and leaning on his sword, had put on the heavy gold crown of Yurt. "He destroyed the invading demons! The wizard has saved us all!" There was another great shout, then an expectant pause as though I was supposed to make a speech.

I didn't have the slightest idea what to say. Paul had something large and shiny in one hand—some sort of medal or award, I thought wildly, which I most certainly did not deserve. "Well, thank you, thank you all," I managed to say, which produced another shout. "But they weren't demons. And I didn't really destroy them. That is—"

Whatever I might have added next was drowned out in more hurrahs. "Step forward, Wizard," said Paul in the formal tone that explained why he was wearing his crown, "and receive the accolades of a kingdom." I could see now that he held a golden medal at the end of a loop of blue ribbon.

It was at this point that Elerius arrived.

❖   ❖   ❖

"It's all right!" I cried as the knights reached for their swords. A castle that has just been invaded by creatures considered demonic does not react calmly to someone shooting down from the sky and landing in the courtyard. "This wizard has come to help me!"

"Came a little late, didn't he?" shouted one knight with a relieved laugh, and, "Didn't notice you needing much help, Wizard!" shouted another.

"He's just in time," said Paul with a determined grin, "to see his fellow wizard honored." He wiped soot from his forehead with an arm and became formal again. "The Golden Yurt award is given but rarely, at most once a generation. Although I have been your king only six years, I need not hesitate or wonder if someone more deserving may aid the kingdom in years to come. Our Royal Wizard has protected Yurt since before I was born, and now that he has destroyed a host of demons it is clear that this award is long overdue. Step forward, Wizard, and receive the praise of a grateful kingdom!"

It was much too late to explain that I had had nothing to do with the warriors' dissolution in sunlight, or that if anyone was honored it ought to be the dead watchman. To his credit, Elerius restricted himself to only the faintest ironic smile as I stepped resignedly before Paul and let him slide the ribbon around my neck.

The medal itself was engraved with an image of the royal castle and had the heavy feel of solid gold. I turned it over and saw the names of all those to whom it had been awarded in the past. My name was at the bottom; the goldsmith must have worked fast. The last name before mine was the king's cousin Dominic, with a small cross to indicate the Golden Yurt had been awarded to him posthumously.

To the repeated hurrahs of everyone, knights, ladies, and staff, I scooped up Antonia, nodded to Elerius to follow me, and retreated rapidly to my chambers, just escaping having to give a speech.

V

Antonia, telling me loftily that she could dress herself, retreated into my bedroom. Elerius asked me nothing about her; he might guess she was my daughter but I did not intend to confirm his guess.

He and I sat in the outer room while I told him about the warriors. He listened in silence, stroking his black beard and following me with intent eyes. At least, I thought, with my white beard and the Golden Yurt award now hanging by an attachment spell on the wall next to my diploma from the school, I *looked* more wise and venerable than he did.

"When I called you I needed to know how to dismantle them," I finished, "but now that they've dissolved in sunlight all by themselves I've realized they probably aren't the worst threat to Yurt: that will be whatever comes next."

"Your success against them," said Elerius, nodding slowly, "was supposed to give you a false sense of security, so you would be unprepared for whatever does come." He smiled then. "And of course whoever sent these warriors must have hoped he *might* win with a single unexpected attack. I am glad you called me, Daimbert. This looks like the exact sort of case for which institutionalized magic was designed: renegade spells which must be opposed by wizards acting together."

Elerius and I had disagreed strongly in the past on the purposes and goals of organized wizardry, but I certainly agreed with him here. It struck me that he might be acting so helpful in part to put me into his debt. But the difficulty with mistrusting Elerius's motives was that he really did believe he always acted for the best—even if I often thought he didn't. Besides, I needed him.

"Our best approach," he said, "is to find out who wants to harm Yurt and why. Otherwise we could end up dealing with a long stream of different magical onslaughts."

I hadn't needed Elerius to tell me that. And it crossed my mind that, even assuming he himself had had nothing to do with the warriors, he was certainly acting quickly to position himself to take advantage of their attack. But it was hard to resent a faint patronizing tone from someone whom I had begged so desperately for help. "Let's start with these bones," I said and lifted them onto the table with magic, not caring to handle them again.

Outside in the courtyard were the sounds of a castle resuming its daily routine, when everyone believes disaster has just been averted and is wondering whether to be worried or grimly glad. I swung my casement windows shut.

Most of the spells that had held the warriors together had disappeared, along with their human shape, in the morning light. But enough of a hint remained that Elerius and I could probe magically, stepping into magic's four dimensions together and communicating mind to mind. Here was a fragment of a spell I thought I recognized from years ago, here a familiar spell given a very unusual twist—

Elerius broke contact and raised peaked eyebrows. "It's not school magic. It does not even seem like the magic previous generations of wizards used to teach their apprentices, although at first I thought it must be."

"I think," I said slowly, with an irrational but deadly cold conviction that I knew exactly what it was, "it's what they call the magic of blood and bone over in the Eastern Kingdoms."

The kingdoms east of the mountains had never had a wizards' school, had never even had the peace that the western wizards had established in their kingdoms after the Black Wars. There the conflicts among wizards which still persisted even here, even between wizards who had gone to school together, had become part of the constant ongoing wars of the region.

"This will be an important project for the wizards' school in years to come, Daimbert," said Elerius. "The school has functioned very well in the past to coordinate magic in the Western Kingdoms, but we will need next to turn our attention to the wizards east of the mountains."

But I was not interested in Elerius's plans for when he eventually became Master of the school. "What this attack must mean," I said, "is that the Thieves' Guild of Xantium has overcome their aversion to the forbidden arts enough to hire a very powerful eastern wizard to pursue a princess." I told Elerius briefly about Justinia's arrival. "If these warriors were made by her enemies," I added, "they must be very good and very fast to have found her within twenty-four hours of her arrival in Yurt. I'll have to get her out of here before the next attack."

But Elerius was shaking his head. "I cannot believe that Xantium's greatest mage would have been so sloppy as to let the princess's enemies know where she was going even before she left. For they would have had to know she was heading for Yurt to be able to start making unliving warriors even before she arrived."

I nodded without speaking, wanting desperately to persuade myself that this had nothing to do with the East. From years of experience I knew that I often leaped to unwarranted conclusions, but I also knew that I had a tendency to try to disbelieve things I did not dare face.

"If the Lady Justinia is *not* the target here," Elerius continued, "then her best safety will lie in staying quietly where she is. And if the warriors were indeed made by the magic of blood and bone, I would not be so quick to assume any mage in Xantium would embrace it."

"I was in Xantium once," I said in exasperation, "but I don't understand their morality and laws at all. I would have considered thieves outlaws myself, but *there* they are an organized guild, with whom the governor negotiates. Who knows? Maybe they really would be fastidious about any magic different from their native magery. But if those warriors had nothing to do with Justinia, where can they have come from?"

Antonia came out of the bedroom at this point, wearing her blue dress, her shoes neatly laced and tied but her hair thoroughly tangled. "Who's going to braid my hair, Wizard?" she asked me accusingly.

Elerius smiled and held out a hand. "I'll do it. There's a little princess in my kingdom who's about your age. Would you like your hair styled like a princess's?"

Antonia stayed put, looking at him in silent suspicion. Undaunted, Elerius said a few quick words in the Hidden Language. "Here, catch."

An illusory golden ball arched through the air. Startled, Antonia reached up to catch it. But just before reaching her, the ball changed into a golden bird and flew, flapping wildly, up toward the ceiling where it disappeared with a pop. A single golden feather drifted down and dissolved back into air.

Antonia laughed and trotted over to climb on Elerius's knee. "My wizard does illusions too," she said. I thought it nice of her not to mention that I, the winner of an undeserved award, couldn't do anything that complicated anywhere near as easily. "His name is Daimbert," she added in explanation, as though Elerius might be unsure who I was. "I'm Antonia."

"My name is Elerius," he said, taking her brush. He was good at everything else; why should I be surprised that Elerius was also good with children? "Hmm, it looks like you've been trying to do some braiding yourself, Antonia, without being able to see what you were doing."

"That's because my friend Celia left yesterday," said Antonia.

Celia! With everything else I had forgotten all about sending her to find out about the Dog-Man. It was too early to expect a message from her yet, but I might soon. And might that man, who performed very strange magic tinged with the supernatural, who had persuaded the bishop he wanted to be a priest, be behind the attack on Yurt?

Elerius finished brushing out the tangles and started braiding Antonia's hair. A few magic words helped keep the strands in place until he could work them in. While he braided she took hold of a handful of his black beard and, humming, started brushing it.

"This may not have anything to do with the Lady Justinia, Daimbert," said Elerius casually. Antonia, having exhausted the immediate possibilities of his beard, was now braiding her doll's yarn hair. "Consider this: it may rather be directed toward you."

"*Me*?"

"Forget Xantium for the moment," he continued, still speaking in a casual voice Antonia happily ignored as she started singing to her doll. "Think about your trip years ago through the area where this sort of magic is widespread. I believe the others who were with you then are either now dead or at any rate not here in Yurt. Did you make any foes among the wizards of the Eastern Kingdoms?"

"I might have," I said reluctantly. But all the hair on my arms and the back of my neck stood on end to hear someone else voice my worst suspicions.

It had been fifteen years ago on our way to the East, when we had met the dark, half-living wizard Vlad. Mostly by luck, I had been able to get us away and out of his snares without giving him what he wanted. Although I had not actually intended to hurt him, when we fled, that eastern wizard's body had been partially destroyed, dissolved by sunlight. . . .

So if Vlad, who had screamed curses after me, had found me at last, what would he try next, now that I had been able to withstand his warriors just long enough for the dawn to come?

VI

There was no message from Celia all day. In early evening I left the castle ostentatiously, standing on the drawbridge talking to Paul for several minutes before flying away. The story Elerius and I put out in the royal court was that I was searching by night for whatever practitioner of black magic had unsuccessfully attacked us, while he stayed on guard in the castle. We were doing more, however: testing to see whether the castle—including Justinia—was the target, or whether I was.

They raised the drawbridge and lowered the portcullis behind me; a lot more than one watchman would be on guard tonight. Elerius also stood ready to put spells, far more powerful than anything I could have managed alone, all around the castle, to stop any further magical creatures in their tracks before they reached the walls. Antonia, perched on his shoulder, waved as I flew away.

I did not go far, only a few miles, before settling myself with my back against a tree. After last night I was exhausted, but there were spells to hold off sleep as long as I was willing to put up with a bad headache. I built a fire and began to work illusions: large, brightly lit illusions, ones designed to proclaim to anyone within miles that there was a wizard here.

If Vlad—or whoever had attacked the castle last night—was after me, then I might not have long to wait. As long as I did not go to sleep, and as long as none of my friends or my daughter was in immediate danger, I should be able to fight back or escape. I hoped.

Unless Justinia, or perhaps some other member of the royal court for reasons I could not even imagine, really was the target. After a few hours in which nothing happened except that I perfected a few details of my illusions technique, I made a particularly large golden phoenix burning with realistic flames, donned a spell of invisibility, and darted through the night toward the castle.

It was quiet except for the knights in the courtyard, patrolling slowly, exchanging comments, lifting their lanterns at the faint thump I made landing on the battlements. Justinia's automaton hovered at her door. I flew silently and invisibly across the courtyard to my own chamber windows. A magic lamp made a point of light within. Elerius sat reading, and beyond him I could just see a rounded shape on the couch that must be Antonia, asleep. Elerius lifted his head a moment, but I was fairly sure that even he, with all his abilities, could not see me. I flew upwards again and back to my slowly disintegrating phoenix.

The hours of the short midsummer night seemed to drag on forever. From being keyed up with anticipation of a magical attack, I went to being tired and bored. I replaced the phoenix with a pair of dragons who placed their claws on each other's shoulders and did a tango, but my heart wasn't in it. As a test, this seemed a dismal failure. I stared vacantly and gloomily out into the darkness beyond my fire. Whether aimed at the Lady Justinia or aimed at me, it looked like the next attack would not come for a while—just long enough to give us a false sense of security.

I had fallen into a doze shortly before dawn when I was abruptly brought back to full consciousness by the crack of a broken stick. My fire had burned down to cold ashes, and all my illusions were long gone. I spun toward the sound to see a huge, dark shape coming over the hill, silhouetted against the eastern sky.

It was in the form of a man, a man who walked heavily and awkwardly with his arms straight in front of him, a man ten feet tall.

I shot away, my heart hammering. The creature followed me, with a drag in its step like something dead that had forgotten how to walk, watching me with yellow eyes the size of saucers. There was an intelligence behind those eyes I did not recall seeing in the warriors. The creature's heavy footfalls seemed to shake the earth.

All right, I thought. We know then that I'm the target. The test is a success. We can stop now!

The creature showed no sign of stopping. I kept ahead of it, but it moved surprisingly quickly for something so awkward. Elerius might have been able to help me against it, but I didn't dare head back to the castle, trailing a creature of nightmare, to get him.

Hovering just ahead of it, I madly tried both binding and dissolution spells, but all were ineffective. Years ago I had been pursued by a creature something like this and had found a way to improvise; desperately I tried to remember the words of the Hidden Language that had worked then. But nothing seemed to work now, and it kept on advancing. When I glanced over my shoulder to see that it was indeed maneuvering me toward the castle, I darted off in a different direction.

"Come on," I muttered toward the dawn. If this creature was made with the same magic of blood and bone that had held the warriors together only as long as darkness lasted, I should be safe in another few minutes.

The creature, ignoring my change in direction, continued toward the castle. I dropped to the ground, yelled to get its attention, and very slowly backed away on foot: slowly enough, I hoped, to focus it on me again.

My foot caught on an uneven tussock just as it made a spring at me. I ducked and rolled, suppressing a scream of terror, and shot up into the air an inch ahead of its grabbing hands. The yellow eyes seemed to be considering me in thoughtful assessment.

Twenty feet above it, I tried taking deep breaths. Showing no more signs of starting toward the castle, the creature watched me patiently. The mouth, a slit in the face, opened in what might have been a smile. Inside were quite real teeth.

I tried probing the spells that propelled it, hoping that if I could discover their structure I might find some way to reverse them. Slipping into the stream of magic, I probed there, and there—and came back to myself to find that my flying spell was disintegrating, and that I had descended almost within reach of the creature's outstretched hands.

Again I dodged away just in time. Sweat poured down my face, both at the closeness of my escape and at what I had found. My quick magical probe had shown me no way that this creature could be dissolved, but it had revealed the sorts of spells that held it together, a mix of spells I had never seen together before: the old western magic of earth and herbs that long predated the school; the eastern magic of blood and bone; and, quite unmistakeable, a twist of school magic.

The rising sun lifted itself over the horizon at last, flooding the creature with pale light. It showed no sign whatsoever of dissolving.

"So some school-trained wizard has gone renegade," I said to myself, "and has trained with Vlad—and may be here as his agent." I would have to telephone the school at once—if I could only stop this creature first.

It had been reaching for me, but now it lowered its arms. Keeping its round yellow eyes on me, it opened its mouth and spoke. "This is a hard spell to keep going from a distance, Daimbert," it said conversationally. "But I am very pleased to see it works."

And with that the creature collapsed. Limbs fell off, the head tipped over, lost all the intelligence in the eyes, then dropped and rolled away, and last of all the torso subsided to the earth.

My heart pounding harder than ever, I cautiously approached. The body parts were no longer those of a ten-foot creature. Most were bits of wood and leaf, but lying among them, inanimate and clearly recognizable, was the dead body of the night-watchman.

And I had recognized the creature's voice. It was the voice of Elerius.

Back at the castle half an hour later, I dragged him out of my chambers and up on top of the tall northern tower, where I could curse him in privacy.

"Damnation, Elerius," I said, low and furious, "*what* could you have been thinking in digging up the watchman's body?! I've just had to rebury him, fast before anyone noticed."

"I needed a body for my experiment," he said mildly. "Your predecessor used old bones back when *he* made an unliving creature, as I recall, but it didn't work as well as it should have. I found his ledgers at the back of your shelves last night, and in reading over his notes, and putting together what I found with what we discovered yesterday from the remains of the warriors, and what I once learned myself from an old renegade magician up in the mountains, I decided that the fresher the body, the better. It isn't as though I was hurting the watchman in any way; after all, he was already dead."

I fumed in silence until he paused, apparently feeling he had answered my objections. "I hope you're pleased that you terrified me with your creature as well as disgusted me with your methods," I said angrily. "This does *not* seem like something the school's best graduate should do—or would want widely known."

He shrugged. "I feel confident you will not tell the school about this. After all, if you did I could mention to them the curious fact that a man without brothers or sisters has somehow produced a niece. . . . And I see no reason why a wizard should let conventional squeamishness influence him. Since it was becoming clear last night that we would not get any answers at once as to who attacked the castle, I thought I might use the time profitably to see if I could make an animate creature and, at least temporarily, put my mind into it. That eastern magic has a great deal of potential, but it was a real challenge to find a way to overcome its susceptibility to sunlight!"

Still furious but without any good answers to what he clearly thought were convincing arguments, I said, "You always have felt the ends justify the means, haven't you. I don't want a grave-robber in my kingdom. Get out."

He smiled indulgently. "I must apologize, Daimbert, for apparently frightening you even more than I intended! I couldn't tell you what I was doing, of course, because I wanted to observe what my creature's effect would be on the unsuspecting, but I counted on a wizard being hard to frighten. And of course I was interested to see what sort of response *you* might improvise. You know you can't be serious in wanting to send me away, not before we finish finding out all we can about those undead warriors, not while your kingdom may still be in danger. By the way, while I was probing again those warriors' bones you saved from the bonfire, I thought I sensed some kind of latent spell in them, something we hadn't picked up before, so we should try to discover that as well. Since it bothers you, I'll promise not to disturb any more graves while I'm here."

"And stay away from Antonia," I growled, no longer ordering him out of Yurt, not sure how I had lost the initiative but quite surely having lost it. He was right: I did need his help.

He smiled again. "Do not be concerned, Daimbert. I would never take a delightful little girl apart for an experiment, or whatever you're imagining. My goal, like that of organized wizardry, is always the good of mankind. And knowledge of magic in all its forms is one of the principal foundations of wizardry."

He turned without waiting for a reply and stepped off the parapet, floating majestically back down to the courtyard. I followed slowly, not sure how to enunciate what was wrong with his approach to magic, yet feeling that, at least for now, I would have to continue to work with him. But I also felt an implacable conviction that his ways were not mine.

PART THREE

The Bishop

I

That morning Justinia announced she intended to take her elephant for a ride. "She's ordered me to accompany her," Gwennie told me, standing in the doorway of my chambers and trying to decide whether to laugh or be irritated. "And you too, Wizard."

Back in my chambers, I had been drinking tea and eating cinnamon crullers. As I ate I picked up one of the warrior's bones I had saved and fingered it, wondering absently what spell Elerius might have spotted in it and whether he might already have a very good idea and be using this as a test for me. But I had no time to worry about him. Resignedly I pushed myself to my feet. Gwennie and an elephant would not be much protection for Justinia if whoever had sent the unliving warriors returned.

"Do I have to go ride on the elephant too?" Antonia asked dubiously.

"Not if you don't want to," I said, relieved that she didn't. An elephant's back struck me as a treacherous place. But if she was not with me, who would look after her? When I had first talked to Theodora about having our daughter visit Yurt, I had not imagined how much attention would go simply into taking care of one energetic five-year-old.

Elerius looked up from his reading. From his manner our quarrel this morning might not have even taken place. He seemed to be planning an extended stay in Yurt, during which he would read through all of the big, handwritten volumes in which my predecessor as Royal Wizard had kept his notes. "I'll watch her for you, Daimbert," he said with a slight lift to his brows, as though understanding and amused by my predicament.

Although I didn't trust him, at the moment he appeared to be interested in my friendship, and it really did seem unlikely that he would harm Antonia while I was gone. When I went out a few minutes later, he was again absorbed in my predecessor's spidery hand, and Antonia, with a quick glance at me and a self-righteous lift of her chin, had pulled down *Elements of Transmogrification.*

The Lady Justinia's luggage had included a sort of double saddle with a roof, almost a little house, that could be strapped onto her elephant's shoulders. The stable boys, grim and determined, managed to get it on, shaking their heads behind Justinia's back. The elephant appeared almost as nervous as they were.

The automaton watched without moving, then sprang up onto the elephant's neck when it was ready at last to go. I lifted the lady and Gwennie with magic into the little house and perched myself behind them on the elephant's back. The leathery skin was scattered with long, coarse hairs that pricked through my trousers. I gave the stable boys a companionable shake of my head. This was supposed to be a small elephant, but I felt disturbingly high above the ground.

It reached its trunk, as supple as a snake, up to Justinia,

and she handed it an apple. The trunk's end, I saw with fascination, was provided almost with fingers, or at least flexible protuberances. It thrust the apple in its mouth and ate it with evident enjoyment, made several rumbling noises that I hoped indicated a happy elephant, and then, at the light touch of a goad on its neck from the automaton, trotted briskly across the drawbridge and out into a lovely June day.

"The sun here is very faint and low in the sky," commented the Lady Justinia.

Staying on an elephant's back was even harder than I had expected. Remaining fairly stable and probing magically for potential enemies kept me fully occupied while the beast's rolling gait took us down the hill and along the brick road that led eventually to Caelrhon. I left it to Gwennie to try to explain that this was a warm day of midsummer and that the sun here was never as high or as hot as the lady was accustomed to.

We entered the forest, and dappled shadows flitted across us. After a few minutes, I was able to work out a spell to keep myself more or less balanced on the elephant's back, while allowing me the attention to keep a watch for bandits or anyone else who might try to attack. When the Lady Justinia, who had fallen silent after exhausting the possibilities of solar intensity, suddenly spoke again, I was so startled I almost fell off.

"Art thou," she asked Gwennie, "the king's concubine?"

Gwennie blushed a dark red from her hairline to the neck of her dress. "Excuse me, my lady," she said faintly, "but I do not find that an appropriate question."

Now she had *me* curious.

"Come," said Justinia breezily, "a vizier may oft keep secrets, but not from a governor's granddaughter—especially not one who wishes to aid her."

Gwennie kept her eyes down. "No, my lady," she said

as though the words were dragged from her, "we are not lovers. And—" She took a deep breath. "—and I think it shows how immoral the East must be for you even to *think* so."

"Nay, O Vizier," said Justinia. It was hard for me simultaneously to stay on the elephant, to pretend to be looking around as though not hearing their conversation, and to follow it avidly. "Does not passion for him burn great within you?"

Gwennie's mouth shaped the word No, but for a moment no sound came out. Then she took another breath and answered fairly firmly, "Such a feeling would not be appropriate. A king can love only a princess or highborn lady, his social equal, someone fit to become his queen."

There was not even a hint in her voice that she thought Justinia would make a terrible queen of Yurt. It occurred to me that Gwennie, not in any position of real power, was much more concerned with maintaining social conventions than was someone like Paul whom those conventions were supposed to support.

"This attitude speaks well for thy training and awareness of thy position," said Justinia thoughtfully. "But I have observed how thou watchest the king, how aware thou constantly art of his presence. I speak now as a woman, not a highborn lady. Many a king has found more solace with a slave girl than his own wife. Would not thy heart's sorrow be eased by entering his bed?"

"I don't have to listen to this," Gwennie replied, in what was doubtless supposed to be a hot defense of morality but came out half-choked. "Turn the elephant back to the castle."

"That may indeed be a difficulty," said Justinia, as though Gwennie had said something quite different. "Thou hast always lived, I ween, here in the royal court— wert thou perhaps even once his playmate? But I have also verily observed *him*, how eager his youthful strength and restlessness is to turn to something deeper and stronger. If he awoke in the night to find thee beside him, it would be but a moment ere his friendship for thee turned to passion—especially when he realized how much thy love could guide him to find what he truly wishes to find."

I wondered myself what she thought Paul was seeking.

"Thou carriest the castle's keys at thy belt, I have noted," Justinia continued. "It will be a simple act for thee to slip into his chamber when all are sleeping, so that none else need ever know. Thy delicacy and inexperience itself should prove an added attraction."

"Turn the elephant back," said Gwennie again, staring straight ahead.

Justinia laughed and said a word to the automaton, which touched the elephant's neck with the goad. It turned obediently, pausing only to strip a trunkful of leaves from an overhanging branch before starting homeward. I remembered somewhat guiltily to probe for bandits.

And realized there was a group of riders approaching, less than a quarter mile behind us. I stiffened, summoning spells of protection. But there was something familiar about them. . . .

"Wait a minute, my lady," I called to Justinia, in a loud voice to indicate that I could not possibly have overheard a low-pitched conversation. "It's the queen mother of Yurt, coming home."

In a moment the riders came out of the trees and pulled up hard: a small group of knights with the queen and her ladies in the center. Several of the horses, eyes rolling white, reared as the elephant turned to look back at them.

Gwennie worked herself out of the housing on the elephant's neck and would have jumped straight to the ground if I had not caught her magically to slow her fall. She sketched a curtsey, and although her cheeks were still blotched red she addressed the queen clearly and calmly. "Welcome home, my lady! This is the princess of which I told you."

There were greetings and introductions all around. Gwennie must have telephoned the royal court of Caelrhon or sent a pigeon-message as soon as Justinia arrived, I realized. The queen and Prince Vincent, her husband, would have left for Yurt the very next day, cutting short what had been supposed to be a several-weeks visit at his family's court. Although at first I thought that Gwennie had told them about the attack on the castle, and the queen had hurried home to assess the damage and the danger, no one in the party from Caelrhon seemed to have heard about it.

When the queen introduced a wide-eyed and rather gawky girl to Justinia, a girl who seemed to have shot up two inches since I saw her last, I understood why Gwennie had been so quick to contact the queen. It was not just the acting constable telling the queen of Yurt that her castle had company, although that was how she would have phrased it. Gwennie must have made an allusion—that the queen had understood very well—to the beauty and charm of the foreign lady. The thirteen-year-old princess of Caelrhon who some, at least, had designated as Paul's future bride was being brought in fast before it was too late.

"And wilt thou be a queen someday, Princess Margareta?" Justinia asked the girl politely.

Margareta, in awe of the elephant, stared open-mouthed for a moment, then remembered herself and said in a slightly squeaky voice, "No! That is, my father is king of Caelrhon. But, you know, if I marry another king, that is—"

The girl stopped in confusion. Justinia, considering

with a twitch at the corner of her crimson lips, seemed to have guessed almost as quickly as I had why Margareta was being rushed to the royal court of Yurt. "In the meantime," she said with a smile, "would it bring thee delight to ride upon an elephant, O Princess?"

"Oh," with a nervous look toward her Uncle Vincent, the prince consort, and toward the queen, "could I?"

Gwennie seemed happy to give up her seat on the elephant's back. In a minute Margareta was seated next to the Lady Justinia, gaping anew at the automaton, and we all started homeward. I yawned and thought I might finally get some sleep once we were back at the castle.

Margareta squealed with real or assumed nervousness when the elephant began trotting, until Justinia told her rather sharply to stop scaring it. Gwennie, riding on the young princess's horse, gave a calm and professional account of the castle's doings in the few days the queen had been gone—except for the most crucial, the attack of the unliving warriors.

"In addition," she finished, "there was one very sad event, and the night watchman is dead. Perhaps the king can tell you about it better than I. No, no, my lady, there is nothing to concern you now."

Glancing surreptitiously at Gwennie, I wondered what, if any, of the Lady Justinia's advice had gone home. That, I knew, would concern the queen if she ever learned about it even more than an attack which was now safely over.

When I awoke, aching and ravenous, in late afternoon, it was to find Antonia and her doll curled up beside me. I had been having strange, rather uneasy dreams, involving Theodora and some bones, and was glad to wake. I tried to sit up without disturbing the girl, but she rolled over and looked at me inquiringly through tousled hair. "I want to ask you something, Wizard," she said. "Are you my father?"

I jerked upright, fully awake, and looked around quickly for Elerius. But if he was still reading old spells it was in my outer study. "What has your mother told you, Antonia?" I asked cautiously.

"She said that my father couldn't live with us," she said slowly, as though trying to remember all the details correctly, "but that he loved us very much, and that I would understand it all when I grew up. I want," she added, fixing me with sapphire eyes, "to understand it all *now*."

I ran a hand over my face and pushed back my hair. "So why do you think I'm your father?"

"I know you love me and Mother," she said with great seriousness, explaining a complicated logical exercise, "and you told me you don't love other ladies. And Mother seems to love *you*, and she hardly ever talks about any other men—except of course the bishop."

If our daughter thought Theodora loved me, then she indeed must. Most of the time I knew this anyway— it was just her reserve and self-reliance, I told myself, that made me sometimes doubt it. "The bishop loves you, too," I said. "He baptized you."

"He's my friend," said Antonia, nodding. "But he just told me to talk to Mother when I asked him about you. Some of my other friends on the street said *they* all knew you were my father."

In spite of Theodora's quiet determination to keep her private life private, her neighbors must long have speculated about Antonia's parentage, and I visited Theodora too often not to have attracted notice. Even the Romneys knew she had a wizard friend.

"So are you my father?" Antonia asked, looking at me expectantly.

There didn't seem any way to get out of answering.

Theodora may have preferred not telling our daughter for fear she would tell the other children, but it seemed too late to worry about that. "Yes, I am," I said gravely, taking her hands in mine. They were bigger than when she had been born but still tiny in my grip. "And I am very glad you're my daughter."

She threw herself against my chest, and I gave her a close hug. "I'm glad too," she said indistinctly against my shirt.

"Your mother wants this to be a secret," I said after a minute, stroking her hair, "so let's not tell anyone here, not even Celia and Hildegarde."

"I guessed the secret all by myself," Antonia said proudly, looking up at me. "But my friend Jen said she thought my father was the bishop."

The *bishop*? I tried to make a sudden jerk seem like squeezing her tighter.

But Antonia observed my surprise. "I think," she said in explanation, "that's because he visits us sometimes, and everyone knows that Mother can go visit him in his palace whenever she wants."

If such a rumor had started, I had to tell Theodora to be a little less secretive about me with her neighbors: far better to have them know for certain what most of them had guessed anyway than to have people start believing wild things about her and Joachim.

A sudden rap on the bedchamber door interrupted us, and Elerius put his head in. "Good, I see you're awake, Daimbert. Your young woman constable just came by with a pigeon-message she said she thought was important."

He handed me a little cylinder of paper, all the pigeons could carry, and ducked back out. "If you're my father," asked Antonia thoughtfully, "does that mean you're Dolly's grandfather?"

I didn't answer. The message was from Celia in the

cathedral city. I rubbed grit from the corner of an eye. I had again almost forgotten she was there. If people and events would just stay where I put them, and new ones would stop showing up in Yurt, and if I ever got enough sleep again, I might be able to keep track of what was happening in the twin kingdoms.

The message was, of necessity, brief. "Have met the Dog-Man. Religious vocation seems genuine. But strange. This afternoon down by the docks he killed a pigeon and brought it back to life."

"But strange" was right. Presumably the pigeon in question was not the same one who had brought this message? I stared unseeing at the little piece of paper until I realized Antonia was trying to read it too, then wadded it up in my fist.

"We'd better get ready for dinner," I said, but my best effort at cheerfulness sounded forced in my own ears. I felt cold from the nape of my neck all the way down my back. Somehow this man had persuaded Celia as well as the bishop that he genuinely wanted to be a priest. What could they be teaching in seminary these days? Even a wizard knew that a humble, holy man would not try to show off his miraculous powers. And someone who had already killed a frog and a pigeon, just to bring them back to life, might have something much worse in mind.

And someone who revived dead animals, I thought, trying without particular success to duplicate what Elerius had done to Antonia's hair yesterday, seemed too close for comfort to someone who made warriors out of dead bones—someone who had killed the watchman and *not* brought him back to life.

II

Princess Margareta came down to dinner with her eyelids painted an iridescent blue like the Lady Justinia's, which earned her an askance look from the queen, and carrying a big porcelain doll. The doll wore a lace and silk dress more elaborate than the princess's own and had golden curls arranged around its placid face in a style that even Elerius might have had trouble matching.

The king's Great-aunt Maria threw up her hands with delight at the sight of the doll, but Antonia frowned. "The wizard told me not to bring Dolly to the table with me," she said to the princess in a low voice, as though warning her against possible embarrassment.

But Margareta tossed her head imperiously and said in her slightly squeaky voice, "Queen Margarithia always sits wherever I do." She ordered a servant to bring up a stool and set the doll in it, next to her own chair. One of the castle hounds, who were not supposed to be in the great hall at mealtime, came up and started sniffing, but Margareta aimed a kick at it and the servant took the animal quickly away.

"Queen Margarithia is a good name for a doll," said Antonia approvingly.

Margareta settled herself with a complacent flounce into the place of honor, at the king's right hand. She had first been given that place by the queen two visits ago and seemed to feel it was rightfully hers.

As the rest of us seated ourselves and started passing the platters, I noticed that the young princess, however, paid less attention to King Paul than to the Lady Justinia, sitting directly across the table from her in the secondary place of honor. When Justinia took a single piece of chicken but several scoops of vegetables, Margareta pushed the three pieces of chicken she had already taken to the side of the plate and tried surreptitiously to fluff up her vegetables with a spoon. When Justinia set down her knife and switched her fork from left hand to right to eat after cutting each piece, Margareta tried to do the same, although on the second effort she dropped her knife on the floor and blushed when a servant slipped over from the other table to give her a clean one.

Paul too gave most of his attention to the Lady Justinia. Elerius was entertaining the knights and ladies with tales of his travels, including a trip right up into the far northern land of dragons, where I had never gone. He seemed so comfortable at an aristocratic table that I wondered vaguely, as I had several times before, if the family background he had always kept secret might include birth in a noble household, or if he, like me, had learned to imitate refined social graces upon taking up a post as a royal wizard. Antonia followed his stories with such rapt attention that she almost forgot to eat, but the king scarcely appeared to hear him.

When dessert came, Elerius graciously refused requests to entertain the court with illusions, referring the company instead to me. My dragons doing the tango got a much more appreciative response here than they had received last night from the renegade magic-worker who might— or might not—have been watching me covertly.

As the servants began clearing away the plates and everyone else started back toward their chambers or else talked in small groups by the hearth, the Lady Justinia put her hand on the king's arm. "I have a question for thee, perhaps even a suggestion," she said with a slow smile, under the sounds of general conversation.

Princess Margareta, picking up her doll, glanced toward them. Justinia, her back toward the table, did not notice either the girl or me. "I have been at thy court long enough, O King, to learn that thou art truly a man and not a boy," Justinia continued quietly, her lips curved into a half smile and her dark eyes holding his. "A man and a king can make his own choices in love: he is not one to let the old women decide for him. Thou and I both know, do we not, that thy own choice would never be a little girl, scarce more than a child, who still plays with dolls?"

The tips of Paul's ears went pink as he started to smile in response. But the effect on Margareta was immediate. She blanched white and stood stark still for a moment, clutching her doll to her. Queen Margarithia's wide blue eyes stared unseeing at the room, and her painted china lips continued to sketch their cupid's-bow smile.

Then Margareta whirled around, the doll swinging from one hand, and stormed from the room. Queen Margarithia's porcelain head struck the table leg and shattered explosively. A number of people turned at the sound, but Margareta, almost running, did not seem to notice.

Neither did Paul, although Justinia glanced briefly over her shoulder. "Who do you think then my choice should be, my lady?" he asked. My liege lord's expression was so intense and so vulnerable that I felt almost ashamed to be eavesdropping.

"The choice is thine to make, O King," she said, looking at him from under long lashes. "But I believe there is a heart in the castle that loves truly, has loved thee a very long time, with a care thou hast ignored for far too long."

I turned away. The queen, frowning, was looking toward Paul and Justinia, but this was something the king would have to take care of by himself. The Lady Justinia might think she was pleading Gwennie's cause, but to me it looked only as though she were advancing her own.

❖　　　❖　　　❖

Gwennie had reasserted her authority as arranger of accommodations in the castle and had told me that a little girl could not possibly stay in my chambers with *two* wizards, and instead would sleep with her in her own room until the twins returned. That was fine with me—it kept her away from Elerius. Antonia had been quite smug earlier about this opportunity to sleep in three different rooms in a castle and said she could hardly wait to tell her friend Jen.

This evening, however, she kept referring to the smashing of Queen Margarithia. Antonia thought Margareta must be especially upset because she had destroyed her beloved doll herself, and when I explained that my magic would not put broken porcelain back together, she suggested earnestly that we send at once for the Dog-Man. I took her to Gwennie's room and sat holding her hand until she fell asleep.

The room was reached from the courtyard by an outside staircase. Gwennie was waiting when I came out. "Could I talk to you for a moment, Wizard?"

We sat side by side on the stone steps, still warm from the day's sun although it was now twilight. The castle around us was growing quiet, but from the stables came faint sounds of restless horses who had yet to reconcile themselves to the company of an elephant. The last swallows darted high overhead.

I looked at Gwennie from the corner of my eye while waiting for her to begin. She had a finely shaped nose and brow-line, if a rather firm chin marked by a slight cleft, and straight dark blond hair that was always escaping its pins. I myself thought she was as lovely as the Lady Justinia.

"All the years my father was constable," she said with strained cheer after a few minutes, "I never realized how difficult his duties must be! Keeping the castle accounts, hiring new servants, assigning them their duties and ascertaining that they carry them out, making decisions ranging from when to whitewash the walls to when to buy new table linens to whether we should plant barley or rye this spring—"

"I'm sure everyone appreciates how smoothly the castle runs under your direction," I said and waited again, knowing this was not what she wanted to talk about. For that matter, I had never really thought myself about the merits of barley versus rye. Gwennie was again silent as shadow filled the castle courtyard.

"This morning," she said at last in a low voice, not looking at me. "Did you hear what that eastern princess tried to tell me?"

It didn't seem worth denying. "I'm afraid I couldn't help overhearing."

"The worst of it is," she said, so quietly I had to strain to follow, "I almost found myself agreeing with her."

"Ahh," I said as noncommittedly as possible. This sounded more like something for which a castle employed a Royal Chaplain than an issue for the Royal Wizard. But then I wouldn't have taken a moral dilemma to our chaplain either.

"I know him so well," Gwennie said bitterly. "He likes me, he trusts my work as his constable, he remembers fondly the times we used to play together as children. If he found me in his bed in the middle of the night, he would be a little surprised, but I know I would quickly be able to find ways to arouse his interest—even having no experience of my own with men. I could even make him believe he was in love with me."

Although I was quite sure this was not the sort of topic on which royal wizards were supposed to give advice, and although I didn't like to think that my king could be so easily manipulated by a woman, I said nothing. At the moment Paul seemed ready to leap to do whatever Justinia might suggest to him, and my own situation was hardly an example of male independence and mastery.

"But what good would that do?" Gwennie continued. "If he did not come to love me by himself, with no help from me, it would not be real love. And," she paused, gulped once, and continued, "and that he could never do, and I as constable of this castle would never allow. He would be the laughingstock of all the neighboring kingdoms if he took a cook's daughter as his wife, and what purpose would there be in becoming his concubine?"

It might temporarily take her misery away, I thought to myself, but even I recognized that would only be temporary.

"If he got me with child," she continued, speaking fast now, her voice trembling on the edge of tears, "I know him well enough to be certain that he would not cast me out."

She seemed to have thought it all through remarkably well for someone who had summarily rejected this option.

"He would find a place for me to continue to live in Yurt, and our son, if we had a son, would be brought up as a pet of the castle, well trained and well educated to serve as a constable or even a knight in some other kingdom, but he could never inherit the throne."

Like Elerius? I wondered.

"Our daughter, if we had a daughter, would be well provided with a dowry to marry some wealthy merchant—even a petty castellan. But any children would be marked all their lives with the stigma of illegitimacy, and he would never truly consider them his."

I was glad it was growing too dark for her to see my face. I thought of my "niece" asleep in Gwennie's room. As she grew up, what stigma would she feel marked her, and would she come to believe I did not think of her as truly mine?

Gwennie had stopped speaking and seemed to be waiting for me to say something. "At least the Lady Justinia seems to have no plans to become queen of Yurt," I suggested tentatively.

"And why not?" Gwennie burst out. "Does she think an eastern governor's granddaughter too fine for the king of a small western kingdom? Where does she think she will find a better man, one braver or more true, more open and generous, or capable of greater love? If she's as shallow as she seems, doesn't she even realize she won't find a man more handsome?"

Since this so completely contradicted everything she had said before, I decided to remain silent.

In a moment I heard the faint sound of a suppressed sob next to me. Gwennie rose abruptly. "Good-night, Wizard," she said unsteadily. "Thank you for listening."

"Good-night, Gwendolyn," I said as her room door shut. I had always liked to think that as a wizard I was enough at the fringes of society's strictures that they did not affect me. But I *was* affected if the young people I loved and served, whether children of king, duchess, or castle constable, could not become the individuals they wanted to be because of the expectations and silent rules that hedged them in. And in Antonia it touched me even more deeply and personally.

III

I woke up all at once, staring around in the dark. It was only a dream, I tried to reassure myself, nothing but a dream, but the scene was still more vivid than my own moonlit chambers. I had been in the bishop's bedchamber only once, years before, back when the former bishop was still alive though very ill. But as I forced myself to settle back down and close my eyes again I could see that room clearly, the candles shining on the wood-paneled walls and on the brilliant red coverlets on the bed.

Emerging from the coverlets in the image before me were two heads above two sets of naked shoulders. Their faces were hidden, their mouths and chests pressed close together. One head had black hair streaked with gray, the other tumbled nut-brown curls. I didn't need to see their faces.

A dream meant nothing, I tried to reassure myself, but found myself unwilling to be reassured. Absolute conviction did not respond well to reason. Suppose the dream *did* have meaning? Suppose my sleeping mind had provided me with an explanation my conscious mind rejected?

I kicked back the blankets, groped for some clothes, and banged the door shut on Elerius's sleepy questions as I went out to fly furiously through the night toward the cathedral city.

I pushed past the bishop's startled servants into his study and slammed the door behind me. He had been reading at his desk after breakfast, but he put his book down at once and looked up.

He's pretending he doesn't even realize there's something wrong, I thought with the fury that had been building all during the long flight from Yurt, I supported myself with a hand against the wall and glared at him. He would learn now that even a bishop cannot trifle with a wizard.

"Joachim, you have been my friend for twenty-five years. We've both saved each other's lives. I love you as the brother I never had. But now I must kill you."

It sounded ridiculous as soon as I said it, but to his eternal credit he did not laugh, which would have been my own reaction. Nor did he do any of the other things I had expected. He did not shout for help, or leap for the door or the window, or drop to his knees to beg for his life.

Instead he turned his enormous dark eyes toward me, but disconcertingly not quite toward me. In a second I realized he was looking at the crucifix on the wall past my shoulder.

Murderous jealousy, I thought with a belated return of the good sense that had eluded me for hours, would have been more appropriate in a boy thirty years younger. Wizards are bound by iron oaths to help mankind, not to kill them, not even false friends who hide their philandering under a cloak of religion. But I had gone too far to back down now, I thought, clenching my jaw. Nothing the bishop could say or do would stop me now.

But then his eyes calmly met mine. He took a deep breath and turned empty hands palms up. "If you must, then you must. I forgive you and shall bless you as I die."

Dear God. My knees were suddenly so weak I could scarcely stand. I leaned back against the wall and put a hand over my eyes. If he had tried to run, I would have paralyzed him with a quick spell. If he had tried desperately to plead for mercy, I would have mocked him to his face. If he had screamed for his attendants, I would have blasted them with magic fire. But by doing none of these things, by surrendering at once, he had unmanned me completely.

He reached past me to turn the key in the door, locking us in together. "Before you kill me," he asked mildly, "could you tell me why?"

Even the wall would no longer support me. Exhaustion and failure hit me together. I found myself on my knees, my face resting on the polished wood of the bishop's desk, unable to speak and scarcely to breathe for fear I would start sobbing. I couldn't do it. I couldn't do anything—not because I had finally remembered the responsibilities that come with wizardry's power, but because my will to act was gone. He had taken Theodora from me and I could not get revenge, could not demand her return, could not even threaten him. In a minute I felt a hand stroking my hair.

Murder victims are not supposed to reassure their murderers. I took a deep, shuddering breath, wiped my eyes with a sleeve, and sat back on my heels to look at him.

"Why do you need to kill me, Daimbert?" he asked again.

Any other man in the twin kingdoms he would have called, "My son." If he had, I might have worked up enough indignation to try again. But it was now too late.

"Don't worry," I said wearily, although he did not look worried. "I'm not going to kill you after all." We looked at each other in silence for a minute. "I would have thought you'd be terrified," I said then. "Did you think I was joking?"

He shook his head, continuing to hold my eyes. "I've known you too long. I still do not always understand your sense of humor, but at least I think I know when you're *not* joking." He paused, then continued thoughtfully, "Maybe I should have been terrified. But as bishop, I need to keep life and death constantly in my thoughts."

I wondered briefly and irrelevantly how terrified another bishop would have been.

"I know my sins," he continued, "and am filled with remorse and the knowledge that I do not deserve salvation. But I also know the mercy and loving kindness of God, Who may save even a sinner like me."

Fury slowly built in me again, but I was too weak to do anything about it, and, besides, I had already said I would not kill him. "Don't be complacent," I said in a low voice. "God may not forgive you quite as readily as you like to think. I should have realized how deeply you were sunk in sin when I heard a demon had boldly entered your cathedral. And this time you haven't merely sinned against God. You've sinned against me."

His dark eyes were genuinely puzzled. "Then I must beg your forgiveness, Daimbert. But you still haven't said why you have to kill me."

I started to speak and changed my mind. How could I have been so wrong?

A short time ago I had been absolutely certain. I had not just thought, not just decided, but *known*. Now that knowledge was gone so thoroughly it was hard to believe it had ever existed. And the bishop was still waiting for me to say something.

I've noticed this before. The earth never opens and swallows you up when you need it. But someone who had just been threatened with murder deserved an answer, especially someone who had been my best friend for twenty-five years.

I tried to say it and couldn't. The silence became long and uncomfortable. At last I was able to force it out euphemistically: "You've made Theodora stop loving me."

He immediately knew exactly what I meant and was immediately furious. His dark eyes blazed, and he half rose from his chair.

This was a new experience. I could only ever remember Joachim truly angry with me once before in all the years I'd known him. He might take my threat to kill him very calmly, but not the suggestion that he had broken his vows of chastity—especially with the woman his oldest friend loved.

"How do you *dare*—" He stopped and took a deep breath then, and I could see him fighting back his anger as though it were a physical presence. "No," he said, quietly and icily.

"I know that now," I said quickly.

He gave me a long, burning look. "I swear to you, by the blood Christ shed for us, that I have never touched her."

I dropped my eyes, deeply shamed. I was fairly sure bishops were not supposed to utter oaths like that. When I finally dared look up again, Joachim was examining his hands as though he had never seen them before.

But he suddenly looked up at me and did the last thing I expected: he smiled. He was certainly full of surprises today.

"No wonder you wanted to kill me," he said. "Well, I am grateful you did not. You were right to call me complacent." He shook his head ruefully. "Sin always awaits us, no matter how carefully we think we guard against it. I had not realized that wrath could overcome Christian charity so easily."

He put a hand on my shoulder. "Forgive my anger if you can, and tell me why you think someone has taken Theodora's love from you." He smiled again. "We talk about you frequently, and I know she loves you dearly."

Theodora and I sat on opposite sides of the gold-ceilinged room. I myself would have preferred to have her next to me, my arms around her, but she seemed to prefer it this way.

After several hours' unconsciousness here in the bishop's best guest chamber, the one where visiting church dignitaries stayed, I felt both rational again and deeply humiliated by my own actions. I had been guilty of some very strange behavior at times in the past, but this had gone beyond all bounds, even for me. In retrospect I could not imagine what madness could have impelled me to do something so eminently likely to lose me both my best friend—even if I hadn't killed him—and the woman I loved. The wizards' school would doubtless have agreed—not even raising a perfunctory request for mercy such as the cathedral would have forced itself to make—when the city authorities condemned me to hang. Theodora's unwillingness to sit any closer seemed only appropriate.

"Theodora, you know I'd do anything for you. I'd die for you."

She smiled and shook her head. "I realize you think you mean it, but that's what the boys always tell the girls in all the songs."

"I'd give up wizardry for you."

"We've already been through that many times. You couldn't give up magic, no matter how much you wanted to, no matter how hard you tried."

I was rapidly running low on sacrifices I could make for her. "Then what can I do?"

She gave the worst possible answer. "I don't want you to do anything."

We sat in silence for a minute. "Can I still visit you and Antonia?" I asked then, trying not to sound abject and not succeeding.

"Of course," she said in surprise. "It would take more than a nightmare to change *that*. You're sure she's all right alone in the castle?"

"I told you I telephoned Gwennie this morning," I said wearily. I had talked to Elerius as well, making sure no more magical attacks had taken place while I was gone, but I did not want to bother Theodora now with undead warriors.

Silence stretched out again between us. "Well," I said then, putting hands on my knees preparatory to rising, "if there's nothing I can do to make you love me, then maybe I should get back to Yurt." I waited to see if she would say anything but she didn't. "At least Antonia seemed happy when I told her I was her father."

Theodora abruptly smiled, with the lift of her brows and the dimple that I loved. "I'm so glad you told her! She had been asking about you the last few weeks, but I thought you would enjoy telling her yourself."

It was as though the cool, reserved tone our conversation had taken had suddenly broken. I did not dare move but waited to see what Theodora would say next. She came across the room, took me by the ears and kissed me. "Maybe even in the bishop's palace it won't be too sinful to kiss the man I love."

I wrapped my arms around her so she couldn't get away again. "I don't understand you, Theodora," I said into her hair, feeling happiness breaking over me in spite of myself. "Why do you have to be so conventional sometimes? Why can't you just tell me what you feel?"

She pushed herself back to look at me, though I kept a grip tight enough to forestall any attempts to escape. "Considering that you call me a witch," she said, a smile twitching the corner of her lips, "I'm surprised to hear myself suddenly accused of conventionality."

"You were just sitting there coldly, listening to me say I would do anything to make you love me, saying you didn't want me to do anything!"

"Of course I don't want you to *do* anything," she said with a hint of a laugh. "I already love you! But it's not respect for 'convention' that makes me feel that I should try to rise above concerns of the flesh here, as the bishop would surely want us to do. It's respect for *him*, as the representative of God. He is so far above all of us—knowing him as well as you do, you must surely feel it too."

It might be nothing like my nightmare, but in some areas she still felt more strongly about Joachim than me. I pulled her tighter to avoid meeting her eyes and maybe seeing something which—I managed to persuade myself—I would not see anyway.

"But I think he might understand now," she said, kissing the side of my face. "When he sent for me he said you were very upset and had had a nightmare that I didn't love you." Her voice took on a teasing note. "Since you came to him yourself for comfort and guidance, why be surprised that I respect him as much as you do?"

It was more than I deserved that Joachim had not told her that I had threatened to kill him.

"But I don't follow your reasoning, Daimbert," she said more seriously. "Somehow I think you're saying that because I have tried to be a mother on my own, acting strong for Antonia's sake no matter how hard it is to be separated from you, rejecting the easy path of tying you down with marriage, I'm being *conventional*?"

"It's because you want me to behave like an ordinary, unmarried wizard, while you try to act like a virtuous, self-supporting seamstress," I said lamely.

"It *is* deliberate, Daimbert," she said quietly. "If I want Antonia to have any sort of normal childhood, I have to be above suspicion of being just one more woman who threw away her virtue—I hope you are not equating convention with morality! And I really don't care what 'ordinary, unmarried' wizards do. All I want is what will make you happiest, and that is *not* being driven out of Yurt by your king and snubbed by your school."

It was clearly no use to argue with her or to point out that she was not giving me the chance to make decisions for myself. And if she worried more about morality than I did— Well, wizards had never had much use for religion anyway.

Something in her comment teased out a thought about Elerius. Would he hold over me threats of revealing all to the school in order to bind me to him for purposes of his own?

But I didn't have the time or energy to worry about

him. I looked into Theodora's amethyst eyes and managed to smile. "I guess I'd better make it up to the bishop for breaking in on him this morning by trying again to find out more about the strange magic-worker here in the city."

IV

Theodora had not seen the Dog-Man, but I hoped to learn more from Celia. Escaping from the bishop's palace, I crossed town to the little castle belonging to the kings of Yurt, where the royal family stayed when visiting Caelrhon. As I hoped, the duchess's daughters were there.

Hildegarde looked irritated and bored, but Celia appeared to be experiencing intense joy. "Thank you for sending me here, Wizard," she said, taking both my hands. "This is the chance I have long waited for, that I feared might not exist, and I would not have it but for you."

"The chance for what?" I said, too startled to appreciate her gratitude.

"To study for the priesthood, of course," said Celia. "I've been so happy that I've been sending pigeon-messages to all the people who have encouraged me over the years in a religious vocation."

And these, I felt fairly certain, did not include her parents.

"She met that Dog-Man all right," said Hildegarde, leaning against the doorjamb and cleaning her nails with a knife. "And now that the bishop has accepted him into the seminary he's promised to come teach her in the evenings everything he learns during the day."

Celia shot a sharp glance at her sister but said only, "I told you not to call him Dog-Man anymore. The children call him that, of course, as a sign of affection, but his real name is Cyrus."

Cyrus. So at least now I had a name to go with the fragmentary and contradictory things about him I had learned from Theodora and the bishop.

"His religious vocation is so strong," Celia went on eagerly, "that he spends most nights in prayer, lying before the high altar in the cathedral."

This, I thought grudgingly, might explain why I had not been able to find him when I was here before. He wouldn't have had to be hiding from me deliberately. In prayer, he would enter the supernatural realm of the saints and be beyond the reach of my magic. "Any particular sins he's trying to atone for with all this penitent prayer?" I asked, half as a joke.

But Celia did not take it as a joke. "He feels terrible urges within himself," she said in a low voice. "That—that is why he has killed innocent creatures. That is what he hopes he will overcome through penitence and through immersion in the sanctity of the seminary."

"Does the bishop know this?" I asked in amazement.

"He—" She hesitated, then pushed on. "Cyrus may not have told His Holiness everything."

And she already had my own authorization to act behind the bishop's back, I thought grimly.

"But his prayers have always restored the creatures," she said in what was probably meant to be a hopeful tone.

I didn't like at all the idea of the duchess's daughter spending time alone with someone with "terrible urges." I started to forbid her, with a sharp rebuke for her lack of sense, ever to see him again.

But too many people had been telling her what she could and could not do. On the other hand, to be killed by someone I persisted in thinking of as demonic would probably be a mild, even pleasant experience compared to what the duchess would do to me if she thought I had allowed one of her daughters to be hurt. Why, if a young woman decided to find her own vocation and her own way in life, must it be by putting that life in peril?

I looked toward Hildegarde, the one sure defense Celia might have. She nodded her blond head slowly and wordlessly, meeting my eyes. She understood the situation even better than I did.

"Oh," I said, remembering what had been happening in Yurt while the twins were gone, "you missed some excitement, Hildegarde." I told her briefly about the warriors' attack.

She cheered up at once. "It sounds like we'd better get back to Yurt right away," she said to Celia. "Paul will want me there in case anything further happens. And don't you think, Wizard, that this might be an attack on the Lady Justinia? After all, she'd just arrived when this happened. So the king may want to post a guard in her bedchamber, and it had better be another woman!"

"Do what you like," said Celia quietly. "I shall remain here."

"But you can't stay here by yourself!" Hildegarde protested.

"Why not? We need not always do *everything* together. And if I went back to Yurt, Cyrus would not be able to teach me what he learns in seminary."

Hildegarde fidgeted, eager to show what a woman's strong arm could do against creatures of darkness, yet unwilling to leave her sister to the Dog-Man. "And we still haven't showed the wizard's niece how to deal off the bottom of the deck," she said to her sister as an added inducement to return to Yurt. "You know you're much better at it than I am."

"Uh, Hildegarde, maybe the two of you can stay here

just a little longer," I said. "I'm going to find this Cyrus and talk to him myself."

"But he won't want to talk to a wizard," said Celia, rising abruptly from her chair. "He has had evil experiences with wizardry. In becoming a priest, he intends to break all ties with magic."

So had this man been at the wizards' school along with everything else? I really did need to talk to him soon, no matter what Celia might think.

I left the little castle a few minutes later to head out of the city. Although the Romneys had denied categorically any knowledge of someone called Dog-Man, they might have information about someone named Cyrus. Both Yurt and Caelrhon were tiny kingdoms, probably unknown to most of the people in the west, much less anywhere else. If this would-be priest had come here intentionally, rather than just wandering into town by accident, he would have needed directions from someone who traveled here fairly frequently, which would mean either the merchants who brought up goods from the great City or else the Romneys.

Although we in the Western Kingdoms tended to consider the kingdoms east of the mountains as "eastern," in fact there was a very long distance past them still to go into the East. The multitude of small kingdoms and principalities where the Romneys were believed to have originated formed a barrier between our Western Kingdoms and the true East. Far beyond that region, in the old imperial city of Xantium, they must consider our Western and Eastern Kingdoms an undifferentiated western mass.

The streets of Caelrhon were packed, as they always were these days, and I had to thread my way carefully toward the city gates. The square in front of the cathedral, once the main market square of Caelrhon, had for several years been full of construction equipment, and now rising from the center was what would someday be the great doors and flanking towers of the new cathedral. So far the doors opened not into a cathedral nave but only onto more piled timbers, stones, and vats of mortar, but every time I was in town I could see that the crew had brought the new church one small step closer.

Beyond the city gates the dense crowds thinned out rapidly, though a number of people besides me seemed to be heading toward the Romney encampment. Today the brightly painted caravans were surrounded by horses. Afternoon sun shone on glistening coats, black, bay, and dapple, and summer breezes ruffled manes and tales. The Romneys themselves in their black and red ducked and dodged their way between the animals, talking confidently to the other people there.

The Romneys, it seemed, were holding a horse-fair. Knights and merchants and a few farmers milled around the encampment, both buying and selling. Horses stamped, kicked, and bared their teeth at each other. Some of these were riding horses, some plow horses, and a few unbroken colts. On every side I heard extravagant claims by would-be sellers of the virtues of horses that looked no different to me than those that were being harshly criticized by would-be buyers.

But it did look as though all the adult Romneys were involved. The children were half a mile away, playing by themselves. I wandered toward them, trying not to draw attention to myself from the adults. High white clouds sat on the horizon, but the sky above was clear.

"There's the wizard!" one of the boys called, breaking away from the rest to run toward me. "Make me another snake!"

It was the same boy, peering at me with shiny black eyes from under shaggy hair, to whom I had first spoken a few days ago. The other children raced to gather around us. Again I made an illusory ruby-eyed snake that curled up his arm and quivered its tongue at him. "Now make it real!" he said.

I shook my head, smiling. "That's beyond the reach of natural magic," I said.

"How about the Dog-Man?" a girl suggested. "I'm sure *he* could do it!" One of the other children elbowed her hard, and there was suddenly a bashful silence.

My illusory snake was fading fast. "When I was here before," I said, looking at the children with a wizardly scowl, "you told me none of you had ever met the Dog-Man. But I think now you really had, even though you might not have realized it at the time." The children shuffled their feet, and I knew I was right. "He's the same man who traveled to Caelrhon with you a few weeks ago, isn't he. He's calling himself Cyrus now; what name did he give you?"

The children, laughed, embarrassed. "When did you find out that the man the children in the city were talking about was one you already knew well?" I pressed them.

"You can't blame us for not knowing who he was," the oldest boy piped up. "He never did things like bring dogs back to life when traveling with *us*! Maybe," he added thoughtfully and unconvincingly, "he knew we'd see straight through his illusions."

I myself had long since given up any hope that what this man was doing was mere illusion. "Tell me more about him," I suggested, jingling coins ostentatiously in my pockets.

"Well, *I* decided to go into town and see him," announced one of the girls, tossing her hair. "We'd heard such strange things about him—and *you* had asked us about him, Wizard—that I went down by the river to find him. And it was Cyrus!"

The oldest boy apparently decided that as long as

the story was out anyway he might as well tell me what he knew and at least get the credit for it. "He always told us his name was Cyrus," he broke in. "But he never told us he was a wizard."

"Where did he join you?" I asked casually, not wanting to show how urgently I wanted to know.

"East of the mountains. We were heading this way for the summer, and he came up to our camp, asking if we'd ever heard of Yurt. . . ."

I went cold. Vlad had lived in the Eastern Kingdoms, far beyond the mountains. Could he himself be Cyrus, here bent on vengeance against me?

"We told him we were going to Caelrhon, which was very close to Yurt," said the boy, taking my attentive silence as an invitation to continue.

But nothing that I remembered of Vlad suggested he would decide to become a priest. Mentally I shook my head. I was letting my imagination get carried away. There could be plenty of explanations both for the attack on the casfle and for this very strange miracle-worker without having to imagine it had something to do with long-ago events or even with me. Elerius had thought it might, but even Elerius, I told myself firmly, could be wrong.

"Did he say anything about wanting to enter the seminary?" I asked. The children were growing restless, finding the topic of Cyrus rather dull and clearly wondering if I was going to do anything with my coins besides jingle them.

"He asked us if we were Christian," said the girl who had spoken before. "I told him we weren't. By the way, are you wizards Christian? Some priest came out from the city last week and was trying to make us go to his church, and I told him to start on wizards before bothering us!"

"Wizards are Christian," I said hastily, not wanting

to go into detail on the millennia-old conflict between magic and religion, and pulled out a handful of coppers. I divided them between the girl and the oldest boy, and when I headed back toward town they were busily counting and assessing how they should be distributed.

So Cyrus had come west with the Romneys, I thought, strolling through the sun-warmed meadows. And he had been looking deliberately for Yurt. This need not have anything to do with Vlad to be distinctly ominous. The dark chill on the summer day had nothing to do with the weather.

But what could have possessed this strange half-wizard to enter Joachim's seminary?

I sat down in the shade of a tree, thinking that I ought to demand that the bishop forbid this man to talk to Celia, or for that matter to anyone, and that he be expelled from the seminary. But it was going to be hard to do so without any information more solid than what I had bought from a group of children not generally credited with high standards of honesty. It would be *especially* hard since I was still mortified enough by behavior I was now trying to pretend had never happened that I was unsure how I could ever face Joachim again.

V

I must have fallen asleep sitting under the tree, because the next thing I knew I found myself half-slumped at a very awkward angle, and the tree's shadow stretched long across the meadow.

Rubbing a stiff neck, I sat up and looked toward the Romney encampment. The breeze that made silver tracks in the long grass was cooler now. The horse-fair seemed over; the last steeds were being led away. Well, I thought, it seemed only appropriate that a day that

had begun with nightmare-inspired madness should end
without my accomplishing anything at all.

I rose and stretched. I had behaved idiotically with
Theodora as well as with Joachim, but it was always so
good to be with her that the attractions of spending
the evening at her house far outweighed the
embarrassment of facing her.

And then I saw a lone figure striding across the meadow.
He was dressed in black, so that his person and his long
shadow seemed to merge into one. He walked with his
head down and hands behind his back, paying no attention
to the Romneys' camp or anything else.

Cyrus! I thought, heading rapidly toward him. Now
was my chance to confront him.

But it was not the mysterious miracle-worker from
the Eastern Kingdoms. It was the bishop.

Joachim glanced up as I approached. He gave a start
as though surprised to see me still in Caelrhon, or
perhaps to see anyone. But then he nodded gravely in
my direction and kept walking.

At least he did not seem frightened of me—but then
he hadn't this morning either. I fell into step beside
him. Something must be very wrong for the bishop to
be out here alone, without any accompanying priests,
without guards or servants.

We walked in silence for several minutes. "I had not
expected to meet you, Daimbert," he said at last, "but
perhaps it is only appropriate that I do. For it is because
of our conversation earlier that I have spent much of
today searching my soul and have now come to a very
difficult and terrible decision. For I know that God first
summoned me to the office of bishop, and it is because
of my own sins that I must now resign."

I stared at him, stunned. What could my wild
accusations have done to him? Or could he— But I
dismissed this idea before it could even form.

"The devil is even more subtle than I had imagined," Joachim continued, soberly and quietly. "I told you this morning that I knew well my own sins, but I was wrong. I have sinned, and sinned willingly, in ways that I kept hidden even from myself. It is only fitting that I tell you first, Daimbert, before announcing my decision to the cathedral chapter."

"Uh, I thought bishops had chaplains of their own to whom they were supposed to confess their sins," I mumbled. At this point, tired, humiliated, and deeply worried about Yurt, I didn't think I was in much of a position to help a bishop through a spiritual crisis.

Joachim paid no attention to my mumblings if he even heard them. "For you were right. It is especially against *you* that I have sinned." He had been avoiding my gaze, but he suddenly turned toward me, his enormous deep-set eyes darkly shadowed as the sun sank toward the horizon. "I began wondering why I should have become so wrathful at your accusations, when it should have been clear that these were only the product of the fears that lurk in midnight dreams. But in turning my thoughts over I realized that it was the wrath of a sin that fears exposure."

We had stopped walking and stood facing each other. Joachim was taller than I, and I had to look up at him. The breeze fluttered his vestments around his ankles and stirred his hair.

"You distrusted Cyrus when I first told you about him," he said. "And then today you said that it was my sins that had allowed a demon to enter the cathedral. Although I am still certain that Cyrus is no demon, you were right that a bishop's sins can put his entire church in mortal peril. If I can no longer sift out evil from good, then I cannot in conscience lead my flock.

"As I told you, Daimbert," he continued quietly, "I have never touched Theodora. And in eschewing sins of the flesh, I had managed to persuade myself of my own purity. Of course I spoke with her often about her duties as seamstress for the cathedral, and even, in quiet moments that each of us might take amidst our responsibilities, we would share a cup of tea and talk about you. I was happy, I told myself, that my oldest friend had won the love of such a woman, and that the two of you could prosper together in chaste friendship, the parents of a fine little girl. But today I have had to ask myself: did I counsel Theodora in physical purity only so that I did not have to think of her loving another man as she could never love me?"

I had to interrupt him, even if he was giving voice to ideas I had unwillingly had myself. I could see his eyes now within the shadows of their sockets, and they burned like dark coals. "Joachim, you're getting yourself all upset for nothing. None of your cathedral priests will understand what you're talking about. Theodora has always admired you, and you, quite naturally, appreciate her fine qualities. I can't believe that a bishop immediately falls into sin if he thinks well of a woman."

He took a deep breath and held my gaze with his as though determined to push through a reluctance to reveal something deeply disgraceful. "But I have not yet told you all. When you first went to the guest chamber to sleep, leaving me with my thoughts, I was almost amused, thinking that I could well understand your murderous intentions. After all, I told myself, for a woman like Theodora a man might well do anything to keep her from pain or harm, even gladly kill another in the full knowledge that he would damn himself for eternity, world without end. And then I listened to what I was thinking. Horrified at myself, I resolved I should never see her again. It was when I realized how much I would miss her that I knew I must leave Caelrhon at once and become a hermit."

"You can't be a hermit," I said weakly before the intensity of his gaze. "You're the bishop."

"And in my misery and sin," he said, looking away at last and seeming to pay no attention to anything I said, "I thought this afternoon to walk to the hermitage in that deep valley at the east end of Yurt. If I started now, I told myself, I could be there in two days. I would leave my vestments and episcopal ring for the Romneys to find. If they kept the ring for themselves—well, it had become too tainted for the next bishop to want anyway. Naked I would reach the valley and beg the hermit with tears of penitence to accept me as a novice."

The picture of Joachim walking naked across two kingdoms in order to shave his head and become an apprentice hermit was almost too much for me. Shoulders quivering, I managed to suppress hysterical laughter. The bishop would probably only consider it appropriate punishment for me to laugh at him on top of everything else, but I could not let it out. The thought of the hermit of the shrine of the Cranky Saint, a man who had been a ragged apprentice hermit himself when I first met him years ago, did not help.

"That was why I was so startled when you walked up to me, Daimbert," Joachim continued after a moment, looking out to what was shaping up into a rather fine sunset. "You appeared like the voice of conscience, telling me by your very presence that a bishop cannot walk away from his duties without even telling anyone that he is going, and that to escape without confessing my sins would be only to embrace them. My true penitence must come in facing my cathedral chapter. They will be surprised when they hear that their bishop—who, I have led them to believe in my own sinful complacency, is a virtuous man—has fallen so far."

I knew I had to talk him out of it if I could only think

of what to say. Somehow my own insanity this morning must have infected him. "Don't do anything you may regret without giving it proper thought," I said inadequately and out of my own experience.

Joachim turned, and we started slowly back toward the city. The sun had slipped behind the horizon, and the whole world now was shadowed. "Would it be better to tell my chapter this evening, in a privacy that would not disrupt the simple faith which Christians have in their priests," he asked, "or would it be best to announce it publicly at the high altar tomorrow morning? Would my sins be more truly atoned for if I suffered public humiliation, or am I only taking a perverse pride in how far I have fallen?"

Considering that I did not feel he had fallen at all I had trouble answering him. But then a light flickering in the distance before us caught my eyes.

It was not a lingering ray of the sun remaining on Caelrhon when gone from the rest of the land. Quickly I shaped a far-seeing spell. At the same time the sound of the alarm bells, one high and desperately urgent, one deep with a note that seemed to enter the blood, rang out from the cathedral tower and across the meadow grass toward us.

"Come on!" I cried, lifting from the ground to fly. "The city's on fire!"

PART FOUR

Cyrus

I

Even before we reached the city walls I could hear the roar of the flames. It was the bellow of a gigantic animal, a wordless, implacable voice, above which human shouts rose insubstantial and confused. Over all rang the unceasing note of the alarm bells.

Flying, I reached the city gates before the bishop, but only by ten yards. The fire had taken hold in the shops and inns lining the high street, just within the gates. The street was jammed with onlookers who had to keep dodging sparks. Flames licked from windows in upper stories, and exploding bottles shot high. The bishop said something beside me, but I could not hear him. A roof went with a roar, the collapsing blackened timbers silhouetted against the lurid light.

Not the cathedral, I told myself desperately, not the artisans' quarter where Theodora lived, not the castle where the twins were staying. Joachim was no longer beside me, but I had no time for him anyway. If I could somehow restrict the fire to this street . . .

The people who lived here must already have emptied the big barrels kept at every corner, for they had formed a human chain to bring more water up from the river in buckets. Ordinary school magic, the magic of light and air, was useless here. I braced myself against a gatepost and tried instead to find in the magic of fire something to slow this blaze.

Originally I had learned fire magic from Theodora. It was slippery and dangerous, bringing one into contact with vast and inhuman primordial forces. Lighting and controlling fires could usually be done by such simple, ordinary methods that wizards stayed away from these perilous spells. But I deliberately left the well-worn tracks cut through magic by generations of wizardry to venture where few successfully went, to skitter through magic's four dimensions and try to find a way to rein in flames now rising twenty feet above a ruined roof.

And found another mind trying to do the same thing. Theodora! I touched her thoughts for a fraction of a second, unsure where her body was but more confident than I had any right to be with her magic joined to mine.

She was still better at fire magic than I was, even though most of her experience lay in lighting candles and cooking fires, *not* in trying to hold back flames which had now consumed a city block and were roaring in anticipation of the next one, flames that could have come straight from hell. Slowly, almost delicately, our minds worked together, darting carefully into the forces of magic, pulling back just before we had gone too far.

And then, suddenly, we turned a flame whose tip had leaned toward an untouched thatch roof. The men and women with buckets threw water at the flame's base, and the water evaporated into hissing clouds of steam. But more water kept coming. The flame's tip wavered again and moved backwards, shrinking, no longer threatening the next house across the street.

The dark evening sky had become orange above us. I took a breath of air that could have come from an oven and tried again. There, and there! Dancing through spells in the Hidden Language, twice almost being sucked so deeply into the forces of magic that I might never have found myself again, I sought a way to turn the next flame, then the next—

I came back to myself with a thump as my legs collapsed beneath me. Hard magic is physically exhausting. Rubbing a bruised hip, I looked up with no idea how much time had passed. But the townspeople had the fire in check. Clouds of white steam still rose with every bucket of water poured, but no more flames flickered in the windows or out the roofs, and the great roar of a lion the size of the cathedral was no more than a growl.

Then I looked around at those people not actively involved in fighting the fire, the groups watching disconsolately the destruction of what had once been their businesses or homes. Many were blanket-wrapped children, staring in horrified fascination. The city mayor was there, grubby and without his chains of office, but I heard him announcing that the covered market would be open for anyone who needed shelter.

I saw Joachim then, speaking to people and helping pass out the bread and ale that someone had brought from elsewhere in the city. The cathedral would doubtless buy much of the food for the families forced in the next weeks to live at the covered market. I wondered, too tired from hard magic to give the idea much consideration, if the bishop still intended to resign, and whether he might decide this fire was somehow punishment for his own sins.

Again I found Theodora's mind. She was as tired as I. "I'll be by later," I told her. "Much later, I'm afraid. Get some sleep. Thank you."

Pushing myself away from the gate, I started walking, finding back alleys to dodge around the area where the fire still lingered. The houses now appeared more black than orange, but it would be midnight or later, I knew, before the last coals were extinguished, and none of the structures was salvageable. People were talking now of how the fire might have started, several men saying confidently that they had heard the problem began with a chimney fire, others speculating whether a child left alone might have allowed a fire to spread beyond the hearth.

A voice stopped me. "I'll bet you it was the Romneys."

I made my legs start walking again, but this man, whoever he might be, was not alone. By the time I left the streets surrounding the area where the fire had raged, I had heard four more people speculating that it was not simply an accident but arson by the Romneys.

Why them? I asked myself, hurrying toward the little castle on the far side of town. They had done nothing to hurt the people of Caelrhon, except perhaps beat them in sharpness of horsetrading.

But they came from the Eastern Kingdoms, spoke their own language, and were not Christian. Those were, it seemed, sufficient reasons to suspect them.

No one appeared to have gone to bed in the city. The smoke had permeated all the streets, and rumors and reports of the progress of the fire ran up and down around me. Celia, who met me in the same hall of the castle where we had spoken earlier, seemed the only person not concerned about it. She set down her Bible and came forward to grip my hands with an excitement that had nothing to do with the fire. In dim candlelight her eyes were featureless smudges against her fair skin.

"This evening, Wizard," Celia said with great solemnity, "Cyrus came as he promised and taught me what he had learned in seminary today. So my education as a priest has begun!"

I thought of asking what good it would do her to have the training if she still could not be a priest, but maybe it would be better to have her think of that herself. My immediate question was more urgent. "Where is Cyrus now?"

"Probably in the dormitory with the other seminary students, if he is not at prayer in the cathedral."

"And Hildegarde?"

She shrugged. "I think she went to join the bucket brigade." So at least word of the fire had reached her. I might have passed Hildegarde among all the shadowed, soot-darkened people and not even recognized her.

I excused myself and hurried away. She stood in the doorway to watch me go, her Bible in her hands again. Celia was here in Caelrhon in the first place because of me, which probably made me responsible for her, too, even though her acceptance of this miracle-worker and her eagerness to follow him made her useless as the spy I had intended her to be.

Carefully I picked my way through the construction site in front of the cathedral. The workmen's huts were empty and dark. But through the stained glass windows of the church I thought I could see lights faintly burning—unless it was only the reflection of the last of the flames.

But when I pushed open the heavy doors I could still see the candles' yellow glow before me, glinting on the inlaid mosaic of the tree of life on the floor of the nave. Slowly, listening for the sounds of someone else in the church, I walked toward the high altar. The pillars were dark, shadowy shapes on either hand, and a dozen people could have hidden behind them. The smell of smoke was faint here, overlaid by incense.

Candles clustered on the altar, glinting on the golden

crucifix. In their light I saw a black-clad figure lying on the flagstones that surrounded the altar. I stopped, reluctant to disturb him, waiting for him to lift his head and see me. When I had waited for several minutes, I spoke at last. "Cyrus?"

He stirred then, rising slowly to his knees to look toward me. There was enough light to see him clearly: dark complexioned, with deep-set eyes and high cheekbones over gaunt cheeks, features that reminded me disconcertingly of a young Joachim. He did not look as though he knew how to smile.

I went down on my heels beside him. "I am Daimbert, the Royal Wizard of Yurt. I understand you don't like wizards, but I need to talk to you."

He stared at me unspeaking for a moment. I traced around a mosaic tile in the cathedral floor with a fingernail, making a sharp right angle at the corner, forcing myself to be patient. Cyrus's eyes darted from side to side, but then whatever he saw in the shadowy cathedral seemed to reassure him. "I shall speak with you, Daimbert."

As the bishop had said, his deep voice had a slight accent, though not quite the same as the Romneys'. He rose, dusting himself off, and walked a few yards to sit in the front pew. Everyone in the twin kingdoms called me Wizard, rather than by my name; the only exceptions were Joachim and Theodora. The one demon I had ever met had also called me Daimbert.

But now that I was sitting beside Cyrus he seemed only very intense and very sober. There was a faint aura of the supernatural about him, but he was certainly no demon incarnate. "I understand," I said cautiously, "that you come originally from the Eastern Kingdoms."

He shook his head. "My past is of no importance. I have determined to become a priest under the direction of a most holy bishop."

A most holy bishop who was threatening to resign, I thought. But could Joachim's reputation have possibly reached into the Eastern Kingdoms? Everyone here revered him—even including me when I wasn't threatening to kill him—but it was hard to imagine that anyone would have heard of him many hundreds of miles away, far past the mountains.

I had the oddest feeling that Cyrus had known who I was, perhaps had even expected to meet me. "But you were trained in wizardry," I said. Now that he was sitting beside me it was unmistakable. He was no more a fully trained wizard than he was a demon, and he was not actively practicing magic at the moment, but it is virtually impossible to erase magic's imprint.

He turned abruptly away, clenching his fists. "Once I thought that magic might impart the power to aid others," he said in a low voice that hinted at experiences he did not want to recollect, "but I know now that wizardry leads only to darkness."

I had no leisure to worry about his sensibilities, not with unliving creatures stalking Yurt and assassins from Xantium doubtless searching for Justinia. "You were not trained in the wizards' school," I persisted. "Did you perhaps serve an apprenticeship east of the mountains, where the school's influence does not extend?"

He turned sharply back toward me, the candle flames glinting in his eyes. "I told you my past is of no importance. And I do not think I should say more to you, Daimbert, about the Eastern Kingdoms. If you have nothing else to discuss, I would prefer to return to my devotions."

I had quite a bit else to say to him. "Then let us not talk of your past," I said hastily, "but only of what has happened since you came to Caelrhon. So far I have heard that you have restored to life or wholeness several animals and a little girl's doll." I paused, waiting for some response, but he looked away from me in silence. My ears strained for other sounds in the shadowy church, but the faint taps and scurryings did not appear to be anything other than the normal sounds of any large building at night. "This is not any magic I know," I continued, "and I would be interested in learning how you did it."

He shot me a brief glance, then turned his eyes back toward the crucifix on the altar. His face was dark and sharp in profile. "I am in Caelrhon to learn the ways of God," he said quietly, "not to teach magic to a wizard."

Careful questioning didn't seem to be doing any good. "Listen," I said harshly, putting a hand on his shoulder. Under the vestments of an acolyte I could feel clearly the shape of his bones. Maybe not the personification of evil, I told myself, but there was evil in this man no matter what he had said to the bishop. "Since you first arrived here my royal castle has been attacked by warriors made by magic from hair and bone, and tonight the high street here in the city burned. Someone with the powerful magic to restore life, even if only the life of an animal, might well be thought to be behind undead warriors, and even more so be suspected of arson."

Slowly he turned toward me again, and his gaunt, sober face was transformed by a smile. It built slowly, working its way from his lips up to his cheekbones. The effect was shattering. I had to dismiss at once my thoughts of him as evil, for there was a joy and a deep love in that smile that confounded me again with the similarity to Joachim.

"I have not prayed here in vain," Cyrus said, putting his own hands on my shoulders. "Whatever ill may have befallen the city will be restored."

I was so surprised that for a moment I could not answer. Then I heard a creak from the hinges of the small side door of the cathedral, and the smell of smoke became momentarily stronger. Someone else had entered the church.

Cyrus and I waited in silence, listening to the approaching footsteps. A tall figure stepped from the shadow of a pillar into the candlelight. It was the bishop.

Now that I saw them together, Joachim and Cyrus did not look anything alike. The bishop was taller, and his face was alive with the power of good. The same good had burned in the other's expression when he smiled, but he again was sober and the effect was gone.

Joachim lifted his eyebrows when he saw us. It must seem to him that I had been showing up all day at the most inappropriate moments. I wondered what to answer when he asked why I was questioning his new seminary student after he had told me not to, especially if Cyrus complained that I had been quizzing him about his experiences with wizardry.

But the bishop did not ask why I was here. "Forgive me for disturbing your conversation," he said instead. "I came to offer thanks to God for the safe deliverance from fire of the city's people, even before the thanksgiving service I shall lead tomorrow. I had not known there was anyone else in the church."

"My devotions kept me overlong, Father," murmured Cyrus, the perfect humble seminary student. He dipped a knee toward the altar and retreated hastily, the side door closing hollowly behind him. It looked like any further conversation with him would have to wait.

"I'm leaving too, Joachim," I said. I thought of trying to say again that he shouldn't do anything rash without giving it more thought, but the outbreak of the fire had put such an effective end to our discussion on that topic that I was not sure how to bring it up again. "I'll be heading back to Yurt first thing in the morning."

"Before you go," he said, not nearly as embarrassed

as I was, "I want to ask you something. The fire died out much more rapidly than anyone had dared hope— was that due in part to your magic?"

"Mine and Theodora's," I said, and was immediately sorry I had mentioned her when the bishop dropped his eyes.

"Then I am glad I found you to thank you," he said gravely, not looking at me. "Convey my thanks to her as well when you next see her. More priests should recognize how often God works through human agents, even wizards." There was an awkward silence for a moment, then he asked quietly, "Are you going to Theodora's house now?"

"Yes." It seemed as though I ought to add more, but I was not sure what. One of the candles on the altar guttered out with a strong scent of hot wax.

"When you see her," said Joachim, now in a flustered tone that did not sound anything like him, "I would be grateful if— That is, unless you think there is a need to say—"

"I did not plan to tell her what you have told me."

There was another silence. Confessors are supposed to maintain the secrets of the confessional, but both of us knew that someone who takes his secret sins to a wizard does so at his own risk.

Joachim raised his enormous dark eyes then to meet mine. "This has been a strange day, Daimbert," he said at last, which seemed an understatement. "Before you return to Yurt tomorrow, come to the episcopal palace and talk with me."

When I walked the length of the nave to the main doors and glanced back, it was to see him kneeling before the altar on the flagstones where Cyrus had lain.

II

The sun shone through Theodora's curtains when I rolled over the next morning, just barely avoiding pitching myself off her couch and onto the floor among the cloth scraps. I had spent quite a few nights on that couch over the last five years, but it really was too narrow. From the kitchen I could hear rattling sounds of someone making breakfast.

"What time did you get in last night?" Theodora asked as I leaned, rubbing my eyes, against the doorframe. She seemed to be tactfully not recalling that the last time we had met face-to-face I seemed to have lost my mind. "I was so soundly asleep I didn't even hear you."

"I know. I didn't want to wake you." I took the piece of toast she handed me and wolfed it down. When I thought back over yesterday's confused events, I couldn't remember eating at any point. "How about if I scramble us some eggs?"

As we sat at her kitchen table in the morning sun, eating eggs and toast and drinking hot tea, everything seemed so safe and normal that for a moment I could merely have imagined the events of the last week. The light brought out golden highlights in Theodora's curly brown hair. But one thing was missing. Antonia should have been here with us.

"Where did you go after the fire was contained?" Theodora asked. "I know I should have tried to help with the families and the children, but I was so exhausted I could hardly stand." A smile brought out her dimple. "How do you wizards *ever* manage to practice magic all the time?"

For a moment I stopped eating to listen to a sound of distant voices carried from elsewhere in the city.

They might have been voicing surprise or wonder, but at least it did not sound like fear. "I finally met the Dog-Man last night. His name is Cyrus, and he's just become an acolyte in the cathedral seminary." I paused for another bite. "He worries me, Theodora. There's magic about him, though he's no wizard, and a hint of the supernatural that seems strangely different than what you'd expect of a devout young would-be priest." She had finished a much smaller breakfast than mine and watched me with sober amethyst eyes. "And I can't help wondering what he's got to do with the warriors who attacked Yurt."

"*What* warriors?"

I remembered just too late that I had never told her about the attack on the royal castle and had in fact been meaning to let it slide until Antonia was safely home again. But the city of Caelrhon, with its fire, fears of the Romneys, and Cyrus, might be no safer than the castle of Yurt, guarded now by a far better wizard than I. I told Theodora briefly about the attack.

"There wasn't enough magic left in their bones for me to learn much about—" I stopped abruptly. "Wait! I just remembered! I handled those bones yesterday— or I guess it would be the day before. I wasn't paying very close attention at the time, so if there was some kind of latent spell in them, ready to infect a wizard who wasn't careful, and through him—" I seized her by the shoulders. "Theodora! Are you feeling all right?"

"Of course I am. Why shouldn't I?" She looked concerned, as well she might.

"I think there was a spell in those bones that affected me, and now I'm infecting other people." I stopped just in time from telling her about Joachim. "You aren't feeling, for example, a wild conviction that I don't love you, or that Antonia is in danger? You aren't fearing that everyone in town knows you for a witch and holds it against you?"

Now she looked alarmed. "Daimbert, what are you talking about? *Is* Antonia in danger?"

"All right," I said, mostly to myself, gulping down the last of the tea. "Everything's fine. It didn't affect you. Maybe it can only infect once. But with the bishop this morning— And I almost forgot, he wanted me to come see him. That reminds me, Theodora. Joachim told me to thank you for your fire magic last night."

The distant sound of voices came clearer again as the breezes shifted, and the cathedral bells were ringing as though for service, although I thought it was the wrong time. Maybe it was the special thanksgiving service the bishop had mentioned. Theodora came around the table to put a palm on my forehead. "Are you sure you haven't become feverish again?"

I pushed back my chair and stood up. "I'm fine as long as you are. I'll telephone Elerius from the cathedral office and tell him to check those bones for spells at once. And I'd better get back to Yurt before Antonia starts to doubt that I really am her father." I kissed Theodora and smiled reassuringly. "In a few days, when I bring her home, I can tell you all about it."

As I walked briskly through the city streets, I noticed that all the smoky smell had dissipated overnight. Somehow I had expected it still to linger. The cathedral bells grew louder as I approached.

The voices grew louder too. Feeling suddenly uneasy, I quickened my pace. There was a disconcerting note to that many people shouting together, a wordless sound that could have been the voice of last night's flames.

The open area in front of the cathedral was packed. People stood in every available spot between the huts and supplies of the workmen and the piles of stones. All sectors of society and all ages seemed to be there; children darted between legs to try to get closer, or begged to be lifted high enough to see. I spotted Celia near the front, Hildegarde beside her, and then was startled to see King Paul's Great-aunt Maria trying to scramble up onto a heap of building supplies for a better view. What was *she* doing here?

The crowd kept pushing forward like the motion of the sea, with a murmur like the sound of waves, and the shadows of the cathedral's new towers lay across them. I couldn't get any closer to either the twins or the Lady Maria without flying. At the top of the cathedral steps, facing the crowd, stood the bishop.

"The miracle is God's!" he called out over that wordless murmur. He wore his formal scarlet vestments and tall episcopal mitre and extended his arms wide. "Come into God's house where we can offer thanks together to Him! Nothing is impossible for Him who rules all!"

But the crowd was disagreeing with him. What miracle? I wondered wildly. We all had reason to be grateful no one had been killed in the fire, but there was much more going on, and I had somehow missed it.

"No, my sons and daughters!" the bishop continued, even more loudly and clearly. His gaunt face was intense, and his eyes focused not on the crowd but on the sky. "It is idolatry to speak like that to a living, sinning mortal!"

What could possibly be happening? I tried again to shoulder my way through toward the front of the crowd, not wanting to practice magic this close to a church with everyone speaking of a miracle. The crowd was too intent on the bishop to pay any attention to me, although several people almost stepped on my toes.

"So if you didn't call down the saints to save our homes," a booming voice shouted from almost next to me, "then who did?"

"The Dog-Man!" someone else shouted, and a dozen voices took it up. "The Dog-Man, the Dog-Man!"

"Cyrus!" called a woman's voice from the front of the crowd. It rose almost to a scream. "Cyrus!" I looked to see the source of the voice and saw that it was Celia.

One big cathedral door opened, and the seminary's newest student popped out like the figure in some child's game. "It was Cyrus who worked the miracle!" screamed Celia as though in ecstasy. I saw Hildegarde take her by the arm, but she shook her sister off. "Praise God! Praise God!"

Cyrus, his sharp face sober, stood beside Joachim with his arms extended in an identical pose. The bishop turned his head and came as close as he ever did to looking irritated.

"Give not me the praise, but the saints who heard my humble prayers," said Cyrus when after a moment the crowd's wordless shouts died away. "My merits are but meager; it is the sincerity of my heart that the saints have answered. Come, let us worship together!" He spun around, apparently finding nothing wrong with inviting Joachim's flock into Joachim's own church, and led the way as the townspeople poured up the steps after him.

Celia was one of the first through the doors, but I reached the Lady Maria before she managed to descend from the building materials on which she had so precariously perched. She gave me a smile when she spotted me. "Right on time!" she announced and launched herself into the air. I was just able to catch her, both with my arms and with magic, and set her carefully down.

"How nice to see you, Wizard," she said conversationally, straightening her dress. "And what a marvelous thing that a miracle-worker has come to the twin kingdoms and that our Celia is studying with him!"

Things were happening much too fast for me. "So you came because Celia wrote you?" I asked, hoping for at least one solid piece of information. Celia had said something yesterday about telling all the people who had supported her in her religious vocation that Cyrus was going to teach her.

"And fortunately I got here just in time to see his first big miracle!" continued the Lady Maria cheerfully. "Come on—we don't want to miss the service!"

"What miracle?" I demanded, blocking her path.

"Restoring the burned buildings, of course," she said blithely. "When I arrived this morning everyone was talking about it. Don't tell me," with a playful smile, "that just because you're a wizard you're going to pretend it never happened!"

"Um, go ahead into the church and I'll catch up," I said and shot off without waiting for an answer.

But she was quite right. The burned street had been restored.

The buildings stood silent and empty now, since everyone was in church, but the charred remnants I had seen late last night were back to their former state, as solid as ever. Wood and plaster structures leaned over the high street, and sunlight glittered on windowpanes I had seen smashed. I wandered down the street, doubting my own eyes, and tried pushing against the timbers in a halfhearted and futile attempt to persuade myself it was all an illusion.

I put my head into the doorway of an inn, blinking in the dimness. There was spilled ale on the wooden bar, filth in the straw on the floor, and dirty plates and mugs on the tables. A brown rat poked its nose out of the straw to look at me and scurried away again. Whatever saint had restored this street seemed to have been very literal. If *I* had been working a miracle, I would at least have cleaned up the place a little.

Flabbergasted, I leaned against the rough plastered wall outside. This certainly let the Romneys off from accusations of arson. The inn sign, its paint peeling, creaked over my head. Perhaps all the events of the day before had been my imagination, I thought wildly. But if so all the townspeople now at the cathedral, treating a quite willing Cyrus as though this was all due to his own merit, shared the illusion.

The air around me almost glittered with the force of the supernatural. The city always had a touch of the supernatural anyway, evident to any wizard, because of the presence of the cathedral, but this went much further.

Mixed with the aura of the saints was the faint but unmistakable imprint of evil.

III

Afternoon sun shone on the polished wood of the bishop's study. Joachim, bareheaded but still in his formal scarlet, sat behind his desk, his enormous dark eyes fixed on me. "I cannot leave my cathedral and my people now," he said quietly, "not until I know what is happening here."

"It's not complicated," I said, irritable because my insides felt so cold my legs were trembling. We could hear, faint in the distance, laughing and singing from the high street, where the innkeepers had announced free ale for everyone in honor of the miraculous restoration of their businesses. "Cyrus is working with a demon." How, I asked myself, could I ever have imagined there was anything good about him? "And as long as you won't let me take him out of the cathedral there's nothing I can do about it."

"It could have been as he says," Joachim said somewhat uneasily. Whatever else I might have done, I seemed to have made the bishop doubt his own judgment. "The saints might have answered his prayers and restored the buildings."

"I thought you just said the saints don't do things like that," I shot back.

He shook his head slowly. "I have never known of such a thing. A saint might act to protect his own shrine, and saints of course keep demons out of the churches as long as the hearts of the priests are pure, but they do not usually concern themselves with the material things of this world."

"Then if it wasn't a saint," I said firmly, "it's got to be a demon."

"Even a demon could not restore a soul from death," Joachim objected. He spoke quietly but his gaze was intense.

"We're not talking about restoring a soul," I said, looking away. This could not be any easier for the bishop than it was for me. Fingernails dug into my palms. "I think he's made time run backwards, very locally. That's how he rebuilt the houses, how he repaired the toys, even how he brought animals without souls back to life. Let me call the demonology experts at the school."

Joachim lifted an eyebrow. "You did not call them from the cathedral office when you said you needed to call Yurt?"

For all I could tell he might have been making a joke. "Of course not. I don't lie to you, Joachim. I called Yurt because Antonia's safety is even more important to me than your demon."

"It is not," he said, no trace of humor now, "*my* demon."

The thought crossed my mind that if Cyrus indeed was working supernatural black magic, then he could not have been behind the undead warriors; that had been perverted but natural magic. Which meant that I had another faceless enemy to worry about as well as the Dog-Man. "Whoever's demon it is," I snapped, "we need an expert to find it and send it back to hell."

The bishop rose with a swirl of vestments. "Let us go speak to Cyrus together then, Daimbert. I will not have you or any other wizard bullying one of my seminary students."

"He may be infecting the rest of your students with evil," I said as we went out through the study door, the same one I had slammed behind me yesterday morning as I came to murder the bishop. A fine one I was to talk about infection—although the madness seemed to have passed off him as quickly as it had passed off me.

"If the saints heard his prayers and truly worked a miracle," said Joachim, ignoring my comment, "he needs my spiritual guidance so that he does not become puffed up and proud. By now the crowds will have dissipated, and I may even be able to call my cathedral my own again."

The only thing I had going for me, I thought as we walked the short distance down the cobbled street from the episcopal palace to the side door of the cathedral, was that the bishop now seemed as disturbed to have the Dog-Man and his purported miracles in his church as I was.

But the crowds had not yet completely dissipated. Cyrus, a thin black form, knelt in prayer at the high altar, and at least a dozen people, mostly women, knelt beside him. Colored light from the stained glass windows washed over them. Among them were Celia and the Lady Maria.

Hildegarde stepped out from behind a pillar to meet us. "They've been like that for ages," she muttered. "I would have thought they'd be stiff by now."

The Lady Maria and several of the others, among whom I now recognized the mayor, were indeed shifting uncomfortably. But Celia, her head lowered and face very white, seemed transported beyond issues of physical comfort.

The bishop went down on his knees beside them. In a minute the townspeople seemed to become aware of him. Several lifted their heads and glanced toward each other uncomfortably. After a few more moments, a man rose and tiptoed quietly away. Joachim, his eyes closed, paid no attention. Two women followed, then another. Last of all the mayor rose, murmuring, "I will not forget," and patting Cyrus's shoulder as he turned to go. Soon Celia and the Lady Maria were the only people left kneeling beside the bishop and his newest seminary student.

Maria looked up, then got to her feet, shaking out her skirt, and came over to the front pew to sit next to me. "Our chaplain never expects us to kneel on the stones like that," she said in a good-natured undertone, "or not us old ones anyway! But then a little suffering may be good for the soul, or so the priests tell us."

Both Cyrus and Celia lifted their heads then. I met the Dog-Man's eyes fleetingly before he looked away, then reached for words of the Hidden Language to try to find indications of evil around him. A blatant but silent spell, worked directly contrary to what the bishop would have allowed me to do if I asked him, revealed no supernatural power beyond that of the saints. Maybe, I thought in disappointment, folding my hands and trying not to look like a wizard, Cyrus had checked his demon at the cathedral door.

Celia did not give me a chance to probe any further. "Holy Father, I am so glad for this opportunity to see you," she said to the bishop, her voice low and vibrant. "My life and my spiritual calling have long been confused, but now at last they are clear. I shall leave tomorrow for the Nunnery of Yurt, there to make my profession as a novice."

Just as I had feared all day. The bones' infection had now gotten to someone else—not to Theodora, but to

Celia. If Cyrus was responsible for the warriors—and the bones—then he had even more to answer for than perverting the people of Caelrhon. But I was also interested to notice that in those with a religious bent, like Celia and Joachim, this strange infection apparently made them want to throw away everything for quiet contemplation. Would the bones make another wizard as murderous as they made me? Perhaps, I told myself, dismissing the question, it was not good to ask too many questions about the differences between priests and wizards.

When I had spoken to Elerius on the telephone, he had reassured me that no one in Yurt had started demonstrating inexplicable behavior. While I waited, listening through the receiver to the distant sounds of the royal castle of Yurt and thinking I might hear Antonia's voice, he had probed the bones again. A subtle, almost invisible spell, very unlike any school spell, had dissolved by itself while he was trying to find a way to neutralize it. That should mean, I tried to reassure myself, that Celia would be the last.

But in the meantime she had just announced, publicly and unequivocally, her intention to become a nun. "If that is your choice, my daughter," said the bishop kindly, "and God has guided you in it, then of course I shall do all to assist you."

"But, excuse me, Holy Father, she can't!" cried Hildegarde. "Mother would kill her."

"Christ said that those who would follow Him must forsake even father and mother," put in Cyrus, "braving the cross for His sake."

"You need her permission," said Hildegarde, ignoring him and taking her sister by the shoulders. "You're supposed to become duchess of Yurt. You can't just throw it all over without even telling her!"

"We shall discuss this further in private," said Celia

in an icy tone that I myself would not have dreamed of arguing with. She dipped her head to the bishop— and to Cyrus?—and hurried down the nave, Hildegarde behind her.

The Lady Maria bounced up from the pew. "I should get over to the castle," she said. "I brought the Princess Margareta with me, and she's probably wondering what's been happening all day. We got in first thing, you realize, and I knew something was up but that it would take a wise head to straighten it out, not the princess's curls!" I had known the Lady Maria twenty-five years and had not yet once thought of her as having a wise head, but it was much too late to explain that to her. "So I'm afraid I've left the little princess sitting all by herself, when my plan had been to give her some amusement by taking her on this trip. I don't think she ever had more than a schoolgirl's infatuation for the king, of course, but after what's occurred I thought it better to provide her with some change of scene."

And she pranced out, leaving me staring after her. *What* had occurred? I wanted to shout. Elerius had not said anything about Paul and the Lady Justinia having eloped, or whatever else they might have done, but then he probably would not see it in the same light as I would. I had needed to get back to Yurt for two days, now more than ever—if it weren't for the matter of an acolyte working with a demon.

Cyrus, left alone now with Joachim and me, made as if to go, but the bishop did not give him a chance. "I need to talk to you, my son," he said gently, "about the miraculous restoration of all the burned houses and businesses. Even the Bible does not record such events."

"Compared to the Lord's parting of the Red Sea," said Cyrus, looking at me suspiciously, "the rebuilding of a few charred structures is trivial."

"But you," said Joachim thoughtfully, "are not Moses."

"No," said Cyrus promptly, "and that is why I am so profoundly grateful to the saints who have listened to my poor prayer."

I bit my lip to keep from saying several things, mostly doubting and sarcastic. This was Joachim's cathedral, and especially now that Cyrus was starting to act as if it was his instead, the bishop would not want the interference of a wizard. "Why," he said, even more gently, "do you credit your own prayers, my son, rather than those of others?"

Cyrus looked up at him quickly, dark eyes shadowed. In his quiet answer there was a trace of something that I would have called smugness. "Because the saints told me so, Father."

I couldn't listen to him anymore. I walked halfway down the nave and leaned my forehead against a pillar. The only point on which I felt unsure was whether he was deliberately trying to mislead the bishop or whether he was deceived himself. He seemed horribly sure of himself, but was that because he did not even know that a demon was working beside him? Suppose the demon, who must be lurking somewhere in the city, waiting for him to emerge from the cathedral again, had deluded him into thinking that it was not a demon but a saint?

I turned my head to glance back toward the front pew where Joachim and Cyrus were talking. If he was now trying to deceive the bishop, then I would take him by the scruff of the neck with my strongest binding spells, regardless of what disrespect I might be doing the church, and drag him to the demonology experts at the school. (This of course assumed I would have the slightest success against someone who used supernatural power to oppose me—a point on which I did not want to dwell.)

But suppose, said a cold doubting voice in the back of my mind, a voice that remembered all the times over the years that my absolute convictions had been absolutely wrong, that the reason my best spells could now find no direct sign of evil about him was because there was nothing to find?

Wizardry could reveal nothing about the state of a man's soul, and might not reveal a demon who was carefully hiding, but it should certainly indicate if someone was practicing black magic in my face. "Let me ask him something," I said brusquely, striding over to where the other two sat.

"Ask me no more questions about wizardry," said Cyrus in a meek tone, his eyes lowered. "I already told you I have left all that behind."

"*But,*" I said, clenching my fists so I wouldn't grab him by the throat and shake him, "you yourself may not be working magic, Cyrus, but you've sold your soul to the devil!" The bishop went very stiff but did not interrupt—maybe he was too shocked to do so. Or maybe he was preparing himself to spring on me if I showed signs of trying to murder Cyrus as I had threatened to murder him. "Admit it!" I said, just below a shout. "You're working with a demon!"

Echoes ran up and down the aisles, then for a long moment there was silence in the church, while I wondered if the bishop would ever speak to me again. At this rate he might still decide to go become an apprentice hermit, just so that in leaving the affairs of the world he would never have to see another wizard.

Cyrus lifted his head, looking not at me but at Joachim. "I have not despaired of my soul or abandoned it to the powers of darkness," he said, quietly but very firmly. This sounded like prevarication to me. "I can swear on whatever saints' relics you like, Holy Father."

Joachim rose abruptly, not looking at me either. "That

will not be necessary. Forgive us, my son. I hope you realize that with a miracle this spectacular it is the duty of an officer of the Church to investigate it fully. And I'm sure you realize that you must acknowledge this miracle with abject humility of soul. You may return now to your studies and devotions." He started rapidly down the nave, scarlet vestments flying behind him, and I almost had to run to keep up.

But the bishop slowed and turned his deep-set eyes on me as we reached the door. "Weren't you saying, Daimbert," he said coldly, "that you needed to get home to Yurt tonight?"

IV

After leaving a message at the little castle for the twins and the Lady Maria, saying I hoped to see them in a day or two back in Yurt, I flew homeward through the twilight, trying to cheer myself up by reminding myself that at last I would be back with Antonia again. It didn't work.

"It's just not fair," I said as though I was presenting someone a logical argument—perhaps Theodora? "Joachim forgave me for trying to kill him. Why should he now be furious with me for being maybe just the tiniest bit harsh with one of his seminary students, when all I was trying to do was protect his cathedral? You'd think he *wanted* to have a demonic acolyte developing a cult following right under his nose.

"Well," I continued, "I just don't care! If Cyrus has sold his soul, that certainly doesn't bother *me*. And since what he apparently wants in return for his soul is to be thought a holy miracle-worker, then there should be no danger to anyone else. And why should a wizard care if some priests are misled? They're confused most of the time anyway."

Whoever I was addressing had no good answers,

except to point out that I seemed to be protesting quite a bit for someone who didn't care at all. And I didn't even want to raise the point that an experienced wizard, one whom the masters of the school trusted to be able to deal with a demon, could not find one in spite of being convinced that it was there.

The drawbridge was up when I reached Yurt, just as dusk was darkening at last into night. I was pleased to be challenged immediately as I flew over the wall, although the knight excused himself when he recognized me.

Antonia would have been asleep for some time, I thought, heading toward the kitchens, remembering that I hadn't eaten since breakfast with Theodora. There I found Gwennie, disconsolately eating leftover strawberry shortcake straight out of the serving bowl. There was still enough in it for at least four people.

The fires were banked for the night, and she ate by the flickering light of a single candle. I took the bowl from her and pulled it toward me. "Did anything interesting happen in Caelrhon?" she asked with complete indifference.

I didn't answer, my mouth full of strawberries and whipped cream.

"It looks like the fine Lady Justinia is planning to stay all summer," Gwennie said after a minute. At least, then, she and Paul had not eloped. "The stable boys tell me her elephant is eating like a dozen horses. I tried to find out, politely of course, how long she planned to stay in our best guest rooms, and she said she could not say until she had word from Xantium that things were safe there again."

I made myself recall the situation here in Yurt. If I was completely wrong about Cyrus—and even if I was right—I was still responsible for defending both those who lived here and the lady who had been entrusted to my protection.

Gwennie sighed and played with her spoon. "Paul is teaching Justinia to ride a horse. Can you believe she'd never learned? She said at dinner today that she could captain a sailing ship, but what good will that do her in Yurt?"

"None," I said, scraping the bowl.

Gwennie looked at me properly at last and started to smile even through her glum mood. "You're very hungry, Wizard," she said, with the recognition of the obvious which any good castle constable had to have, "or else you're depressed. Or both."

I didn't ask which of these explanations accounted for her sitting by herself, polishing off the leftovers after the cook and the kitchen maids had all retired. She found me some cold meat and salad from dinner.

"Could you contact that mage in Xantium?" she asked with more of her accustomed energy, sitting across the table from me again while I ate. "It seems a shame for the lady to have to wait without any word from home."

I wasn't fooled by her concern for Justinia's peace of mind, but it was a good idea. "I don't think there are any telephones in Xantium, Gwendolyn," I said thoughtfully. It was a different experience eating dinner at the kitchen table, in a room usually full of bustle and activity but now dark and quiet—and also different to have the dessert before the meat course. "Telephones work by western, not eastern magic. But I can try to find out tomorrow how the merchants in the great City manage to get important messages through to their representatives there."

I rose and stretched. It seemed much more than two days since I had left. "Is Elerius still in my chambers? And is Antonia still in with you?"

"The wizard is still in your chambers," said Gwennie in a neutral voice. "But," with more animation, "your niece is in the Princess Margareta's room—did you see her down in Caelrhon, by the way? The princess decided she wanted the little girl with her after she'd broken that precious doll of hers, and Antonia stayed when she left."

I supposed wearily that a good wizard should protect those he served from their own folly as well as from undead creatures. Maybe it would be a relief to worry about whether the princess whom everyone (except of course Paul himself) expected the king to marry still liked playing with dolls rather than about whether a demon was loose in Caelrhon with Theodora.

"I'm glad you're back, Wizard," said Gwennie with almost her usual good spirits as we left the kitchens together. "If you'd let me eat all the strawberries by myself I probably would have gotten sick—and a castle can't function with a sick constable!"

Elerius finally went home to his own kingdom in the morning, reassuring me that there were no more latent spells in the bones and no undead warriors within a three kingdom radius. "This was an unexpected but most enjoyable opportunity to meet your friends in Yurt," he said before he left, stroking his black beard and fixing me with his tawny eyes. "It was an especial pleasure to meet your niece." Did he put an extra emphasis on that last word? "What a charming little girl, and intelligent too. I am happy to do you a favor any time, Daimbert, so be sure to call if any more problems arise. After all," with a smile, "I may want *your* help someday."

The twins, the Lady Maria, and Princess Margareta all returned to Yurt in the afternoon, accompanied by the knights Maria had taken with her, so Hildegarde ended up being escorted like a lady across the countryside after all, rather than getting to be a knight herself.

Celia closeted herself at once with the royal chaplain,

but Hildegarde came to my chambers to see Antonia. "Have you been practicing your riding while I was gone?" she asked, swinging the girl up over her head until she shrieked with delight. "Is it time to start you on your swordplay?"

"Will you mind too much if I don't become a knight?" Antonia asked once she had her breath back, looking up at Hildegarde with a serious frown. "Because I've been thinking. Maybe I should be a wizard after all."

When I entered my chambers the night before the rooms had nearly reeked with magic—as well as being scattered with enthusiastic if strangely proportioned drawings of wizards. Although Elerius had said nothing about it, it was clear to me that he had been entertaining Antonia with flashy spells in my absence.

"That's the way," said Hildegarde approvingly. "If you're going to learn magic, be a wizard. Don't let anyone make you settle for being a witch."

"My mother's a witch," said Antonia proudly.

Hildegarde started to say something and changed her mind. She looked at the girl thoughtfully a moment, then shrugged and turned to me.

"I haven't been able to talk Celia out of it," she said quietly. "By evening yesterday she'd lost that possessed look she had earlier—you must have seen it—but she said that now that she had announced to the bishop her intention to become a nun she had to take her vows. I must admit that miracle of Cyrus's staggered me too, Wizard; I'd been on the bucket brigade, and I *saw* those buildings consumed. But I tried to remind Celia that she'd always wanted to be a priest instead of a nun— suggested she disguise herself as a man and go to some other seminary, even got so desperate as to offer to go in disguise as an acolyte myself and then come home and teach her what I'd learned!—but nothing would budge her."

"When does she plan to take her vows?" I asked uneasily, thinking of the duchess's wrath.

"I think that's what she's discussing with the chaplain." Hildegarde shook her head. "I'll send a pigeon-message to Mother and Father tomorrow—I'd just as soon not try to explain this to Mother over the telephone. But I believe the nunnery has some sort of novitiate period, during which women can change their minds. So it's not hopeless yet. The real problem, Wizard, is that Celia is nearly as stubborn as I am."

During dinner that evening all the conversation was about the miraculous restoration of the high street of Caelrhon. Celia said virtually nothing and only played with her food, but the Lady Maria was in her element. "It's like something out of the old stories of the saints," she said enthusiastically. "The holy man walks out of the wilderness into the city, and no one recognizes his power except the children, until at last a great miracle puts everyone in his debt and silences all doubters."

"I saw it too," said Princess Margareta. She seemed, at least for the moment, to have forgotten both Paul and Justinia and basked in her position as assistant bringer of wonder-stories. The chaplain expressed an interest in making an immediate pilgrimage to meet Cyrus, and several people said they would join him.

But I had other concerns. After dinner I drew the king aside. He had listened politely to Maria's stories, but most of his attention was still given to Justinia. They had gone riding that afternoon—he on his red roan stallion, she on an old white mare—leaving before I realized their plans. I did not like the idea of them roaming the countryside without a wizard's protection against whatever magical enemies might be pursuing Justinia.

But I was supposed to serve King Paul, not order

him around. "Could you do me a favor, sire," I asked diffidently, "and take me along if you give the Lady Justinia any more riding lessons?"

"So you think I need a chaperone, Wizard?" he said with an amused smile. He glanced across the hall to where the Lady Justinia was talking to the queen. The eastern lady this evening was wearing an iridescent blue silk dress that matched her eyelids and left her shoulders bare. The Princess Margareta stood a short distance away, trying to appear uninterested in their conversation. "Did my mother put you up to this?" Paul added.

"Of course not!" I said in irritation. "It's none of my business who my king decides to marry! But it *is* my responsibility to protect both you and her from black magic."

"I thought you and that wizard friend of yours had cleared up that problem," said Paul, still looking amused. "Or should I ask you for the return of the Golden Yurt?" He laughed and slapped me on the back. "You can tell whoever is worrying about me that I'm not planning to marry the Lady Justinia. Of course she's an attractive woman, but I'm merely trying to keep her entertained during what must be for her a rather tedious stay in a foreign land."

While I was relieved to hear this, it crossed my mind that the mage Kaz-alrhun, in sending Justinia to Yurt, may have had some such plan of his own. He was always calculating how to make events redound to his advantage, and he may indeed have intended the king of Yurt to fall in love with the lady. In spite of his immense shrewdness, Kaz-alrhun had become convinced, due to a rather improbable series of events, that I was one of the Western Kingdoms' greatest wizards, and it was possible that he hoped an alliance between his niece and my king would bind me to him.

Paul looked past me, smiled again, and ran a quick

hand over his hair. I turned to see the Lady Justinia coming toward us. But she turned her almond-shaped eyes not toward the king but instead toward me.

"Come thou this eventide to my chambers, O Wizard," she said in her melodious voice. She turned slightly as she spoke, addressing me over a naked shoulder. " 'Twould seem the time is ripe for thee and me to hold conversation.' "

"Of course," I said. I should tell her that I was trying to get in contact with Xantium. Now that I had met Cyrus, perhaps it would be possible to find out if she knew anyone like him who might be involved in the plot against her. And perhaps I could persuade her, even if I could not persuade the king, that she really needed a wizard with her whenever she ventured outside the castle walls.

As we left the hall together, I glanced back to see Paul glaring after us. If he had not just told me he had no romantic interest in the Lady Justinia, I would have said he was jealous.

V

Justinia's automaton had a fire blazing, even though I would have called the evening warm. She seated herself gracefully on the carpet by the hearth and motioned me to join her. I recalled as I lowered myself much less gracefully that this was a flying carpet, although at the moment it showed no sign of going anywhere.

"I've been trying to find a way to talk to the mages in Xantium," I said. "But the City merchant I reached this morning assured me there are still no telephones in the East. He was rather huffy about it, feeling it was somehow the wizards' fault. Now, I know that some of the eastern mages communicate through images in deep pools of water, so I was thinking that if I was able to telephone someone in the furthest east port where the western merchants have telephones, then I might—"

But she interrupted with a look of horror. "Thou must not attempt to contact anyone in Xantium! Any magic would be traced in a moment, and then my enemies would pursue me even unto Yurt!" Her automaton rose at the alarm in her voice and approached me in slow, silent menace.

"All I want to do is talk to Kaz-alrhun," I said in surprise. "He already knows you're here."

"But he remains the only one." She leaned toward me and gripped my hand. "Even my most trusted slaves did not learn my destination. Please, I beg thee in God's name, do not play at chances with my life!"

"Well, I think I could find a way to call without it being traced," I started to say, then trailed off. The automaton retreated again. Justinia leaned closer, still holding my hand, close enough that I was almost overwhelmed by her perfume.

"And I was *also* going to say," I continued quickly, trying to keep from babbling, "that it may be dangerous for you to leave the castle without an escort. I know the king never takes any knights with him when he rides, but if I came with the two of you—"

Her red lips curved into a smile. "This is better. Let us speak no more of Xantium, where my enemies are and I am not. Let us speak of Yurt and of the king."

"Well," I said, feeling flustered and wishing she would release my hand, especially since her rings were starting to bite, "he doesn't seem to think he needs any magical protection. But since I don't want to play at chances with your life any more than you do, I would appreciate it if you would ask him yourself next time if I could accompany you."

"Or perchance there may not be a next time," she said, shifting on the carpet so that our knees touched.

I drew my knee back fractionally and she pressed hers forward fractionally. "I would fain persuade thy young King Paul that he would do far better to take his woman vizier as his concubine thán to pay his attentions to me."

"You *said* this to him?"

"Of course not," turning her head on its fine neck in a scornful attitude. "Men will do naught, are they not persuaded they have thought on it themselves."

And what did she hope *I* would think of myself?

"But he has awakened through my presence to his manhood and his position, and I trust that he will now find the strength to tell the old women that he will ne'er marry the little maid." It took me a second to realize she meant Princess Margareta, not Antonia. "I think my hints have already made him aware of the vizier's willingness to share his bed." I had no reply. She gave me her slow smile again. "Now, all I must do is persuade him that he need not pay *quite* so much attention to me, that my own feelings may not be as immediate and as warm as his."

I had never had a chance, I recalled through rising panic, to tell Theodora about the Lady Justinia. First I wished she was here, then I was just as glad she wasn't.

"So wilt thou join me in my plan, Wizard," she asked, still smiling and brushing my shoulder with her black hair as she leaned even closer, "to convey to thy king, obliquely of course, that he should pay me no more attention?"

I had to get out of here. She was so close now that I could feel her breath on my cheek. Neither my relations with Theodora nor with my king would be improved in the slightest by giving the eastern princess a passionate embrace, and her automaton had come silently forward again, staring at us voyeuristically with its flat metallic eyes.

"Gracious!" I cried, wrenching my hand out of her grip and leaping to my feet. "I'd lost track of how late it is! I have to go say good-night to my daughter."

Justinia looked up at me in silence, blinking iridescent eyelids, as it dawned on me what I had just said.

I stood silent and stiff, waiting for her to say something. In a moment Justinia rose to her feet in a single smooth motion and took my hand again, much less tightly. "Why didst thou not tell me at once, O Wizard?" she said, to my relief looking amused. "Antonia, is that not her name? I understand, then, that the maid's mother is someone most precious to thee, and here is the reason thou hast always been so awkward in my presence." I wouldn't have put it that way, but I was at the moment incapable of speech. "Is the mother here in Yurt? Does King Paul know of thy love?"

I found my tongue again. "Nobody in Yurt knows Antonia isn't my niece," I said, looking at the floor. That is, for the moment no one else but the queen mother knew. It didn't seem worth asking Justinia not to tell anyone; she either would or would not as she chose. "The girl's mother does not live here, but yes," lifting my eyes determinedly, "she is very precious to me."

"Then I must choose another if I desire the king to wax jealous," said Justinia lightly, "or would convince him that *I* at least will ne'er be his concubine. I feel foolish now, not to have guessed that little Antonia was thy daughter. I ween that the purpose of her visit here is to commence teaching her magic? It is regrettable, O Wizard," she added with something between a chuckle and a sigh, "because thou art passing handsome. Thy face and form are yet those of a young man, in despite of thy white beard, and thy wisdom and authority are of surpassing attractiveness in themselves."

"Um, I really do need to kiss Antonia good-night," I said, backing away.

"Of course, Wizard," she said agreeably as the automaton, with a suspicious look, opened the door. Had she tried this on Elerius, too, I wondered, or would his much greater powers have put her in awe of him?

"Do not be shy to sit thee again by my side in spite of thy awkwardness this evening," Justinia added. "Give the girl a kiss from me, and be assured that thy secret is safe." She gave a slow smile. "I am well schooled in the keeping of secrets."

I spent that night and much of the next morning composing conversations with King Paul, in which I combined plausible and nonchalant explanations for why I had never told him I had a daughter with assertions— assertions that never, of course, seemed forced or defensive—that my silence on this matter in no way implied embarrassment or shame about my relations with Theodora. None of these conversations seemed to come out right.

And yet, I reminded myself, I had brought Antonia to Yurt in the first place partly because I hoped to find some way to end the secrecy. This just didn't seem the best way to do it.

If the Lady Justinia said anything to Paul, he gave no indication to me. He went riding by himself in the morning while I took a stroll with Antonia.

Her hair had been curled and ribboned elaborately by the Princess Margareta, who seemed to be treating her as a substitute for her broken china doll. Antonia's Dolly too had a pink ribbon around her cloth neck. I realized, walking through sunlit meadows with my daughter's small hand in mine, that her visit to Yurt was nearly over.

"Maybe I should take Celia and Hildegarde home with me," she told me thoughtfully.

"Take them home?" I asked with a smile. "What will you and your mother do with them?"

"Here in Yurt everybody is always telling them they can't do what they want to do. Mother wouldn't tell them that."

"She doesn't let *you* do everything you want," I said, amused at Antonia's concern for the twins. Larks sang around us, and I was able to push to the back of my mind the voice which was trying out, "Wizards, of course, traditionally keep their private and their professional lives separate, so I therefore never happened to . . ."

"But Mother never told me I can't be a wizard," said Antonia. "Is that better than being a witch, by the way? And nobody will let Hildegarde be a knight, and now Celia thinks she'll have to be a nun because she can't be a priest. Maybe I should find out who keeps telling them all these things and turn him into a frog. What's a nun, Wizard? Is it fun to be one?"

"No, I don't think it's fun to be nun," I said, deciding to ignore the question about the relative values of wizard and witch—and even more so the issue of frogs. "But I'm afraid the twins were just down in Caelrhon, and they got the same answers there they got in Yurt."

"Then I'll have to find a better place for them to go," said Antonia in determination.

We walked for a moment in silence. "Do you like my hair like this?" she asked then, turning sapphire eyes on me.

"Well, the bows are very nice," I said cautiously, "but I like you in simple braids too."

She nodded emphatically. "That's what I decided. But I don't want to hurt Margareta's feelings. She broke her doll by accident, and now she has no one to play with but me. And this makes *four* different rooms in the castle I've slept in! I can't wait to tell my friend

Jen. Margareta's unhappy because she doesn't think the king loves her."

I wondered whether Princess Margareta had told her this, or whether Antonia, with her mother's quick insight, had worked it out for herself.

"I know what I can do, Wizard!" she said with a sudden skip. "I can take them all to see a dragon!"

"Well, since school-trained wizards are considered wedded to magic, it seemed best . . ." said the voice in the back of my mind with forced casualness. I pushed the voice away again and smiled at my daughter. Everything, the pain of being separated from Theodora, the deception, the embarrassment now that that deception seemed about to be found out, was worth it because of her. "Where will you find a dragon? I don't think your mother has any around."

"I'll find one someplace," she said confidently and enthusiastically. "Then Hildegarde can be a knight and kill it, but first the dragon will hurt Margareta so that she'll be sick in bed and the king will realize he always loved her, and Celia will give the last rites so that she can be a priest."

"It's a complicated scenario," I said, trying to keep from laughing.

"What's a complicated scenario?"

"Your plan. While you're at it, why not take Gwennie along too? I must say I'd never really considered, Antonia, that all that these women need is a trip someplace to see a dragon."

"That's right," said Antonia. "Gwennie is sad too. How about Justinia?"

I thought about the lady's self-possession. "She's in fear for her life—reasonably well concealed—but I wouldn't call her sad. But while you're trying to find ways to help people trapped by their circumstances and other people's expectations, how about King Paul?"

Antonia appeared to be turning over my bigger words

in her mouth for a moment, but rather than asking about them she said, "I don't think Paul needs to go see dragons. He could see them anytime he wants all by himself. After all, he's king!"

I found myself wondering if Cyrus, in whom the bishop saw no evil and who had, at least for a moment, turned on me a smile brimming with goodness, had somehow found *himself* trapped by circumstances. But I didn't want to think of him sympathetically.

Antonia plopped herself down in the grass by the path. "I'm getting tired of walking. Could you carry me—maybe carry me with magic? Or could you teach me to fly?"

Princess Margareta took Antonia off with her after lunch while I settled down for some serious magic. I could find traces of no one else's spells anywhere in the vicinity, but just at the edge of my attention I could occasionally catch hints of something in the distance, in the direction of Caelrhon. A demon, of course, with access to supernatural forces, would have no trouble hiding from me. I circled the outside of the castle, making sure that the big white lumps of chalk, surrounding us with a giant pentagram, were still in place. It was ironic, I thought, that the pentagram had originally been set up to confine a demon, but could now be just as effective in keeping one out.

Back in the courtyard, I spotted the Lady Justinia talking animatedly to Princess Margareta while Antonia watched and listened with interest. Margareta made only a few awkward comments of her own but seemed to be observing Justinia with even more thorough attention than my daughter. The princess, I thought, couldn't seem to decide whether the eastern lady was someone glamorous to model herself after or a dangerous rival for the king's affections.

Antonia waved to me but I just waved back and kept walking toward my chambers, feeling reluctant to speak to Justinia again just yet.

Sitting by my window, leafing through the *Diplomatica Diabolica* in an unsuccessful attempt to find something more useful to do, I saw Antonia dart away across the courtyard, but as I reached my chamber door, wondering what was happening, she returned to the others, pulling Hildegarde by the hand. Celia trailed behind her sister. The whole group disappeared into Justinia's chambers.

I smiled as I went back to my books. They could use the distraction. In a day or so Hildegarde's message would reach the duchess, relayed through several sets of pigeons, and then there would be no more time for the twins to play with Antonia. I ought to telephone Evrard, the Royal Wizard of Caelrhon, I thought, to tell him there was a demon loose in his kingdom—unless of course there wasn't. But at least I would be able to tell him my doubts and uncertainties more easily than I could tell the wizards' school, though he would be just as displeased when I told him the demon seemed involved with the cathedral.

There were shouts of laughter from the courtyard. I glanced up to see Hildegarde dragging something out through Justinia's door at Antonia's direction, while the automaton watched uneasily. It looked like a carpet. Margareta and Celia clustered around. Gwennie, crossing the courtyard with her arms full of clean linen, stopped to watch.

So Antonia was going to pretend to take her friends far away from here on a flying carpet, I thought affectionately, somewhere they could leave all their problems behind and maybe even meet a dragon. Sometimes it was hard to believe someone so imaginative and good-natured was really my daughter. She stood with one small fist on her hip, using the other hand to point, ordering them into their places. They laughed as they moved to obey; even Celia had shed her serious look to join in Antonia's game.

I had been reading for several more minutes and had just gotten to a part discussing how someone who had summoned a demon from hell might be able to make that demon do his bidding even from a considerable distance, when there was a loud *whoosh* from the courtyard.

Jumping up, I ran to the door. The courtyard was empty except for Justinia and some clean towels, drifting slowly out of the sky.

The lady's normal self-possession had been driven out by fury. "What manner of thing is this, O Wizard?" she cried. "Thy daughter hath stolen my flying carpet!"

PART FIVE

The Wolf

I

"How canst thou expect me to carry myself home from this benighted little kingdom without my flying carpet?" Justinia shrieked at me, but I was gone, shooting upward into the sky after a rapidly dwindling speck of color.

Theodora was going to kill me. That is, unless the duchess got to me first. Both Paul and the cook would cheerfully join in stripping the flesh from my bones when they learned Gwennie was gone. The Lady Justinia probably planned to work over whatever of me was left. And I hadn't even allowed yet for the royal court of Caelrhon.

The carpet was heading in the general direction of the city of Caelrhon, far faster than I could fly, but that didn't keep me from trying. Eyes streaming from the wind, I tore across the sky with every ounce of magic I had. But I realized in a few minutes that desperate, exhausting flight was not going to catch a flying carpet fueled by spells far more powerful than anything of mine.

I hovered in midair, desperately putting together a

167

tracer spell, then hurled it after the disappearing carpet so I that might have some hope of finding it—or its remains.

How could Antonia have stolen a flying carpet? She had heard me say the words of the Hidden Language to fly it a short distance, but could a five-year-old have remembered the strange, heavy syllables? And what must the others be thinking, hurtling through the air with a little girl supposedly in control, a girl who was surely at this moment sobbing with terror herself? Suppose they fell off, or the carpet tipped them off? Would it keep flying without further direction, over land and sea, circling the globe until it struck a mountain?

I tore my eyes from the speck that might be my last sight of Antonia to race back toward Yurt. I would do what I should have done at once and telephone ahead for another wizard to stop them. The flight to the castle seemed endless. Below me several villages whizzed past, none with telephones. How could I have been Royal Wizard here for twenty-five years and never installed magical telephones in them, imagining that pigeon-messages would continue to serve, never thinking that I might want a telephone to save my daughter?

Wheezing and dripping sweat, I staggered into the castle telephone room, ignoring the shouting and the questions. The story had gotten around fast that Justinia's carpet had taken off with a crown princess, the acting castle constable, the heiresses to a duchy and a principality, and a little girl. I slammed and leaned against the door as I gasped out the magical coordinates for the royal castle of Caelrhon.

It was not in the city itself but ten miles past it, on the far side from Yurt. But Caelrhon's Royal Wizard would be able to get there much faster than I could if Antonia had intended to take her friends to meet

Theodora. My mouth was so dry I had trouble making myself understood to the liveried servant who answered the telephone.

After what seemed a wait of several hours but could only have been a few moments, Evrard appeared. He gave me a cheerful smile over a bushy beard that failed in looking properly wizardly because it was so thoroughly red. "Nice to hear from you, Daimbert," he began.

But I had no time for pleasantries. "Quick! Do you remember how to stop a flying carpet?"

"A *what?*"

He had flown on a carpet years ago when we had been in the East together. I tried to refresh his memory of the spells to command one, taking deep gasping breaths between words. I had no idea how much time had passed or just how fast the carpet was going. By this time it might be well past Caelrhon anyway.

"Stay by the phone," Evrard said briskly. "I'll call you right back." The glass telephone went blank.

I kept my back against the door, in no condition to answer anyone's questions. The wait seemed interminable. I thought I could hear the king's voice among the rest, but if I didn't hear his orders clearly I wouldn't have to obey.

Should I call the school in case Evrard couldn't intercept them? But the masters of the school were unlikely to know anything about flying carpets. And they certainly would not understand why every wizard in the Western Kingdoms had to be mobilized to stop a runaway carpet. They wouldn't understand even if I told them my daughter was on it—after all, none of them were fathers.

How about Elerius? Or—and my heart, if possible, beat even harder—had he somehow put Antonia up to this? Or if not Elerius, had someone else insinuated his magic into the castle, putting a spell on Justinia's carpet so that it would fly off by itself as soon as someone sat on it?

This seemed improbable—after all, I had sat on it myself just last night, though I had been too distracted to spot renegade spells. But if someone was watching the castle and waiting for another chance to attack, the person who had sent the undead warriors, this would be a golden opportunity. If Evrard couldn't catch the carpet and bring them home, I would have to go after them myself, all the way around the globe if necessary, even if it meant leaving Yurt unprotected.

I put my sweat-covered forehead against the stone wall and closed my eyes. My best bet might be to go straight to the cathedral, grab Cyrus, and tell him I was ready to sell my soul to the devil. Saving Antonia would be cheap at the price.

The phone rang, making me jump convulsively and scrape my forehead. I snatched the receiver up.

"I couldn't catch them, Daimbert," said Evrard, looking haggard. I closed my eyes and wiped blood from my eyebrows. "I saw the carpet shoot over the city and was able to fly within fifty yards of it, but I just couldn't catch it. I'm sorry! I don't know what else to say. There were four women and a little girl on it—is that how many were on it when they left Yurt?"

"Yes," I said dully because he seemed to be waiting for an answer. At least none of them had fallen off yet.

"The girl waved at me."

"*Waved*? Desperately?"

"No," said Evrard slowly. "As if she were enjoying herself."

"Dear God," I groaned. Antonia, unable to slow the carpet, did not yet realize the danger she and all the others were in. She might not have even recognized her city from the air. If they continued in this direction, within an hour they would be over the coast. . . .

And very near Elerius's kingdom. "Get off the phone," I barked. "I'm going to call Elerius."

Evrard made a contrite mouth and hung up at once. Elerius too had been in the East, I remembered as I desperately placed the call. He must have some knowledge of flying carpets. Even if he had put Antonia up to this—*especially* if he had—he had to help me.

He came to the phone immediately. Had he been lurking nearby, I wondered suspiciously, waiting for a call he knew would come? But like Evrard, he seemed to want to begin with pleasantries, though his hazel eyes looked at me calculatingly from under peaked eyebrows.

I didn't have time to worry about it. I told him in a few words what had happened. Let him derive any pleasure he liked from knowing Antonia had taken his suggestion. But he said blandly that he still recalled perfectly the commands for a flying carpet. I gave him the magical coordinates of my tracer spell so he might have a chance to spot the carpet coming if it wasn't there yet.

"I'll be there as fast as I can," I said. "But it's all up to you." He nodded as he rang off.

But did I dare leave the people here in Yurt unprotected, especially Justinia? And what was I going to say to them all?

I burst out of the telephone room, scattering those who had clustered close, hoping to overhear. "Sire!" I shouted at Paul, spotting him toward the back of the crowd. "Another magical attack may come while I'm saving the kidnapped women! Be ready!" I lifted myself to fly over everyone's head, through the courtyard, to the stables where we kept the air cart tethered.

Justinia's elephant trumpeted in loud terror as I brought the purple flying-beast skin out past its stall. The lady was at the front of the crowd outside, black eyes snapping. "Wouldst thou care to tell me—" she began with barely controlled passion.

I didn't wait to hear the rest. I lifted her with magic, dumped her unceremoniously into the air cart, and leaped in myself. As I shouted the command to take off, her metallic automaton sprang in after us and grabbed me by the throat.

The air cart, responding to my final gurgling words, rose majestically as I was thrown onto my back. The shouting of the knights, ladies, and servants was replaced by a stunned silence as we sailed off to the strong beats of purple wings. I could feel blood oozing from under the points of the automaton's fingers as I struggled vainly, trying to find enough words of the Hidden Language to free myself before the world went black.

"No, kill him not," said Justinia quickly to her automaton. The pressure on my throat eased at once. I collapsed on the bottom of the cart, sucking in air. "At least," she added, "until I have questioned him."

The automaton moved to the far side of the cart. I rolled over and sat up slowly. "I am trying to save you, my lady," I gasped. "Someone kidnapped those women knowing that I would have to go after them, knowing that with no wizard in the castle you would be helpless. I'm only taking you along to protect you, in case anything else like that army of undead warriors attacks the castle again."

"Nonsense," she said crisply, maintaining her balance easily with a hand on the edge of the cart. "No one kidnapped them. I *heard* thy daughter give the commands to start the carpet flying. And I would ne'er be helpless with my automaton near."

She might have a point there, I thought, using my handkerchief to wipe the blood from my neck. The flow seemed to be easing; at least it hadn't hit an artery.

"Then think of it this way," I said with as much dignity

as I could. "I am taking you to reclaim your carpet, after the unfortunate incident in which a little girl's game got out of hand—and you'd better hope to the saints that no one is killed."

I turned away, looking gloomily at the landscape passing—so slowly—beneath. It would have been faster to fly myself, but I was still badly winded from the desperate attempt to catch the carpet and might not have made it. Justinia had probably told everyone in the castle that Antonia was my daughter. I wondered why I had ever thought it mattered.

After a minute I felt a gentle hand on my arm. "Did my automaton wound thee very grievously?" she asked.

I turned and lifted my chin to let her finish wiping away the blood. It didn't seem worth answering.

"Realize this, O Wizard," she said after a minute, "that thou hast distressed me exceedingly. Verily the mage Kaz-alrhun thought that I would be safe in thy little kingdom, yet I have ne'er felt completely at ease here, and then to be carried away so forcibly when I had just lost my only method for e'er returning home!"

"Well," I said grudgingly, "then we're even. Your automaton distressed me exceedingly when it tried to kill me."

At this rate, I thought, maybe I should just plan to stay away from the castle for a few days. Even if I got everyone off the carpet safely, Theodora would never forgive me for allowing Antonia to take it from right under my nose. And when the story got around that I had carried off the eastern princess, kicking and screaming, doubtless with plans to rape her, the king would not leave enough skin on my body for the duchess to have a decent turn. There wouldn't be enough of me left for a proper burial—but then the bishop would tell them I didn't deserve a Christian burial anyway.

Elerius had better have caught them, I thought

gloomily. Otherwise it was right back to Cyrus and his demon.

We flew on in silence. Justinia stood close beside me, her shoulder against mine. I kept staring ahead, trying to turn clouds, birds, and wisps of smoke into flying carpets.

And then at last I saw a rapidly moving speck, one that did not disappear when I blinked. It was deep red and heading toward us.

II

"That was terrific," said Hildegarde enthusiastically. "If you had a dozen of those carpets on the battlefield, no one could ever stand against you."

"God heard our prayers," said Celia quietly. "We must all give our thanks to Him for preserving our lives."

"I didn't know you wizards could do spells that powerful," added Gwennie, "stopping a flying carpet dead from a hundred yards away." I certainly couldn't have done that myself—otherwise the carpet would never have gotten away—but I did not want to dwell on how much better Elerius's magic was than mine.

We all ended up having dinner crowded around the table in his study. When his king, twice as formal and august as Paul, learned that one of his unexpected guests was a crown princess and two more the daughters of a prince, he came up personally to meet them. He welcomed them to his castle with a few well-chosen words and complimented Princess Margareta as though she had been ten years older, but he paid no attention whatsoever to Gwennie and me and only looked quizzically at Justinia, clearly curious about the automaton hovering at her shoulder but not wanting to ask.

"This is Daimbert," said Elerius, "the wizard who invented the far-seeing telephone."

His king looked momentarily interested but not very much so, and in a minute he wished us all a pleasant dinner and left.

Antonia, exhilarated and exhausted, fell asleep in the middle of the soup course. I cradled her on my lap, too relieved and too weary to feel much like eating myself, and wondering how one little girl could at the same time be so adorable and so exasperating.

"Lady Maria thought she was giving me a 'change' the other day by taking me to Caelrhon," said the Princess Margareta excitedly. "But how many times have I been to that city before, a thousand, a million? Where does she think I *live*? But this!" She giggled. "This really was a change! And now I know all about flying carpets, Justinia, just like you do."

"I hadn't realized you were teaching your niece magic, Wizard," said Gwennie. "Isn't it rather unusual for girls to learn magic?"

Elerius caught my eye, lifting one eyebrow but saying nothing.

I had telephoned Yurt as soon as we reached the castle. The queen had answered the phone herself, emerald eyes concerned. "Everyone's fine," I had said quickly. "No problems at all. You'll hear all about it when we're home. Anything happening there?"

But everything was quiet in Yurt. I called Evrard next, to reassure him as well. Theodora I would tell when I saw her. One more thing, I thought with a sigh, that I was keeping from her.

"When I take over Father's principality," said Hildegarde, "I think I'll get a flying carpet of my own. But will I need an eastern mage rather than a western wizard? Just think, Celia, if you don't go into the nunnery you can ride on my carpet whenever you come to visit, once you're a duchess."

Elerius was the perfect host, serving us himself.

When I asked, in a low voice shielded by the general conversation, if he had taught Antonia to fly the carpet, he only smiled and said, "I have never taught anyone the spells for a flying carpet."

Gwennie looked more cheerful than she had in weeks. "I must say, Wizard," she said to me, "that I didn't think Antonia meant it when she said she could take us to see a dragon! We didn't actually see one," she added regretfully, "and considering that she didn't seem to be able to steer maybe it's just as well the wizard came along when he did, but it certainly made for a more interesting afternoon than putting away the laundry!"

Elerius's constable was able to find rooms for all of us in the castle, and in the morning we set out to return to Yurt. "Antonia," I told her firmly in my best wizardly voice, "I think it's time for you to go home. I've really enjoyed having you at the castle this week, but you took off without telling me where you were going. I'm afraid I just can't allow that."

"But I *told* you I was going!" she protested, giving me a sidelong look, as though knowing perfectly well she had been disobedient but confident she could still get out of it. I had sometimes felt that way myself.

Justinia directed her own magic carpet, her automaton riding with her, keeping its pace slow to match the air cart where the rest of us were crowded. Quite understandably, she insisted that the girl was not to ride on the carpet again.

"You said that your friends would like to see a dragon, Antonia," I said, not about to be won around, "but you didn't say anything about taking them there on a flying carpet, and you didn't even give me a chance to come along if I'd wanted."

The sky was overcast, and I hoped we would make it home before it rained. Antonia whirled from me to Hildegarde. "But I want to stay with *her!*"

Hildegarde shook her head. "I'm afraid Celia and I are going to be busy for a while. By now our parents will have heard that she wants to be a nun, and they're either furiously telephoning Yurt or else riding right down from Father's principality."

"Then I'll stay with *you!*" cried Antonia, turning to Gwennie.

I turned her around toward me again. "We'll drop everyone else off and go straight to Caelrhon," I said slowly and clearly.

Antonia frowned darkly for a moment, but then her expression cleared. "I can tell my friend Jen all about the castle. And I can see the Dog-Man again!"

It grew darker as the day moved on, and the air felt much too cold for this time of year. The air cart's pace slowed as its wings had to beat against a strong east wind. The women shivered, though I kept Antonia warm in my arms—she did a good job of keeping my chest warm too. But whatever storm was building did not yet break. We landed in the castle courtyard under a lowering sky, and everyone turned out to greet us. They were too pleased to see us all safe to start taking me apart at once, though I was discouraged to see the king showing more solicitude to Justinia than to Gwennie.

I paused only long enough to collect Antonia's things, then took off for the city, leaving the others to give the details of our adventure. The duchess had indeed telephoned, leaving a message that Celia was not to do *anything* until she arrived.

The sun never had shone through the clouds, and I wanted to get to Caelrhon before it really did begin to storm. Besides, the sooner I faced Theodora the better. Probably I should go around to the cathedral and apologize to Joachim too if he'd even agree to see me. He'd forgiven me for a lot of things in the past, although in this case I hadn't just insulted the bishop himself but someone under his direction.

Antonia was not reconciled to going home in disgrace—she kept hoping I would change my mind until we were actually in the air—and hugged her Dolly rather than me as we flew along. "It's for your own good," I tried to reason with her. "Your mother said you should do what I said, and you didn't. Suppose Elerius hadn't been able to stop the carpet, and you'd ended up flying for days and days across the Outer Sea until you either fell off or died of hunger?"

"You never *told* me not to fly the carpet," she replied indignantly, her chin trembling only the slightest amount.

But she sprang from the air cart with a glad cry and threw herself into her mother's arms when I set the air cart down in the quiet cobbled street of the artisans' quarter of Caelrhon. And she agreed only slightly reluctantly to kiss me good-night once she had been fed and washed.

I told Theodora everything that had happened, sitting again on her couch with my arm around her, the room bathed in the glow of the magic lamp. The only part I didn't tell her was the bishop deciding that he had had lustful thoughts about her for years without realizing he did. It began at last to rain, a cold, fitful drizzle, and the wind howled in the chimney. At several points Theodora took a deep breath and started to lean forward, but she always settled back again against my arm without speaking.

"Well," she said at last, her cheerful tone sounding almost normal, "it sounds as though Antonia's visit to Yurt was a little more exciting than I had expected. But everyone is fine now, and that's what's important. Shall I make us some tea?"

As we sipped our tea, its warmth welcome this cold night, she suddenly said, "I'll have to try to find out what spells Elerius taught her."

"But he said—" Then I realized Theodora was quite right. When I returned to Yurt two days ago, my rooms had been thick with magic. Elerius would not just have shown off for Antonia. He had decided to win her affection by teaching her spells.

"Were *you* learning magic when you were five?" Theodora asked, pouring more tea.

"I must have been twelve or so," I said slowly, remembering back. It had been years since I'd thought about this. "An old magician who sometimes worked the street corner for pennies showed me how to make an illusory gold coin in return for quite a pile of real copper coins. As I recall, I'd been saving them for months." I promptly made Theodora an illusory gold coin of her own to show I hadn't lost the knack. "But remember that I grew up in the great City, nearly in sight of the wizards' school, where it perched on a pinnacle at the center of town. I'd always dreamed about learning magic, of being one of the very wise masters we would occasionally see, or even one of the student wizards who were always getting into trouble with the city Guardians after spending too long in the taverns. After my parents died and it was clear that the choices were to help my grandmother run our wool import house or else go up to the school and beg the Master to take me on, the decision wasn't difficult."

"And what would the Master say," asked Theodora, "if our daughter asked him to take *her* on?"

"Well, they've never had a woman there. I've told you they mention the possibility from time to time, but either no women have applied or else they haven't been the right ones."

"That is," said Theodora, mostly to herself, "they haven't been women who are in fact men."

"That may change, though," I continued thoughtfully. "They've always thought extremely well of Elerius, and

I know he's got plans of his own to start revitalizing the school once he has a position of power there—which he's certain to have soon. Maybe he was teaching Antonia magic because he intends to have women in the school when he's in charge."

"Or maybe," said Theodora, giving me a quick look, "he's trying to get a hold over you through her. Didn't you just suggest something of the sort yourself?" The rain tapped against the dark panes, and somewhere down the street a dog howled mournfully. I wondered irrelevantly if it was the dog Cyrus had brought back to life. "She is *good*, Daimbert. I've taught her a little of what you call my witch magic, and she learned it far faster than I ever did. If she starts on school magic too she'll soon be far ahead of me."

"If I came and stayed here more often I could give you private tutoring in school magic," I suggested with a smile.

"Maybe I've already learned just about all of your magic I particularly care to learn!" she replied saucily.

I pulled her to me, nuzzling her hair, but thinking about Elerius and Antonia. I could try to teach our daughter myself, but if she really had a flair for magic she deserved to be taught by a better wizard than I was. I had never trusted Elerius, but if he was planning to get women into the school he might be Antonia's best chance for the education she deserved.

But then I chuckled. "Maybe we're getting ahead of ourselves here. She's only five."

"Yes," said Theodora. "A five-year-old girl who already knows enough magic to steal a flying carpet."

III

The clouds were even heavier the next morning although the rain had ceased. Theodora settled down to her sewing almost on top of the magic lamp. "Couldn't you try some weather spells on this?" she asked. "Nobody's going to be able to see anything all day."

"Well, I don't like to affect the weather unless it's for something important like saving a crop," I started. "After all, the spells can have unexpected results—"

But then I stopped. Suppose Cyrus was affecting the weather for his own purposes? I felt very reluctant to try to question him any more, especially since I was quite sure I would get no answers out of him, but the Romneys should be able to tell me if he had worked weather spells for them.

Antonia was still asleep, worn out from her adventures. I bent to kiss Theodora. "I'm heading back to Yurt."

She turned around to kiss me properly. "I'm very glad Antonia visited you. We'll have to do this again." No mention of missing me but I would take what I could get. I thought as I went down the street that allowing oneself to love someone always gave that person the power, intentional or unintentional, to inflict pain. Maybe the wizards in renouncing marriage wanted to avoid any pain that would distract them from their spells.

But if so it was much too late for me. I stopped by the cathedral office and left a note for Joachim. An acolyte told me rather loftily that the bishop was much too busy to see me without an appointment, but I didn't know if that meant that he had left orders to keep all wizards away or if he really was very busy—I tried to reassure myself that most of the times I had seen him the last five years had been in brief interludes he could snatch from his duties.

The Romney circle of caravans was still at the edge of town, smoke rising from their chimneys, but on this cold, raw day no one was outside, and the ponies looked at me disconsolately. I thought I saw a brown rat disappear into the grass ahead of me. But the bright blue door of one of the caravans swung open as I approached, and the Romney woman I had first spoken to a week before called to me.

"Come to have your fortune told?"

I laughed and mounted the wooden steps. "Wizards can manage much better fortunes than I expect you can." I'd never get the Romney children by themselves today. "Isn't this terrible weather!" She stepped back as I ducked my head to enter.

Inside her caravan was smoky from the stove but laid out very compactly and neatly, with copper pans gleaming on the wall and all the cupboards painted blue like the door.

"Not like summer at all," the woman agreed, giving me a gold-toothed smile. "At this rate we'll have frost! We haven't seen weather like this since we left the Eastern Kingdoms this spring."

"Did Cyrus help you with weather spells as you came over the mountains?" I asked casually.

Her expression changed at once and so did her tone, from friendliness to the resonant and artificial note of someone telling a mysterious fortune in which she herself did not believe. "I will look into the future for you, Wizard," she said, "and see shadowed doings beyond even the knowledge of the wise, but you will have to pay me first."

Puzzled, I reached into my pocket and pulled out some coins, substantially more than what I had paid the old magician to teach me my first illusion when I was twelve. Had Cyrus ordered her not to tell me anything about him, even threatened her with his dark magic if he did?

She dropped my money into her own pocket without counting it, then opened a cupboard to take out a crystal ball. In sunlight a crystal will make rainbows and weird reflections of everything around, but today it showed only dark blues and grays, with at the center a flash of light from the fire in the stove. She put the ball on the little table in the center of the caravan, and I obediently sat down across from her.

She stared into the crystal for a moment, playing with the long whisker on her upper lip, while I wondered if she was going to try to impart actual information through an alleged fortune or was just doing something that would plausibly explain my presence and also get rid of me.

The caravan was silent except for the crackling of the fire. The smoke in the room seemed to become denser. At last she spoke, so suddenly and loudly that I jumped. "Someone is coming. Someone from far away. Someone who travels by night."

She spoke with such conviction that I stared into the crystal myself, seeing nothing. Irrational fear made the cold day even colder. "Is this anyone I know?" I asked after a minute when she seemed reluctant to add anything more. "Will he be here soon?"

"He comes slowly, and he comes by night," she said again. Abruptly she rose and put the crystal ball back into the cupboard. "And that," she said loudly, a poorly concealed nervous tremor in her voice, "is all the fortune you will have from me."

She swung open the caravan door in case her point wasn't clear enough. I thanked her and left, glad to breathe fresh air again, even if damp and cold, after the smoky atmosphere of the caravan. As I retrieved the air cart I wondered if this was recent information the Romneys had acquired, or if they had heard while still in the Eastern Kingdoms of someone heading this way. The Romney children had told me Cyrus had asked them about Yurt; had someone else in the East also inquired about us?

As the air cart flew slowly against a dank wind I

thought about the princely wizard Vlad and his obsidian castle, guarded by wolves. Once I had been reassured that Cyrus was not Vlad in disguise, I had tried to dismiss fears of the dark wizard I had made my enemy many years ago. But suppose Cyrus had been sent as Vlad's agent, to find me, even to kill me? Cyrus however had shown no sign of wanting to kill me on the two occasions when I met him.

But *somebody* had sent unliving warriors to attack Yurt, warriors that had dissolved in daylight although a spell had lingered in their bones, a spell to drive men—and women—mad. And Vlad's black castle in the East lay under a permanent bank of clouds, to make even day as dark as night. Sunlight was the one thing he could not bear, even with all his powers.

I leaned back against the edge of the air cart and shouted the heavy words of the Hidden Language at the black clouds overhead. If Vlad was trying to make the twin kingdoms of Yurt and Caelrhon as dark as his own principality, he would not succeed.

The wind swirled stronger, and a small scudding cloud dumped hail on my head. But then the sky split open, and the sun's rays shone placidly down. The thick clouds started to swing together again, regrouping, but I replied with more shouted spells, and they scattered, dissolving as they slid away over the horizon.

There, I thought, looking down at the fields below washed with light. That was better. The air was becoming warmer by the moment. If Vlad came to Yurt after me, we would meet on *my* terms.

The air cart flew faster now with the wind no longer against us. The sun beat down on my hair. Now that summer weather had returned, it was easy to think of the cold and the clouds as something trivial. I smiled, recalling how quick I had been to assume that some enemy would attack the castle as soon as I took off

after Antonia. In fact, there had been no problems at
all since I overcame the undead warriors, other than
those directly due to Antonia's high spirits.

As the air cart and I flew on I tried to plan my
next move. The Romney woman had certainly wanted
to warn me against somebody, and there might be
other spells I could try in order to detect a distant,
evil presence. Certainly I could telephone some of
the other wizards stationed closer to the Eastern
Kingdoms to see if they had heard of someone who
came by night.

We came over the forests and fields that surrounded
the whitewashed royal castle of Yurt. Looking ahead,
I saw that the drawbridge was up, which seemed overly
cautious for daytime.

But then I saw the wolf.

It was a fenris-wolf, huge and white, as tall at the
shoulder as a man. The only shading on its coat was a
ruff of black guard hairs around the neck. Long yellow
teeth protruded from the jaws, and its eyes were a light
china blue. It paced before the moat, ears forward,
growling low and steady. I had seen a wolf like this in
the Eastern Kingdoms, in fact outside of Vlad's obsidian
castle, but this was no time for reminiscences.

I dropped the air cart fast into the middle of the castle
courtyard. The knights, heavily armed, stood along the
battlements, watching. The wolf stared back at them,
sunlight flashing like fire from its pale eyes.

King Paul came up to me, looking very serious, though
an expression lurked at the corner of his mouth that
suggested he was enjoying this. "Has anyone been hurt,
sire?" I asked urgently. "Where did the wolf come from?"

"No one's hurt. The saints only know where it came
from, though it must be another attack on the Lady
Justinia. It first appeared when I was out riding about

an hour ago. The sky was so dark it could have been evening, and it was getting darker and colder by the minute, so I had just turned Bonfire back to the castle when I heard a howl."

Down below the walls the wolf howled, and inside the stables Justinia's elephant trumpeted wildly.

"Like that," said Paul. "Bonfire was spooked, of course, and in the darkness I couldn't even tell where it was." It sounded to me as if he had come extremely close to being killed, but he seemed almost cheerful about it. "But then the sun broke through the clouds, and I saw that beast looking at me. It didn't take much persuading to get Bonfire to run! What's most impressive is that the wolf was—almost—able to keep up. But I was fifty yards ahead when I reached the moat, and they'd seen me coming and were cranking up the drawbridge even before I was off it."

It looked as though I had saved my king's life with my weather spells. I took a deep breath and let it out again. "We should be safe then. It won't be able to get over the walls unless it can fly."

"That's all very well for us," said Paul, no longer sounding as though he was enjoying this. "But there are no stone walls around the village. If it gets bored here it can trot down and have its pick of the villagers' herds—or of them."

"Has anyone tried shooting it?"

"We did. But it seems to be able to dodge arrows easily."

I had been probing the wolf as we spoke. It was a real wolf all right, but with a faint magical aura about it. Bigger and stronger than a normal wolf, it also appeared to have faster reflexes—and doubtless stronger jaws. I could try transforming it into something innocuous, but if it was a creature from the land of wild magic the spell would blow up in my face.

"Now that you're here," said Paul, "we'll try a sortie

against it. If you could put a binding spell on it we should be able to capture or kill it. But we'd better move fast in case those clouds come back—or before it really becomes night."

"Not you, sire," I said. "I'd certainly like a few sword arms at my back, but not yours. As your mother keeps on telling you, you don't have an heir. If you get yourself killed by a wolf, who's going to be king? You don't want Yurt run by some fourth cousin from somewhere who doesn't even worry about his villagers."

Paul frowned, but I wasn't going to wait for an argument. I might be pledged to his service, but a wizard could never be expected to obey with absolute, unquestioning loyalty. Our highest oaths were not to our kings. "Let's get a few people down to the postern gate," I called to the other knights. Hildegarde was among them and turned eagerly at my voice, but I ignored her. "You, you, you! I'll distract the wolf on this side of the castle while you get out the back."

"Wizard," Paul began ominously, but then he stopped without countermanding my order. The three knights, delighted to be chosen, ran to let themselves out the small postern gate and to cross the moat on stepping stones while I flew over the wall to meet the wolf.

I needn't have worried about keeping its attention while the knights came around. It sprang at me with a howl, and only by rapid midair backing was I able to avoid getting my throat ripped out.

"That's right," I told myself, hovering twenty feet above it. The red gullet and teeth were improved by distance, but not by much. "Remember that it has fast reflexes. And can jump." I lifted to thirty feet.

I started on a paralysis spell, something to freeze it in place. From the corner of my eye I spotted the knights coming around the corner of the castle, spears at the ready.

The wolf plunged through my paralysis spell as though it wasn't there and tore toward the knights. Flying madly behind, I tried a quick and dirty binding spell with no better result. This wolf had been sent here with counterspells all ready to foil a wizard.

The startled knights had their shields up and spears braced for the onslaught. Abandoning my binding spell, I turned the air to glass in front of the wolf.

It bounced back with a snarl of pain and rage. So you weren't quite ready for *that* spell? I thought in grim triumph.

But already it had sprung up and around the solid air, again toward the knights of Yurt. They might not be the king, but I couldn't let them get killed either. Easily dodging the spears with which they tried to impale it, the wolf knocked the first one down and went for his throat.

I yelled behind it, trying to remind it that it had been sent to kill a wizard. It whirled away from the fallen knight and at me, a mass of furious teeth and fur. I snatched up the spear the knight had dropped and flew rapidly backwards.

The wolf ran right along with me. This was a beast, I reminded myself, able to match paces with the fastest stallion in a dozen kingdoms. Taking long bounds, it snarled again, baring vicious yellow teeth. I tried to fly faster, but it still had no trouble keeping up.

Once all the way around the castle. I was almost back to the knights. Should I go around again and try to tire it out? I could hear faint distant cheers from the battlements. But this wolf might not tire in twenty circuits of the castle, while I myself would long before then. This was no spectacle or race where the viewers cheered for me—or the wolf? I stopped fleeing and stood my ground.

One last bound and it was on me, trying to evade

the spearpoint and going for my face. The two quick words of the Hidden Language that should have knocked it backwards had no effect, and it was a struggle to keep clear in my mind the words to speed my own movements. Whoever had sent this wolf had spelled it against western school magic.

My magically aided reflexes were nearly as fast as the wolf's, but it was appreciably heavier. It ran straight up the spear, not even seeming to feel the point driving into its chest, and knocked me flat. Protection spells seemed to have no effect. Dropping the spear I threw both arms across my face and throat, feeling the wolf's hot breath and the slash of fangs cutting into my flesh. For a second there was no pain at all, then the wounds began burning like fire.

What an ignominious way for a wizard to go, I thought, feeling a rush of hot blood pouring past my ears. An enormous weight landed on my chest, and as consciousness left me I realized that I could no longer hear the wolf's growls. Maybe I'd killed it after all. My last thought was that at least now I might deserve the Golden Yurt.

IV

I did not get better.

I regained consciousness while being carried into the castle, just enough to realize that the wolf was dead. In the evening, after the village doctor had salved and bound up the slashes on my forearms, the king came and sat beside me on the bed, long booted legs stretched out before him. He told me how the knights had struck the wolf from behind with sword and spear while it was trying to kill me; the blood I had thought came from my own throat was in fact the beast's.

"Damnation, Wizard," finished Paul, sounding relieved

and irritated at the same time, "aren't you ever going to let me do *anything*?"

Groggy but comfortable, I fell asleep, resigned to general stiffness for a few days and bandages for a little while longer. I had really worn myself out the last week or two, I thought, and being heroically wounded was a good excuse to catch up on my rest.

But in the morning the fire was back in the wounds and my head ached so badly I could barely think. The doctor, returning, pronounced that there might be "some infection." When I tried to explain to him in a voice that didn't sound anything like my own that there was a certain blue-flowered plant he had to find, one good for healing infection through herbal magic, he shook his head, told me to try to stay calm, and went to talk to Gwennie at the doorway without even listening to the plant's description.

All that day I kept sliding in and out of evil dreams in which the wolf leaped at me again and again, causing me to jerk convulsively, throwing off the blankets and almost falling out of bed. Behind the wolf I could now clearly see Vlad's face, dead white and with eyes of stone.

"The Romney woman told me he's coming," I told Gwennie when she put cool cloths on my brow. "You have to keep watch for him. Tell the wizards' school he's coming."

"Of course we'll tell them," she said in the voice of someone humoring a child.

"And stop putting cold water on me," I said irritably, stirring a bandaged arm enough to throw the cloth away. It felt like the scab had ripped free under the bandage. Just as well. I didn't trust the doctor and whatever he had been putting on me, and I would tell him so. "This room is freezing already!"

"This room is very warm," said Gwennie. "But you have a fever."

Unconsciousness washed over me again. When I again felt cold water dripping into my ears—maybe later that day, maybe the next day—I tried to tell Gwennie that Vlad and the doctor had conspired to kill me. But it wasn't Gwennie bending over me. This time it was Celia.

Nuns, I thought vaguely, nursed the dying. If I died from my wounds, would that count as having been killed by the wolf? But there was something wrong with Celia being at my bedside in Yurt.

"You're not here," I told her. "You're a nun."

"Not according to my mother and father," she said with a sad smile. "Do you feel any better?"

"No." And I passed out again.

Later I was never sure how long I wandered through fever and nightmare. I couldn't keep my eyes open, but when I closed them demons leered at me while my body, especially the arms, seemed to grow distorted and enormous. Elerius kept slipping through my dreams, always one step ahead of me, looking back from under his peaked eyebrows and giving an ironic smile. Various people nursed me and tried to feed me soup as I slumped, only slightly conscious. At one point I became convinced that Theodora sat beside me, holding my hand, but when at last I was able to open my eyes all my fist clutched was the edge of the pillow.

"I'm sorry," I came to myself to hear my own voice mumbling. "Won't you forgive me? I thought priests were supposed to forgive people. I just wanted information, and I know he's evil. You can tell because he tried to kill me."

Whom was I addressing? It sounded as though I thought I was talking to the bishop. I got my eyes open and saw not Joachim but a man over seven feet tall, whose blond beard was streaked with white.

"Good," I told him confidently. I knew who this was. No more nightmare illusions for me, I thought with assurance. "You can go hunt the wolf." It was Prince Ascelin, Hildegarde and Celia's father and a noted hunter. He bent over the bed, paying more attention to what I was saying than anyone else seemed to have lately, his blue eyes dark with concern. "The wolf poisoned me when it tried to bite me, but if you kill it I'll recover. Just don't let the doctor in. He doesn't know anything about infection."

I sank back beneath the surface of consciousness, but not as far or as long this time. They seemed to be doing something with my arms. Probably cutting them off, I concluded. The wounds must have become so infected that the doctor had decided to amputate before gangrene spread to the rest of my body. Little did anyone realize that this was all part of Vlad's plot against me.

Well, I wasn't going to let them do it. With a roar of anger, I forced myself to sit up and awake, jerking my arms back.

But it wasn't the doctor who had taken hold of me. It was Prince Ascelin, and, this time, truly and not in a dream, Theodora.

"That sounded like a fairly healthy yell," said Ascelin. "And it looks as if the wounds are healing at last."

"His forehead doesn't feel as feverish," said Theodora, putting a cool palm against my head.

"Don't talk about me as though I'm not there," I said pettishly. "Who said you could cut off my arms?"

"I already tried to tell you," said Ascelin patiently. "I have no intention of cutting off your arms. But nothing the doctor had seemed to be working, so I've been attempting a little of your own herbal magic. Don't you remember that blue-flowered plant you found on our trip to the East? It's *hard* to find around here, let me tell you, and I don't think it works as well without a wizard to mumble magic words over it, but I think it's drawing the infection out at last."

"I tried to tell the doctor," I said, sinking back against the pillows, "but he wouldn't listen."

"Either that," said Ascelin with a quick smile, "or you weren't making a lot of sense. You haven't the last few weeks, you realize."

"Few *weeks*?"

Theodora pushed me back into bed again with a hand on my shoulder. "Lie still and I'll try you on the soup."

I let her spoon chicken soup into my mouth, trying to sort out what was reality and what nightmare. My head felt strangely light, which I decided was the absence of headache. The wolf, it seemed quite clear, really was dead, and Ascelin and Theodora assured me that nothing else had attacked the castle.

"I tried to get some help in herbal magic from the wizard of Caelrhon," said Ascelin, "but he told me nobody teaches it at your school anymore." He was right. I only knew what I did from my long-dead predecessor's rather grudging lessons. "So let's hope I remembered that plant correctly!"

Something else was nagging at me. I identified it at last. "What are you doing here?" I asked Theodora, swallowing soup. "And where's Antonia?"

"She's staying with her friend Jen. And I'm here because your queen sent me for me when—when she thought you were dying."

"Was I?" I asked, interested. "Am I still?"

"Considering that this is the first time you've been coherent in a very long time," said Ascelin with his quick smile, "I trust you aren't." After a moment he added soberly, "But the bishop came last week and gave you the last rites."

So I hadn't entirely imagined Joachim being here. I wondered if he'd actually heard anything I tried to say to him. And if he'd forgiven me, would I stay forgiven even if I didn't stay dead? "But Celia should have given me last rites," I said, remembering my daughter's plan to give everyone a chance to do what they most wanted.

A shadow passed across Ascelin's face at his own daughter's name. "She nursed you as assiduously as anyone, but—" He stood up abruptly. "You need to sleep. Come on," to Theodora. "We can talk to him more in the morning."

That night I slept deeply, without the nightmare of fever chasing me, and when I awoke toward dawn I almost felt like myself, though very weak. I took a quick glance at my arms—still there—and then looked across the room to see Theodora dozing in a chair.

She awoke when I stirred and came to sit beside me. Her amethyst eyes were gentle. I took her hand, an action which seemed to require an enormous amount of effort. "I'm so glad you're here," I whispered. "But how did you know?"

"I told you," she said gently and bent to brush her lips across my forehead. "Your queen sent for me. She knows about you and me."

"It's a secret," I said, trying to open my eyes enough to look at her properly. "Nobody else knows."

Theodora shook her head slowly and kissed me again. "I think just about everyone in the castle has worked it out. After all, when a mysterious woman is sent for as a wizard lies dying, and everyone recalls that he very recently produced a 'niece' no one knew he had, one who seems remarkably adept at magic for a little girl, a secret is hidden no longer."

"I'm sorry, Theodora," I murmured. So much for the privacy she had worked so hard to maintain! "I didn't want to have them all get to know you thinking of you as some—"

"As some fallen woman?" she said with a smile tugging the corners of her mouth. "Since they do, at least nobody has questioned whether it's suitable for me to spend the night watching you alone in your chambers."

"What does King Paul think about it?" I asked as though casually. Inwardly I was thinking gleefully that now Theodora would have to marry me. It would be the only way to restore her reputation, and although this wasn't the best way to have told Paul about her, now that the secret was out he would have to agree that I could stay on as Royal Wizard once we were married. This should take care of Theodora's final objections.

But from her reply she hadn't looked at it quite the same way. "I'm not sure what your king thinks about me," she said slowly. "He has gone out of his way to talk to me, almost as though wanting to demonstrate that he is *not* passing judgment on a fallen woman. In the same way, he has been struggling to act as though he considers you no differently than he ever did—which suggests of course that at some level he must be." Theodora, I thought, had always had a quick insight into other people's thoughts—due to being a witch, or maybe only to being herself.

"King Paul has been extremely concerned about you, of course," she continued, "and has been at some pains to tell me all the wonderful things you've done for the kingdom over the years, going back to when his father was still alive. He's even grateful for the times you've kept Yurt's knights—and him—from fighting as they were trained to do! It was touching, Daimbert: as though he hoped that by talking about you he could keep you alive. Since I don't live here in Yurt, maybe he thought I was the best person to tell, the one least likely to know all the stories already. And I must say some of the events sounded better in his telling than when you've told me about them!" She squeezed my hand. "He was very happy last night to hear that you were improved—nearly as glad as I."

I blinked against the early light coming through the window. Maybe I would try tea and cinnamon crullers this morning, I thought—my mouth tasted like old chicken soup. Well, even if Theodora and Paul hadn't realized yet that she would have to marry me and come live in Yurt, they would soon.

"The chaplain is planning a thanksgiving service for when you're a little better."

"I don't want the chaplain to have anything to do with it," I said peevishly. "I want the bishop."

Theodora smiled. "I'm sure he'll be offering his own thanks to God in Caelrhon. You don't want to act as though you thought only one priest had access to God and His saints!" Actually that was exactly what I thought, but I kept quiet. "I know he's been your friend for years, Daimbert," she continued, "but he's even busier than usual with his duties this summer." It sounded then as if Joachim had given up his plans to resign, I was pleased to hear. "Especially with the rats in the cathedral—"

"*What* rats?"

I had been lying comfortably, holding Theodora's hand, but now I tried to sit up with a great deal of thrashing.

She pushed me down again easily. "It's just that the river rats seem to be fairly numerous this summer," she said in a casual voice that immediately made me suspect this was much more serious than she wanted me to think. "They've always lived along the docks, but now they're getting into houses and a whole swarm seem to have settled in the cathedral. An acolyte even found one chewing on the altar cloth! So you can understand why the bishop is concerned."

"It's Cyrus," I said darkly. "He summoned the rats."

"The Dog-Man?" said Theodora in surprise. "After his prayers restored the burned buildings, I doubt if anyone in Caelrhon would suspect him of such a thing.

There are some who have blamed the Romneys— But I'm sure everyone realizes it's just a result of higher water along the river this year," she finished briskly.

"It's Cyrus all right," I repeated obstinately. "But the bishop won't believe any evil of him, and neither will Celia. Maybe if I tell her that he's behind the rats she'll give up this notion of being a nun. She never wanted to be one anyway."

Theodora looked somewhat pained. "I think Celia is taking this hard," she said quietly. She tried then to smile and added, "It feels so strange to be meeting all these people properly at last. You've told me about them, of course, and some of them I saw at King Paul's coronation, but the twins were just overgrown girls then, not young women."

But I wasn't going to let her change the subject. "What is Celia taking hard? The rats?"

Theodora shook her head fractionally, looking somewhere over my head. "Finding out that Antonia is your daughter. I think she'd gotten the notion that wizards should be as pure as priests. And she had trusted you, Daimbert, with her religious vocation. . . . She won't speak to me at all, though her sister does all the time, as though to make up for it. Hildegarde told me she's afraid that Celia is talking herself into really wanting to be a nun, in part to avoid having any more unpleasant discoveries in the secular world."

Feeling irritable because I was so weak, I said, "Then if she can't handle a glimpse of a little sin—and six years ago at that, I hope you told her!—then it's a good thing she won't be a priest. See if the cook made any crullers this morning."

As I ate my breakfast, deciding that I would have improved much faster if they had spooned tea into my mouth these last few weeks along with the chicken soup, I had the vague feeling that I had discovered something important shortly before the wolf attacked me. And something Theodora had told me about our daughter was worrisome. I wondered what it was.

V

I was able to recall enough herbal magic to assist the natural properties of Ascelin's healing herbs, and within a few days fresh, pink skin was growing on my arms where the wolf had bitten. The Lady Justinia, to my relief, showed no sign of trying to win my love by assisting in nursing me. The bishop telephoned from the cathedral office to tell me how grateful he was that I was alive, his voice and face giving no hint that he had ever been angry with me. He said nothing about Cyrus, and I decided it was most diplomatic not to ask.

Hildegarde came to my chambers to talk to me. I was out of bed now and spent part of each day sitting by the window, enjoying the warm air and leafing through my predecessor's books. Since I seemed to owe my life to the old magic, I thought I ought to learn a little more. It was startling to find in the margins in several places annotations in Elerius's small, neat hand.

"It looks to me, Wizard," said Hildegarde, "as though you and the knights overcame that wolf through raw strength, not wizardry."

"Not quite," I said slowly. A lot that had happened in the days before the incident was still confused in my mind, but my memories of the wolf were crystal clear. "He was bigger and faster and stronger than any ordinary wolf, and that was wizardry." Cyrus's magic, I thought. Or someone else's? This was one of the points on which I was still unclear. "Without my own magic, I don't think the knights would have had a chance."

"Well, it died just like any beast once they got their swords into it," said Hildegarde. "And that's what I wanted to ask you. Why didn't you take more knights with you?"

"Including you?" I asked good-naturedly. "I took enough to overcome the wolf, I hoped—and it turned out I was right—but no more, because one death this summer, the night watchman's, was already too many."

"But you might have been killed yourself," she said accusingly. "Why should *you* be able to face death but no one else?"

"Do you think it's actually *good* to be killed?" I asked, startled. "Has it been so long since knights in the western kingdoms were involved in wars that horrible pain and raw terror are actually appealing?"

"Well, maybe not," she said reluctantly. "But it *is* what knights are trained to face. I think I could be brave in the face of mortal danger. But now you wizards have taken all the danger for yourselves."

"Of course. That's because we're pledged to serve humanity."

"All right, then, Wizard," she said, as though she had been carefully constructing an argument and I had just conceded a key point, "are you going to let your daughter face death to save the lives of some knights?"

"Antonia?" I was horrified. "Certainly not!"

"Then what are you doing," she continued, bending closer, "teaching her magic?"

That was a very good question. But I didn't have time to consider it. The point that had been nagging me for several days came to me at last. Antonia was staying with her friend Jen while Theodora was here in Yurt. And Jen's mother let her play with the Dog-Man.

"Antonia is a delightful little girl," said Hildegarde conversationally. "Celia is just being silly. Because you're good friends with the bishop, she had somehow convinced herself that you should be almost a priest yourself. I know she won't be happy as a nun—she's got the same desire for action as I do. Saying she wanted to be the West's first woman priest was bad enough, but to go into the cloister! She's overreacting, of course, but it will be hard for Mother to stop her from entering the nunnery, because we will after all be of age this month."

I was no longer listening, but Hildegarde didn't seem to notice. "Theodora is a charming woman—intelligent, too, in spite of being unaccountably willing to be involved with you. Why don't you just marry her, Wizard?"

"Did Celia tell the Dog-Man that Antonia is my daughter?" I interrupted, heaving up out of the chair and seizing Hildegarde by the arms. Several times during her visit Antonia had hinted that she had met him earlier, in spite of Theodora's attempts to keep her away.

Hildegarde eased out of my grip, looking puzzled. "Celia hasn't told Cyrus anything. Don't you remember? My parents have forbidden her all contact with him, convinced that he's the one who made her decide to be a nun."

If someone had told me this, it must have been while I was delirious. I settled back slowly into my chair. But if Antonia went and played with Cyrus, maybe asking him to repair a broken toy—or, even worse, to take her to see a dragon—that strange, sharp-featured man would learn soon enough that she was my daughter. And what better way to get at me, now that his warriors of bone and hair and his fenris-wolf had failed, than through Antonia?

"Quick!" I cried. "Find Theodora and bring her here!"

"Well," said Hildegarde, bemused, "you mean my little suggestion has made you abruptly decide to propose marriage at last?"

"No! I mean, of *course* I want to marry her, but she won't marry me. She has to get back to Caelrhon right away."

"I'm not sure it's a good plan either," commented Hildegarde, "to send her away just because she has too much sense to want to tie herself to a wizard. She *did* take very good care of you while you were sick. *I* would never fall in love with a crotchety old wizard myself, but she gives every sign of it."

"Just get her!" Hildegarde shook her head with a grin and went. I pushed myself out of the chair to find my shoes. I should be able to fly the air cart, even in my weakened condition, and it would get Theodora home faster than a horse. I hated for her to go, leaving everything between us more unresolved than ever, but we had to make sure Antonia did not come into further contact with Cyrus.

Now that he had been accepted into the seminary, rather than living on the docks, he might have no more time to play with the children, I tried to reassure myself as I tied my shoes. I even took the time to wonder if I really had become a crotchety old wizard. Maybe I should have told Hildegarde that Justinia, for one, thought my face and figure youthful and my power highly attractive.

Antonia skipped down the street to meet us, braids bouncing on her back. "Guess what!" she called. "Jen and I caught a baby rat and we're going to raise him and teach him tricks. We'll make him a little house to live in and keep him in our bedroom at night. We named him Cyrus."

Theodora caught the girl up and hugged her hard. "I'm afraid a rat won't make a very good pet," she said then. "Does Jen's mother know about this?"

"Well, *if* Jen's mother won't let us have the rat at her house," said Antonia slowly, as though the girls had already thought this through, "can we have him in *our* house?"

A rat named Cyrus? I thought. It seemed a good choice.

Antonia hugged me too. "I'm getting a new tooth," she told me proudly. "Are you all better? Mother said you were sick. The bishop took me to church with him one day and we prayed for you. Did I make you better?"

"You might have," I said, smiling just from the pleasure of seeing her.

Antonia paused in skipping down the street to look back. "I asked the bishop if he had any little girls or boys of his own," she informed us, "and do you know what he said? He said he was the father of everybody in Yurt and Caelrhon, including the grown-ups. Doesn't that sound strange? Is he really?"

We went to see Jen and her mother and to get Theodora's things. The two women presented a united front against the concept of a rat as a pet.

"So have you come back for the ceremony?" Jen's mother asked. "You mean you didn't hear? Cyrus is going to receive the key to the city. They're holding the ceremony at the covered market this evening."

"Is that the Dog-Man?" asked Jen.

"That's right," said her mother. "The same man who fixed your doll this spring." It chilled me to hear her speak so matter-of-factly about a supernatural event.

"*I* knew that," said Antonia. "That's why I wanted to name our rat for him."

It didn't sound then as though the girls had seen him recently. That was a relief. I wondered if receiving the key to the city was like getting the Golden Yurt. "I'd better go to this ceremony," I told Theodora as we walked back to her house. "I want to see what's been happening here."

The Lady Maria had returned to the city from Yurt last week, once again bringing the Princess Margareta with her. I wasn't sure of the details, but my guess was that the royal court of Caelrhon had decided that the chance that Paul would marry some foreign lady was preferable to the chance that their crown princess would be eaten by a wolf. I met the two at the castle and we went together to the covered market, me leaning on my old predecessor's staff. On the way, I saw a woman chasing three rats out her front door with a broom, using words that I hadn't even realized respectable Caelrhon housewives knew.

"Cyrus is so spiritual!" Maria told me enthusiastically. "Even though he worked such a striking miracle, it hasn't made him at all puffed up and proud. When all of us come to revere and honor him each day, he just sits quietly or else speaks of God and the Last Judgment." Princess Margareta looked bored, trailing along behind.

The streets around the covered market were packed. Townspeople in their finery moved through the warm evening air and between the pillars into the market, where clear-burning torches provided the light. Straw and bits of fallen vegetable lay underfoot. Something seemed unusual about the crowd, but I could not immediately place it. I managed to find a place at the back to lean against the wall, supporting myself on the silver-topped staff. The crowd spoke in quiet voices, but their words still bounced, magnified and jumbled, from the ceiling.

"I have to tell you, Wizard," said the Lady Maria with a coy smile, speaking low so that Margareta could not hear us over the general din, "that I was the tiniest bit *shocked* when I learned you had had a daughter out of wedlock!" Her wide blue eyes glinted at me in the dimness. "That really was naughty of you, especially to take advantage of *such* a nice young lady. I've kept it from little Margareta because I think she may be a bit too young to understand. Now, *I've* seen and heard enough in my day that very little shocks me, but you know sometimes one imagines one knows someone very well, yet they still have secrets! That's why Cyrus is so remarkable. I think he understands *everything*."

I rather hoped Cyrus didn't understand me. I saw him now, dressed all in black, his face sober and intent. He did not spot us in the crowd. But I felt a sudden chill on the back of my neck, as though a breeze were stirring on this still evening. "You haven't told him about Antonia, have you?"

"*I* don't tell secrets," said Maria placidly. "I may have hinted that there was a certain wizard, not very far away, with sins that even a holy man might find hard to forgive, but as you can imagine I said nothing else!"

Before I had a chance to ask more, the mayor stepped up to a rostrum, flanked by candles, which had been erected at the far end of the market. He had been mayor for years, a solidly built and honest man who always sought a way to keep his city's life and commerce functioning separate from the cathedral, although literally in the cathedral's shadow, and with the goodwill or at least tolerance of the priests. The light glittered on his chains of office. He waited a minute until conversation died down, then began, simply and informally.

"I don't think I need to remind all of you what we owe to Cyrus," he said. With wizardry I could hear him clearly, but the Lady Maria beside me strained to listen. Margareta, examining the cracked finish on one nail, seemed to be suggesting rather pointedly that she would rather be somewhere else. I thought I could detect a faint nervous tone in the mayor's voice, which seemed rather surprising in someone who must have to give hundreds of public speeches.

"Cyrus has proven himself a true friend of the city of Caelrhon," he continued. "We could make him a citizen, for all he's foreign-born, but many men are born or made citizens. So the council has decided to offer

him something we haven't offered anyone in years—
not even our own king!"

There was an appreciative chuckle from the crowd.
King Lucas of Caelrhon had been known to grumble
when visiting us in Yurt that the city seemed remarkably
adept at evading his tolls and taxes, and apparently it
looked much more amusing from their side than his.

"Cyrus, we want to give you the key to our city."

Cyrus stepped forward then, a gratified look in the
angle of his shoulders even though he did not smile. A
gust of wind stirred the candles at the rostrum, and the
torches flared. This was it? I asked myself as the mayor
handed him an enormous ceremonial key, glittering with
rhinestones. This was worth someone selling his soul to
the devil, so he could have the mayor of a small city
make him a presentation?

With my magically enhanced hearing, I was able to
catch the mayor's next words, although they did not
seem intended for anyone but Cyrus. "Next time you're
talking to the saints," he said, not quite as though he
were making a joke, "how about if you mention our
problems with the rats?"

But then the crowd began to murmur appreciatively,
yet in a low note, as though too deeply in awe to shout
as they had shouted last month in front of the cathedral.
Cyrus turned from one side to the other, holding up
his hands as though in benediction, smiling but without
the shattering goodness I was now able to convince
myself I had never actually seen.

Instead he seemed to be soaking in the praise—and,
I was almost afraid to say, worship—of the crowd like
a lizard soaking in the sun's rays. What had the Lady
Maria said about people coming to honor and revere
him? But this simple reverence did not now seem
enough for him.

"Give God the glory!" he called, and the crowd

repeated it. "Prepare for Judgment!" and his words were repeated again. "Hunt out sin!"

The evening breeze continued to rise, and in the torches' glare his face was shaded red. The candles on the rostrum cast shadows from below that made his eyebrows enormous. Demonic, I would have called the effect, except that everything he said could have been said by Joachim—the words, but not his way of saying them.

"Overcome evil!" he shouted, and I clutched the silver-topped staff tighter. "Root out all sin! Destroy the works of the devil! Seize paradise as God has promised us!"

The crowd seemed almost choreographed, now starting to sway together, no longer repeating his phrases but steadily chanting, "Cyrus, Cyrus." Their chant had the steady hard beat of a heart. The mayor, looking somewhat uneasy, slipped away into the night. The shouts from the crowd went higher as Cyrus lifted his hands, lower as he lowered them. The Lady Maria beside me joined in enthusiastically.

This, I thought, adulation like this might all be worth it.

And then I realized what was so odd about a crowd this size in the city of Caelrhon. It included no priests.

PART SIX

Rats

I

"I have spoken to him, of course," said the bishop gravely, "and spoken more than once. But he always says his only interest is to bring himself closer to God by carrying the divine message of judgment and salvation to His flock."

"You should stop him, Joachim. A bishop can certainly forbid Christians from listening to a charlatan who preaches false religion."

We sat in the bishop's study, where candlelight reflected on the dark windowpanes and made the wood paneling ruddy. There was a faint sound of scurrying in the walls that might have been rats, though I had certainly never heard any in the bishop's palace before.

Joachim answered me quietly, light and shadow flickering across his face. "But *is* he preaching false religion, Daimbert? I wish that I could say. It is true that I have told the cathedral priests not to attend his prayer meetings. But is a bishop who lacks the will to resign fit to judge a man who after all only teaches God's message? *Can* there be sin in Christian preaching, even if done more spectacularly than by most and without the license of a sinful bishop?"

Joachim could sometimes be even more exasperating than Antonia. "Don't tell me you're still thinking of resigning! Didn't I explain it to you? You and I were both infected by some spell of madness left in the bones of those undead warriors by whatever renegade wizard made them. I *hope* you realize I wouldn't normally try to kill you any more than you would harbor lustful thoughts."

"I was under a *spell*?" The bishop looked slightly ill at the idea.

"So was Celia—that's why she suddenly decided to become a nun after insisting that she would never retreat from the world to the cloister, but instead become an active priest. And I think Cyrus is behind it. You know I've suspected him all along of working with a demon. Wait!" as Joachim seemed about to interrupt. "What I'm trying to ask you is, if he repented of his evil ways, including his attacks on Yurt, would he be able to save his soul after all by becoming a preacher?"

"It is very difficult for someone who has sold his soul to reclaim it," said the bishop dubiously. "But I would not be so quick to condemn or to assume—"

"And I also had another question," I said hastily, not wanting any lectures about forgiveness of one's brother, since I had no intention of being Cyrus's brother. "If someone sold his soul from pure motives, to save another's life, would he regain it?"

I had told Joachim briefly about Antonia's flying carpet ride when he asked after her. He looked at me a moment from his enormous dark eyes, then slowly started to smile. Whatever he had that passed for a sense of humor appeared at the strangest times. "If one were acting from completely pure motives, the devil might not accept the bargain. Do you know why,

Daimbert," he added in apparent inconsequentiality, "priests do not marry?"

"To avoid sins of the flesh, I presume," I said in surprise, hoping he was not about to start confessing yearnings for Theodora *again*.

"There is certainly an element of that," he said, still with a faint smile, "a belief that only those who are purified as much as any son of Adam can be should assume spiritual leadership. But that is not the only or even principal reason: after all, married couples sin less than a celibate priest with a perverted imagination. But priests must never allow attachment to a single person or persons to obscure their duties to *all* Christians."

"Oh," I said, suddenly realizing what he was talking about. "And you think that wizards traditionally don't marry either because we could be distracted from our oaths to help mankind by personal affection?"

"Someone who would cheerfully sell his soul to save his daughter," said the bishop dryly, "would break wizardry's oaths just as cheerfully." I hadn't told him that part, but Joachim knew me too well. "Priests give up the love and companionship of families of their own to lead all of God's children to salvation. A wizard gives up a family for knowledge and power. Tell me, Daimbert: is it worth it?"

I studied the surface of the bishop's desk. So far I had a modicum of wizardry's knowledge and power—far less than Elerius, but far more than the twelve-year-old boy who had used his pennies to learn a few illusions. Was magic worth Theodora refusing to marry me and my king looking at me askance? I had not before thought of it in these terms, but I did know that at one level Theodora was right: magic was as much a part of me as breathing. But Antonia was even more important than my own breath.

It was no use asking either Joachim or the school

how to resolve this. They would both tell me that as long as I was a wizard I could not also have a family, and this was an answer I had no intention of accepting.

But I was distracted from these thoughts by another, by a sudden realization that something I had pushed to the back of my mind as part of my delerious dreams was actually real: the old Romney woman's "fortune." "He's coming by night," I told the bishop, leaning abruptly toward him. "Vlad, the dark wizard from the Eastern Kingdoms."

Joachim had been on that trip to the East and certainly remembered Vlad. "When will he arrive?" he asked soberly, the faint spark of humor gone from his face. It was doubtless a tribute to the abilities he thought I had that he did not ask how I knew.

"The Romneys told me," I said excitedly, not wanting to take credit for extra powers, "but fighting that wolf knocked the memory out of me. But it all comes back now and it all makes sense. Vlad probably hoped that if he could make our days as dark as night he could travel more easily—light destroys whatever holds his half-dead body together. And that was one of his wolves he sent ahead. But when I dispersed his clouds he realized it would be too dangerous to try to travel by day, because I or any other wizard could bathe him in sunlight with a few weather spells."

"And this has something to do with Cyrus?" asked the bishop with an air of trying to understand what I was suggesting.

"Of course." But even as I spoke all the certainty went out of me. "That is, I don't know. The undead warriors did appear to be made with Vlad's form of eastern magic, and the wolf seemed specifically spelled against a western wizard. . . ." I paused and looked at Joachim uneasily. "Vlad has had reason to hate me for years, and he may finally have decided to come after me as he threatened to do. Cyrus seemed to know who I was, but . . ."

"Would Vlad have summoned a demon?"

This was the same problem I was having. Just when I thought it all made sense, it stopped doing so. "I don't think so, Joachim, not if he's coming by night. There was nothing demonic about the warriors. If Vlad had gotten supernatural assistance in rebuilding his body, he would no longer have to fear sunlight or anything else—except of course hell. . . ."

"Too many wizards have no respect for either heaven or hell," said the bishop in disapproval.

"Well, that's probably true from the Church's point of view," I said slowly. "But wizards still try to avoid black magic: supplementing their powers with those of a demon. If nothing else, it's considered a sign of weakness not to be able to gain results with unaided magic. Vlad wouldn't be hiding in darkness if he had a demon working with him, so he must be relying on natural magic." I stared into the candle flame, disturbingly reminded of Cyrus's face in the market. "So I don't know what this has to do with your cathedral, Joachim, or for that matter with the Lady Justinia. But if a bishop can ever listen to a wizard, listen to me and make Cyrus stop."

Before he could answer we were interrupted by a rising murmur of voices. It seemed to be coming from the square in front of the cathedral.

The bishop and I looked at each other. "I've got them!" came a man's voice, loud and harsh, over the general murmur. "I've got the sinners! Let's put them to death *now*!"

Joachim and I raced out into the night. I hadn't moved this fast since the wolf attack. Many of the same people who had been with Cyrus at the covered market now milled around in the building site before the cathedral, carrying torches. Cyrus himself stood halfway up the church steps. He turned smoothly, as though acting a part, his eyes coming to rest on a heavyset man at the back of the crowd.

"I've got them, Your Holiness!" the man called triumphantly. His voice was harsh and a little slurred, but it made up for it in volume. My heart gave a hard thump when I realized that by "Your Holiness" he meant not the bishop but Cyrus.

Each of the man's big fists clutched a Romney by the collar. One was a gray-haired old man, the other the woman who had told my fortune. They hung limply, their feet dragging the ground, and their black eyes wide with fear. There was a faint squeaking from the piled building materials that might have been rats. The torchlight glinted incongruously on the bristle on the old woman's upper lip as the two captives were dragged forward.

"They're sinners, all right," the burly man continued. The two Romneys seemed to be putting up little resistance, but he had a bruise coming up across his forehead and her dress was half ripped off under the shawl she clutched around her. Joachim beside me drew in his breath sharply.

"Sin, sin, drive out sin," murmured the crowd together. The mayor reappeared at the back of the crowd, as though drawn against his will.

I could have paralyzed the heavyset man with magic and snatched the Romneys from him, but with the crowd in a potentially ugly mood, acting too quickly could make the situation even worse. Panting from sudden exertion while still weak, I silently started putting the first words of a spell together.

"These are the ones who brought all those rats to town!" the man shouted. "They confessed it themselves when I applied a little, shall we say, *persuasion*. Let's hang them at once! It's the Christian thing to do. Then we'll go set fire to all their caravans!"

At that the bishop strode forward through the crowd, his dark eyes ablaze. The people stepped aside for him with surprised faces. What had started to be general sounds of loud agreement were abruptly cut off. Maybe I wouldn't have to use my spell after all.

Joachim, reaching the front, did not hesitate. He put his own hands on the heads of the Romneys and met the man's gaze. "Let them go, in God's name," he said quietly but very firmly.

The man was taken aback. Joachim was as tall as he was even if only about half as bulky. But after a second the man tightened his grip again. "Why do you care about these people, Father?" he sneered, giving them a shake. "They're not even Christians! Killing them would be like killing an animal—a rat!"

There was a murmur of assent from the crowd but with the slightest note of uncertainty.

"*All* men and women are God's children," replied Joachim clearly. "Rats do not have immortal souls; humans do. No one, Christian or not, can be put to death without a legal judgment, and no one but yourself believes that the Romneys have anything to do with the vermin in our city."

The torches hissed in the sudden stillness, and the sky above lowered heavy and black. The people stood motionless, watching the burly man and the bishop stare at each other. A few rats darted out into the crowd but immediately disappeared again.

"Don't you believe in overcoming sin, Your Holiness?" the man said after a moment. His voice was not so loud or so assured, and I noted he had returned Joachim's title to him. "Don't you think—like Cyrus!—that God wants us to root out evil?"

"To kill the defenseless," replied the bishop, his hands still resting protectively on the Romneys' heads, "is to embrace evil, not drive it out."

"Are you so sure, then," said the man doggedly, "that you always recognize evil yourself when you see it?"

Joachim winced at that. Before he could answer, another voice came from the crowd, a woman's voice.

It was the Lady Maria. "Oh, let them go!" she called. "Of *course* we have to overcome sin! But rats aren't sin. And aren't you just the *tiniest* bit ashamed of yourself for dragging an old man and woman out of their homes? I am not, of course, *nearly* as old myself as they are, but I can imagine how frightening it must be!"

Cyrus had been standing silently, without moving, as though waiting to see the crowd's mood before reacting. His expression had been very strange, one moment distant and ethereal, but the next alert and almost cunning. At the Lady Maria's words he resolutely stepped forward, hands held high. "Praise God!" he shouted. "For He has spoken through His humble handmaiden!"

"I'm no handmaiden!" the Lady Maria snapped back, her voice loud and clear. "I was born the daughter of a castellan lord and am the aunt of the queen of Yurt!"

After a second's startled silence, there came a new note to the sound of the crowd, a note of surprise, almost a giggle. Although it passed away again almost immediately, the tension was broken. Cyrus looked as though he wanted to stare Maria down. "Well, if you want to use the term in the *Biblical* sense," she said defensively, giving her skirt an indignant flounce. "But I'm glad you have the wit to realize I'm talking sense."

"See how the devil tempts us all!" Cyrus cried, raising his eyes from the Lady Maria to the black sky above. "God's daughter has spoken truly! Sin comes masquerading as goodness, luring even the most righteous into error! Repent, my children! Repent!"

"You mean I have to let them go?" the burly man asked truculently.

"Yes!" said Joachim and Cyrus together.

He thrust the Romneys from him with disgust. "All right, Holy Father," he said, and it was not clear which man he was addressing. "But don't blame me if the rats get worse!"

The Romneys stumbled and would have fallen if the bishop had not caught them. He put an arm around each and, sweaty and grimy as they were, gave them the kiss of peace on both cheeks. "Let me apologize to you on behalf of all the priests of Caelrhon," he said, loudly enough that everyone could hear. "I see the mayor is here, and I am sure he expresses the same sentiment on behalf of Caelrhon's citizens." The mayor made an incoherent sound that was more assent than anything. "One misguided and overzealous Christian is not representative. Would you like some assistance returning to your caravans?"

But the Romneys, their eyes still wide, wanted no assistance. The crowd, shamefaced, parted for them as they hurried away.

I turned from watching them go to see the bishop standing sternly in front of his newest seminary student, his left hand extended at waist level. After only a moment's hesitation Cyrus knelt and kissed the episcopal ring reverently.

"Praise God!" he shouted then as he rose to his feet, as though wanting to reassert his authority over the crowd. "For He has given us a truly holy bishop to lead us!"

"Cyrus," said Joachim, not at all mollified, "I shall speak to you in the cathedral office first thing in the morning."

The bishop strode away with a swirl of vestments. "I see," said Cyrus behind him, uncowed, "that before any other Christians are tempted into sin I shall have to do something about those rats."

II

It was just before dawn when a sound woke me. I lifted my head from Theodora's couch to listen, unsure at first if it was dream or reality.

It was reality, all right. Faint but clear, from the direction of the docks, came the sound of piping.

As I listened the music grew louder, as though the piper was coming this way. The notes rose and rose again, wild and compelling, a music that entered the brain and called the body. That piping had me swaying on my feet with my hand on the doorknob before I even realized what I was doing. It tugged at the magic within me with a call that overcame all feeling, all will, nearly all thought.

"No," I gasped, and the sound of my own voice gave me back a little of my senses. I made a desperate effort and pushed away from the door. No magic I knew could oppose this. Theodora emerged from the bedroom in a long white nightgown, her eyes only slightly open, and brushed past me, reaching for the knob.

I seized her and held her to me. She struggled but as though only dimly aware of my presence. Faint light from the curtained window fell on pallid cheeks and tumbled hair. "Theodora. Wait. Stop. Don't follow it," I managed to choke out.

But it was Antonia, clutching Dolly and stretching to unlock the door, who seemed to make Theodora aware of where she was. She shook herself, gave me a quick look, and pulled our daughter back into the middle of the room. The three of us clung together desperately as the piping came closer.

"It's a spell," I said in a low voice, hoping that the sound of a human voice would keep us anchored here in this room. The notes were mixed with another sound now, almost a squeaking. Antonia had ceased struggling but was crying silently. "Someone is working a summoning spell. I don't recognize his magic at all, but I think—I hope—it's not for us."

Summoning was specifically forbidden by the masters of the wizards' school as the greatest sin a wizard could commit.

"It's only because we all know magic that we're more susceptible than most people to spells," I tried to continue in a calm, explanatory tone.

But now the piper was directly outside Theodora's door. I stopped speaking as it took all my effort just to keep myself from abandoning my family and all my reason to follow that music.

There was a moment in which I must have squeezed Theodora's arms painfully, because she had purple bruises later, but with my eyes tight shut I was unaware of her, only of my desperate need to follow and equally desperate determination not to. But after what seemed an endless time, though it could only have been a few seconds, the piper passed by. I took a deep breath that was almost a sob as the power of his spell diminished.

Antonia plopped down in the middle of the floor, crying hard, and Theodora tried to comfort her. I lifted the curtain to look out. The piper was gone, and I did not see any of Theodora's neighbors following.

"It looks like that was only a spell for magic-workers," I started to say, trying to make it a joke.

But then I saw the rats. Hundreds of them, thousands of them, brown rats poured like a river down the middle of the street, their hairless tails arched over their backs. More came scampering out of cellars and alleys to join the stream. Theodora joined me at the window and stared in amazement. I had not realized how thoroughly the city had been overrun with rodents until I now saw them all together.

"Well," I said when I could speak again. "It looks like Cyrus really has done something about the rats."

We bathed, dressed, and had breakfast to give ourselves time to calm down. "It wouldn't have to be a demonic spell," I said to Theodora as we went out two hours later. I leaned again on my predecessor's silver-topped staff.

There was a narrow crevice at the center of the cobbled street where rainwater drained. The thin layer of mud on the bottom was marked with the prints of thousands of rat feet.

"The school doesn't teach summoning anymore," I continued, "in part because such spells are almost impossible to resist, even for a skilled wizard, and they don't want the students practicing on each other. I wouldn't even recognize an eastern summoning spell, especially one designed for rats, but it still almost captured us."

"Where did all the rats go?" asked Antonia with interest. She had cheered up quickly once the music of the piper had passed. "Will they come back? Do you think our pet Cyrus was with them?"

"I thought Jen's mother and I told you to let him go," said Theodora reprovingly.

"Well, he probably got out of his box anyway," said Antonia, skipping ahead.

Everyone in the city seemed to be out in the streets, talking excitedly about the rats' disappearance. I caught snatches of conversation as we headed toward the cathedral, and it appeared that, according to the bargemen, an enormous number of rats had appeared downstream from the city this morning, many drowned in the river, the rest looking confused but showing no sign of returning. Although quite a few people had heard the piping, no one had actually seen the piper. That did not keep everyone from assuming it had been Cyrus.

"He tried to tell me he'd given up magic," I told Theodora. "But it looks like his purportedly religious desire to put his past behind him is less important than his desire for acclaim—especially with Joachim reasserting his spiritual authority."

No one else seemed to have been lured by the magic. The question flashed through my mind whether it might be not Cyrus but Vlad who had come into Caelrhon with the magic to summon rats. But I could imagine no reason why that dark wizard would care about the city's rodent population, and piping at dawn would be too dangerous for someone liable to disintegrate in daylight.

We found Joachim in the cathedral office. The acolyte outside the door at first feigned ignorance whether the bishop was even there, then claimed he wouldn't want to see us—most of the cathedral attendants had looked at me dubiously ever since I burst in on him last month, and that was not even knowing that I had intended to kill him—but I pushed past.

The bishop sat without moving, staring at nothing in particular, and looked up in surprise when we were already halfway across the room. He rose then and came to meet us, his face gaunt and troubled, without even an attempt at a smile. Theodora knelt to kiss his ring, which made me wonder if Cyrus had left some sort of infection on it with his lips, and then of course Antonia had to as well. Joachim rested his hand on her head a moment in blessing.

"Did you talk to him?" I asked, too worried not to be brusque, even though Theodora kicked me in admonishment. "Did you hear about the rats?"

Joachim nodded his head fractionally. "I am not so removed from the cares and concerns of the city as you appear to think, Daimbert," he said, and just for a second humor glinted in his eyes. I might not be able to do much about black magic, I thought bitterly, but I seemed to be good at cheering up bishops. "Yes, Cyrus came and spoke to me—apparently, as I learned once he left, almost immediately after leading the rats out of town."

"What did you tell him?" I demanded. "Did you tell him he can't keep on preaching if he's going to encourage townspeople into all sorts of excesses, including worshipping him?"

Joachim turned to Theodora, the faint humor again in his eyes. "Do you have the same problem with him?" he asked conversationally. "Does he keep acting as though you couldn't carry out your own responsibilities without his supervision?"

"But what did he say?" I cried impatiently.

Joachim opened a drawer with infuriating deliberation and gave Antonia some paper and colored chalk. She sat down happily to draw at the far side of the room. It looked as though she was drawing a crowd of rats following a man. The bishop, completely serious now, pulled up chairs for Theodora and me.

"I did tell Cyrus that it was inappropriate for a seminary student to be preaching so regularly," he said quietly, "especially in a cathedral city where the faithful never lack access to God's word. But when he pleaded with me it was hard to resist him. It was, after all, his prayers that miraculously restored the burned street."

"I already told you what I think of that 'miracle,'" I said grumpily.

"And he *did* help return the townsmen to the voice of their consciences last evening, when that man tried to turn them against the Romneys."

"That wasn't Cyrus, Joachim. The Romneys were saved by you—and the Lady Maria."

"I could not sleep last night," the bishop continued slowly, "so I slipped out of the palace in the darkest hour and went toward the Romney camp. I am not sure why I went—perhaps to apologize again or to be sure those old people suffered no serious hurt. But it did not matter. They had left."

"*All* the caravans?" I asked, and he nodded. I could see the Romneys' point; I would have left too.

"Sometimes I have thought," Joachim went on, "that God sent the Romneys to Caelrhon for a purpose, so that I might be able to win them for Christianity. But now what must they think of a faith in whose name a man would threaten to murder them without cause?"

"But did Cyrus say anything about the rats?" I asked, not wanting to get into questions of God's hidden purpose and also not wanting to bring up the point that I myself had once threatened to murder the bishop, equally without cause.

"He said nothing," Joachim replied shortly.

"Well, I still think he's deceiving you with a pious façade. That was very powerful magic to summon those rats—it almost trapped Theodora and me too." I paused a moment but then went on, because whatever else I had always tried to be honest with Joachim. "It wouldn't have to be a demon this time. In fact, I keep being convinced that he brought the undead warriors to Yurt, but that wasn't black magic either. But if he won't admit to wizardry of any kind he's concealing a lot from you."

"Then I shall speak to him again, Daimbert. You know my concern has always been whether he was truly working miracles or practicing renegade magic in the guise of miracles. A summoning spell is scarcely the work of the saints."

Theodora had been listening to us in silence. Now

she said, "It sounds to me as though he's confused popular approval with real goodness. He won the friendship of the children by mending their toys and pets, and he received the keys of the city from the mayor for restoring the burned buildings. What will he want for cleansing Caelrhon of rats?"

III

The old king of Yurt, Paul's father, had spent much of his time sitting on the throne in the great hall, dispensing justice, talking to other members of the court, or reading rose growers' catalogues. Paul, on the other hand, only used his throne on the most formal occasions.

So my heart sank when he sent for me upon my return to Yurt and I found him seated there, resting his chin on his fists. This could be it, I thought, squaring my shoulders, my dismissal from Yurt for having a family contrary to all the traditions of wizardry. Well, I had always told Theodora I would happily do magic tricks on street corners if I could do so with her. I might now be emulating the man who had first taught me illusions.

But King Paul did not speak at once of dismissal. He appeared uneasy and kept crossing and uncrossing booted legs. The warm air of a summer evening washed through the room's tall windows. "So Theodora is safely home now?" he asked vaguely, giving me a quick glance and looking away again.

"That's right," I said cautiously, waiting for what was coming next.

"Why didn't you ever tell me about her, Wizard?" he demanded almost accusingly.

"Well, I must apologize," I said stiffly. "I realize now I should have told you at once, but I met her the summer of your coronation, and you will recall a lot happened that summer."

Paul gave a quick grin. "Only adventure you've ever let me go on," he remarked. "But why not tell me about the little girl?" he continued, looking uneasy again. "You didn't need to pretend she was your niece!"

"As I say, I know now I was wrong," I said, standing with my arms straight down my sides and heels together. "Organized wizardry does not want wizards to be fathers, and out of cowardice, I'm afraid to admit, I decided to say nothing. Once I had begun the deception, it was difficult to end."

Paul had stared off toward the other end of the empty room as I started speaking, but he now turned back and grinned again. "So I'm not the only person in the castle who has others planning for him if and whom he's going to marry, with or without his consent!"

It slowly dawned on me that Paul had been asking me about Theodora not as a prelude to requesting my resignation but to avoid talking about what was really on his mind.

He took a deep breath, planted his boots on the throne's footrest, and faced me squarely. "How would you like to be Celia's spiritual sponsor?"

"Her what?!"

"I knew you'd react like this," he said, shaking his head. "That's why I agreed to talk to you myself. I tried to tell her that wizards have never had much respect for the Church, but she insisted she wanted you. I wish you would at least consider it. It would mean a lot to her."

"Excuse me, sire, but I don't know what you're talking about."

"Celia comes of age in two weeks," said Paul gravely. "She has told her parents that on her birthday she will ride over to the Nunnery of Yurt and make her maiden vocation. The chaplain and I have checked into the requirements for her. They won't, of course, let her take her final vows until after a year as a novice, but there's a ceremony when she enters, and she needs a sponsor. Preferably a man, the abbess told me, someone of mature authority. Prince Ascelin won't do it because he's still not reconciled to his daughter becoming a nun. I offered, of course, but Celia said she would rather have you."

"But if she's going to be a nun, Paul, she doesn't want a wizard! Especially me. The abbess won't want me either. I don't know what Celia told you, and she hasn't talked to me herself for weeks, but . . ."

"She told me you'd raise these objections. But listen, Wizard. This is very hard on Celia. First she decided to become a priest, but no one would take her seriously—not her parents, not her own sister, and not even the bishop. Then she met that miracle-worker over in Caelrhon—Cyrus, isn't that his name? Studying with him was the first thing I think she felt she'd ever done that she chose for herself, rather than having others choose it for her. Then somehow *that* didn't work out. I'm still not sure what happened, but at some point while trying to learn from him she decided to give up her plan for an active spiritual career and become a nun instead."

She had run straight into a spell of madness, but I wasn't going to mention that now.

"Then she found out—excuse me, Wizard—that you weren't always as pure as a priest yourself, which only confirmed her desire to retreat from anything worldly, in spite of increased opposition from her parents. So you see," he finished somewhat shamefacedly, "that she considers it a suitable act of forgiveness and penitence to begin her life in the cloister with you beside her."

It sounded to me as though King Paul was going out of his way not to say anything judgmental about my conduct. Of course, it was rather irritating that people here in the castle seemed to be trying to demonstrate how broad-minded they were by overlooking something which, in fact, had not happened for years.

But if I was not dismissed then I should be able to stay on in Yurt, I thought with a flood of relief that surprised me by its intensity. Perhaps the Golden Yurt award really did mean that Paul respected me and my service to the kingdom, no matter what. But I had to concentrate on Celia. "So what does a spiritual sponsor do?"

Paul turned his emerald eyes fully on me. "Then you'll do it? This is wonderful, Wizard." He jumped down from the throne and clapped me on the shoulder. "I *knew* you'd agree if I explained it all to you. I'll go tell Celia. She'll be delighted."

As he hurried out I found myself wondering which would be harder to explain to Zahlfast at the wizards' school: that I had a daughter or that I had agreed to sponsor a novice nun.

"You realize," commented Joachim, "that you're probably the only wizard in the western kingdoms who worries about seminary students." His face in the glass telephone looked unworried, even amused. I wished I felt the same.

"But what is Cyrus *doing?*" I demanded again. It had been two weeks since I returned to Yurt, and I had heard nothing from Caelrhon beyond a few pigeon-messages from Theodora, saying little more than that she and Antonia were fine and sent their love. I had tried again to get help from Zahlfast, but he had said even more frostily than before that if there was indeed a renegade eastern wizard holed up in Caelrhon's seminary, then the wizard of Caelrhon and I would just have to keep an eye on him.

"Cyrus is attending seminary classes," said Joachim, "studying, praying, the same as any other student."

"I hope you've made him give up those meetings of his where people come and revere him." I knew as I spoke that the bishop would think this one more example of my not trusting him to carry out his own duties, but I had to know. "The Lady Maria's returned to Yurt now, but she won't say anything about him—just tells me my mind isn't pure enough to understand true holiness."

Maria had come back looking pleased with herself but was surprisingly untalkative, except to say that the Princess Margareta had decided to stay on in Caelrhon for a few weeks. The princess, finding her own royal castle, Yurt, and the city all filled with ennui or embarrassment for one reason or another, seemed to have decided that, overall, the city offered the most possibilities.

Joachim hesitated for a moment, as though wondering himself if the topic of a seminary student's behavior was fit for a wizard's ears, but then continued as though there had been no pause.

"After the incident with the rats, of course, I ordered him to stop preaching or even speaking on spiritual issues to anyone but a priest. He could not deny that was magic, and he understood why I could not allow someone practicing wizardry to pass as the Church's representative. I suspect he is irritated with me, in spite of his penitent attitude, as well as with you for detecting his spells." Joachim seemed remarkably unconcerned about it. "But he is studying hard and making good progress, I hear. Many seminary students come in these days with the impression that they are already spiritually advanced, scarcely needing our guidance, so if he's had a few rough spots in his early training he has company."

"We're not talking about rough spots. We're talking about someone who works with a demon."

"I know you believe that, Daimbert," said the bishop

good-naturedly, "but I have yet to see the slightest sign of anything of the sort. If there is black magic in his background, he has struggled hard to overcome it."

"Has the mayor made him any more presentations?"

"No—why should he?" Joachim looked amused again. "Cyrus already has the key to the city, something the council has granted no other seminary student or priest—not even me."

I thought but did not say that I would find menace rather than humor in someone trained in eastern magic, someone who had had demonic help with at least some of his spells, whatever the bishop might think, and who was doubtless now furious with the organized Church, with the mayor and council of Caelrhon, and with me. Even if he were trying to break away, through prayer and study in the seminary, from a demon he had unwisely summoned, he had set himself a very difficult task. The demon would haunt him whenever he was not actually in church, magnifying his sense of wrongs done to him, and tempting him with spectacular ways to get even.

"I hear you will be Celia's spiritual sponsor at the nunnery," Joachim continued, having put concerns about Cyrus behind him. "I plan to ride over myself for the ceremony, so I shall see you tomorrow."

Celia, Hildegarde, and I rode down to the Nunnery of Yurt together. Given the circumstances, I had decided not to wish the twins a happy birthday. Their parents had announced at the last minute that they would accompany us. Celia, looking at the resignation and reluctance on their faces, which they made no effort to hide, took them away for a few minutes' private conversation and returned without them, silent but with red eyes. She did not speak the whole journey.

The nunnery was only a few miles from the royal castle, but it could have been located in another kingdom for all the contact we had with it. One could see its church spire, rising above some trees, from the road, but I had never gone any closer. It was a hot day of midsummer, and the sun beat down on us and our black clothing, so I was relieved when we turned down the lane, bright with asters, that led to the nunnery.

The lane took us around the shoulder of a hill and into the nuns' valley. A low wall, its gate open, circled the nunnery complex. The church itself, surrounded by its claustral edifices and farm buildings, looked peaceful and prosaic. In the surrounding fields the nuns' tenants, stripped to the waist in the sun, were bringing in the hay. They waved to us cheerfully as we rode past.

"There's still time to change your mind," said Hildegarde hopefully. She had been itchy and uncomfortable in her black dress since we left Yurt. "You know they don't want women who aren't absolutely sure of their vocations. No one will think any less of you."

Celia shook her head without bothering to reply.

A priest came out to meet us as we clattered over the paving stones in front of the church. Roses bloomed by the entrance: nearly as good, I had to admit, as in Yurt's royal garden.

"The Lady Celia, I believe?" the priest said, having no trouble distinguishing her, with her sober, weary eyes, from her flushed and irritated sister. "The abbess awaits you within. And this must be your spiritual sponsor."

"My name is Daimbert." I had done my best not to look like a wizard, having even borrowed a belt from one of the knights so as not to wear mine, with its self-illuminating emblem of the moon and stars on the buckle.

The priest noticed me admiring the roses. "Those were a gift, many years ago, from old King Haimeric of Yurt," he told me proudly. "He sent us the rootstock."

Our horses were led away and the priest led us inside. Celia was whisked off to meet with the abbess, while two elderly nuns sat down with Hildegarde and me, to spend the next hour making sure we were clear on the details of our roles in the ceremony as family member and as spiritual sponsor.

What am I doing here? I wondered. I didn't believe any young woman should be a nun, I didn't think Celia herself really wanted to be one, and I was having trouble taking seriously the words and symbols that the elderly nun was trying to explain to me.

"Then, after you have spoken these words," she said, looking at me over her spectacles, "dip your finger in the sacramental water and touch Sister Celia three times, once on each eyelid and once on the chin. Use your forefinger." She was tiny and would have appeared fragile were it not for the cheerful energy that flowed from her. "But remember, don't speak and certainly don't dip your finger in the water until the priest has finished the initial prayers and the abbess has led the Amen twice."

I heard the sound of more hooves outside and concluded that the bishop had arrived with his attendants. Why couldn't he have been spiritual sponsor instead? I asked myself in irritation. He probably was used to performing rituals like this all the time.

"And you know, I hope," the nun continued, "that you have to take her by the hand to lead her up to the bishop when it is time for her to make her maiden vows before him. We are very honored that the bishop himself will perform the office today, rather than one of our own confessors. We want everything to go perfectly." She looked at me intently. "Will you be able to remember all this?"

Hildegarde's role, I gathered from snatches of conversation from the far side of the room as I repeated

my instructions back, would be much simpler. After
the rest of the ceremony was over—so that it was clear
that the nuns had accepted Celia for herself, not for
any payment—Hildegarde would convey to the abbess
the stone, the clod of earth, and the applewood staff
that symbolized the property which the duchess had
agreed to give the nunnery if her daughter really did
insist on joining.

"Come," said the nun briskly. "It is time to go down
to the chapel."

IV

The chapel was hot and stuffy, a small room with an
altar at one end and rows of nuns packing the sides. In
their black robes and headdresses, they looked very
much alike in spite of variations in size, shape, and age.
All had wedding rings on their left hands—brides of
Christ, I reminded myself. Their faces wore identical
expressions of reverence.

Hildegarde and I took our positions at either side of
the door, opposite the altar. I looked for but did not
see Celia. The room was heavy with the scents of
lavender and incense. The nuns must have received
some signal I didn't catch, for they abruptly began to
sing in unison, a sweet hymn of praise.

When the hymn ended, the abbess swept in, three
priests scrambling to keep up with her like small boats
in the wake of a ship. Even in a nunnery, I thought,
they used men for priests. It looked as though Celia's
original plan never had a chance.

The abbess was even taller than the twins, and her
piercing blue eyes didn't look as though they missed
much. She nodded rather distantly to Hildegarde and
me and went to stand by the altar. There was a stone
font next to it, like a baptismal font, that I assumed

must hold the sacramental water. Forefinger, I reminded myself, both eyelids and the chin.

Then Joachim entered, formal in his best scarlet vestments that Theodora had embroidered for him. He caught my eye for a second but gave no other sign of greeting as he joined the abbess. Each of them gave the other a slight bow, but she showed no sign of kissing his ring. He might be the chief spiritual authority in two kingdoms, but this was still her nunnery and he was here on her sufferance.

The nuns began to sing again, and then the novices entered. They made a striking contrast with the nuns, for they were dressed in white rather than black and thus sprang into relief against the background of the older sisters. They wore no wedding rings. All carried white wax candles that flickered in the still air as they walked.

Although the novices wore identical, very simple white robes, and all had their heads shaved, the differences between them were much more pronounced than between the adult nuns. Many were girls, who would remain novices until they were sixteen and old enough to choose their own vocation. One didn't look much older than Antonia; she walked with great solemnity, keeping her eyes on her candle. Another, a graceful girl about the same age as the Princess Margareta, had somehow managed to pin or tie her plain white robe in a way to suggest great elegance, without doing anything blatant enough to draw the abbess's censure. Her shaved head was carried at an angle that suggested that she personally knew that women without hair were much more alluring than women with hair. She looked at me a moment longer than necessary as she passed, raising an eyebrow in a way I would have had to call coquettish. *She* at least would not be here once she turned sixteen.

The other novices were older, one or two young women like Celia, and a handful of mature women who were probably widows. These would all be full nuns within the year, unless the abbess found them unsuitable or unless they changed their minds.

The novices, holding their candles, lined up in ranks in front of the black nuns. They began a new song then, one that startled me so much when I heard the words that I nearly spoke out. This had *better* just be something symbolic out of the Bible.

"Let him kiss me with the kisses of his mouth: for thy love is better than wine. Because of the savour of thy good ointments, therefore do the virgins love thee. The king hath brought me into his chambers: we will be glad and rejoice. His left hand is under my head, and his right hand doth embrace me." I almost felt I should rush over to the girl Antonia's age and cover her ears—but she was singing too.

The door beside me opened, and Celia came in: dressed like a bride and carrying roses.

She walked very slowly, not looking at Hildegarde and me or at anyone else. Her black hair hung loose over the shoulders of a white lace gown and down to her waist in back. It would all be shaved off by nightfall, I thought. White ribbons and white rosebuds formed a headpiece. The singing continued until she reached the middle of the chapel, facing the bishop and abbess, and halted.

Joachim stepped forward. First the bishop's address, I thought, then the prayer by the abbess's chief priest, then, right after the Amen, I would say my piece. *Two* Amens, I told myself. Don't be hasty. Then the second prayer, then Celia would pronounce her vows, then—

The bishop had just opened his mouth to speak when there were quick footsteps in the passage outside, and the door burst open. The abbess took a step forward, eyes snapping at this interruption. A woman hurried into the chapel but froze when everyone turned to look at her.

She wore a dark blue dress and a white apron— housekeeper, I thought. Before the abbess's glare she became silent and rigid, even started to walk out backwards. The novices' candle flames swayed in the slight breeze from the open door.

But after only a few seconds the housekeeper remembered the reason she had come with such urgency and stepped forward again. "Excuse me, Reverend Mother, but it's a very important message for the bishop from the cathedral."

Joachim crossed to stand beside her. She spoke quickly and in an undertone, which a quick and highly irreverent spell allowed me to overhear. "I'm so sorry to interrupt, Your Holiness, but a pigeon-message just came in, and it said at the top that you must receive it *at once*. It's something about your goddaughter."

The blood turned to ice in my veins. Antonia!

"Excuse me just for a moment, Reverend Mother," said Joachim quickly and hurried away. Without excusing myself at all, I was right behind him.

The housekeeper led us up flights of stairs and down echoing, vaulted corridors to a little enclosed courtyard off the kitchens. The pigeon loft was on the far side, and several maids stood there, looking uneasy. One smiled with relief when she saw me. "Oh, are you named Daimbert? A second pigeon just arrived, with a message to you from the royal castle. It says it's urgent."

Both messages, Joachim's and mine, were ultimately from Theodora. She had, it appeared, bullied the cathedral priests into letting her use the telephone in the office there to call Yurt. When Gwennie told her I wasn't home, she had instead sent a pigeon-message to Joachim, at the same time as Gwennie was writing a message conveying the gist of the phone call to me. "She was nearly hysterical," Gwennie wrote at the end.

Hildegarde came panting up. "There you are!" she said cheerfully. "When you both left the chapel so abruptly I knew it had to be something pretty important! I'm afraid I don't have my weapons with me, but it shouldn't take long to stop back at the castle for them. What's happening?"

I felt almost hysterical myself. "It's Antonia," I managed to gasp. "And all the other children of Caelrhon. Cyrus has piped them out of town and no one can find them."

My heart was pounding so hard it was almost impossible to think clearly. The flying carpet, I told myself over the roaring in my ears. It could fly a lot faster than I could. Even with a detour back to the castle to get it, I would still reach Caelrhon faster than by my own unaided flying. And if we had to quarter and search all the rivers and forests and fields around the city, it would be good to have the fastest transportation possible.

"Tell Celia I'm sorry, but she'll have to have a different spiritual sponsor," I said to the bishop and shot off, not even caring if it was irreverent to fly within the precincts of the nunnery.

This was so horrible I couldn't let myself believe it. It had to be some mistake. The children had gone for a picnic and someone had started a foolish rumor. They would all be home, laughing to hear how frightened everyone had been, by the time I reached Caelrhon.

The pit of my stomach didn't buy any of this.

A summoning spell like the one Cyrus had used on the rats, I thought as I flew madly back toward the castle, but a spell with a subtle change to summon children instead. Feeling aggrieved at the bishop for making him give up the prayer sessions where people

essentially came and worshipped him, at me for exposing
his use of magic, and at the mayor and council for not
coming to find him in the seminary with some even
better reward than the key to the city, he—or the
demon—had decided to take his revenge through the
children. His piping would have drawn them all as surely
as it had drawn the rats; Antonia, whose flair for magic
made her particularly susceptible, wouldn't have stood
a chance.

Now I just had to try to find some clue to show where
they had gone. *Not* taken downstream and dropped off
like the rats, either to drown or wander away, I tried
to persuade myself. According to Gwennie's account,
fuller than what Theodora had written the bishop, Cyrus
had invited a number of his old friends, the children
from the artisans' quarter, for a country stroll. Antonia's
friend Jen had apparently been one of them, and Antonia
had gone along. Adults had heard piping in the distance,
but only Theodora had realized, when she felt a faint
tug herself, what it meant, and by then other children
were leaving their chores and their games to race through
the city streets and out the gates. By the time the
grown-ups went after them, every child under fourteen
was gone.

But was there even more to this? Had Cyrus been
especially interested in *my* daughter? He had seemed
to know who I was when we first met, and if he was,
as I intermittently suspected, part of Vlad's planned
revenge on me, then seizing Antonia would be doubly
sweet, since he was already furious with me. Any of
several people could have told him I was Antonia's
father—Theodora's neighbors, even the Lady Maria,
who had been so uncharacteristically closedmouthed
since coming home. Was summoning the rest of the
children both generalized revenge and also a chance
to conceal his nefarious plans for one particular child?

I flew over the walls of the royal castle and went straight to the Lady Justinia's chambers. "I need your flying carpet, my lady," I said with minimal effort toward politeness. "And I need it *now*."

Her automaton leaned threateningly toward me. "This is passing abrupt, O Wizard," Justinia said coolly. "The carpet is mine, given me by the mage Kaz-alrhun for my own transportation to safety, *not* for the convenience of western wizards and their daughters."

I didn't have time to explain properly or to respond to the sarcastic note in her voice. "Antonia's been kidnapped by an evil wizard, and I have to go after her."

Justinia immediately looked much more sympathetic. "She is always getting herself into one difficulty or another, of a certainty! I give thee leave, then, to use my carpet to help in the search for her, on this condition: that I myself accompany thee."

I didn't have time to argue. All I said was, "In that case, please leave your automaton behind—last time it tried to kill me." It already seemed as though hours rather than minutes must have passed since the pigeon-messages arrived at the nunnery. We dragged the carpet, with the automaton's help, out into the courtyard. Gwennie and Paul, hearing the commotion, came running.

The king must have gotten the details from Gwennie. "I will help you, of course," he said, very sober and very concerned. "Move over. Are there handles or anything on this thing?"

"You just sit on it and hope it doesn't tip," said Gwennie from experience.

I didn't want them along but I really didn't have time to argue. The automaton glided nervously around the courtyard, and Justinia's elephant trumpeted from the stables, angry at being left behind. The flying carpet shot off toward Caelrhon carrying, besides the foreign princess to whom it actually belonged, the king, the constable, and the wizard of Yurt.

V

"When I couldn't reach you," said Theodora, fighting to keep her voice steady, "I telephoned Elerius. He seemed to know who I was without my having to tell him. I know you don't trust him, Daimbert, but you've always said he's the best wizard of your generation, and—" Her mouth quivered, making it impossible for her to go on.

I put an arm tight around her. "We'll find her. Everything will be just fine." I wished I believed it myself.

"And the mayor's just phoned the royal wizard of Caelrhon," she continued, trying to compose herself. "It turns out that the Princess Margareta is among the missing."

"Poor kid," said Paul, showing unexpected sympathy for the girl he mostly referred to in the context of not wanting to marry her. "She must be terrified. And she's started developing a woman's form—what will an evil magic-worker want with her?"

"Come *on*. We'll find them," I said with a desperate effort to sound assured. "Cyrus won't be able to hide from three wizards."

The carpet shot off into the air again and out over the city walls. I had probed for and not found any lingering trace of Cyrus's magic by which we might have followed him. He'd covered his tracks, which meant we had to assume the children could be anywhere. There might once have been footprints, but any physical traces of their passage had been obscured by the feet of desperate parents. The fields near the city were thick with the citizens of Caelrhon, shouting their children's names, thrashing their way through clumps of bushes, dragging every body of water. A few looked up and pointed as we sailed past.

It was a good thing, I thought, that the Romneys had been gone for two weeks. Otherwise the people who had already been suspected, at least by some, of setting fire to the high street and of bringing the rats to town would probably find themselves killed by hysterical parents.

"I hope the Thieves' Guild in Xantium does not learn of this stratagem," commented Justinia. "They could win an exceeding number of concessions from my grandfather the governor in return for the city's children."

"It's all my fault, Daimbert," said Theodora, breaking down completely. "I told her she could spend the day with Jen. I should never have let her out of my sight. Will you ever forgive me?"

"It's not your fault," I murmured, holding her close. "There's nothing you could have done. The piping would have drawn her just as surely as it drew all the other children."

We were now some two miles from the city, beyond where the parents were beating the underbrush. They probably assumed their children could not have gone far. I, on the other hand, realizing the force of a summoning spell, knew that they would have kept running, following the piper, even with their legs worn down to bloody stumps. "We'll circle the city by air, and if we don't see them on the first circuit we'll go out a few more miles and try again." My attempt to sound calm and rational was a failure in my own ears. "That many children can't have disappeared without a trace."

The flying carpet turned at Justinia's command and briskly traced a wide circle around Caelrhon. All of us lay flat, our heads over the edge, desperately searching the land below with our eyes. Gwennie and Justinia, on either side of the king, kept giving each other surreptitious glances over his head, but I had no time for them.

I had never realized before how much forest covered the hilltops and river valleys of the kingdom of Caelrhon, dense stands of trees that could have hidden hordes of children and were impervious to my magic unless I probed each clump individually. In spite of a far-seeing spell my vision kept blurring—wind, I told myself.

We saw nothing on the first circuit and started on a second, larger circuit. How much time, I tried to calculate, since Cyrus's piping had summoned the children? The sun was well down the western sky. They could be miles from home by now, or they could be concealed in some cave only a short distance from town. On this circuit we spotted the towers of the royal castle of Caelrhon—Evrard, I thought, was probably now somewhere looking for *us*. Well, let him and Elerius start their own hunt. I had no time to try to make contact with them. Maybe they'd have better luck than we were having.

Gwennie nudged me. "Wizard," she said in a whisper, "don't you think it just a little *suspicious* that someone you say knows eastern magic should show up in Caelrhon at the same time as an eastern princess shows up in Yurt? Especially since she seemed to know Antonia was your daughter before anyone else did?"

"I don't find it suspicious at all," I whispered back. Justinia had done nothing I could see to make me suspect her of evil. She was just a woman in hiding from her enemies—who, assuming the undead warriors and the wolf had been aimed at me rather than her, had so far hidden successfully.

"Wizard," said Paul briskly as the flying carpet approached our starting point again, "I know this is the most systematic way to search the whole area, but we'll only be able to spot them if they're out in the open. And it's going to be dark before very long. It's time to make a guess and go that way."

"What do you suggest?" I asked bleakly.

"The river road heading upstream from the city. It's a good road, so even children could travel fast on it, and it's tree-shaded most of the way. Because it's not a major trade route, Cyrus might hope he wouldn't meet anyone to bring the tale to Caelrhon. If we fly low we may be able to pick up something."

It was worth a try. We swooped down over the treetops and swung back near the city, then started following the road from just beyond where the parents were dragging the river. Justinia ordered the carpet to fly more slowly, and I probed magically as we flew, trying without success to pick up some indication that the children had come this way.

The direction we were following took us slowly and obliquely toward Yurt. After several miles the road emerged from the trees and ran a short distance in the open, among meadows where cows grazed unconcernedly. Justinia set the carpet down, and Paul and I leaped off.

The road was hard-surfaced, but the margins were damp from the proximity of the water meadows. "Lots of feet," said Paul, "an enormous number of feet just today. And look. Most of them are very small."

"Then you were right, sire," I said, springing back onto the carpet, suddenly feeling enormously more hopeful. "We may still catch them by nightfall."

The carpet moved faster now. If Cyrus kept to the road, we should be able to hear the children even if we did not see them, as long as we stayed close over the treetops. It was a good thing we had the carpet, I thought, or my own flying powers would have been exhausted hours ago.

Theodora still sat disconsolately, but Paul and I stared eagerly ahead. Gwennie, who had taken Theodora's hand reassuringly, looked up at me. "Is there any chance Antonia has turned Cyrus into a frog?"

"What?!"

"When she stayed in my chambers, she boasted she knew how to do transformations. Does she?"

I looked inquiringly at Theodora but she shook her head. "Not that I know of," I said. "It would certainly make things easier if she did." But even as I spoke I thought that if Cyrus knew she was my daughter, he might be especially careful around her and have counter-spells all arranged. I kept probing for his mind, but he must have his counter-spells all ready for me as well.

Justinia suddenly shivered. "I still am not accustomed to what ye of the West call summer weather. It is scarce this cold in Xantium in winter!"

She was right. Although I hadn't been noticing, after being hot all day the air had rapidly grown cooler. Ahead of us, dark storm clouds loomed, trailing curtains of rain. "It's going to be dark even sooner than we thought," said Paul concernedly.

"Not if I have anything to say about it," I replied grimly and started on weather spells. Did this mean, then, that Vlad had finally arrived? And if so, had Cyrus taken the children of Caelrhon straight to him?

The clouds began at once to lift, but in a moment they rolled together again, and lightning flashed directly in front of us.

"There's a mind behind this weather," I said through my teeth, "and he's very close. Theodora, do you know any weather spells?"

She shook her head, still not speaking. But Gwennie asked her with interest, "Do you know magic too? I hadn't realized that. Are there women wizards, then? Or are you a witch?"

All of Theodora's and my secrets were now on display. It hardly seemed to matter.

I redoubled my spells, trying to force the storm clouds apart. But someone enormously powerful was trying just as hard to keep them together. This had better not be Vlad, I thought with the grim conviction that it was. I had overcome his weather spells twice, but the first time, in the eastern kingdoms, he had been badly wounded, and the other time, just before I met his wolf, he had still been a great many miles away.

The others huddled together in the middle of the carpet as the temperature continued to drop. The king had his arms and wide cloak around both Gwennie and Justinia, though looking only at the latter, a faint smile at the corners of his mouth.

Cold rain started falling, first a few drops, then a downpour. Rivulets of water ran down our hair and clothes and across the carpet to drip off the edge. "This was my finest silk dress," announced Justinia, "but now it is ruined." We flew on, slowly now, through heavy darkness as thunder rumbled around us. I wondered uneasily what a direct lightning strike would do to a flying carpet.

As near as I could tell through cloud and rain, we were approaching the headwaters of the river that flowed through the city of Caelrhon. The road veered away as the ground rose abruptly into rocky cliffs. Justinia, huddled in on herself and shivering in spite of Paul's arm, muttered that I might as well fly the carpet myself. We circled once over the tops of the cliffs, then I directed the carpet to follow the road out across the plateau.

Theodora suddenly stirred. "Daimbert!" she cried excitedly. "I think I've found her! I've found Antonia! She's alive!"

Paul and I let out identical triumphant whoops. I

turned the carpet at once to head back toward the cliffs, where she said she had sensed our daughter's mind.

But now she seemed confused. Probing myself, I found no hint of any humans in the vicinity. "But I know I sensed her," Theodora said doggedly. "Unless it's some kind of trick—"

"Wait a minute," said the king, peering over the edge of the carpet at the nearly invisible naked rock below us. "There's supposed to be a castle here."

"*What* castle?" I cried.

"There's always been a ruined castle right below us, on top of these cliffs," said Paul patiently, trying unsuccessfully to wipe rainwater from his face. "Or at least I assume it hasn't always been ruined—but it must have been since the Black Wars. We're close to the border of the kingdom of Yurt here. This is the castle I told you about that I was exploring earlier in the summer."

I did remember now that he mentioned it. "Well, you must be mistaken," I said wearily, not even trying to wipe the streams of water from my face. "I know it's hard to tell distances from the air."

Suddenly I stopped and grinned. Maybe we had them after all.

"You're absolutely right, sire. A ruined castle would be exactly the place to hide a large group of children. And all the easier if you're a wizard with the powerful spells to make a whole castle invisible." Vlad's obsidian castle in the eastern kingdoms had been invisible unless he wanted someone to see it. If it weren't for Theodora's witch-magic breaking through his defenses for a brief moment, and for Paul's knowledge of local geography, we would have gone right by these cliffs without a second look.

"Now I just have to find the way in," I said fiercely.

Antonia was still alive. "The castle's stones are here though hidden, and we could rip the carpet landing on a jagged wall even if we can't see it." With the heavy darkness and the rain, we wouldn't have been able to see much of the castle even without a spell of invisibility.

"Down at the bottom of the cliffs," said Paul, "there's a back entrance that was probably where they once brought up goods from the river." I immediately directed the carpet slowly downward. Rain was now falling so hard it bounced from the carpet's surface. "Do you think, Wizard," the king added as we descended, "that they'll know we've arrived?"

"They'll have a pretty good idea," I said shortly.

Would it just be Cyrus we had to face, I wondered as I gently landed the carpet amid jagged rocks that must have fallen from a ruined wall above, or did he have Vlad with him now? And had these two dark wizards brought a demon along?

"The rest of you had better stay outside," I said quietly, setting my jaw determinedly. "I don't know how long this may take. But if I'm not back by dawn, Justinia, take the carpet and—"

But none of them wanted to be left behind. Theodora cared as little about her personal safety as I cared about mine when it came to Antonia, and Paul flatly refused to wait patiently for the adventurers' return. Justinia insisted she would freeze to death if forced to stay out in the driving rain for five more minutes, and Gwennie had no intention of being left alone on a night of magical darkness and hidden evil.

It was going to be hard enough to get myself out of this alive without worrying about all of them. I should have dumped them all off miles ago. But then I would never have located the castle. "Come on," I said. "Let's try to find the way in."

PART SEVEN

The Ruined Castle

I

"Here's the door, Wizard," called Paul, feeling his way along a cliff face streaming with water. "I can't see it but I can touch it." Standing next to him I could feel it as well, a half-open old door, falling from its hinges, with a musty passage beyond.

I had groped for and found pieces of driftwood that had come ashore here where cascades from the hills above flowed together to form the river: torches if we could discover a way inside out of the storm. "Hold hands," I told the others over the rumbling of thunder, and led them straight into and straight through what looked, in what little light we had from lightning flashes, like unbroken rock. Theodora was right behind me, and I could feel the bite of her fingernails as we passed through the illusion of solid cliff face, but no one spoke until we were all inside and wringing out our hair.

At least this castle was perfectly visible once we were within the walls. "God be praised, it is dry in here," said the Lady Justinia.

Paul blew out the air between his lips and commented,

"Glad you never decided to make *my* royal castle invisible, Wizard."

Theodora and I lit the torches with fire magic; they never would have burned properly without a spell. With me in front and she in back, we started cautiously up the tunnel before us. The torchlight showed a shadowed and dismal passage, hung with dusty festoons of cobweb, its floor strewn with rubbish where animals had denned.

"It's not very far," Paul said in a low voice, "a straight way leading slightly upward, and then the big storage cellars. It's possible the children are there."

Sitting in the dark, I thought, in utter terror. Would we see them even if they were there, or would they be as invisible as the castle itself was from the outside?

The light flickered on the uneven walls, and our footsteps echoed hollowly. It really would be night soon, I thought, and the night would be Vlad's, with nothing to stop him before the dawn. The weight of the cliffs above seemed to press down on us, and a fetid odor rose in the stale air from beneath our feet.

I kept straining, both with my ears and my magic, for indications of life, and at first found nothing, either good or evil. The sound of the thunder was very distant here, and I could hear nothing beyond our footsteps and our rapid breathing. *Were* the children even in this castle, or was it all an elaborate feint? But after only a few dozen yards I picked up the sound of distant moaning.

We came to an abrupt halt. "Antonia!" Theodora whispered.

But I shook my head. "Wait," I whispered back. The floor before us came alive in the torchlight: glossy black cockroaches, spiders, and a six-foot viper that looked at us with glittering eyes, then slithered away. Gwennie was at my shoulder, and I could feel her trembling. In any of the others' position, I would have run screaming back down the passageway, with a new appreciation for spending the night in the pouring rain, but no one moved.

Then, faint in the distance, I picked up a sound like the rattling of dry bones.

"What was that?" hissed Paul.

"Oh, Christ," I said, mostly under my breath. It sounded to me exactly like a skeletal apparition, the residue of death and evil left over in this old castle from the time of the Black Wars, now given life by a demon. It seemed to be getting closer.

The slightest whiff of brimstone, I said to myself, and I'm gone.

As if in response, the roughly quarried stones on either hand rapidly began to grow warmer. Justinia, in relief, started to lean against the wall, but she pulled away with a sharp intake of breath as it grew hotter and hotter. Raw horror, even beyond what was rational given what I had just seen and heard, seemed to roll down the tunnel toward us. And wafting through the air came a small cloud of stinking smoke, poisonous yellow in the torchlight.

"Right," said a rational voice in the back of my brain. "Zahlfast can't argue with you anymore. Time for the demonology experts. Fly the carpet back to Yurt and telephone the school."

"And when will they arrive?" I asked myself testily.

"Tomorrow," said the rational voice, sounding less certain. "And in the meantime, while we're waiting, you can try to locate Elerius and Evrard—they must be around somewhere, looking for *you*." But I couldn't wait for tomorrow. Antonia was in this castle *now*.

And could she and all the other children be sitting, not just in the dark, but in a dark they shared with vipers, with brimstone, with skeletal apparitions, and with a demon that was even now killing them one by one with terror?

"No, of course not," babbled the rational voice. "Cyrus loves children. He may use a demon to help his magic, but he doesn't want to hurt them. He's always wanted the children to love him back."

The voice had a point. If Antonia was indeed still alive, then Cyrus must have brought the children here for a reason, rather than dumping them into the first convenient widening in the river. He therefore wanted them for some specific purpose—ransoming perhaps, or a refined revenge—even if he did not love them for themselves.

And I therefore had to find them before his purpose took effect.

This mental argument with myself had taken only a few seconds. "The children are not in the big storage cellars," I said in a low voice, not mentioning what I was fairly sure *was* there. "Sire, is there any other way up to the rest of the castle without going through the cellars?"

"There's a narrow staircase on the left," said Paul, "just a little farther on." I noticed he'd drawn his sword—not that it would do any good. "It's partially blocked by fallen stone, but it's passable."

"Theodora," I said, "light the others back to the doorway and stay there until I get back. And if—"

But it was no use. In spite of what we had seen so far, and in spite of having to assert through chattering teeth that they were not at all frightened, Paul and Theodora had not given up their intention of accompanying me. Gwennie and Justinia claimed they preferred staying with the rest of us, even if it meant advancing through giant cockroaches, to waiting alone with hot walls and the moaning and clattering and no magic to keep a damp torch lit. Three of them, not knowing magic, might not be as susceptible as I was to the disembodied and demonic terror pouring out of the storage cellars—but Theodora was.

No time to argue. "Then let's hurry," I said and strode forward. Pushing against waves of horror was like pushing against the tide. I kept my feet moving with sheer will. The rattling of bones kept coming closer, as insects scurried out from underfoot. Paul's narrow stairway was an empty black opening in the tunnel wall.

Good thing it wasn't any farther or I might not have made it. I felt inside the opening with my hand—not as warm as the tunnel where we stood. When I thrust in the torch it was to see worn and cracked stone stairs spiraling upwards. There would be halls, chambers, and passages higher up, some certainly roofless, but some doubtless still whole, and Antonia had to be up there.

I led the way again, climbing as quickly as I could on the uneven steps, my heart pounding wildly. The staircase was so narrow that there was scarcely room for my shoulders between the stone central post and the outer curved wall. A little rivulet of water found its way down the spiral, making surfaces slick and forcing me to be careful when I wanted to do nothing but run and run. The moaning and the rattling faded behind us. Someone slipped but caught themselves after a hard thump.

"Do you think the children had to climb all these stairs?" Gwennie whispered.

"I'm sure they were brought in the front way," I whispered back. Wild terror receded as we climbed—unfortunately rational terror did not. "But we couldn't even *find* the front way, and I'm still hoping we can get to wherever they're being held without being discovered."

I spoke confidently, but whatever hope I had was a desperate one. Someone who went to the trouble to make his castle invisible and to surround it with dark clouds would certainly have set up spells to detect a wizard sneaking in.

How far had we come? It was impossible to tell distances, except to know that we had climbed high enough that my legs were aching. My wet clothes had begun drying on my back into clammy stiffness. This had once been an expensive black wool suit, I recalled, bought just for Celia's vocation at the nunnery.

Ahead I thought I could pick up the smell of rain-washed air over the general mustiness, and then I began to hear a louder dripping. We came around a twist of the stair and saw Paul's "partial blockage" before us.

Part of the wall had collapsed inward, leaving a gaping opening looking out into night. Rain still lashed down. I redoubled the fire spell on my torch and put it and my head outside—still sheer cliff above and below, but we must be getting close to the top.

The collapsed wall covered the staircase with chunks of stone, but beyond it continued to spiral upwards. The stones cast heavy shadows in the torchlight—had that been another viper? No, I tried to reassure myself, just another shadow.

"You have to climb carefully over the loose stones," said Paul. "It was daylight when I did this before, but—"

I stopped him and lifted myself with magic to fly up and over. One at a time I then lifted Gwennie, Paul, and Justinia to bring them past the obstacle and up beside me. Theodora flew unaided, holding the flaring torch well away from herself. Gwennie, impressed, started to say something but didn't.

Flying spells, I thought as Theodora found her footing, would announce to any wizard paying attention that another wizard had arrived. I would feel more comfortable about this if I could pick up the slightest trace of *him*—or if I didn't keep imagining what might already be working its way up the stairs behind us, heating the stones as it came until the rivulets of dark water vanished into steam.

"We're almost there," said Paul quietly. "We'll come out in what was once the kitchen. The roof is long gone, but there's another passage—still covered—that should take us to the great hall in the central keep. That's the most intact part of the castle: the children may be there."

A final turn of the stair, and we staggered out onto a level if gritty surface, next to an enormous fireplace. Ducking under the stone mantel to shelter from the rain, now falling harder than ever, we all paused to catch our breaths.

I kept straining to pick up any sound over the rain's steady drumming or any magical indication of who else was in this ruined castle, but still found nothing. I lifted an eyebrow at Theodora, but she shook her head. "I haven't sensed her again since that one time."

"This way," said Paul. Back under an arched roof, we tried to walk quietly, but five sets of feet on flagstones sent echoes running up and down the passage around us. The light from our torches was too dim to see any distance ahead or behind, though it made our shadows on the stone walls grotesque and gigantic. Little puffs of wind tugged at our damp hair.

Suddenly the torches went out. We all crashed together in the dark, then Theodora and I desperately tried to relight them. It was no use. Plenty of unburned wood remained, but our fire spells no longer seemed effective.

And then, down the passageway ahead of us, I saw a small yellow light, like a candle flame. As we all held our breaths we could hear the steady tap of approaching feet.

The dead torch fell from stiff fingers. "No use running," I said quietly. "They've found us."

✧   ✧   ✧

Paul and I stood with the women behind us, waiting for whomever was coming. The cold knot in my stomach already knew. Someone dressed in black satin emerged from the shadows. Just before he came close enough to pick out the features on the white face, Paul gave a sudden, startled grunt and dropped his sword.

I looked down. The blade had transformed itself into a black and white striped snake that now slithered away. Paul reached for the knife at his belt but I nudged him and shook my head.

The person kept on coming. I could see his face now clearly, dead white, split by a smile that showed an unusually large number of sharp teeth. One of the cheeks was just a little crooked; the eyes, behind half-lowered translucent lids, were expressionless stones.

"Daimbert, we meet again," he said in a friendly tone.

One of the women behind me gave a brief moan of terror. I took a deep breath. "Greetings, Prince Vlad," I said.

II

"As I recall," he said, looking me up and down and still smiling, "we had not finished our negotiations when you left my castle so abruptly, the last time we met. I believe I was explaining to you why you should bring me the treasure from the eastern deserts that a certain ruby ring would reveal. . . ."

As I recalled it, when we had last met I had nearly killed him and he had called down curses on my retreating back. But if he wanted to talk for a while before he murdered me that was fine—it gave me time to try desperately to think of a way to get the others out of here.

"You were about to agree to bring whatever you found

back to me," he continued. I wished he wouldn't keep showing his teeth as he talked, or that his stone eyes would blink, or *something*. "Since you still appear to be the Royal Wizard of Yurt—a tiny kingdom which, I shall gladly admit, was *very* hard to find—and have no startling new powers, I assume you didn't find it. Well, I am here now, ready to forget our little differences in the past, even ready to give you some assistance if you want to look for the treasure again."

For a second I considered agreeing with him, telling him that I would be happy to have his company searching the East for treasure, and that when we split what we found I would even let him have the larger share.

But I dismissed this as a ploy. Spending weeks or months crossing the eastern kingdoms and the deserts beyond by night, probably with all the others brought along as hostages for my good behavior, and then having to explain to Vlad at the end why there was nothing there to find, would only postpone the problem.

"It's no use, Prince," I said, trying to keep the tremor from my voice. "We found it fifteen years ago, even without your assistance. But both the treasure itself and the ruby ring that unlocked its secrets are now gone beyond recovery, sunk in the deepest part of the Outer Sea."

A faint expression of disappointment passed over his white features. Under that living mask, I thought, must be the face of a corpse.

"Then we shall need to discuss other arrangements," he said suavely, "by which you and the kingdom of Yurt might compensate me properly for what you have done to me over the years. Otherwise, I shall have to kill you. Nothing personal, of course!" holding up a white hand. "Just scientific curiosity: how long does it take a western wizard to die? And of course sound political practice: I would not want it known widely in the eastern kingdoms that someone had done to me what you did and gotten away with it.

"But I am forgetting my manners!" he continued, turning toward the others. His very politeness made it even worse. "Who are these friends you brought with you?"

"Don't tell him!" I said sharply.

This intrigued Vlad. "So at least one of them is someone important," he said thoughtfully, "someone in whom I might be very interested if I knew their identity. Let me look at them." He lifted his candle higher, and his pebble eyes looked us over. "A rather bedraggled group, I must say. I had hoped for a minute for a member of the royal family itself, but no. . . ."

Just when I thought that Paul's creased and filthy tunic had fooled him he shot an arm past me and put his hand on Justinia's shoulder.

"But this one!" he said triumphantly. "She is darker complexioned than most of you in the west, and this was once an extremely expensive silk garment. Much more than a townswoman looking for her lost children. Who then could she be?"

He stretched it out, enjoying the suspense. Lost children, I thought, desperately trying to find reason for hope. Then they really *were* here in the ruined castle! But *where* were they, and where was Cyrus?

Justinia shrank away from Vlad's touch, but her almond-shaped eyes flashed. I was afraid she would tell him defiantly that she was a governor's granddaughter, but she had been brought up amidst intrigue. "My name is of but the smallest import to *thee*," she shot at him.

"A Xantium accent!" said Vlad, even more interested. "That I find most unusual. Could she be . . . ?"

Paul grabbed the wizard's arm to wrench it away from Justinia, but Vlad lifted the little finger on his other hand and the king staggered backwards, doubled over in pain.

"Do not interrupt me," Vlad said chidingly. "She is clearly important, a princess perhaps?" He enjoyed the suspense a moment longer, then said, "I think, my lady, that you are none other than Justinia, granddaughter of the governor of Xantium! The Thieves' Guild is looking very hard for you."

Paul, gray-faced in the candlelight, caught his breath and wiped sweat from his forehead but showed no sign of trying anything else.

"And who informed thee I was here?" Justinia snapped. "Who hath betrayed me?"

Vlad widened his mouth in a tooth-filled smile. "Then you *are* the Lady Justinia! Thank you for confirming my guess. The Guild will pay me extremely well for discovering you."

She pulled her lips together angrily, either at him or at herself for letting herself be taken by such an old trick. The mage Kaz-alrhun had entrusted Justinia to me, I thought bitterly, and I had brought her straight to someone who would deliver her to her worst enemies.

"When they could not find you in Xantium, my lady," Vlad continued pleasantly, "they put out the information all over the East that they were looking for you. News even crossed the Central Sea and the mountains to reach my own little principality. A rumor or a guess that you might have fled to the western kingdoms was all they had to go on. I promised, of course, to help in the search for you during my *own* quest to the kingdom of Yurt. The Guild should pay me enough when I deliver you to them that I may be able to buy the services of Xantium's greatest mages, thus making up at least in part for the loss of that which Daimbert so carelessly let disappear in the Outer Sea."

"If thy plan is to hire Kaz-alrhun to assist thee in making the simulacrum of life from dead flesh and bones," said Justinia haughtily, "thou shalt be most gravely disappointed. These are forbidden arts, and even the greatest of Xantium's mages will not follow their dark ways."

"He may change his mind when he sees the Guild's money," suggested Vlad.

"By now," I interrupted, "Kaz-alrhun must have all the money he could possibly want and more."

Vlad dismissed these concerns with a shrug. "Then my money shall buy whatever *does* still interest him." He took a step backwards and motioned with his arm, like a genial host inviting in his guests. "In the meantime, I need to keep you safe—I am quite sure you will be worth more to the Guild alive than dead. And all these other people may have secrets of their own. If not, I shall still want to keep them secure until after Daimbert and I have finished our, shall we say, *negotiations*." He blinked once. "Perhaps there *is* some personal feeling after all in what I would like to do to Daimbert. Some of that feeling might be assuaged by giving him the opportunity to watch his friends die slowly—but that is a matter for later. Come with me, and I shall take you to a dry chamber."

The second he turned his back I threw together a spell of light that should have lit up the passage in a blinding flash. Light, the light that broke down the magic of blood and bone, was the only weapon I had against him.

But the words of the Hidden Language twisted and turned to dust before I could finish formulating them. "I must say I am disappointed, Daimbert," said Vlad without turning around. "How could you have thought I would not be prepared for the spell with which you defeated me last time?"

We reluctantly followed Vlad, holding tight to each other, because there didn't seem much else to do. The chattering of my teeth was due to much more than the chill of the night, and from the sound of Theodora's breath she was again on the verge of hysterical tears.

Lit only by Vlad's candle, the tunnel was nearly black, but at least I saw no giant cockroaches and heard no bones rattling. The demon must still be down in the bottom of the castle. The children had *better* not be down there with it.

Vlad opened a heavy oak door and motioned us within. "I am afraid I moved into this castle very recently," he said apologetically, "and have not yet had a chance to install suitable furnishings." The candle showed a cold and empty but dry room, its only window very far up and much smaller than a human could squeeze through.

As he motioned the others inside, lightning flashed for a second from the high window, followed by a sharp clap of thunder. Vlad flinched at the lightning. "Your weather is not as tractable as I had hoped," he said. "I wanted clouds but not lightning. I am afraid we shall have to postpone our conversation at least briefly, Daimbert, until I have restored suitable conditions. You will be so good as to wait for me, I am sure."

He handed me the candle and slammed the door, and I heard the bolt going across. His feet tapped away down the corridor.

All of us let out shuddering breaths. I counted to twenty to give Vlad time to get away, then started on a lifting spell to slide the bolt back again. But it was no use; he had put a magic lock on it.

"Shall we try kicking the door down?" suggested Paul, his jaw set.

"A magic lock strengthens the door itself as well as the locking mechanism," I said, shaking my head and thinking fast. "But we might be able to set it on fire—"

I immediately began working on fire spells, and Theodora, who had been trembling and clinging to Gwennie, took a deep breath and started on her own magic. But our spells were no more effective on the door than they had been on our torches. Vlad must have wanted to be sure there were no sources of light in his castle other than the small candles he lit himself.

We were safe and even dry for the moment, safe from Vlad, safe from the demon. But the safety only lasted until Vlad returned. And I still had no idea how, even if we escaped alive, I was going to find Antonia.

"How about the window?" said Paul, low and urgent. There was another lightning flash and more thunder. Good, I mentally said to the weather. Keep Vlad occupied as long as possible.

"I could transform us all into birds so we could fly out," I suggested halfheartedly. Keep thinking, I told myself. Don't dwell on the demon downstairs. Don't think about how evil Vlad is. Think of a plan. "But I couldn't shape the words of the Hidden Language as a bird, so we'd all have to stay transformed unless another wizard realized who we really were and broke the spell. Or I could transform the rest of you and stay behind, and then when you were all safely through the window break the spell from in here. . . ."

"Leaving us sitting on the roof in the storm?" asked Paul.

"No," I agreed, "we'd all still be trapped. Maybe all becoming birds is still the best plan. We'll get away from here and wait somewhere along the road for Elerius—he's bound to find this castle eventually," I heard myself babbling. "And when he comes maybe we can spell out a message in birdseed or something. . . ."

"This is the most stupid plan I have ever had assail my ears," said Justinia, her voice ragged.

Theodora took my arm. "Vlad has not harmed us yet in spite of his threats, and we know we must be close to the children." At least she didn't say my plan was stupid.

We huddled together in a corner, my arms around

Theodora, Paul again with an arm each around Gwennie and Justinia. A corner of my mind was interested to note how social conventions did not stand up against true danger; this was not a king embracing a foreign princess and his own cook's daughter, but three people trying to deny their fear by clinging together desperately. Rain pounded above our heads, and the candle flickered as the wind blew in. For a minute the storm seemed to be weakening, but then three lightning flashes in a row cast glaring blue light into the room. Vlad should be occupied for a while yet.

Justinia seemed to be struggling between fury and despair. "I should have been far wiser than to let Kaz-alrhun ever send me into the western kingdoms," she muttered. "I should have known that I would stand out to the first person who came seeking me, and that the local magic-workers would have no protective spells."

I declined to mention that if she had let me take the carpet myself she would now be safely home in Yurt.

"Perhaps the path of wisdom is to cast myself from this castle to the rocks below," she continued determinedly, "so that the Thieves' Guild will not have a live prisoner with which to pressure my grandfather, and so that I need not submit to the caresses of a dead man!" Paul held her tighter and made soothing sounds—as he would to one of his horses, I thought.

"*Is* he even alive?" Theodora asked quietly. "And do you know why he captured the children?"

"He's alive," I said, "and he's not using the supernatural power of a demon himself, but that's all the good I can say about him. I don't know if capturing the children was his idea or an independent plan of Cyrus's."

For a minute I paused, waiting for some sort of reaction from Vlad if he were listening. But weather spells, I thought—as well as maintaining his defenses against fire and light here in the castle—must be taking all his attention not already devoted to keeping the castle invisible. "I think half of his body is made from the flesh of others," I went on, "and much of the rest from stone. The flesh must rot; I don't want to think where he gets more. . . . He is aged beyond reckoning, animated only by spells darker and more subtle than any I know."

"I remember hearing your tales about him," said Paul, "years ago, when you and Father came back from the East." He turned to Justinia with the good-natured assumption that she would want to hear the story too. "They were maneuvered, by wiles that set the eastern kingdoms aflame with war as I recall, to a black obsidian castle. And there lived a princely wizard who had once, a great many years earlier, betrayed my uncle, an uncle who died long before I was born."

I nodded slowly. "When we met him in the East he already felt injured by the royal family of Yurt, and since then he's had an especial reason to hate *me*. He has wanted for years to find Yurt."

"And it was the will of God that he find it when I was there," said Justinia gloomily.

We fell silent, listening to the thunder continue to rumble around the ruined castle. Gwennie suddenly spoke up. "Do you remember, Paul," she said, not bothering with his title, "one time when we were little, and it started to thunder like this, and you put your arm around me like this and told me you'd protect me?"

Justinia looked past the king at the other woman, her eyebrows raised as though in approval. He gave a low chuckle. "I certainly do remember. I was just as scared as you were but I didn't want to admit it. What would we have been—maybe about five?"

Antonia's age. And there was no one to comfort *her*.

Theodora shifted and spoke as though deliberately trying to distract her own mind from Antonia. "So Cyrus, you think, is Vlad's pupil?"

"He must be. The unliving warriors who attacked the royal castle were made by the same magic. I think now that Cyrus was sent into the West as Vlad's agent, to find Yurt and to attack the castle for him, and to send word back when he found it. If the warriors— and the spell of madness in their bones—or the wolf succeeded in killing me or the king, all was well; or, if not, Vlad himself would soon arrive. At the time I thought those attacks a little too easy to overcome."

"What do you mean, easy?" protested Theodora. "You were almost killed!"

"Well, yes, but I *did* overcome them. I still haven't found a way to oppose Vlad's magic directly." With this depressing thought we all fell silent.

Then, over the sound of the storm, I heard approaching steps. Here he comes, I thought, pushing myself to my feet. If I could take him off somewhere for a private conversation, he might not guess who King Paul was, and maybe I could stall until morning or until such time as Elerius ever got here—

But it was not the regular tapping of Vlad's feet. It was someone running.

He hit the door hard, and then I felt more than heard a sharp crackle. Blue light flared for a second around the doorframe, and I could sense a powerful spell breaking up. I hadn't known it was even possible to break a magic lock.

"Elerius?" I called with a wild surge of hope.

The bolt shot back and the door swung open. "No, it's me. Cyrus."

III

The others pressed into the doorway behind me. "*Where,*" said Theodora between gritted teeth, "have you taken my daughter?"

"She's fine," said Cyrus with an expansive gesture. "You'll see her very soon. But you have to come with me."

I spread my arms protectively, keeping the others back. Paul reached for his knife again, but I distracted him with an elbow in his ribs. "We're not going anywhere with you, Cyrus," I said defiantly. "You've already tried to kill me twice, and you're working with a demon. You denied it to the bishop, but your 'miracles' owe more to the supernatural power of evil than to the saints. And you'd need a demon's power to break Vlad's lock."

He shrugged. "Well, the demon might have helped me there. But he's not with me—he's somewhere else," he added vaguely. "And this is the last spell on which I'll need his help!"

"Why hast thou come to unlock our door?" said Justinia fiercely. "Didst thou not think we would recognize such a trick?"

"No trick! I am here to save your lives. Vlad wants to kill you all, but I don't."

How did he, Vlad's accomplice, expect us to believe that he would save us from Vlad? The candlelight glittered in his dark eyes. He was, I thought, completely mad.

"Dost thou intend instead to obtain all for thyself the reward from the Thieves' Guild?" demanded Justinia.

Cyrus shook his head. "I know nothing of the Thieves' Guild. Come at once! All of you! You have to trust me if you want to escape. Do you not wish to preserve your lives?"

"Well, *I* do," said Justinia with sudden decision. "I am dead if I stay in Vlad's captivity."

"And if you have my daughter," said Theodora, intense and low, "I don't care how many demons you're working with."

"Then follow me!" said Cyrus and turned to walk briskly

down the corridor. Justinia and Theodora followed as surely as if he had been playing his enchanted pipes, and the rest of us, after only a second's hesitation, hurried behind. At least we were no longer locked in, I thought grimly.

"Vlad told me he sensed you arriving at his castle, Daimbert," said Cyrus over his shoulder. Thunder continued to rumble loudly over our heads. "He says he's wanted to see you again for fifteen years! But I was fairly sure his intention was evil. That's why I knew I had to provide a distraction in order to rescue you."

"You mean the lightning is due to you?"

Cyrus chuckled. "You can do a lot when you've got a demon on your side! The thunderstorm shouldn't let up before morning. Of course," he added, "that was the next-to-last spell on which I had the demon help me. Breaking the lock was the last."

Somebody who had sold his soul to the devil, I thought, didn't stop asking a demon for favors. There was always just *one* more thing. The demon would happily provide him all the favors wanted as long as he asked—or until the demon became bored and decided to play tricks of his own on the man who had summoned him.

We darted down a maze of corridors, several times coming out from under shelter into a roofless area where the driving rain soaked us again. I didn't dare use a spell to shelter us against the wet for fear of attracting Vlad's attention, and Cyrus seemed neither to notice nor to care. In a few minutes we reached a wide staircase. "You'll be safe here," said Cyrus confidently, leading the way up.

"I think the chambers up here were built for a visiting dignitary," said Paul as we climbed. "It's some of the newest construction in the castle, and it's rather separate from the rest. The roof is still intact."

"You know the castle too?" asked Cyrus, pleased. Paul

bit his lip, but Cyrus did not ask more. Instead he seemed eager to show us into the chambers.

We all stopped and stared. The large room beyond the door at the top of the stairs was furnished with soft couches and tapestries, and a fire crackled in the fireplace. I blinked and tried the two words that would end an illusion, but this was no illusion.

"It should be nice and comfortable for you here," Cyrus said, watching our reaction. He was hoping, I thought, for more praise and adulation. "Aren't you pleased? Aren't you impressed? And Vlad won't find you. It will be for him as though this part of the castle didn't even exist."

"*This* certainly didn't exist before," said Paul, entering slowly. Justinia, however, rushed straight to the fire and held out her hands. The flames seemed real enough.

"The demon helped you out again?" I asked cautiously.

"Of course! It was the second-to-last spell on which I had his help. You'll all find some dry clothes on that couch over there. Vlad told me there were some people with you, Daimbert, but I wasn't sure how many or what sizes you were, but something should fit."

He smiled, his eyes strangely bright. "And if you're still worrying that I'm evil just because I occasionally have a demon help me, let me assure you that the saints help me as well. You implied that the miracles that made me famous in Caelrhon were all demonic, but I'll have you know that rebuilding the burned street was due to the saints. I certainly prayed over it, and as I was walking home from the cathedral, thinking about it, an angelic messenger came and whispered in my ear."

I looked away, feeling sick. The demon had started to toy with him already.

"Now!" Cyrus said cheerily. "I need to go show myself an obedient pupil to Vlad, appear to be helping him with his weather spells, so that he won't be suspicious.

But I'll return soon. We'll go see the children together when I do—the dear little things. You see how much I trust you? I'm not even locking you in!"

He hurried away, leaving us staring at each other. None of us, not even Justinia, showed any interest in dry clothes conjured up by a demon. "At first I didn't believe it," said Gwennie in a small voice. "But how else could he . . . I've never known anyone who sold his soul before."

"Summoning a demon and asking for favors is certainly the surest way to damn yourself," I said quietly. "I don't think even the saints can help you then. But it's still not the quickest or easiest way to damnation. If Vlad imagines his soul can still be saved just because he's stayed clear of demons himself, he may have a nasty surprise on Judgment Day. At this point, a demon wouldn't even be interested in him—no use making bargains for a soul that already belongs to the devil."

"If we really aren't locked in," said Paul, trying the door, "let's get out of here."

"No," said Theodora, short and hard. I noticed that, under the pressure we all felt, she too no longer treated Paul with the respect usually offered a king. "He said when he came back he would take us to the children. It may be our only chance to find Antonia, and we don't dare make him angry. He and his demon will certainly be able to find us wherever we are in the castle, and if he's telling the truth then at least for the moment we're safe from Vlad."

I nodded glumly, although the last thing I wanted to do was to wait, in a room filled with comforts a demon had provided for us, for a madman: one who had imagined that a demon's soft voice in his ear was an angel's, or for that matter that there was any way he, with human power alone, could break free of the devil.

The three women and I seated ourselves on the couch

by the fire, our clothes steaming in the heat. The king remained standing, tapping his foot, ready for a fight that was not there. "I wonder if I'll ever see my sword again," he muttered, "and whether it's still a snake."

"Steel won't do any good against wizards like these," I said resignedly, "much less a demon. This castle was ruined by armies during the Black Wars, but the same armies that were able to do this much destruction were stopped by wizards who had become sickened by the carnage—and that was only wizards like me, practicing white magic. Come sit down."

The storm continued unabated outside, but in this warm room it seemed far away. "I thought Cyrus was a preacher in Caelrhon," said Paul, settling himself between Justinia and Gwennie. "Celia said he was studying in the seminary. What's he doing practicing black magic?"

"He was a seminary student, all right," I said slowly. "It makes no sense whatsoever. It never has. It's almost as if he were two different people, one of whom wants to be genuinely pious, and another who has learned magic from Vlad and relies on a demon's help for his most spectacular effects." I didn't add that it looked to me as if the conflict between these two personalities had pushed him over the edge into madness.

Theodora roused herself to tell the others about Cyrus's first appearance in Caelrhon under the name of Dog-Man, his apparently miraculous healing of the children's toys and pets, and his evolution, once he had been accepted into the seminary, into someone who preached Christian doctrine to large and reverent crowds.

"And who kidnaps little children," said Paul grimly. "Since they're all from Caelrhon they aren't my own subjects, but it doesn't make any difference. It's a good thing you didn't try to leave me behind *again*, Wizard.

I couldn't consider myself a king if I didn't go after someone who did that to a group of helpless kids."

I had no idea how Paul and Joachim managed to consider themselves fathers to entire kingdoms; I had enough trouble being the father of one five-year-old. "Just don't kill Cyrus quite yet, sire," I said. "For one thing, I don't think you could. For another, at the moment he's all we've got."

"You don't *trust* him, do you, Wizard?" Gwennie said incredulously.

"Of course not. Not even for a second. The third reason I don't want Paul to kill him yet is that I want the pleasure of doing it myself. But in a ruined castle now harboring a wizard who is genuinely and unequivocally evil, a demon, and my daughter, I've got to use whatever fragile leads we may have to free her."

We sat in silence then, listening to the thunder and the fire's crackle. I wondered how long we had been in the castle and how many hours there might still be of night—or if the clouds would ever lift at all. We may even have dozed a little, warm and exhausted, but all our heads came up abruptly when there were quick footsteps on the stairs and the door swung open again.

"Good, I'm glad you didn't try to slip away!" said Cyrus cheerfully. "Then I would have had the trouble of finding you all over again."

"To deliver us to Vlad?" I asked fiercely.

"Of course not," said Cyrus, coming to warm his own hands at the fire. "He still thinks you're locked up where he left you. Weren't you listening? I'm trying to protect you! I brought you to this nice room so you'd have a chance to start thinking better of me, but it doesn't seem to be working. And you haven't even put on the clothes I prepared just for you. You'll have to learn to trust me."

The others looked at me as though expecting me to

know what to say or do. "If you want us to trust you, Cyrus," I said carefully, "then we'll need to understand a little more clearly why you should want to rescue us from your master, the man who taught you magic, to whom you brought the children of Caelrhon."

"I told you all that back when we first met, Daimbert," he said, flashing me a happy, crazed look from his deepset eyes. "Vlad was my master once, it's true, but when I entered the seminary at Caelrhon I decided to put all magic behind me."

"This," I said accusingly, motioning at the comfortable room around us, "does not look to me like putting magic behind you. Nor does putting a summoning spell on children." Keep him talking, I thought. Find out all I could about him: his reasoning, his motivation, his magic. So far I hadn't seen anything that could help.

"Are you just not paying attention, Daimbert?" he asked and shook his head in a scolding way. "I really have given up magic. Your bishop inspired me. So if I've worked just a few little spells since then . . . Have you ever worked with a demon yourself?" he added suddenly.

"No." It came out harsher than I intended; I was, after all, trying to seem friendly, at least until he took us to Antonia.

"My, you sound dismissive. You're as bad as Vlad. It's quite a challenge, I'll tell you! You find yourself doing things you hadn't quite intended, like killing a frog and bringing it back to life to impress the little ones. That's why I've decided not to do magic at all anymore."

"Are you sure the demon will be as willing to break away from you as you are from him?"

"Willpower, that's all it takes," said Cyrus airily. "After all, while I was in Caelrhon I often went several weeks without practicing magic of any kind. But I remember well the arguments Vlad gave me when I first asked him about black magic. He tried to tell me that *he'd* never had demonic assistance with his spells, that it would be a sign of incompetence if he couldn't get results with unaided magic, and that as well as taking your soul demons will often make your life miserable even while supposedly granting all your wishes. My guess," and he gave a broad wink, "was that Vlad had tried himself to interest a demon in helping him and got turned down flat. Why should the devil offer anything valuable for a soul already on its way to hell? Mine, of course," with a smug smile, "was different."

Something he'd said caught my attention. "Are you sure," I asked cautiously, "that Vlad wasn't trying to goad you into summoning a demon because none would work with him, or did he still hope to shield himself from the effects of black magic? It sounds as though he was hoping to put all the burden on you but get the benefits himself." .

"If so, it didn't work," Cyrus replied, still smug. "He *did* hint that I should ask the demon to repair his body for him, but I refused, of course. I knew already that I planned to save my soul, and helping such an evil old man couldn't do any good!"

"Have you," I asked in amazement, "said any of this to the bishop?"

"Not yet. I intend to surprise him once the saints assure me that I'm truly saved."

If this wasn't the only man who could take us to Antonia I would have fled. Horror and revulsion filled me—both at him, with his self-absorption, complacency, and pathetic belief that he could save his soul through willpower, and especially at the demon, who had allowed him to believe he still had the slightest chance.

Cyrus became serious suddenly. "I know you've studied magic a lot longer than I have, Daimbert, but haven't you sometimes felt its inadequacies?"

"Magic," I said carefully, "is part of the same natural forces that shaped the world, but even the best wizards can do no more than tug at its edges."

Cyrus looked at me a long moment, and for once his eyes looked both sober and sane. "You've put it better than I could. Though I might add, magic's other limitation is that it only works in this world. To transcend material limitations, you need religion. *That's* the message I learned in Caelrhon's seminary. The bishop will be very happy when he hears I've rescued you."

"What about kidnapping the children?" demanded Theodora. "The bishop wasn't happy about that! And you told me you'd take us to them."

"Soon, very soon," he replied, his expression once again wild. "Piping them out of town was actually the demon's idea, not mine. It was a good one, though!" with a chuckle. "I certainly taught a lesson to all those citizens of Caelrhon who couldn't even say thank-you politely after I'd cleared up their rat problem for them. But you see, that's the beauty of Christianity. You can sin, but it's all right if you're penitent and make restitution afterwards."

It sounded to me as though he had not been paying very close attention to basic concepts in seminary.

"So I'll make restitution by letting them all go again! I have to tell you, Daimbert," with almost a giggle, "that I was especially pleased to get revenge on *you*. It was your meddling that made the bishop distrust me in the first place, when my ultimate purpose was always so pure! Once I found out you had a daughter in Caelrhon, I knew my piping would bring her along with the rest. Vlad especially thought that was a good idea—he's planning his own revenge, of course. It did occur to me that she might know a spell or two, so I was on guard. Good thing I was, too! Do you know, Daimbert, she tried to put a transformations spell on me?"

"What have you done with Antonia?" cried Theodora.

"Nothing at all," said Cyrus, turning to look at her. "I haven't even pointed her out to Vlad. I just broke her spell before it took effect. Pretty good spell for one so small!"

So Antonia *did* know at least the elements of transformation—could Elerius have taught her?

"And of course," Cyrus continued, "I told her *very* sternly not to try anything again with a man who was friends with a demon. Are you then this girl's mother? Curious, Daimbert. I had assumed the blonde"—with a nod toward Gwennie—"was your sweetheart."

Gwennie blushed pink, but Cyrus wasn't paying attention. "We should go see the children now. Vlad is still occupied with the lightning storm I settled over the castle. This has been a fascinating discussion, Daimbert, but I sense your sweetheart is growing impatient. Come, and I will take you to where the children are hidden."

IV

Again we hurried down stairs, corridors, and twisting passageways, scrambling through narrow openings mostly blocked by fallen stone, at one point descending a staircase set within a wall: probably once a secret stair before the wall that concealed it had fallen. In the damper passages our hands brushed against mold-encrusted stones, in dryer ones the sharp, sticky threads of giant cobwebs. A distant moaning could have been the wind or could have been the calls of evil apparitions of men long dead. At least we never seemed to approach the cellars where the demon lurked.

There had to be an easier way, I thought, to get where we were going. Either Cyrus was deliberately confusing us or else he was staying out of Vlad's part of the castle.

I tried to keep track of our many turnings and, looking at Paul, thought he was doing the same. It must be easier for him—after all, he had explored this castle by daylight.

"Now, you won't be able actually to talk with the little girl," said Cyrus, "but—"

Theodora whirled on him so fiercely that he backed up a step. "You said we could see her! You said she was all right!"

"Yes, yes!" he said quickly. "You can see her, but she won't see you. Vlad has imprisoned all the children behind an invisible shield."

I didn't want to dwell on what Vlad's plans might be for them. Would he think children's flesh, because younger and fresher, better for rebuilding his body than that of adults? "How hard would it be to break this shield?" I asked, thinking fast. I might be able to improvise a way to dismantle the spell—if doing so didn't bring Vlad racing through the castle at once to stop me.

"Very hard," said Cyrus, looking concerned for a moment, but he immediately cheered up. "I know! I can have the demon break it!"

"You said you'd done your last demon-assisted spell," Gwennie pointed out, her lips white.

"Whoops! So I did. See how difficult it is, Daimbert?" he said, hurrying ahead of us through an arcade. "You have to be constantly alert."

Beyond the arcade was a final passageway, shadowed and reeking with menace. But the light from Cyrus's candle bobbed down it without hesitation, and after a second I reached for Theodora's hand and followed. The passage opened onto what must have once been a chapel. But the stained glass windows were gone and the cracked stone altar had a rooks' nest built on it. Desecrated long since, I thought—no aura of the saints lingered here. And in the chapel were the children.

There were at least a hundred of them. Theodora threw herself forward with a cry, to be stopped by air turned to glass. I probed the spells even while straining to see Antonia beyond the barricade. It was complicated magic, seemingly built on different principles than what I had used against the undead warriors and the wolf.

The chapel was lit only by a few candles. Most of the children were asleep, curled up in heaps like puppies on the stone floor. Their shoes were worn to ribbons. "The poor little things," said Cyrus, as sympathetic as though it hadn't been his own piping that had brought them here. "They must be exhausted!"

The few who were awake seemed unable to hear or see us. I spotted the Princess Margareta, who must be the oldest person there, sitting with two very small children on her knees.

Margareta's slightly squeaky voice was loud in the ruined chapel. "And of course the children were frightened in the dark house," she said in the voice of a storyteller. "But they would have been much happier if they had only known that, just a few miles away, a brave knight was on his way to rescue them!"

Nobody was going to rescue these children unless I found a way through this barrier. I looked toward Theodora, wondering if she might have a possible approach with her witch-magic, but she was still trying to spot Antonia.

"The brave knight was very handsome and very strong," Margareta continued. "He had blond hair and green eyes, and he rode a red roan stallion." I caught Paul's eye; his jaw was set in angry determination.

"But did he *rescue* the children?" piped up the little boy on her lap.

"Of course. I'm just coming to that part."

Theodora put a hand on my arm. "There she is."

Antonia was on the far side of the room, sitting up

talking to an older boy and drawing a horned figure on the wall with a piece of chalk. We hurried around to be closer. "You see, you really can't be *friends* with a demon," she was saying seriously. "My wizard has a book that tells all about demons. So therefore the Dog-Man must either be a very bad person—though I don't think he is—or else in big trouble."

Cyrus giggled beside me. "What a sweet little girl, Daimbert! Big trouble! You'll have to teach her magic—and a little more accurate demonology—when she gets older." He turned to Theodora. "But now, my dear, I'm afraid we have to get back to those nice chambers I prepared for you."

"No!" I said brusquely. "I'm going to get my daughter free!" And, not caring anymore if it did attract Vlad, I plunged into the forces of magic, trying to find a way to unravel this spell.

"Stop! Stop!" cried Cyrus. "Don't call Vlad's attention to the children now! There's still time to rescue them if—"

He was trying to put a paralysis spell on me, but I really had studied wizardry a lot longer than he had. School magic worked just fine blocking the not-quite-thoroughly understood spells of someone who had only been Vlad's apprentice, learning from him the magic of blood and bone but never completing his studies.

In a few seconds I had Cyrus tied up in a binding spell. "Now!" I said firmly. "That should keep you from interfering any more while I find out how Vlad put this invisible wall together and take it apart again."

Cyrus looked desperate. "Don't do it, Daimbert. I'm serious! If you start dismantling Vlad's spells he's bound to notice. Don't you know what he plans to do with the children—doubtless starting with *your* daughter? I've got him practicing weather spells all night, but you and I have to work together in the meantime on a plan to free these children. Let's go back to those comfortable rooms where Vlad won't even find us! We can plan there."

I had stopped to listen to him, but now I started on magic again. This was an arcane, highly convoluted spell and might take a while. "I can't wait any longer, Cyrus. I can't trust the man who kidnapped my daughter to help set her free."

"But how will I make restitution for capturing the children if you don't give me a chance to release them?" His mouth was pulled into a grimace. "Don't make me do this, Daimbert! I know you think you're going to help them, but you're putting their lives in immediate danger! I've stopped asking the demon for his help, but I'll do it again if it's the only way I can stop you from hurting the children." He dropped his eyes. "Amen, ever and forever, glory the and power the and kingdom the is thine—"

"Stop," I said harshly. "All right. Let's go back. You've made your point." He didn't even have to say the whole Lord's Prayer backwards. The demon would come aid him with only a single mental call. I sniffed but smelled no brimstone—yet.

Nothing, I thought bitterly, would do any good at this point. Vlad might hold off whatever plans he had for the children for a few hours yet, but as soon as Cyrus and I figured out a way to free them—assuming we could, and assuming I could trust Cyrus's assistance—he would be on us. I broke the binding spell that held him.

"This is much better, Daimbert," said Cyrus, rubbing his arms to restore circulation. He started back down the passageway, and Theodora took my arm, her amethyst eyes sober, as we followed. "I realize," Cyrus said gaily over his shoulder, "that wizards always have trouble working with those who follow the path of true religion, but you and I should be able to manage!"

I turned for what might be my last glimpse of my daughter. Antonia had again taken her colored chalk out of her pocket—the same chalk the bishop had given her a few weeks ago, I thought—and was drawing something else on the floor, to the evident interest of the boy with her. "And so they were rescued," came Princess Margareta's voice. "There! Wasn't that a good story?"

Paul, I could see, could hardly contain himself. Cyrus and I, back in the chambers the demon had provided us, became involved in a rather desultory discussion of magic and whether it was possible to break Vlad's spell from here, where theoretically Vlad would not spot us at work. There didn't seem to be any way. The king, on the other hand, was ready to act, to act *now,* to start on a bold plan to rescue us and a hundred children, and waiting for something to happen was not an acceptable alternative.

The women, exhausted by fear and the long night, huddled together, half-dozing, but after a while I looked up to see Justinia slowly rise. She met my eyes for a second, put her finger on her lips in silent warning to Paul, who had also glanced toward her, and advanced toward Cyrus.

"If there isn't a way to dismantle the barrier without Vlad noticing," he was saying, "maybe we'll just have to give him even more to think about than the thunderstorm."

Again, while discussing strategy and spell structure he had become, at least for the moment, disconcertingly sane. "Could you come up with a diversion to make him think this castle is under attack?" he continued. "Illusion won't do, I'm afraid. And I'm also afraid I used my whole supply of spell bones attacking *your* castle." He gave a chuckle. "But almost any commotion might work if it was over on the far side of the castle. Your manservant," meaning Paul, "seems to know this castle, so he can guide you. If you could try something, then in the meantime I—"

He noticed Justinia then. Her long black hair, damp and uncombed but still magnificent, swung over her shoulder as she came closer, hands on shapely hips. "I have not yet had a chance," she said with a slow smile, "to thank thee for saving us all from Vlad."

Cyrus was even more startled than I was. "Well, you're welcome," he said, flustered. "I'm glad you're starting to trust me at last." In a moment he recovered his composure and leaned suavely back, a gratified-but-humble expression on his face.

"Perhaps," Justinia continued, her head tilted sideways, "thou and I might step into one of these other rooms and I could thank thee more personally."

What could she be planning? To distract him from everything around him just long enough for Paul to stick a knife into him? The king, standing in the background twitching with readiness, seemed to think so.

"Well, my lady, you seem to be making a very attractive offer," said Cyrus, blushing a little, "but at the moment Daimbert and I are busy planning our strategy, and you should also know that I am in training to become a priest."

Before Justinia could make her offer of thanks even more attractive, the entire castle shuddered. There was a clang, as though from an unimaginably huge bell, and the castle shuddered again. All around us we could hear falling stone, as half-ruined walls and roofs subsided further. But the distant sounds of falling seemed to take place in the heart of a strange and eerie silence.

"What—" cried Cyrus, but his words were cut off. The fire, the fireplace itself, the couches and tapestries were abruptly gone. Cyrus and I smacked to the stone floor from the chairs on which we had just been sitting but which no longer existed.

He jumped up, looking wildly around a room now as bleak and bare as the one where Vlad had originally put us. Only one candle still burned—the rest had been upended. I reached wildly for Theodora, my heart pounding horribly, as raw, unfocused terror poured through the room.

"The storm!" cried Cyrus. "The storm!" That explained the strange silence. The thunder and the lash of rain had abruptly stopped, though the night was just as dark.

Panting hard, Cyrus started mumbling, too low and too fast for me to follow though it sounded like the Hidden Language. Nothing happened.

"My demon!" he cried in heartbroken despair. "My demon is gone!"

"Then let's *go!*" cried Paul, jerking the now-rotten door open.

I sprang in front of him. The primeval terror I felt made it seem that a demon had just arrived, not gone, but I would try to understand that later. "Wait, Paul! It's the demon's magic that has protected us from Vlad!"

That demon's thunderstorm and comfortable room had disappeared, and it was no longer answering calls from Cyrus. Vlad, suddenly not tied up with weather spells and able now to spot us with his magic, would be on us at once.

"Then it has also protected the children!" the king shot back. "We have to get to them before Vlad does!"

Theodora evidently agreed with him, for she grabbed my hand to pull me along. Cyrus glanced up from the floor and appeared to decide at the last second to accompany us. I thought briefly of binding him again and leaving him behind, but it wasn't worth it. If he'd been abandoned by his demonic helper, all he had left was an irretrievably lost soul.

I tried a spell of light as we hurried out into the corridor, but it still didn't work. The demonic spells were broken, but Vlad's magic seemed to be operating fine. "This way," said Paul, running down the broad stairs with the candle in his hand, the rest of us hurrying to keep up. Cyrus, at the rear, had begun sobbing uncontrollably.

"I am exceeding glad," muttered Justinia beside me, "that this distraction came before rather than after I had to kiss him."

Down the first corridor, through an open-roofed chamber where heavy clouds, no longer raining, hung overhead, down another passageway, Paul led us at a trot. He was right. Without a demon's supernatural power hiding us from Vlad, that wizard would know at once that we had eluded his capture. He would also know that I had been trying to tamper with his spell that kept the children imprisoned and would guess that torturing them, especially when he found out which was my daughter, would make me grant him anything he wanted far faster than torturing *me*.

But *what* could have happened to the demon? Could—and for a second I felt wild hope—this mean that the bishop had arrived and overcome it?

I shook my head even as I ran. Even Joachim wouldn't be able to make a demon obey him. Humans had been given free will in this world, which meant that saints and angels were very unlikely to step in and dispose of demons that humans had summoned.

Might Vlad have somehow caught the demon and imprisoned it in a pentagram? It was ironic, I thought, hurrying across an open area where I looked in all the shadows for Vlad, that I didn't know whether that wizard might protect us from the demon or the demon from him. But if Vlad had caught the demon, it had been done extremely rapidly. According to the *Diplomatica Diabolica* it might take days even for demonology experts to capture and imprison a demon someone else had summoned. The quick way required negotiations—in hell's currency of human souls.

And when I delicately probed with magic I could still sense—in the second before my mind drew convulsively back—the black evil of an active demon lurking somewhere in the ruined castle below us.

We reached the old secret stair in the wall, squeezed in, and started down. The candle flame flared wildly as we groped our way.

Except that we were suddenly not standing on broken steps but on air.

V

We all grabbed at each other, and the candle smashed and went out. But it too lay on what appeared to be solid air. My shoulder touched what felt like stone, yet my straining eyes saw no stone. All around us was a gray dimness, and the ruined castle, the stairs, the stones, and the eyeless windows, no longer seemed there.

"Cyrus?" I began fiercely.

He had been ranting to himself as we came down the narrow staircase, but he now paused and looked around. "Vlad knows where we are," he said in desolation. "And he's made the castle invisible from the inside as well as from the outside."

This went *far* beyond any capabilities of mine. At least, I thought grimly, keeping such a powerful spell operational would require an active mind; this wasn't the kind of spell you could set up and then walk away from. Maybe his own magic would distract him for the moment from catching us.

"How do we get down to where the children are, Cyrus?" I demanded urgently. "You know the way—take us there, invisible or not."

But he had begun to babble, swaying on an invisible step, looking wildly at the empty drop beneath his feet to the cliffs.

"Don't look at it," said Gwennie suddenly. "Close your eyes. It's no worse than going into the storeroom for something and not bothering with a light. Paul, you know where the children are. Keep on going."

He gave her a quick grin. "You're better at this than I am. Hold my hand. Down to the bottom of the staircase, over that pile of stones—we'll have to do it by feel—and then turn left."

Our progress, already terror-ridden, now became a nightmare. Unable to see where we were, we groped by feel down invisible passageways, moving what felt incredibly slowly as Paul tried to recreate in his mind what he had seen both on earlier exploring jaunts and on our previous trip to the ruined chapel. Cyrus was no use at all. I tried it both ways, keeping my eyes squeezed tight shut and leaving them open. Neither seemed to work, especially as with every step we seemed closer to raw evil and to despair. The sky above, I noticed, was moving toward dawn at last, but Vlad's cloud cover kept growing thicker, to keep any sunlight from reaching him.

I stopped abruptly, causing Cyrus to smack into me from the rear, but I hardly noticed. "Paul, wait," I said desperately. "We're going in the wrong direction. You aren't taking us to the chapel. You're taking us down to the storage cellars."

He looked back at me. "This is right," he said quietly but firmly.

"Don't you smell it?" I cried. Faint on the air before us was a whiff of brimstone.

And then, as suddenly as it had come it was gone again. The demon coming up for a quick peek? But he seemed to have abandoned Cyrus and all the spells he had been helping him with. I shook my head. "I'm sorry, Paul. Keep going."

We crept onward. The king was leading more and more slowly now, stopping at every intersection to grope, to pace off distances, to consider whether to turn or continue straight. I listened, both with my ears and with magic, for either children's voices or Vlad's footsteps, but heard nothing but our own breathing. He had not come after us at once, not even to get revenge on his own pupil who had so recently tried to thwart his magic. That meant— I didn't want to think what it meant, but I feared the logical conclusion was that he was starting with the children.

"Wait," said Paul, so quietly I hardly heard him. He stood facing an invisible wall, feeling along it in both directions with his hands. "There's supposed to be a door right here, into the last passageway that goes to the chapel. I can't find it."

Then we had taken a wrong turning someplace, I thought. "Back the way we just came?" I suggested.

Paul shook his head. "No, this should be it. I know that last turning was right. Unless—" We all waited. Fatigue and the strain made the king's face hard and tight in the dim predawn light. He did not curse, he did not shout at Cyrus, who should have at least as good an idea as he did where we were. Instead he said after a moment, "Wait for me. Let me retrace our steps just a little way—"

And abruptly the castle was back. We stood in a dark, enclosed passageway, without even a night sky above us. The solid rocks under our hands were no longer invisible.

Without even thinking I tried a spell of light. And it

worked. The corridor lit up for a few seconds as bright as day.

"Ha!" cried Paul, the tension gone from his face. "I knew I was right! I'd just forgotten we had to turn left and walk twenty feet along this arcading first. Come on! We're almost there."

Spells of light were too hard to keep going constantly; a flare would glow for only a few seconds unless there was something to burn. In the dark again, our eyes too dazzled to see at all, we followed Paul as quickly as we dared.

Cyrus's hand closed around my shoulder. "How did you *do* that? Vlad spelled this castle against the magic of light!"

"I don't know," I said truthfully. Vlad had also made it invisible just a short time before. Were he and the demon engaged in some gigantic clash that had diverted both their attentions?

"And down here to the chapel," the king called back cheerily. "I think I may see some light at the end of the passage— perhaps the children have lit a bonfire?"

But Vlad, if he had truly overcome the demon, would have had plenty of time to reach the ruined chapel before us. I had no idea what might be happening, but that did not keep my mind from churning out terrifying possibilities.

We stumbled forward, almost running. Paul, in the lead, tripped and hit the floor hard. "Watch it," he gasped, waiting to catch his breath before even trying to sit up, "there's something big and damp in the middle of the passage."

A pool of blood? I cast another spell of light to see for a moment. Sitting in the middle of the passageway, looking at us with mournful eyes, was an enormous green frog.

I lifted it slowly, staring in disbelief as my magical

light faded. "Ugh!" cried Justinia. "How did it arrive here? Put it down, Wizard!"

But I did not put it down. I turned it slowly, probing with magic now. The frog was held by a transformation spell that trembled just over the line into success. The transmogrified creature was strangely misshapen, and something was wrong with its eyes. "Daimbert?" asked Theodora quietly.

"Sweet Jesus," I said at last. "I think it's Vlad."

I stuffed the frog into my jacket pocket; I would have to strengthen the spell that held him, but it would do for the moment and even more urgent things demanded my attention. Squaring my shoulders I pushed ahead of Paul, down the passage toward the chapel. Whatever was there, I thought a wizard ought to see it first.

As I came cautiously nearer, I too saw the light that Paul had thought might come from a bonfire. But the chapel itself at the end of the passage appeared completely dark other than that ghastly orange glow. The light did not flicker. Vlad kicked in my pocket, but this wasn't his magic; as a frog, he wouldn't be able to shape the words of the Hidden Language. This was something far more powerful—and even worse—than anything of his.

Panting as from a long run, I reached the doorway and stopped, holding on to the doorframe with both hands. The chapel was very quiet except for the sound of one small person sobbing. My heart suddenly felt as though it had been crushed inside my chest, for that voice was Antonia's.

In the center of the chapel were two pentagrams, drawn with colored chalk. One of the pentagrams was empty, though a little yellow brimstone floated in the air over it. Glowing bright red in the middle of the other was a being with curved horns, an enormous bloated belly, two writhing snakes for legs, and eyes that burned with real flames.

The demon smiled, revealing twice as many teeth even as Vlad, a smile suggesting that we were old friends and he was delighted to see me again.

When I stopped dead in the doorway Paul and Theodora, behind me, first tried to push forward, then froze themselves. "May God be merciful," murmured Justinia in horror.

But the sobbing continued. The pentagram was closed, I saw, holding the demon trapped. Theodora, Paul, and I wrenched ourselves from the doorframe and sprang forward. It was one of the hardest things I had ever done.

The demon turned avidly to follow our progress. I didn't like the way he looked at me—meeting Vlad had already been one reunion too many with an old enemy—but I averted my eyes for something far more important. On the far side of the pentagram, chalk clutched desperately in one small hand, sat Antonia.

Theodora and I nearly ripped her in half as we both snatched her up. Somehow we managed on the second try. The chalk dropped from her fingers to roll away into darkness. The demon continued watching but had not spoken; maybe he couldn't while trapped unless addressed by the person who had summoned him.

I saw then, all around, the still forms of the other children. Dead? I thought, my insides going to ice. But they were breathing, rapidly and shallowly, but breathing.

"Gwennie!" called Paul, his voice an octave too high. "We've got to get these kids out of here!"

She might not have entered a room with a staring demon in the center for anyone else, but she did for the king. She ran toward him, gasping for breath. Theodora and I, selfishly ignoring any child but our own, carried Antonia back up the passage as fast as we could go, but behind us I heard Paul say, "Just grab as many as you can. We've got to get them away from here. Justinia! Cyrus!" I didn't wait to see if the others obeyed.

Antonia stopped sobbing as soon as we were out of the chapel, but she clung to me like a burr, her face in my beard. Now that we could see the castle again, we were quickly able to reach a window and collapse with real light, the light of a summer's early dawn, breaking through. The heavy clouds that Vlad had summoned were now dissipating and rolling away.

Gently I pried Antonia's hands out of my beard and turned her around. Her face was filthy and streaked with tears, but she managed half a smile for us. "I'm sorry if I scared you," she said.

Theodora started crying herself, kissing her hard. "We *were* scared, dearest," she murmured, "but it wasn't your fault. We're just so happy to find you alive and well. Could you tell us—tell us what happened back there in the chapel?"

"I didn't think it would be so awful," said Antonia, squirming around to get comfortable on her mother's lap. "Your book should have explained it better, Wizard." Suddenly she looked very pleased with herself. "But when everybody else fainted I didn't. And I saved the Dog-Man."

"What, exactly, did you do?" I asked, very quietly and afraid I already knew the answer.

"The Dog-Man made us all follow him," she said, enjoying having two adults follow her every word with rapt interest. "I didn't like that. It was as though we were rats! And we got *so* tired and he hardly would let us rest. But then he said he had a demon for a friend, and I started thinking. You have that one big book that tells all about demons, though Elerius didn't want me to read it. And my friend the bishop told me that demons make people do bad things. So I knew that the demon wasn't really his friend at all and had made him whistle his magic pipes at us. That's when I decided to get the demon away from him."

"All right," I said slowly and carefully. "I agree, the demon was responsible for bringing you here. But Antonia, could you explain to us how you managed to *capture* the demon? There are masters at the school who can't do it as easily as you just did."

"That wasn't *his* demon you saw," said Antonia complacently. "His demon is back in hell. That was mine."

Theodora and I exchanged stunned glances. "Just— Just tell us," I said, when I had my voice working again, "tell us what happened, starting when all of you reached the castle."

Antonia settled back, yawning and smiling at the same time. She was, I saw, totally exhausted, but she didn't want to go to sleep while there was anything exciting going on. "We were very, *very* tired by the time we got here," she said. "And the Dog-Man took us to the room where you found us. Then another man came and stared at us. Or do you think he might have been another demon?" she asked thoughtfully. "He looked like he wanted to hurt us, though he didn't try anything then. But the Dog-Man kept trying to push him back out of the room, and his eyes didn't look like real eyes."

"He was human, all right," I said. "Go on." As I spoke, I felt in my pocket for Vlad. Not there. He must have fallen or hopped away while Theodora and I were getting Antonia out of the chapel. For that matter, I wasn't entirely sure how he had become a frog in the first place. Could Antonia possibly have transformed him? But that was unlikely; it would be very hard to put a spell on a wizard that powerful.

It didn't matter, I tried to reassure myself, who had transformed him and where he was now. A quick magical probe didn't find him, but my probes weren't set up to find amphibians. He shouldn't be able to break a transformations spell himself, even a somewhat weak one, while he was a frog, and Cyrus was unlikely to break it for him. I'd catch him later.

"After we were left alone almost everybody went to sleep. Maybe I did myself for a while," Antonia added reluctantly. "But when I woke up I started thinking. I wanted to save the Dog-Man because I knew he was in big trouble, and I thought if there wasn't a demon around pretending to be his friend, maybe he would take us all home. But I didn't know how to catch a demon—that part of your book is *hard*. So I imp—imperv—"

"Improvised?"

She shot me a smile. Her sapphire eyes were still bright but her lids were drifting shut. "I remembered the way the book told to draw things in chalk and say magic words to call a demon from hell. I thought maybe because there was already one so close they'd just send *him*, the Dog-Man's demon, into my pentagram." She managed the word on the first try and looked pleased. "But they didn't. That was the part where everybody fainted except me."

When the masters had summoned a *very* small demon, just to show how it was done, in demonology class at the school, several wizardry students twenty years older than Antonia had fainted.

"They sent this different demon," she said around a long yawn. "And he's *really* scary. I didn't want to cry because I'm a big girl, but I couldn't help it. He asked me what he could do for me, and I told him to catch the other demon and make him go back to hell. He tried to argue with me but I told him he had to obey because I was 'Mistress of the Pentagrams.' Doesn't that sound good?"

And with that she fell asleep in Theodora's lap, her eyes shut tight and mouth slightly open. We sat still for several minutes, hardly breathing. Theodora spoke at last.

"God in Heaven, Daimbert. Our daughter has just sold her soul to the devil."

PART EIGHT

Demons

I

I scrambled to my feet. This all had to be a mistake. A mistake! I stopped myself just in time from driving my fist against the stone wall. Of course she *had* summoned a demon, and asked it for favors, a process that both wizardry and religion agreed led to eternal damnation. But she was only five years old!

Unlike Cyrus, she'd had the sense to keep it imprisoned in a pentagram rather than letting it run around loose. But that reminded me. There must still be unconscious children in the room with it, awash in the terror beyond terror of death which flowed from a demon, even an imprisoned one.

I hurried back to find that Paul and Gwennie so far had been able to shift about two dozen of the children. I needed to do something, *anything*, even worse than the king did. A demon, even an enormous horned demon who kept giving me a knowing smile, was not the most terrifying thing I could imagine. Lifting limp boys and girls with magic—I could manage five or six at once—and carrying them away from the chapel was an excellent alternative to dissecting Cyrus bone by bone and nerve by nerve.

He sat huddled in a corner by the arcading, his hands over his head, and Justinia, sitting a dozen yards from him, seemed to have given up trying, but Gwennie and the king kept grimly running up and down the passageway. She was strong and could easily carry two children at a time. Theodora settled Antonia in a corner and came to help.

The others made wide detours around the demon, but I, running with my head down, didn't care—until my foot skidded and almost slid across the chalk line, which would by breaking the pentagram have let the demon out.

I wiped cold sweat from my forehead with a damp sleeve. All the things they had taught us in demonology class came rushing back. Someone who has sold his soul is even more dangerous to those around him than someone who has damned himself through ordinary sins. Cyrus had barely begun. First the demon fills a person with anger and bitterness, then offers spectacular ways to harm those with whom he imagines he is angry. And why worry about a few murders? His soul is already long gone.

And, if the demon is loose and able to work his own tricks, the situation only grows worse.

The children started to revive once they were away from the chapel. One little boy opened his eyes to find himself in Paul's arms and asked with delighted surprise, "Are you the brave knight?"

"I guess I'd better be," he said with a grin, ruffling the boy's hair for a minute before putting him down and starting back for more.

In ten minutes we had them all spread out in the arcade, well away from the passage that led to the chapel. The king flopped to the floor and leaned back against the wall. He reached up with one hand to pull Gwennie down beside him. Her face was running with sweat and looked exhausted, terrified, and grimly satisfied. "You've always been the best friend I've ever had," Paul said, meaning it. He gave her a hard hug as she settled herself on the floor, with no more romantic passion in it than the dozens of hugs he had just been giving children. "Once we're home I'm changing your title from acting castle constable to permanent constable. When you told me you thought you could handle the duties, did you ever expect them to include facing a demon?"

We caught our breaths for a minute. All a big mistake, I told myself again. Baptized children went straight to heaven, as long as they had not yet reached the age of reason and therefore could not commit intentional sin. Didn't they? What *was* the age of reason? Seven for sure. Yes, that was right. Seven. Antonia was only five.

Did demons recognize how old a person was in human years, or did they ask only if they had functioning reasoning abilities—if, for example, they could read and work magic?

"When I was little," said Paul, "I always thought it would be exciting to meet a demon. Now that I have met one, I can't say I particularly care to repeat the experience. Did you see that belly? Those *eyes*? But I do remember learning about pentagrams. Looks like your daughter, Wizard, must have drawn a pentagram to imprison it—she's an amazing little girl, and you have *no* reason at all to hide her. One of her chalk lines, I couldn't help noticing, looked scuffed, but it was redrawn carefully. And the demon appears pretty well trapped now."

"Yes," I said reluctantly. "It can't move away or hide, and it can't make itself invisible. As long as no one lets it out, it shouldn't be able to do anything to terrify us, such as bringing more vipers and apparitions."

"Oh, I'm terrified quite enough already, if it asks," said Paul cheerfully. "But it looks like we've won, then!

Cyrus seems to have broken down completely without his demon to help him," with a glance in his direction, "and Vlad's a frog, so once it's a little lighter outside one of us can fly the carpet back to Caelrhon and tell the parents all their children are safe."

That reminded me. I had better try to find Vlad again.

"And I guess sending the demon back to hell is something you wizards know how to do," Paul continued lightly. He looked around at children starting to sit up groggily, many of them apparently deciding the whole episode had been a nightmare and lying down to sleep again. The Princess Margareta was awake but lay silently, as though trying to make it all make sense in her own mind.

"Maybe Mother has a point," the king went on. "If I got married *I* could have children. Maybe not a hundred. Say, a dozen or so. Wouldn't that be great, to have a dozen little princes and princesses running around the castle?"

"You'd better consult your queen on that." Gwennie managed to say it as a joke. Margareta, looking startled, rose on her elbows.

Paul laughed without seeming to notice either's reaction. For him, all our troubles were over rather than just beginning. "All right. Maybe I'll settle for three or four. Too bad I don't have any brothers or sisters of my own, or I could have nieces and nephews. And if the duchess's daughters aren't going to marry—" He stopped. "That reminds me, Wizard. Is Celia a novice nun now?"

I had completely forgotten about the twins since leaving them at the nunnery. "I suppose so. They would have had to finish the ceremony without a spiritual sponsor."

"I'll ride down there in a few days," said Paul lazily. "They probably won't let me see her, but at least I can find out if everything is going smoothly. I was looking through some old ledgers—thanks again, Gwennie, by the way, for helping me find them—and it looks as though previous kings of Yurt sometimes made gifts to the nunnery, so maybe I should too."

Suddenly, unexpectedly, a voice floated through the window. "Hello!" It sounded magically amplified. "Is anyone there?"

I knew that voice. I jumped up so fast I almost slipped and leaped to the window. Outside, hovering somewhat tentatively in midair, were two wizards, one black-bearded and one with a red bandit's beard: Elerius and Evrard.

Paul joined me at the window and waved enthusiastically. "What's that older wizard's name, Elerius, is that right?" he asked me with a low chuckle. "It seems like he's always showing up just a few minutes too late, just after you've finished disposing of the enemy. You're going to make him jealous at this rate, Wizard!"

I didn't have the heart to tell him how wrong he was.

"We'd been combing Caelrhon almost inch by inch for any sign of you and the children," said Evrard. "At first Elerius"—with a nod toward the other wizard—"was able to pick up the remnants of the tracer spell you'd put on the flying carpet earlier this summer, but the spell disappeared as we came upriver. And we could have sworn this castle wasn't even here!"

Elerius meanwhile was introducing himself to Theodora. They had spoken on the telephone but never actually met. "So this is the witch of Caelrhon," said Elerius pleasantly, regarding her from under peaked eyebrows, "for whom Daimbert has been willing to flout all the traditions of wizardry."

"But about half an hour ago," said Evrard, continuing his story, "Elerius said he could sense a major spell breaking up somewhere in this direction. And as we approached a ruined castle suddenly materialized before us, towers, battlements, and all!" His cheerful blue eyes looked concerned for a moment. "And there wasn't much question about the presence of the supernatural. . . ."

I flew down to the base of the cliffs to retrieve the carpet, and Paul and Gwennie began loading children. Justinia, with no desire whatsoever to stay in this castle, agreed to pilot it back to Caelrhon. "We should be able to take them all in three or four trips," said Paul. "Princess Margareta had better be in the first group, or it could provoke an international incident!" He laughed at his own humor. "Yes, that's right," to one of the children. "You'll be back with your mother very soon."

"So the demon's already trapped in a pentagram, I gather," said Elerius, looking at me thoughtfully. "That certainly saves the hard magic of chasing it around the castle. We won't need the demonology experts from the school; the person who summoned it can just send it back." He waited expectantly.

The first carpetload of children took off, awake and laughing now. The king and Gwennie accompanied them, while Theodora stayed with the rest. Antonia was still asleep, curled up on the hard stone floor with her chestnut hair loose across her face.

I turned back to see Elerius still looking at me. I realized slowly that he was wondering just how desperate I had been to rescue her. Evrard himself was just working out that I even *had* a daughter and seemed shocked— at least in part, I thought, because everyone here but he seemed to know about it.

I took a deep breath. This was going to take all the wizardry we knew between us. "I didn't summon the demon myself," I said, not mentioning that in only slightly different circumstances I might have. I went on to tell them how Cyrus had long been working with a demon, ever since his apprenticeship days in the eastern kingdoms with Vlad—who I still hadn't found—and how Antonia had decided the easiest way to save him from it and to get all the children rescued was to summon a demon herself.

"What did you say she was, five?" said Evrard. "Too young to have to worry about her soul, then. Pretty sharp move, Daimbert!" giving me a punch on the shoulder as though it had all been my idea. "Let's wake her up and have her return it to hell. If she could lisp out the words to call it she should be able to send it back all right."

Elerius had known Antonia; Evrard had not. The former had the good taste not to take for granted that there was no problem. He gave me a long, sober look from his tawny hazel eyes. "I swear on all the powers of magic, Daimbert," he said quietly, "I did not teach her any demonology."

Evrard looked back and forth between us, realizing there was more going on than he realized. I shook my head. "I didn't think you had. That's not what's bothering me."

Elerius nodded slowly. "If someone has sold his or her soul, the only chance to get it back is through negotiation, before rather than after the demon returns to hell."

Evrard wrinkled his forehead in surprise. "Aren't the two of you getting a little overexcited here? Wizardry doesn't worry about people's souls. And even if she *didn't* get off for being so young, she'd still have seventy years or so to worry about it. And—"

Before he had a chance to tell me reassuringly that she would probably damn herself a dozen different ways in the next seventy years anyway, Evrard found himself propelled backwards hard and fast through the air. He hit the wall and subsided slowly.

"All right, all right, I get the hint," he said good-naturedly.

"Daimbert!" said Theodora, who had been following our conversation from a little distance away.

But that hadn't been my magic. That had been Elerius.

We sat quietly, close together, our eyes locked. "Why are you doing this?" I asked. "Why are you trying to help me?" In part I realized I was stalling; as long as Antonia was asleep, as long as the demon down in the ruined chapel was imprisoned in the pentagram, things could not get any worse than they already were. But in part I wanted to understand.

"We all take oaths to help humanity," he said slowly. "A little girl is part of humanity. But there is of course more, Daimbert, as you and I know. If we called the school, the demonology experts would doubtless tell us that the theoretical danger to a girl's soul, a danger they would have to discuss with the priests to assess properly—which they have no intention of doing—is nothing compared to the very real danger of a demon loose in the world. Back to hell with it at once, the school's masters would tell us, before it breaks out of the pentagram, and if one girl is sacrificed it's still worth it."

The castle was quiet around us. The children dozed again while waiting, and the only sounds came from Cyrus, who sat a short distance from us, his head in his hands and muttering. Evrard and Theodora were listening but could have been miles away. "That sounds like the kind of logic that would appeal to you, Elerius," I said. "You always claim to be working for the greater good of humanity, even if a few standards or a few people have to be sacrificed along the way."

He was not insulted. "I am speaking openly, Daimbert. I know perfectly well that in trying to help Antonia—

and she *is* a delightful little girl, one that anyone of any sensitivity would want to help—I am not following the school's standards. But there is a higher good here. I have spoken to you of this before. Someday, probably sooner than they think, the masters of the school will have to step aside for younger leadership. It's no secret that everyone assumes—including me—that I shall be part of that leadership. And when that time comes I will want your help."

I looked away, not able to meet his calculating gaze any longer. "You said all this once before, but I would have thought it would be clear now that I could never join the school faculty. They don't want wizards who have families."

"Because such a wizard would let his judgment be swayed by personal considerations?" said Elerius with half a smile. "It is a good policy, but I may have to make an exception here. Certainly I will not now tell the school what you yourself have managed remarkably well to keep hidden from them. By the time I assume the leadership I will be in a position to make my own rules. I don't know what it is about you, Daimbert. Your grasp of academic magic is scarcely better than Evrard's"—the redheaded wizard cringed—"and yet somehow you are always in the right place at the right time."

I seemed at the moment to be in the wrong place at entirely the wrong time, but I didn't interrupt.

"And you have imagination and a flair for improvisation, and you have a daughter who knows more magic at five than most first-year wizardry students—someone who, if she is not perverted by a demon, could be very useful to organized wizardry herself when just a little older. Yet you have always been suspicious of me. Call this calculation if you like, but I want your friendship. Trying to save Antonia is but a small price to pay for that friendship."

I was not quite persuaded yet. "You realize," I said slowly, "that if these negotiations go the way I think they may, I won't even be around to help you in your plans and projects."

"That is why you need me now, Daimbert: another wizard to give you a chance to get both of you out of this alive. Unless your mistrust of me weighs heavier than your fears for Antonia?"

"I'd deal with the devil himself to save her," I said, looking at him quickly and then away. "And it looks as though I will."

We woke Antonia gently. She didn't want to wake up and kept digging her knuckles into her eyes and trying to turn away from the light. But when she spotted Elerius she sat up in my lap and gave him a broad smile. "I remembered everything you taught me about frogs," she said with enthusiasm.

I myself had nearly been forced to leave the wizards' school because of all my trouble with those frogs in Zahlfast's transformations practical. She had to get this ability from Theodora.

"So that was you who turned the man into a frog?" Elerius asked. We had sent Evrard off to scour the castle for Vlad.

"That's right. He really was a bad man. After I'd summoned the demon he came running into the room where we all were, very excited. I think he was looking for the Dog-Man. He had been very quiet and pretend-polite when I saw him before, so it made me even more scared because he was shouting and threatening— That's when I turned him into a frog." She smiled happily. "I think he was surprised."

"I'm sure he was," said Theodora from across the room. "I still can't do transformations myself." So the Lord knew where she had gotten this ability.

And the devil knew where she would get her next startling abilities if we couldn't reclaim her soul.

"But I want to hear more about how you summoned the demon," said Elerius gently.

Antonia would clearly have preferred to discuss the frog some more, but she reluctantly agreed to provide details. "When he appeared in the pentagram I told him I wanted a dem—a demastr—a *demonstration.* The book said sometimes they would do one for free. And I said for my demonstration he should catch the other demon and make him go back to hell." She laughed. "That's like a joke—demon, demonstration."

"And what did he say?" I said, abruptly hoping against hope. Maybe Evrard was right, and I'd gotten myself all worked up for nothing.

"He said that was too hard to be a demonstration. That's when I told him I was Mistress of the Pentagrams and he had to do it whether he wanted to or not. He did, too," she said, pleased at the memory of wielding such power. "I had to make an opening in the pentagram to let him out, but I told him I only did it if he promised to come right back. I made the second pentagram to hold the demon he caught while I was waiting for them." She sighed. "That was probably the worst part of all, with two demons right there in the room, before the Dog-Man's disappeared and I was able to redraw the line to keep mine in."

Elerius and I exchanged glances. We might be able to persuade the demon to return to hell with no one's soul, to convince him that all of this fell into the category of demonstrating demonic powers before reaching agreement on a soul's sale. I doubted it.

"Don't you think," suggested Antonia, "that now that the Dog-Man doesn't have a demon anymore he'll be happier?" Cyrus was making low whimpering noises at the moment. It was a nice thought on Antonia's part, but it hadn't worked: with the demon back in hell he had simultaneously lost his power to do black magic in this world and any hope for the redemption of his soul in the next.

I stood up, clenched and unclenched my fists, and walked over to Theodora. I had been kissing her for over a minute before she realized that this public display of affection meant that I was saying good-bye.

II

"Should we ask Cyrus for his help?" asked Elerius. "He's certainly had experience dealing with a demon." He paused. "I never have."

We both looked toward Cyrus. The Dog-Man, the miracle-worker with the key to the city of Caelrhon, the failed seminary student, was huddled in on himself: a broken man without the demon who had long accompanied him. "Not unless we think we could pass off his soul in trade," I said in disgust. "But at this point I doubt even the devil would want it if it wasn't long since his."

"You and me, then," said Elerius, and we started down the passage toward the ruined chapel. Antonia reluctantly accompanied us, holding both our hands. Either one of us could have sent the demon back to hell at once since it was already imprisoned in a pentagram, but we needed Antonia to start the conversation if we were going to try to negotiate.

At the last minute Cyrus looked up and rose to slink along behind us, but he had the good sense to stop well short of the chapel. A hundred reasons why it would be much better to put this off struck me, but I kept on walking, teeth tight together to keep them from chattering. Knowing the feeling of raw terror was about to strike made it no easier when it did.

The chapel was pitch black, even though outside the

windows it was now early morning. The only light came
from the demon himself. He was alive, glowing, yet
essentially motionless. Our feet slowed and dragged
as we crossed the room toward the pentagram. Antonia
faced the demon squarely, visibly struggling to keep
from sobbing again. He gave her a wide and evil grin,
as if she were a dainty morsel he was about to consume.

"By Satan, by Beelzebub," she brought out between
trembling lips, and my heart wrenched to hear her have
to say it, "by Lucifer and Mephistopheles."

At these words of summons he abruptly became twice
as alive, twisting in a veil of smoke within the pentagram.
"I am yours to command, Antonia," he said pleasantly—
or his best attempt. "What can I bring you? What
enemies of yours can I destroy?"

"I don't want anything," she said stubbornly, keeping
her eyes on the floor. "But you have to talk to these
wizards."

Not quite the language recommended by the
Diplomatica Diabolica, but it would do. "Quick, get
back to your mother," I whispered, giving her a push.

"But I have to help you, Wizard," she whispered back,
retreating only a short distance. I glanced over my
shoulder and saw Theodora halfway down the corridor
and motioned to her.

But before I could make sure Antonia was well on
her way the demon spoke again. And he spoke to me.

"Daimbert, what a surprise! Are you back to take
me up on some of the offers you rejected last time we
met?"

The final scraps of my courage vanished. Just as I
had feared. Thousands of demons in hell, and Antonia
had summoned this one. Maybe Yurt was his territory
just as it was mine.

The demon fixed me with a malevolent eye. "Before
we begin," he said conversationally in his high voice,

"you'll have to let me out of this pentagram so I can work for you. I can take your soul, of course, if you'd like to hand it over, but I assume you'll want some benefits in return? I thought so. They usually do."

"No 'benefits,' Demon," I said harshly, trying to make myself furious because it was the only alternative to abject terror. "You're staying right there until we've finished negotiating."

"But *I* know someone who would like something from me," said the demon coyly—or as coyly as something red and bulging could manage. "Antonia," he called, "come erase the pentagram, even just a single chalk mark as you did before, and I'll bring you something you'll really like. Haven't you always wanted to see a dragon?"

"A dragon? Really?" She turned and took half a step toward us, then looked fully at the enormous mouth and fiery eyes and raced up the passage toward her mother.

I let my breath out all at once and had trouble catching it again. A good thing this demon didn't have experience trying to be tempting to little girls while trapped inside a pentagram.

"We have come to bargain with you," I said as firmly as I could. "Let us begin with nonbinding conversation." I glanced toward Elerius, wondering when he was going to add something, and saw *him* trembling hard. In some ways that was the most terrifying thing I had seen yet.

"Nonbinding conversation," agreed the demon good-naturedly, showing a remarkable number of pointed teeth. "That way you can ask me for whatever you want without worrying about the results." This was actually not accurate, but the *Diplomatica Diabolica* did make it clear that one was less likely to be tricked by a demon if the conversation had been declared nonbinding.

"You say you want to negotiate," continued the

demon, "but you have, I fear, caught me in a position of weakness." He gestured at the pentagram with an enormous hand. "You see me imprisoned here. If you and all your friends just walked away, I wouldn't be able to play any of my little tricks that seem to annoy you so much, I wouldn't be able to whisper suggestions in Antonia's ear, and, in short, you could forget I even existed! So your coming around talking of negotiations suggests you'd actually like something from the devil but are just too shy to ask."

"Not at all," I said sternly. So far, so good. The temptation to leave him in the ruined chapel and run lasted for only a second. "You know you'd like nothing better than to be left right here." I glanced surreptitiously at the pentagram; it appeared well-drawn, without flaws. "Sooner or later the chalk would wash away, or dry up and blow away, or someone would come exploring the castle and break the chalk lines without realizing the danger. Leaving you here would only postpone the problem—or make it a hundred times worse if we had to chase you and capture you. I'm not going to walk away and leave you here and I'm not going to let you out. And I'm also not going to ask you for favors in this world."

"If you keep on rejecting what I could offer you before I even offer it," said the demon with a flash of fire from his eyes, "you risk getting nothing at all!"

"Fine," I said shortly. "I only want Antonia's safety." The negotiations seemed to have begun. "Now, you claim to want no benefits from me," said the demon, settling himself comfortably in the center of the pentagram, "but you and I both know that's not true. You'd like to be a better wizard, you'd like to find a way to combine marriage to a witch with continued association in organized wizardry—and, oh yes, I don't want to forget, you'd like some assurance that your daughter has not yet 'lost' her soul, as your so-called religion so quaintly puts it." He grinned evilly. "This sounds to me like a lot to expect in return for one soul that's already fairly well stained!"

It was better not to ask how a demon gained knowledge about someone. "You're starting from the wrong assumptions," I said roughly. "I don't want—" I stumbled over the words and started again. "I wouldn't want any of the rest if I only had it because of you. All I want is the assurance that you have given up any hold over Antonia."

"That sweet little girl will make an especially tasty mouthful for the devil," said the demon, licking his lips in anticipation. "Why should I assure you of anything of the sort? After all, she summoned me herself and has already asked for a *very* large favor. Don't tell me you think she's not capable of making her own choices!"

Not yet, she wasn't, I told myself desperately. She was still only five. And that the demon had tried to tempt her further, with an offer to see a dragon, suggested that he had at least some doubts himself.

Either that or he was toying with me.

"You are not entitled to her soul, Demon," I said with as much confidence as I could muster, "and you and I both know it." The room grew slowly but steadily hotter as we talked. "Don't interrupt! Three reasons. First, she is well short of the age of reason, which is seven, and therefore cannot yet damn herself by her own actions. Second, she may have asked a single rather simple favor of you, but it was from the purest motives: she wanted to save another mortal. And third, if she 'sold' her soul to you she didn't get what she wanted in return, for Cyrus is as thoroughly damned as ever."

The demon waved his hand airily. "You ought to know that the reckoning of mortal years means little to us. Do you imagine that a child who plotted and executed the deaths of all his playmates would be safe just because he desisted the day before his seventh birthday? And, as I am sure she will confirm if you ask, she did not actually ask me to 'save' Cyrus, which I would have not done anyway. She only asked me to return another demon to hell."

"*And* she asked for your help only from the purest of motives," I insisted again. "Someone who selflessly gives his life to save another goes straight to heaven. How much more then someone who gives his soul?"

"Nice try, Daimbert," said the demon, showing all his teeth. "But how could the devil take one soul in exchange for another if you claim that the second thereby saved itself? You'll be trying to assert that hell has no claims to *anyone* at this rate."

"She didn't even know she was selling her soul," I said, retreating to a backup position. "Souls are always judged on intention. If you now claim her it is on the merest technicality."

I had nearly forgotten Elerius was there. Concentrating on the demon and on withstanding my own fears left me no time for anything else. When he suddenly spoke I jerked convulsively.

"The protocol between wizardry and demons has always been clear on this point," he said, managing to sound impressively calm and assured. "A soul that might be forfeit, although only on the shakiest grounds, can be redeemed by the offering of a human *life*, not another soul."

"And therefore," I said, fast before my lips could freeze in terror, "I am here to offer my own life in return for Antonia's soul."

Both Elerius and the demon spoke together. "Not you, Daimbert!" Elerius hissed. "I'm trying to give him Vlad."

"Not this bargain again, Daimbert!" said the demon

with a laugh that made his enormous belly shake. "I unwisely agreed to such a bargain with you once long ago, and you managed to wiggle out of it. Did you think I would be so easy to mislead a second time?"

"All right, then," said Elerius briskly. I was for the moment unable to speak, filled both with bitter despair that the one way I hoped I might have to rescue Antonia wasn't going to work, and with a wild, desperate, and shameful relief that I might still live. "We'll offer you another life instead, the life of a wizard right here in the castle."

"Elerius, I'm so pleased to have a chance to meet you at last," said the demon, the flames shooting from his eyes spoiling the effect of his friendly words. The room by now was as hot as a stove. "I can see you'll be much more engaging to deal with than Daimbert, who always seems suicidally bent on throwing away his life. But you do have to understand something first. If you want me to take the life of this wizard-frog in return for the girl— and that *was* what you had in mind, was it not?—then it would have to be his *own* sacrifice. You could if you like give your own soul to the devil by murdering that wizard in cold blood, but if you want to bargain with me there must be less messy ways to do it."

"There are other protocols to turn to in that case," said Elerius, sounding abruptly much less assured.

Both my life and my soul, I thought. I could offer them together for Antonia's release. That might do it. If I was dead as well as damned then I wouldn't need to worry about the evil I would do to all the people I loved for the next two centuries. I found my mouth too dry to speak.

"Unlike Daimbert," said the demon to Elerius, shifting his belly to a more comfortable position, "you have never paid much attention to the prattle of your religion. I'm sure you assume you'll be going to hell in the end anyway, and therefore would be more than willing to gain some spectacular benefits in this world in exchange for a soul that would never have much chance for salvation."

Suppose, because I was trying to save Antonia, the devil thought my motives were too pure and wouldn't accept the bargain, even when I offered body and soul together? I might have to have an additional and entirely impure motive. Maybe I could stipulate murdering Cyrus as part of the agreement: an appealing possibility.

"Do not try to tempt me with talk of benefits, Demon," said Elerius sternly. "We are here to talk about Antonia."

"And I am delighted to do so. Since you seem so concerned about her, why don't we arrange a simple trade, your soul for hers? Now before you start to tell me this is an unequal trade," holding up a huge red hand, "wait until I tell you what *else* I can give you as part of the bargain."

"You cannot give me anything I could not obtain on my own," said Elerius. It came out low and thick.

"Elerius—" I started to say, but he motioned me to silence.

"Don't interrupt," he said in an undertone. "I should be able to negotiate better than you can, because I don't have personal feelings to interfere."

"You wizards must be the most exasperating mortals there can be to deal with," said the demon with an evil chuckle. "Even priests aren't nearly as stubborn, once they get past their initial hesitation. Of *course* there are things you want, Elerius, that you could not obtain without me. To start with, how about the immediate leadership of the wizards' school?"

There was a long pause while I waited for Elerius to answer, and he did not.

So far my knees had been holding up fairly well. Now they started to shake so badly that I had to sit down quickly before I fell.

"The school already has a Master," Elerius brought out at last in a thin, tight voice, completely unlike his normal way of speaking.

"Your choice then. Shall he have a little accident, or will he suddenly decide that failing health makes it necessary for him to step aside?" That was the problem of trying to deal with a demon. He might not know someone's higher thoughts and aspirations, but he knew all too well the dark imaginings and cravings that one tried to hide even from oneself.

"I choose neither one," replied Elerius after only a brief pause, appearing to rally slightly. "I plan to take over the school's direction with my own unaided powers, but not for some years yet."

"You're certainly quick now to reject what you know you've always wanted," said the demon softly. I tried unsuccessfully to speak, but this had nothing to do with me. "Why waste the best years of your life, the years of your greatest strength and mature abilities, waiting for an old man whose only real skill is an unusual ability to prolong his own life? Daimbert, I see, would like to give you an argument, but he'll come around quickly when he realizes that I'll let his daughter have her soul back as part of our bargain."

Elerius ran his tongue along dry lips and barked out a very unconvincing laugh. "If I take over the school it will be to help humanity, not to further your own evil plans. This bargain will not help me at all."

"Just too dismissive," said the demon, shaking his horned head, "that's your problem, just too dismissive of good ideas if they don't accord with your own prejudices. Suppose we add a little rather unusual twist to our agreement? I'll make sure you take over the school at once, but then I'll step aside. I won't try to tempt you further or direct your plans; you'll be able to do all the 'good' you want without my interference. I promise!" He laid a heavy hand over what would have been his heart if he had one.

Dear God, I thought, unable to say anything, shouting mentally at Elerius to refuse at once and getting no response. All the damage a master wizard could do if he had sold his soul flashed through my mind. Between his own powers and the added abilities of black magic, not all the western wizards combined could stand against him. And someone like Elerius, who had always thought that one needed to bend a few rules to reach the final good and justifiable end, would find himself bending more and more rules, and would be quite surprised to find that he was entirely alone in believing that his goals were good.

I had come here intending to find a way to save Antonia. Now it looked like I would have to save Elerius's soul as well—and it was almost too late.

III

There was a small, very serious voice behind us. "Don't listen to him. That's not a real promise. He's not your friend."

Elerius gave a great start as though coming out of a trance. I whirled around, finding my voice again. "Antonia! What are you doing here?"

She buried her face in my shoulder to avoid looking at the demon, who appeared *delighted* to have her back. Her voice was indistinct but confident. "Mother was trying to calm down some of the littlest children," as though she were not one of them. "So I tiptoed away. You didn't hear me coming, did you! I got here just in time."

I looked over at Elerius, still on his feet but swaying. His face was ashen and running with sweat—not just from the heat of the room. He broke his gaze away from the demon and sat down very suddenly. "Thank you, Antonia," he murmured.

"I *told* you that you needed me here to help you," she said, starting to tremble now.

She had tried to help Gwennie and the twins by taking them off on a flying carpet ride, tried to help the Dog-Man by summoning a demon of her own, and really had helped Elerius by showing up when she did. But my stomach knotted as I thought what she might do in the very near future, still convinced she was helping her friends, once the demon's influence began to work fully on her.

"You've— You've negotiated with a demon before, Daimbert?" said Elerius hesitantly. "Somehow I never heard about that."

"I don't think anyone but Zahlfast and the Master ever knew," I said shortly.

"I know all the protocols from the *Diplomatica Diabolica*, of course, and I was aware that one had to beware of temptations, but somehow I had imagined them taking the form of wealth and pliant maidens."

"When you're in charge of the school, Elerius," I said quietly, "be sure the demonology courses make it clearer that power can be the greatest temptation of them all."

"We're *negotiating* here, remember?" interrupted the demon. "If you start talking to each other instead we'll never reach an agreement!"

And maybe we don't want an agreement, I thought, but that idea too was a temptation. Doing nothing would mean Antonia's will slowly turning to evil even while the demon remained imprisoned, and at some point, far in the future or very soon, an escaped demon roaming gleefully through Yurt and Caelrhon.

"You have to come now, Wizard," said Antonia to me. "That's why I sneaked away from Mother, to tell you the people are here."

"The king is back with the flying carpet?" I asked, keeping my face resolutely turned away from the demon.

"Not him. I couldn't tell who they are. But a whole group of people are climbing up to the gate, and I think some of them have swords. You have to come see them."

Just a short delay wouldn't hurt anything, I thought, leaping to my feet. Antonia was right; a group of people arriving unsuspecting at a castle with a demon in it was the last thing we needed. "Come on," I said to Elerius. "Now that we've gotten the initial temptations out of the way, we can continue this negotiation shortly."

"You go ahead, Daimbert," he said, shaking his head. Antonia was tugging now at my hand. "We don't dare leave the demon, even imprisoned inside a pentagram, now that we've started nonbinding conversation. He could talk to anyone who wandered into the room— do you want him asking one of the other children to erase the chalk lines?"

Logically it made sense. But I didn't dare leave him alone. "I'll stay, then. You go with Antonia."

The demon was growing more and more irritated that we weren't paying attention to him, but at the moment I only had eyes for Elerius. "You don't trust me, do you, Daimbert," he said quietly. "At least give me credit for the intelligence to realize the flaw in what he's offering. He's right that I've never worried overly about the eventual fate of my soul, but I really do intend to use my magic to help mankind, and the first thing a demon would do is to make me unable to tell the difference between helping and harming." He managed a grim smile. "And I've always been admired for my wizardly skills; don't you realize how galling it would be to know that my future abilities would not be mine but a demon's?"

"But I have more experience—"

"And are much more likely," commented Elerius dryly,

"to throw away your life and soul together in a reckless effort to save your daughter. Now that I have seen the dangers, I shall attempt what other means might be found."

"I want *you* to come, Wizard," said Antonia to me, tugging harder.

Still I hesitated. "If I leave you here, Elerius," I said slowly, "and I find that you've deluded yourself, like Cyrus, into thinking that you can use a demon's help without it affecting your own judgment and will, then I shall have to kill you: quickly, immediately, before the powers of black magic make you invincible."

Elerius's face had slowly regained its color. "I don't think I'll be in any danger of death from you," he said, managing a smile. I wondered if he meant it as equivocally as it sounded.

"Hurry up!" Antonia cried. "If you don't hurry the people will be here, and if you make Elerius go instead I'll stay here with you."

That decided me. I scooped her up and found myself running flat out up the passage away from the ruined chapel, almost tripping over Cyrus, who was huddled by the door. A voice in the back of my mind asked if this urging from Antonia might be the first sign of the devil's influence, taking me away from where I really ought to be.

It felt so good to be out of the demon's influence, back in cool morning sunlight, seizing a startled Theodora and kissing her again when I thought I had done so for the last time, that I almost didn't care.

Briefly I told her of our progress—or lack of progress—so far and looked out the window. A group of people had left their horses at the base of the cliffs and were climbing up the broken causeway toward the castle's front gate. And with a far-seeing spell I recognized them: Celia and Hildegarde, their parents, and the bishop.

❖   ❖   ❖

For a few minutes I could imagine that everything was going to be all right after all. I flew down and met them outside the gate, telling them immediately that all the children were safe but leaving out, for the moment, any mention of demons.

Prince Ascelin sheathed his sword and slapped me on the shoulder. His face was gray with exhaustion, and all the lines in it had deepened, but he still managed a laugh. "Thought you could slip away without my knowledge, Wizard? You may have wanted to protect me from what you would find here, but it's not so easy when you've got the best tracker in a dozen kingdoms on your trail!"

I managed a smile in return. Let him think I had left him in Yurt out of concern for his safety. In fact, I hadn't thought about him at all, only wanting to get to Caelrhon myself as fast as I could.

"I used to be able to hunt all day and all night— even on foot when everyone else was mounted—without getting this tired," he said, shaking his head ruefully. "Age is the best tracker of all; he gets on your trail and you never lose him. But by now I presume you've captured this Dog-Man and have the children all ready to go home?" he added cheerfully, looking up at the jagged turrets of the castle. "Terrible place, I must say, for children; good thing the twins didn't know about it when they were twelve. It looks like your man used a spell to hide their tracks a lot of the way, but he was going fast and must have had gaps in his spells—plenty there for me to follow."

I looked past him and the duchess to their daughters. "Celia?"

She gave me a grin. She still had all her hair and looked happier and more at peace with herself than she had all summer. "When you abandoned me like that, before I even had a chance to make my maiden vows, what choice did I have but to chase after you?"

"And," put in Hildegarde, "she wanted to help me find Antonia." She, like Ascelin, was wearing a sword.

Joachim stood at the rear, not saying anything. The part of me that wanted to be optimistic thought that bishops dealt with the supernatural every day, so Elerius and I could safely turn the demon over to him.

The part of me that was realistic knew that the aura of the saints around the bishop would so terrify the demon that he would refuse to talk to him at all—maybe retreating back to hell, but if so taking Antonia's soul irretrievably with him.

Before I could say anything to him, I saw past his shoulder a flying dark red shape approaching rapidly: the flying carpet. Justinia dipped it over our heads and Paul and Gwennie waved. "You're just in time to help out!" called the king. "There are a lot of eager parents waiting back in Caelrhon."

The carpet shot in through a broken window high above us. Everyone clattered through the gates and up the stairs to join them. It was *much* easier finding our way through the castle in daylight, and without having to worry about Vlad, than it had been at night, especially with the castle invisible around us.

But it had been, I thought, a cold sweat breaking out down my back, a very long time since Evrard had gone off in search of Vlad. . . .

The duchess went straight up to Justinia. "A pigeon-message arrived in Yurt for you about half an hour after you and the wizard flew off. It looked like it had been transferred a number of times: it was from Xantium."

"Didst thou mark who had sent it?" said Justinia eagerly.

"I did more than that," said the duchess, slightly shamefaced, producing it from her pocket. "I'm afraid

I read it. Well, everyone else who transferred it probably read it too, so why shouldn't I? It's from a mage—I can't pronounce his name—and he says that your grandfather and the Guild have worked out their differences. He's going to come to Yurt himself to accompany you home."

"This is joy and gladness!" cried Justinia.

So, I thought, Vlad wouldn't have gotten anything from the Thieves' Guild for Justinia anyway. There were distinct disadvantages to traveling slowly and only by night: one's information could be seriously out of date.

Antonia ran to greet the twins, and Hildegarde swung her high over her head. "You had everybody worried, you scamp!" she said with a great laugh.

"I know," said Antonia seriously. "I didn't *want* to leave town without telling Mother. But I couldn't help it."

"That even happens to grown-ups sometimes," said Celia, smiling. She turned to Joachim. "Your Holiness, I have been thinking ever since yesterday, when we all left the nunnery so abruptly. I don't really have the vocation to be a nun. What took me there, I now realize, was only despair. Don't think—" she added hastily as though the bishop had been going to interrupt, which he hadn't. "Don't think that I look down on women who want to devote their days to prayer. But I want to help others, not just worry about my own little sins. I intend to serve God but I will have to do so actively in the world."

"Are you certain this is your own decision, my daughter?"

Celia smiled again. "Well, it's certainly not my parents', if that's what you're wondering. You've been with us the whole time, so you know they haven't said anything one way or the other."

"Though I had to bite my tongue more than once," said the duchess with a grin. "And the fact that you're twenty-one now did nothing to stop me. Rather it was the memory of all the things that people used to tell *me* I couldn't do."

"I shall have to write to the abbess," said Celia more seriously. "She was very kind to me. And, Mother, we really ought to give the nunnery *something*. It's not their fault I changed my mind."

Paul and Gwennie were getting a second load of children onto the carpet, with Hildegarde's assistance. Justinia, delightedly reading and rereading the letter from Kaz-alrhun, was no help. Most of the children were awake now, and some of the boys suddenly decided it would be exciting to race off and explore the castle rather than traveling home again, even on a flying carpet. Hildegarde's long reach and her offer to let children who did *not* run off hold her sword stifled an incipient break.

"Maybe I should rethink those dozen children," said Paul to Gwennie, prying loose from his leg a sobbing girl who had been more terrified of the carpet than anything else until she saw Hildegarde's sword. "Even aside from what my queen would think . . ." He looked at her silently a minute. "Though I don't think I'll be getting myself a queen for a while. It's going to take me a very long time to find another woman who could be half as much my friend as you are." He let it hang, still looking at her, then suddenly turned and shouted to some boys, "Sit down again! Don't you know how dangerous it can be to stand up on a flying carpet?" This was a curious comment given that they had, for once, been sitting demurely.

"You realize," the bishop said to Celia, "you still cannot be a priest."

"I thought you would say that," she said soberly. "How about visiting the sick as your representative? How about talking to women who are confused and want spiritual guidance but have good reason to feel uncomfortable around men? How about just sitting very quietly in the back of classes in the seminary?"

Joachim lifted an eyebrow. "You seem to have thought of a number of possibilities. I shall have to give the question of seminary classes some consideration. Many of the students are still trying to reconcile themselves to giving up close association with women. . . . But then they will have to deal with women as well as men through their ministry for the rest of their lives," he added briskly. "Yes. When we are all home again, come talk to me at the cathedral office, and we will see what can be arranged."

Celia kissed his ring with a barely concealed look of glee and hurried over to finish settling children onto the carpet. At last I had the bishop to myself.

For several minutes, surrounded by people who, if not reaching their hearts' desire, were at least working out compromises that might temporarily satisfy, I could put the demon out of my mind. But he was still there, trapped in the pentagram in the ruined chapel, not thirty yards away. He still had Antonia's soul. And unless I did something very soon, my nerve would fail me completely.

"I'd like you to give me the last rites, Joachim," I said quietly. "Though it's not going to do much good. Antonia has sold her soul to the devil trying unsuccessfully to save Cyrus from his demon—Theodora can give you the details—and it's going to take my life and soul together to redeem her."

He was going to give me an argument. I just knew it. "There's nothing you can do," I said, speaking rapidly. "You know priests can't exorcise people who have summoned demons themselves, only those who have been invaded by free-roaming demons. And you could use the liturgy to drive the demon out of this castle, certainly, but he would have her soul just as certainly."

Before Joachim could reply—and he looked very ready to do so—I heard a step in the passage leading to the chapel and whirled to see Elerius emerging through the doorway.

He was so haggard he could hardly stand. "Maybe you'd better try again yourself, Daimbert," he gasped. "That demon intends to drive a hard bargain." He noticed with vague interest the others who had arrived and then looked back at me from dark-rimmed eyes that had lost all their irony and calculation. "I haven't given in to his offers, if that's what you're wondering. It's the raw terror, I think, that wears you down, until he hopes you'll agree to anything just to get away. Watch! I can still walk right up to a bishop."

He staggered more than walked. "Even Cyrus can walk up to the bishop," I snapped, not completely sure whether to believe him, then stopped.

"Help me!" a voice echoed down the passage from the chapel. "Help me!" That was Cyrus's voice.

What could I do? For twenty-five years I had been trying to help mankind, sometimes with limited success, but trying. Without even making a conscious choice I flew down the passage into heat and darkness, gritting my teeth against the wave of evil waiting for me. And then I realized that Cyrus was not calling for my help.

"I can't go on without my powers! Help me get them back!" He was calling to the demon.

I dropped to the ground just inside the passage from the chapel and leaned my forehead against the stone doorframe. This was it. No matter what Cyrus was trying to talk the demon into, successfully or unsuccessfully, when I went in there to join him I wasn't going out. I hadn't gotten the last rites from the bishop, I hadn't said good-bye again to Theodora, but twice was all I could manage. If I had to face that raw terror and raw evil a third time, I would just have to let Antonia be lost.

"And why should I grant any particular powers to you?" the demon was saying. "It is not as though you still possessed a soul with which to bargain!"

I looked a last time up the passageway, in the direction of daylight and the people I hoped I would never see again, because they, unlike me, would be in heaven. Elerius put his head into the passage but I waved him back, and he retreated, looking relieved.

"But I used to be able to do things!" cried Cyrus. "Good things! I helped children! I rebuilt the high street of Caelrhon, and they loved me for it! And now," his voice cracking, "the angels won't listen to me, and my demon is gone, and I can't do *anything!*"

Let the demon explain it to him, I thought, trying to take deep breaths to steady myself. The poisonous fumes floating across the room didn't help.

"You wizards really are difficult to deal with," said the demon, sounding irritated. "You always try to pin us down with specious protocols and bargains you have no intention of keeping, and then make ridiculous demands. Can't you understand that the demon who used to help you is no longer here?"

I was barely listening, trying instead to rally what little strength I had left. No more of this nonbinding conversation, in which a demon might blithely offer anything. I would force him to accept binding negotiations, in which he would swear by Satan's name to release Antonia in return for my immediate death and the reception of my soul in hell.

IV

There was a step behind me, and I whirled to see Theodora striding determinedly toward the chapel. She saw me but didn't stop until I wrapped my arms around her.

"Please, Daimbert," she said in a very small voice. "The bishop thinks I'm here to talk you out of it. My courage is going to evaporate in about thirty seconds. Let me go."

I knew immediately what she meant. "Joachim told you? But you can't! You don't know the terms for binding negotiations!"

"Then tell me," she said against my chest, "and tell me quickly. If one of us has to die to save Antonia, it has to be me."

"No, I can't let you!" I whispered. "Theodora, my last happy thought before descending into eternal torment is going to be knowing that you and Antonia are safe. I couldn't go on living if I knew that either of you was in hell."

"And you think I could if you were there?" she said, almost angrily but also in a low voice. "The demon may be satisfied with my life and not insist on my soul. The bishop and Elerius told me that this demon already knows and distrusts you, but he's never met me. And listen," wiggling an arm out of my embrace to cover my mouth, "even in this world you're a lot more important than I am. I've thought all this through, so don't argue. The whole kingdom of Yurt needs you. The only person who needs me is Antonia, but she can live with you. The king might still be uneasy about a married wizard, but he'd be happy with the wizard's daughter."

She didn't want me to argue so I didn't, but there was no possible way I could agree. I held her so close that for a moment I imagined we might fuse into a single person. Life, even in a dark and fetid passage, seemed at the moment almost unbearably sweet. "I've loved you ever since I met you," I murmured. "In six years you've given me more delight than most people experience in their whole lives. I do wish we might have been married, just so I could say before God and all our friends how much I love you, but it's still all been worth it."

She tried to struggle but not very convincingly, and she couldn't speak with my mouth on hers. In the chapel, Cyrus and the demon were still talking. "Well, maybe there is something you could offer," the demon said cunningly. "I could at least *consider* giving you all the powers of black magic again, but first you have to let me out of this pentagram."

I spun around so fast that I knocked Theodora bruisingly against the doorframe. She gave a brief cry, but the sudden terror in her eyes was not of me. Still holding on to her, I plunged into the chapel.

It was too late. As I raced across the floor Cyrus finished rubbing out one of the main chalk lines. "I have indeed 'considered' giving you your powers back," said the demon to him with a leer that showed all his razor-sharp teeth, "and I have decided not to!" And with a white flash and a smell of brimstone, he vanished.

Cyrus gave a heart-wrenching cry as daylight reasserted itself in the room. No demon in the pentagram meant that the miasma of evil was rapidly draining away from here—and going wherever the demon was hiding now.

I advanced toward Cyrus, slowly now. He was huddled on the floor, his face on his arms, but he looked up as I reached him. I must have looked even worse than I felt for he gave a screech and fled up the passageway.

Theodora and I collapsed where we stood. She rubbed her shoulder absently. "I'm sorry if I hurt you," I said. It seemed so inadequate a comment that she didn't even respond.

"Does this mean—" she asked instead, not daring to hope.

I shook my head. "It only means we have to have this whole discussion over. Now that the demon is loose there are all sorts of evil tricks it may try—and doubtless will—and it still has Antonia's soul. We'll have to negotiate again once we corner it." As I spoke I wondered if I would have the energy for anything, much less chasing a demon, but I didn't have much choice. "If it doesn't want to talk to us that could take days. We'd better get everybody else safely out of here as fast as we can and call for the demonology experts from the school."

We walked slowly, hand in hand, up the passageway. The demonology experts would never let Theodora in on the negotiations, I thought. It was the single bright point.

Voices reached us as we walked up the passage, excited and cheerful; I wondered vaguely if I myself had ever felt that way. Only Elerius sat against the wall, his face in his hands. I wondered if he was regretting not taking the demon up on his offer of the leadership of the wizards' school. But everyone else seemed fully occupied.

The second load of children was gone, and the twins and their parents were busy trying to keep the rest together until the carpet returned for its final trip. Theodora took Antonia aside and held her in her arms, not speaking, until the girl started to become restless and wanted to join the other children in running around, but still Theodora held her. "Some of these youngsters are almost as rambunctious as you two were," said the duchess to her daughters.

They still didn't realize what was happening in the chapel, and I had no intention of telling them. "Prince Ascelin," I said, my voice coming out indescribably weary, "could you do me a favor?"

He looked up, extremely weary himself, but nodded.

"Somewhere, probably down in the lower, darker parts of the castle, there's an ensorcelled frog. Find him. But if you start to smell brimstone at any point or hear bones clattering, get right back here and tell me. The frog may have started turning back into a wizard, so he could be dangerous. I sent Evrard to find him—you remember Evrard, the redheaded wizard of Caelrhon—but he's not returned."

"I'll go, Father," said Hildegarde, jumping up. "You did all the tracking but I haven't done anything yet this trip." She hurried happily away before either Ascelin or I could say anything. He took two steps after her but then turned back with a smile. "I think Hildegarde can manage a frog on her own, even an ensorcelled one."

Joachim lifted his eyebrows at me from across the room, where he stood a little distance away from the rest. I walked slowly over to him. Cyrus lay on his face at the bishop's feet.

"All I ever wanted to do," the Dog-Man choked out between sobs, "was to be recognized and admired for doing well. When I realized how evil my master was I decided to break away from him and help little children to make up for killing Daimbert, which of course I had promised my master to do. I didn't *mean* to do magic in the guise of religion. That's why originally I avoided you when the people of Caelrhon started to talk of my doing miracles. But when I finally met you and realized that if I became as pure as you I really could do real miracles, and when the angels told me I had restored the burned street—"

"You have sinned, my son," said Joachim gravely, "and sinned grievously. You have fallen through your pride and false belief that you can become truly good through your own, unaided human efforts. But—"

"*I'll* say he's sinned," I growled, not caring if I was interrupting a confession. "He's just let a demon loose. And it's still got Antonia's soul."

"But God always listens to the prayers of a contrite heart," the bishop continued as though he had not heard me. "He who sent His own Son to die for our sins will not forget us, if we are truly penitent and seek the redemption He offers." I decided not to mention that Joachim himself had once told me that someone who sold his soul to the devil would not be saved until the devil himself was redeemed, at the end of time.

"I want to make restitution for all of it," Cyrus babbled. "For kidnapping the children, for my pride, for attacking Daimbert—even if he did have it coming!—for endangering sweet Antonia, the dearest of little girls." I didn't like the way it sounded on his tongue, even though I agreed with the sentiment. "If I can only become worthy of you again, Holy Father—"

"Do not try to be worthy of *me*," said the bishop sternly, "a sinning mortal like yourself. Prepare yourself rather to accept God's grace, which He brings to all of us though none of us are deserving."

I turned away in despair and disgust as Cyrus began kissing the bishop's ring in abject gratitude. "Elerius," I said. "We've got a new problem. The demon's loose. I don't think I could fly a hundred yards, so we've got to wait for the carpet. But when we get everybody out of here and back to Caelrhon, you're going to call the demonology experts at the school. You're the one who plans to be in charge over them, so you can just find a way to persuade them that after they catch the demon again, they've got to negotiate for Antonia's soul before sending it back to hell."

He glanced up, looking disoriented. "That sounds like a good idea," he said without any conviction.

"Unless you and I and Evrard can catch it first," I said with even less conviction.

"Where *is* Evrard?" he asked.

Maybe I should look for him while waiting for the

carpet. I pushed away from the wall, against which I had slumped, and headed for the stairs. I realized I probably hadn't eaten in twenty-four hours, so part of the hollowness in my belly might be hunger—but most of it was fear. My feet felt encased in lead, and I didn't even have the will left to keep going, only an inertial movement that wouldn't let me stop.

But I hadn't even left the room before Evrard himself staggered in.

He was covered with mud and trembling. But he managed a grin. "Who did you say transformed that wizard into a frog? You sure it wasn't you, Daimbert? Because I remember that mess you made way back in Zahlfast's exam, and this looks like your work. He must have gotten himself at least halfway turned back into a man."

Just what we needed: Vlad at large in the castle again when the demon was already loose. Evrard settled himself gingerly next to Elerius and me. His good humor had not yet deserted him. "A pretty sorry spectacle we make," he commented, "for three Royal Wizards."

He had found the damp prints of a frog on stairs going down to the storage cellars and followed them, finding his way through the dark passages by repeated spells of light. When his spells suddenly wouldn't work he knew that Vlad must have recovered enough of his powers to be able to block them. He never actually saw him, having quite sensibly retreated, but in the darkness he had become lost and at one point thoroughly mired in what must once have been the castle's cess pit. He had not seen Hildegarde.

Elerius and I looked at each other. "We can't wait for the demonology experts," I said. "We've got to find Vlad at once, now, before he finishes breaking out of Antonia's spell and gets his own weather spells working again. If we have to deal with him and a loose demon at the same time . . . Light's the only advantage we have. Torches might do: not damp ones kept alight by fire magic, but clear-burning ordinary torches."

"There are some dead pines growing out of the ruins lower down," said Evrard. "Some of the wood should have been protected from the rain. I'd have thought of that myself, but I didn't realize I'd need a torch until it was too late."

I put a hand to my aching head, trying to plan. If I could just put everything in the right order, it might make sense. First get the final carpet-load of children out of here, along with the bishop and the duchess with her family. Then go after Vlad. Three western wizards ought to be able to catch him, even three as weary as we were, as long as any of Antonia's spell held. Then contact the demonology experts and, with luck, have the demon back in the pentagram by tomorrow. Then make the bargain for Antonia's soul that Elerius had kept me from making today.

So I still had a day to live. Instead of feeling grateful for the reprieve, I just felt at this point that I wanted to get it over.

Or maybe we should look for Vlad first, even before the carpet returned from Caelrhon. And we had to find Hildegarde. I shook my head. My thoughts felt so fuzzy—

Antonia trotted over. "Is Vlad that bad person I turned into a frog? I can help you catch him. The demon said he could do things for me, so I'll make him do it. He *has* to obey me because I'm Mistress of the Pentagrams."

"Antonia, no!" Elerius and I shouted together.

"I would just have him do it as a demonstration," she said, puzzled.

Theodora lifted her up. "Remember, you yourself said a demon can't be someone's friend," she said sternly. "Don't even think of talking to him again."

At the moment we still had some hope of saving Antonia. But at this rate, I thought grimly, the best negotiators from the school wouldn't be able to save her—if they even cared to try.

"Vlad first," I said to Evrard and Elerius, managing to get back on my feet after only a brief struggle. "Come on."

"Where has Cyrus gone?" asked Elerius, looking around. The bishop was by himself now, standing by the window with his back to the room, his head bowed. "He must have been listening to our entire conversation with the demon."

"He's probably off in a corner somewhere vainly praying for forgiveness," I said with supreme indifference. "Evrard, once we have the torches you'll have to lead us, as well as you can, to where the magic of light failed you."

But we had gone only a short distance when Hildegarde came toward us at a dead run. She didn't even slow down as she passed, blond hair flying out behind her. In one hand she held a naked sword, streaked black with blood.

I turned back at once. The children screamed to see her, some in fear, some in simple excitement. Hildegarde stood for a moment looking wildly around, as though not seeing whom she was looking for or not even knowing who it was.

Then she spotted her sister. Letting the sword fall from her hand she threw herself onto her knees. "Celia," she gasped, "you've got to help me. I've sinned horribly. I've just killed somebody."

Celia dropped to her own knees and wrapped her arms around her sister. "Tell me," she murmured.

They immediately drew an intensely interested audience of a prince, a duchess, a bishop, and three wizards. But Hildegarde paid no attention to any of us. "It must have been the ensorcelled frog," she got out, her breath coming in great gulps. "I'd made a torch from a dead pine branch and was well down in the dark part of the castle. Several times I spotted what looked like damp frog tracks, and at one point I heard somebody cursing."

"I think that was me," muttered Evrard, "when I fell into the cess pit."

"But I still didn't spot anybody. Then I climbed over some fallen stones and saw—it was horrible! It was partly like a man, but it had legs like a frog."

"Yes?" prompted Celia.

"He was mumbling to himself, and I don't think he'd heard me coming. But then he saw me, and he jumped at me with his frog legs, and his face was all white but he had these pointed teeth—"

"And so you killed him," said Celia quietly.

"Not yet. I threw the torch at him. That's when he started to come apart. But he was still coming. He was disintegrating, but the teeth especially, as though they themselves were alive— *That's* when I put the sword into his heart."

Hildegarde started to sob then. "God still loves you," murmured Celia, rocking her like a child. "He loves us all, even terrible sinners."

Vlad had been preparing his spells again as fast as he could transform himself back into a man, I thought. He was ready for a wizard but not for a young woman carrying a torch. And it never would have occurred to him that she had a sword.

"As soon as he was dead," Hildegarde continued in a minute, lifting a tear-streaked face from her sister's shoulder, "he stopped being a frog at all, but he fell apart. That might have been the worst part of all. His arm fell off, and half his face. . . . There's nothing left of him now but scraps. And those started to stink, as though he'd already been dead for months." She looked up toward Prince Ascelin. "Father, have you ever had to kill someone? When they're teaching you to fight, why don't they tell you how horrible it is? He might have been awful and half a frog, but at least he was alive until I got through with him!"

Vlad was dead. I turned away, not wanting Hildegarde to see the intense relief on my face. Now that we'd gotten rid of one nearly hopeless problem, the dark wizard, all we had left was the impossible one, the escaped demon.

Antonia put her head out from behind the bishop; I hadn't even realized she had been listening. With an expression of deep distress, she went over and put a hand gently on Hildegarde's shoulder. "Maybe you shouldn't try to be a knight after all," she said. "It sounds too scary."

Ascelin swung her up and passed her, protesting, back to Theodora, who had been desperately trying to keep the rest of the children calm. But then he said soberly to his own daughter, "I think it's too late to make that choice. You *are* a knight now. There's a lot more to it than knowing how to fight. It looks like once we're home again I'd better start you on real training."

Hildegarde, still clinging to her sister, appeared not to hear, but Celia gave their father a quick smile over her head.

"Do you think," suggested Evrard in my ear, just as though I might need something else to worry about, "that the demon will try to reanimate Vlad?"

Before I could shape a reply, the castle shuddered to the clang of what might have been an unimaginably huge bell. For a second a wind reeking of evil fumes whirled through the room, then it whooshed down the passage toward the ruined chapel. I heard Cyrus's voice, but this time it was raised in a frenzied cry of pure triumph.

"I have my powers again!"

V

The air at the entrance of the ruined chapel, when I slammed into it, had turned to glass. Of course. With the powers of black magic restored to him, Cyrus would have no trouble recreating Vlad's spell which had created an invisible barrier around the chapel.

I clawed at it frantically, then tried to calm myself enough to start on spells. The chapel was dark again, lit only by a deep, orange glow. If Cyrus had been able to locate the demon and persuade it to work with him, then it must now be there. If I could reach it I could bargain for Antonia's soul before anything else happened to stop me. I gestured for everyone else to go back and then turned away from them. This was between Cyrus and me now.

The spell that made the air solid remained impervious to my magic. But as my eyes grew accustomed to the dark I could see the pentagram glowing and the demon in the middle of it.

But the demon looked strangely different. He had been deep red with an enormous, quivering belly. Now he was cadaverously thin and colored a pale orange, although the fiery eyes and razor-sharp teeth remained unchanged. "Thank you, Master," he was saying, and even the voice sounded different. Its tone could have been mistaken for pleasant. "It is much more interesting on earth than in hell."

I stared until my eyes stung. When I had spoken to the demon, he had been in the right-hand of the two pentagrams Antonia had drawn. He was now in the left. It wasn't the same demon.

Dear God. Now we had *two* demons in the castle: Antonia's, merrily running around loose somewhere, and Cyrus's, trapped for the moment—but I feared *only* the moment—back in the pentagram in which Antonia had imprisoned him before returning him to hell, from where Cyrus had once again summoned him.

At the moment I would almost have been willing to sacrifice *all* of us, me, Antonia, Theodora, Joachim, the duchess's family, and all the children, if the saints would just appear and open an enormous hole and send the entire castle, with both demons, down to hell. But this seemed very unlikely. If I was ever in a position to give advice on the metaphysics of creation, which had seemed less and less likely for some time, I would say that this business of free will had gone entirely too far.

"I want you to do something for me," said Cyrus urgently to the demon.

"Of course, Master," he replied suavely. "Do not doubt for a moment I am yours to command. As long"—and he showed all his teeth—"as I have the opportunity for evil!"

"There's another demon in this castle," said Cyrus, talking fast. "Yes, the demon who captured *you*. I'm going to free you from the pentagram but only for a minute. You have to bring him back and put him in this other pentagram, and return here yourself."

And send Antonia's demon back to hell, her soul with it. I pounded desperately on the invisible barrier with my fists, without success. They couldn't hear me. Cyrus had doubtless taken tips from what Antonia had done and deluded himself that capturing the demon she had summoned would somehow be helpful. He did not realize that he would thus destroy the one chance we still had to save her.

"There's a flaw in the other pentagram," commented the demon. "It would never hold him."

Cyrus looked around, frustrated, then spotted Antonia's lost piece of colored chalk, lodged against the base of the cracked altar, and snatched it up. Quickly

he redrew the line that he himself had erased when
Antonia's demon had lied to him, suggesting the
restoration of his powers in return for freedom. He
then turned and made a tiny opening in the pentagram
around his own demon.

"Now, go!" he said when the demon seemed to
hesitate. "And return at once. You *have* to obey me."
And with a blinding flash, the demon vanished. There
would be, I thought grudgingly, one advantage to selling
your soul. No more having to negotiate with demons:
they had bound themselves to obedience.

The chapel was now completely dark. Behind me I
could hear people breathing, but none of them spoke.
The only ones who could save us now were the saints,
I thought, but they still seemed remarkably slow to
become involved. We were reduced to waiting and
watching Cyrus.

For a second the passage stank of brimstone, and a
sudden onslaught of new terror made my bones feel as
if they were made of water. With a loud bang and two
flashes of light, two demons appeared in the pentagrams
in the chapel. Cyrus redrew the line to imprison his.

"I order you," he cried, "as your Master, to return
to hell!"

There goes Antonia's soul, I thought, closing my eyes.
I wondered if it would be better to kill her with my
own hands than to have her grow up to a life of evil. I
doubted I could do it.

My eyes flicked open again. No! He was commanding
his own demon. And it was already far too late to worry
about *his* soul.

"But I've barely returned from hell, Master," replied
the demon, sounding peevish and pulling thin lips back
from his teeth. "I thought you were delighted to have
your powers back!"

"And I intend to use them for good!"

"Doesn't that seem a little foolish? It's not as though you could still 'save' your soul, as that bishop you so admire would put it. Since doing good will help you not in the least, whereas doing evil—"

"I don't care!" shouted Cyrus. "As your Master, I command you! Return to hell at once!"

"All right," said the demon reluctantly. "But don't expect me to answer so quickly the next time you summon me." With a flash and a thundering that shook the entire castle, he vanished.

The barrier collapsed before me. I started to leap forward, but a hand grabbed my collar and jerked me back. I spun around, furious, thinking it was Elerius.

It was Joachim. He shook his head and held on tight, with far more strength than I could have resisted at this point. There was just enough light for me to see the intensity in his eyes.

Cyrus staggered, almost falling. But with his powers of black magic gone, he whirled toward the other demon with nothing more than the strength of half-learned eastern magic and sheer human stubbornness. "By Satan, by Beelzebub," he cried, "by Lucifer and Mephistopheles. Binding negotiations!"

The bulging red demon came to life, and a sudden cloud of brimstone made all of us in the passage start desperately coughing, but Cyrus did not appear to hear. "Don't you realize you're negotiating from a distinctly weak position?" asked the demon with a leer. "Your soul already belongs to the devil!"

"I'm not offering my soul!" Cyrus shot back. "I'm offering my life!"

"Are you sure you wouldn't prefer nonbinding conversation?" asked the demon. He seemed to be growing more and more enormous, until his horns brushed against the ceiling. "A life for a soul is not a bargain I would care to accept."

"For a soul to which you are not fully entitled," Cyrus said clearly, "I offer my life: a life which should have been long, eventful, and filled with whatever I most desired, because of the soul I long ago sold. You can kill me now, but you must return to hell at once, and as you go you must release Antonia's soul."

Vlad might never have dealt with demons himself, but he had certainly taught the art of demonology to his apprentice—who must also have been listening closely to Elerius and me.

The chapel and passage had become almost suffocatingly hot. "Those other wizards were also arguing about Antonia's soul," said the demon with a deep and resonating laugh. "I've never seen such stubbornness." He looked past Cyrus and showed his teeth. He knew very well we were there.

Joachim's grip tightened like steel, and his hand stayed perfectly steady.

"No!" cried Cyrus, furious. He was shaking so hard he could hardly stand, but fury and a kind of strange exultation kept him going. "She is below the age of reason, she never intended to sell her soul, she acted only from pure motives, and she did not even get what she requested of you, the other demon thoroughly back in hell, because I was able to summon him again. On any of these points you might argue, but not on all of them. She is not truly the devil's, and a life can redeem her."

"There are quite a few other people who are more than willing to throw away their lives for her," said the demon slowly, shifting his bulging belly. For the first time I even dared hope: by not denying what Cyrus had just said the demon had agreed with him. "Why should it have to be you?"

"Binding negotiations!" he almost screamed. "You have to answer!"

There was a long pause during which I was afraid the demon would not say anything at all, but then he began to speak. "By Satan, by Beelzebub," he said slowly, fire shooting from his eyes, "by Lucifer and Mephistopheles. In the space of what you in the natural world call one minute, I shall return to hell, not to return to this world unless deliberately summoned by woman or man."

I couldn't have moved even if I wanted to. This was so close to being me. All I could do was listen, my eyes squeezed shut, for the slightest deviant word.

"I release, give up, and free Antonia's soul," the demon continued. "But before I go, you shall die. Agreed and accepted?"

At the last moment I thought Cyrus would change his mind. I opened my eyes to see him stiff and white. Any promptings from his conscience would have been the promptings of a conscience perverted by evil.

But then he turned his head and looked toward us. His eyes slid past me and stopped. Twice he opened and closed his mouth. Then suddenly his face took on, just for an instant, that look of shattering goodness that I had seen in him once before. He gasped out, very low but still intelligible, "Agreed and accepted."

The demon's booming laugh came one more time as he bent his mouth, huge now and filled with hundreds of teeth, toward Cyrus. "See you in hell!" he cried, and the air exploded.

When our ears stopped ringing and we could see again, the chapel was empty of life. Part of the outer wall had vanished, letting in morning sunshine on the two still-smoking but empty pentagrams and Cyrus's decapitated body. The bishop strode forward without hesitation and began reciting the last rites over him.

With only minimal hesitation, I followed him and dropped to my knees to begin rubbing out the pentagrams.

If anybody *else* wanted to summon a demon to this castle, they would have to draw their own. I found the stub of Antonia's chalk and hurled it with all my might out into the empty air.

Joachim finished the words of the liturgy as I rose shakily to my feet from the flagstones. They were empty now of all but Cyrus's blood. The others had retreated back up the passage. "I should reconsecrate this chapel," said the bishop distantly. "Not today. I should come back with some priests next week and do it."

"Why did you stop me from going after Cyrus?" I asked, uninterested in consecrated chapels. "I presume he told you exactly what he intended to do?"

"No." Joachim held me with his dark eyes. "But I guessed his heart. He wanted somehow, desperately, to make amends for at least some of the evil he had done."

I grew weak all over again. "I thought you knew what you were doing the whole time and didn't want me to give up my life and soul needlessly when Cyrus, after all, had already forfeited his."

He was silent for a moment before answering. "I am the bishop, Daimbert. I could not have made a choice between you, if that's what you mean, even though I would have wanted to. All I knew was that he intended to atone for his deeds, and I had to give him the chance to do so." He paused briefly again. "And I think he has."

"He didn't think he could still save his soul at this point, did he?" I asked incredulously.

The bishop shook his head. "He wasn't trying to save his soul. He was trying to save Antonia's. He had finally come to the realization of just how deeply he had sinned in embracing evil: especially against the children and against you. He was trying to do good to you and to one particular child for the sake of goodness itself."

"That sounds like pure motives to me," I said slowly. "So what happens to his soul? He's not going to make heaven after all, *is* he?"

Joachim shook his head again, and for a second the angles of his cheekbones gave the faintest approximation of a smile. "Religion is not like wizardry, reducible to formulae and protocols and spells learned from books. Only God can know a soul's ultimate destination. I myself, Daimbert," he hesitated briefly, "I think he might possibly be in purgatory."

We slowly returned to the others. Theodora was squeezing our daughter tight and crying hard. Antonia waved me over. "Why is Mother sad, Wizard? She says she isn't sad at all but she just keeps crying and crying. You can tell me what's wrong. I'm a big girl."

I put my arms around both of them, very close to crying myself. "Nothing's wrong at all. In fact, everything's right."

"Grown-ups are very strange sometimes," pronounced Antonia. I had to agree.

There was a cheerful shout outside, and the flying carpet sailed in again. "I think we can get the rest of you on here," said Paul, his usual vigor apparently completely recovered. "Whoof, what's that smell? Have you gotten the demon back to hell yet, Wizard?"

"Yes," said Elerius, answering for me.

"It was scary again while you were gone," said a little boy accusingly to the king.

Paul looked around in assessment, at the twins sitting by the window hugging each other, at the haggard looks on everyone's faces, at me clutching my family. "You didn't wait until I was gone to have adventures behind my back, did you, Wizard?" he asked suspiciously.

I shook my head. But the king, I knew, would feel that I had cheated him once again. This might be the last adventure I would ever be allowed to have where

he himself wouldn't run a serious chance of being killed.
The only solution, I thought hopefully, was to have Yurt
go back to being the peaceful kingdom it always used
to be.

As we were getting everybody onto the carpet,
suddenly I said, "Wait. I need to get Cyrus's body. I'll
tell you about it later, sire."

"We could always drop him into the old cess pit,"
suggested Evrard, loud enough for me to hear but not
quite loud enough that I had to respond.

"He should be buried with honor in the cemetery at
Yurt," I said firmly. "But I need something to wrap him
in."

Paul handed me his cloak without a word and Gwennie
added her apron. They waited while the bishop and I
returned a final time to the chapel. Cyrus's head had
rolled into a corner. We put it with the rest and wrapped
him up carefully, making sure no bits were left exposed
to terrify the children. When I lifted him with magic
he hardly seemed to weigh anything at all.

"I'm sorry, my lady," said Paul to Justinia as the carpet
shot away from the castle at last, "that you weren't in
Yurt at a more propitious time. Usually it's not nearly
this dangerous! But it will be good to have a chance to
meet the mage; I heard all about him when I was little.
You'll have to come back for a visit just to see us again,
not to hide from your enemies. How about Christmas?"

"I fear," said Justinia with a shudder, "that it would
be quite cold at Christmas."

"But I expect you've never seen snow," said Paul,
somewhat uncertainly. "You might like it."

She shuddered again but did not answer. Gwennie,
sitting on the other side of the king, gave a small smile
intended for no one but herself.

Theodora squeezed my hand as we flew along. "I've
been thinking, Daimbert," she said, very softly. "You

know you have— For six years now you—" She paused, apparently embarrassed to go on.

"Yes?" I prompted.

She put her face on my shoulder and laughed a little. "That's it. You know what I mean. That's what I'm saying. Yes."

I pushed her away to look at her, feeling a great surge of hope. The dimple came and went in her cheek. This was not exactly the most private place to have this conversation, sitting on a flying carpet surrounded by thirty children and several of the chief dignitaries of two kingdoms, but I didn't care. "Yes, you'll marry me?"

Elerius glanced toward us then discreetly looked away. Theodora laughed and hid her face again. "We know we love each other," she murmured, "and for a while we were competing for who would die for the other. Everybody knows about us now, or at least everyone in Yurt and Caelrhon. Your king," dropping her voice even lower, "doesn't seem to plan to dismiss you for having a liaison with a witch. And your school's best graduate has been nothing but gracious to me. I said for six years that I didn't want to marry you because marriage would destroy your career. Now that it's clear that it won't, it would be churlish of me to refuse."

I held her tight, too happy to speak for a moment. Warm summer air whipped past us as we flew. "I don't know where we'll live or what we'll do," I said then, "but we'll work out something. As soon as we get back to Caelrhon, or tomorrow for sure, after we've recovered, we'll have Joachim marry us."

Over her head I caught the bishop's eye for a second. On his lips was a genuine smile.

"And maybe," she added shyly, "we could think about a brother or sister for Antonia. Maybe not a dozen children like your king wants, but wouldn't it be exciting to have two?"

I looked over toward our daughter. She had climbed into Hildegarde's lap and was trying to cheer her up. "If you stop being sad," she promised, "I'll teach you how to turn somebody into a frog."

"Exciting," I said, "is not the word for it."